"It'...

Logan said, shifting his weight to get more comfortable on the fallen log. His shoulder touched hers, and when he glanced down at her, the firelight shone on her face.

"You're right," she said, her voice throaty. She gazed surreptitiously at him. No wonder women chased after him. "I always found the sky lovelier here than anyplace in the world."

A log shifted and sent sparks flying into the sky. Logan noticed that Eve's face was turned up, her eyes glittering in the firelight. Before he could stop himself, he brushed her lips with a gentle kiss. "Eve," he whispered against her hair.

He kissed her again, this time more deeply, urgently. Her fragrance surrounded him, blending with the aroma of smoke from the fire, tantalizing and taunting, coaxing him to deepen the kiss. "Eve?" he whispered again.

Her heart pounding, she moaned and slid her arms around his neck. *What was happening to her?*

Reach for the Stars is dedicated to William Alexander, the TV artist who convinced me I could paint. Mr. Alexander's vision, teaching the world to paint, gives hope to aspiring artists every day. For that, he has my undying gratitude. This book is also dedicated to Charlotte Adams, my first art teacher. She showed me how to discover the artist within me. I'd also like to thank Buck Paulson, Lynne Pittard, and Brenda Harris, very special artists who've shared their talents with millions of people everywhere.

All of these wonderful people have had an impact on my life, as well as on my writing. I feel that God has blessed me by making these people my friends.

My thanks and love to you all.

REACH FOR THE STARS

NANCY KNIGHT

ZEBRA BOOKS
KENSINGTON PUBLISHING CORP.

ZEBRA BOOKS are published by

Kensington Publishing Corp.
850 Third Avenue
New York, NY 10022

First Printing: September, 1994

Printed in the United States of America

One

"Why did I ever think this would work? You're a dreamer, Eve," she told herself, crying out in surprise when a fat green grasshopper landed on her bosom. She thumped him off her shirt and scowled as he landed on a tall weed and seemed to stare at her as if she were the interloper. "And, I don't need the likes of you to welcome me."

Eve Travers stared at the desolate camp in disbelief. How could such a happy place have turned into something out of a horror movie? Offering a silent prayer that her fears wouldn't actually materialize, she snatched her purse from the front seat, leaned across to the floorboard on the other side, and removed the pastel plastic work bucket with her sponges, cleansers, rags, and assorted cleaning paraphernalia.

She glanced around her, wondering if

there were snakes. "Of course there are," she groaned and snatched the broom from the backseat. It wasn't much of a weapon, but it would probably be more effective than a pink sponge, which was her only other choice.

Humming a jaunty tune to allay the tension, she closed the door of her car and stepped cautiously into the tall grass that grew more than knee high in the deserted parking area behind what had been the dining hall. She sighed with resignation and moved along the now nonexistent path to the door.

Eve Travers was not afraid of a little hard work.

The padlocks were long gone, along with the screens and windowpanes. She'd have to get rid of all that broken glass first. It wouldn't do for anyone to get hurt. Once inside, she stared at the expansive dining room with dismay. What she remembered as a cheerful gathering spot for meals and announcements and social events simply didn't fit with the somber silence of the mausoleum cloaked in dust and spiderwebs that she now surveyed. She gazed at the items in her bucket. Little good they would do her here. What she'd brought was the equivalent of a Band-Aid; this place needed major surgery.

Eve decided that the best place to start would be in her own quarters. If she cleaned and repaired them first, then she'd at least have a place from which she could operate. She couldn't afford to stay at the motel any longer than necessary.

She crossed the compound to the little two-story building that had been her summer home when her father ran this camp. As with the dining room, she saw that the locks and windows had been broken, the door left ajar. Still, the building seemed to be sturdy enough—until she started up the stairs, that is. The third riser gave way, and her foot dropped suddenly. The fourth riser scraped her leg as she fell.

"Damn!" she exclaimed, extricating herself from the rotted wood. Eve checked the other steps carefully as she crept up the remainder of the stairs. When she reached the landing, she set her bucket on the banister and moved upward cautiously. At the top of the stairs, she examined the floor and stepped forward confidently. Every board seemed to be in good condition, with the exception of that third riser.

That much was good news on a day that had thus far brought nothing but bad news. Her plea to the soft-drink distributor for funds had been answered with a resounding, "Sorry, but we can't help." She was running out of corporations to ask for the support she desperately needed to make her venture successful. So far, she'd received all negative responses, though some of them indicated that if she'd applied sooner, she might have met with more positive results.

A worthy cause wasn't enough; she needed a *timely* worthy cause, or at least a timely application for her worthy cause. Maybe next year, she thought. But that left this summer. She already had more than a hundred applications for the programs she'd advertised, with more requests coming in every day.

She dropped into the only chair in the room, sending dust motes flying into a dense cloud all around her. What was she going to do? The situation looked hopeless, even to an eternal optimist.

"Sitting here moping won't make this place livable," she chided herself and hefted her trim one hundred and twenty-five-pound figure to a standing position. Once more, she surveyed the living quarters of her new home. "I never knew that dust could be so thick."

Eve fumbled through the contents of her bucket and retrieved her rubber gloves. As much as she hated dirt and dust, she wasn't going to sacrifice her fingernails to her cleaning ritual. That was her only vanity: perfect fingernails—all her own.

By dusk, the living quarters sparkled, but the cool air blowing through the windows reminded her that living on King's Mountain this winter would require her to install new windows and a heater in the caretaker's cabin if she planned on remaining there. With that last thought, she closed up the building as well as she could and drove to her motel where she collapsed into her bed without even having dinner.

As she closed her eyes, she recalled the remarkable change in the camp, from desolate to almost livable. With a weary smile, she thought, not bad for a forty-five-year-old who just a few weeks ago was acting like she was sixty.

* * *

Logan Mallory took one look at the flashing light on his answering machine and groaned. Another bill collector, he decided and moved on to the refrigerator without listening to the message. He stared at the growing supply of mold inside the appliance, enough to supply the nation's need for penicillin for the next thirty years.

He started to clean out the mess, but grimaced when his fingers made contact with something mushy that might once have been fruit. "God, it looks like pigs live here. Worse. I doubt if even pigs would eat that stuff."

He searched for a utensil to aid him in the disposal of the toxic waste that was waiting for him in the 'fridge. Every spatula was immersed in a sink full of liquid that must have been there for a month. "I swear I cleaned this place up . . . let's see, last . . . month."

Drastic measures were called for. He strode to the closet and rambled until he found a tennis racquet that should have been junked years ago. With a deep sense of purpose, he returned to the kitchen and used the handle of the racquet to pry the stopper out of the sink. The strange

slurping noise of the smelly liquid draining away disgusted him.

"Logan, old boy, now that you're offi-
cially retired from everything, you're going to have to change your ways."

The condition of his kitchen ran a
close parallel with the condition of his
love life. For many years, he'd been smart
enough to bring his dates home with him
after an evening of wining and dining.
Most of the women he dated would clean
up his kitchen before they made breakfast
for him.

For the past few years, he'd really disliked himself. Not just for using women
in that way, but for a lot of things. He
drank too much, caroused like a college
freshman, and exerted as much control
over his life as a crazed Tasmanian Devil.

Not anymore. Logan Mallory was turning over a new leaf. He'd made plenty of
New Year's resolutions and he intended
to keep them. The problem at hand—the
condition of his kitchen—was a direct result of not dating for three months. His
resolve to avoid the airheaded socialites
who were attracted to him had a definitely negative impact on the cleanliness
of his house. He simply hadn't considered

that. He was going to take control of his life—right now.

"Who needs a woman anyway?" he asked himself, wishing he'd waited until after the place was cleaned up before declaring a moratorium on dating.

He grabbed a box that almost fit across the width of his refrigerator and opened the door. After a moment of planning his strategy, he wedged the old tennis racquet between a plastic container of milk that looked about ready to burst open and the wall of the refrigerator. He jerked as hard as he could, sweeping the racquet forward in an arc that shoved an entire shelf full of unidentifiable items crashing into the box.

"Well, that was simple enough." He surveyed the gook coating the metal rack. "Get to that later."

After he'd cleaned out the refrigerator, he took the box out to the dumpster. Then he went into the backyard and poked his garden hose through the kitchen window. He waved at a neighbor who was staring in unabashed curiosity and returned to the kitchen without offering an explanation.

Logan finished cleaning his refrigerator with the car-washing attachment to his hose, catching the flood of water in a pile of dirty towels strategically placed on an old shower curtain. Within the span of a day, his kitchen was respectable, if not spotless. For two days, he ignored the ringing of his phone and bulldozed his way through the remainder of his house with a vengeance.

When he finally slumped into his favorite chair, he closed his eyes and leaned back. Logan wasn't sure whether all this was a price he was willing to pay to keep his resolutions. "It's got to be easier next time," he declared with a confidence he didn't necessarily feel.

The sound of someone pounding on the front door woke him with a start. Logan leaped from his chair, glanced down at his dust- and grime-streaked tennis shorts, and hurried to the door. "All right, all right, don't knock it down."

"Open up, Logan!" came a voice through the wooden door.

Logan swung the door open and stood facing his business manager. "Jerry, what in hell are you—"

Jerry Kent brushed past Logan and looked around. "What's going on? Where is she?"

"Who? What are you talking about?"

"I know you. There's only one reason you don't answer the phone." Jerry rushed from one room to the next and finally stopped to peer out the sliding glass doors.

Logan chuckled and followed his friend. "I don't know what you're talking about. You know I swore off women *and* booze. I've been a very good boy."

"Oh, no. You're not tricking me this time." Jerry smirked and gestured at the clean living room. "I suppose you expect me to believe you did this yourself."

"I do and I did."

Jerry proceeded to the kitchen and looked at the sparkling sink and then the refrigerator. "Give it a rest, Logan. I've managed you for twenty years. You've never had a kitchen this clean unless a broad did it."

"I swear, Jer, there's no woman involved in this." Logan smiled proudly. "I did all this myself. Took me three days, non-stop."

Jerry stared at Logan in disbelief. "You're serious, aren't you." He looked around the room again. "You really cleaned the place yourself."

"Yeah, I did and I'd just settled down

to rest when some obnoxious bastard pounded on the door."

"Obnoxious bastard am I?" Jerry started toward the front door. "Then I suppose you're not interested in the deal I've negotiated with Tennis Pro Athletic Equipment."

Logan caught his friend's arm. "What deal? Gimme a break. I've been working like a slave here."

Jerry settled onto the sofa and propped his feet on the coffee table. "So, if there's no broad involved, why didn't you answer the phone?"

"Because I was too busy cleaning this place." Logan sat back in his chair and laced his fingers behind his head. "So what deal? Do I have to beat you with my broom to find out?"

Jerry shook his head. "Guess not. Looks like you've been a good boy."

"Damnit, Jerry, my patience is running out." Logan threw a cushion at his manager. "Tell me about this deal."

"Sounds like you've got PMS, fella. You oughta see a doctor." Jerry grinned and shrugged. "All the dust and stuff must be getting to you."

"Give me the details of this deal or you

die. You have no idea of the torture quo-
tient of ordinary household implements,"
Logan shot back and waved a corkscrew
threateningly.

"Okay, okay, don't get all violent on
me." Jerry held up his hands in surrender. "I've seen what you can do with a
tennis racquet and I have no urge to find
out what you can do with a corkscrew.
Besides, I don't really know much."

Remembering the several uses he'd discovered for old tennis racquets, Logan
chuckled and raised his eyebrows suggestively. "My dear friend, you've no idea
what I can do with a tennis racquet."

Eve smoothed her hair for the fifteenth
time, breathed deeply, and opened the
door to Tennis Pro's corporate office. She
went to the security desk and told the
young man who she was. He smiled and
directed her to the bank of elevators.

Within seconds, she stepped from the
elevator onto the plushest teal-colored carpet she'd ever had the occasion to walk
upon. Everything in the spacious reception
area was decorated with the purple and
teal signature colors of Tennis Pro. Trying

to appear more assured than she felt, Eve strode confidently to the receptionist and smiled. Before she could state her purpose for coming, the young woman smiled and said that she was expected.

Feeling a little more at ease, Eve followed the receptionist to a private waiting room. The pretty young woman offered a variety of refreshments, but Eve declined. She was simply too nervous to trust herself to drink coffee when her entire future depended on this interview with Tim Carlisle, president of Tennis Pro Athletic Equipment.

After she'd waited no more than five minutes, the receptionist brought two more guests to the waiting room. Eve smiled vaguely as the two gentlemen took seats near her. Neither of them accepted the receptionist's proffered refreshments either. The taller man gazed at her, smiled slightly, and leaned back with closed eyes, apparently ignoring her.

After studying the two men for a moment, Eve concluded that they were there for the same reason as she: to ask for money to finance a charitable project. That thought was sobering. Ever since she'd received the letter naming the date and hour of the appointment, Eve had danced along the edge of giddiness, trying not to collapse into it completely. If she succumbed to the capricious state that threatened to erode her plans completely, she'd be lost to her tasks.

She was still working desperately to repair the damage to the camp. With so little money, she was doing most of the work herself. In the past few days, she'd discovered how very little she knew about carpentry and landscaping, not to mention plumbing and electricity. Not even the Time-Life books she'd checked out of the York County Library had helped.

To divert her attention from the upcoming interview, she studied the two men who were sitting quietly across from her. The man nearest her was tall and slender with thinning hair crowning a cherubic face. Nothing about him seemed to fit. Because he was so slender, his slightly chubby face was at odds with the rest of him. He smiled at her as if he knew something she didn't, but she wasn't annoyed by that demeanor. On the contrary, he seemed more like a prankish child than a man near her own age. She'd had enough experience with this kind of mentality when she'd taught school.

The other man was more interesting. She was sure he was an athlete of some sort, though not football because he wasn't brutish looking enough. Maybe baseball, she thought. Eve knew she'd seen him somewhere, but she couldn't remember where.

A tremor went through her body. Eve wasn't the kind of woman who chased after men, but she didn't mind looking at one who was as handsome as this one. A sport-star, she labeled him mentally.

He was good looking; there was no doubt about that. His evenly tanned skin told her that he was an outdoor person, confirming her speculation about sports. Perhaps he was there to sign some sort of promotional contract. Lots of sports figures did that these days—and got millions of bucks for their precious time.

Eve glanced at the man's eyes. They were open now, studying her with an intense umber gaze. Whoever and whatever he was, this was a man who was used to being adored by women. Forcing herself, Eve stared at the magazine resting on her lap. Every now and then, she caught her-

self snatching a glimpse of those marvelous dark brown eyes or appraising his
neat dark hair that was burnished with
silver at the temples.

Food. That might get her mind off
the man sitting so close to her. Eve
thumbed through the pages of the magazine until she came to a picture of a
perfect dinner table laden with some
sort of pasta, steamed vegetables, a
salad, and a bottle of wine.

"Excuse me, but could I look at that?"

Eve jerked her chin up to stare at him.
She looked at the sport-star for a moment,
surprised at his deep voice. Somehow, she
hadn't anticipated such a resonant bass.
"Are you speaking to me?" she asked, willing her voice not to quiver.

"Yes," he answered, grinning warmly.
"I, uh, well you see, I'm looking for a
good pasta recipe and . . . and . . ."

His voice trailed off as if he were embarrassed, but the laughter that erupted
from the man sitting next to him caught
Eve's attention. The sport-star caught the
other man's eye and joined in the laughter. She felt as if she were the butt of a
private joke.

Without a word, she handed the man

the magazine and grabbed another. Eve glared at the door, wishing that Mr. Carlisle would hurry up. She didn't want to spend one minute more than necessary with these two men.

She risked another glance at the athlete. As good as his word, he was jotting down the recipe in a little notebook. Maybe he wasn't really laughing at her after all. If he was, he was going to an awful lot of trouble just to make his joke work.

Logan could have killed Jerry. The woman's face had colored when he and Jerry laughed. She had no way of knowing that Jerry was still trying to adjust to the changes Logan was making in his life. She probably thought they were a couple of buffoons having a good time at her expense.

He studied her as she flipped through the pages of the magazine she'd picked up after giving him the first one. Any idiot could tell that she didn't give a damn about what was in the magazine. She was simply passing time until she could escape this room—and him. He considered that, finding it interesting since he usually had the opposite effect on women.

The door opened and Logan glanced at the receptionist entering the room. "Mr. Kent? Mr. Carlisle asked if you would step into his office for a moment."

Jerry elbowed Logan in the ribs, grinned, and then followed the receptionist. Logan glanced at the slender woman sitting across from him. She was a looker, even if she was kissing distance from middle age. He used to believe that middle age encompassed the third decade of life, but since he'd passed the thirties and was late into his forties, he'd revised his assessment. Now, middle age comprised the years from about forty-five to sixty-five. Logan might be a little generous on the top end, but a man nearing fifty had to have some ego-protecting mechanisms.

He thought back over the past few years, years when he'd tried to maintain some semblance of being a tennis pro. He'd played a few tournaments, but hadn't earned enough to pay his legitimate expenses, not to mention his excesses. And he was tired. Tired of hotel rooms, restaurant food, and the women who followed the circuit. Not to mention that in the years since he'd been a real pro, he'd gone through all his meager savings plus charging a small fortune on his credit cards.

Logan simply couldn't play professional tennis anymore. He sure as hell didn't want to coach tennis to the arrogant bunch of pros that wanted him. They were too much like him. And he was damned sure he didn't want to teach team tennis to a flock of giggling teenage girls at the elite country clubs around the country.

What he wanted to do was kick back and enjoy these years of his life, play a little seniors tennis, and maybe settle down. He groaned aloud. The woman's attention riveted on him, and he shrugged nonchalantly, yawning as if to pretend that the origin of the sound she'd heard was one of boredom.

She smiled slightly. Damned if she wasn't pretty when she smiled. Her short dark hair didn't have any gray and it was sort of perky looking, as if she was a no-nonsense kind of person who liked to look neat without a lot of hassle. She wasn't wearing makeup either. He liked that. Leftover makeup on his pillows was as unappetizing as anything he could think of—especially now that he was doing his own laundry.

Logan met her puzzled gaze. Her eyes were a soft blue and very appealing. He opened his mouth to explain the groan, but thought better of it. Some things were simply better left unsaid.

Logan scribbled the remainder of the recipe in his notebook and held the magazine out to her. "Here you go, ma'am. And, thanks."

Eve took the magazine from him and tried to smile. His southern drawl was as charming as anything she could remember lately, though she wasn't really feeling too friendly toward the man who'd just moments before laughed at her. "You're quite welcome."

"You . . . eh . . . you come here often?" he asked, with a lopsided grin.

Taken by surprise, Eve laughed at his use of the often-quoted pickup line. "All the time."

Logan smiled at her. What a beautiful laugh she had, like the tinkle of silvery bells on a sultry summer night. Then he sobered. "You do? You know Tim Carlisle well?"

Eve stared, confused by the sudden change in his demeanor. "Well, no, I've never even met him. I thought you were teasing me when you asked—"

His eyebrows arched gently and he grinned again. "I guess I was at first, but when you said . . . so you don't know him at all."

"No, I've only spoken to his secretary. When I confirmed my appointment." She glanced at her watch. Mr. Carlisle was late by twenty minutes—exactly the amount of time that had elapsed since the other man disappeared through the door. "Do you?"

"Do I what?"

"Come here often?"

"Oh, no. I've never been here either. Jerry . . . that's my friend who's in with Carlisle now, he's been here several times." Logan gazed at her. He could see that she was a little angry, perhaps about Jerry's laughter, but probably because Tim Carlisle had sent for Jerry before her. Logan didn't know how long she'd been waiting. "I'm sorry. I can be dense sometimes. My name is Logan Mallory."

Logan Mallory. Now it came back. Bad-boy tennis player who had a habit of throwing tennis racquets and screaming obscenities at the referees and sometimes at the fans. "I thought you looked a little familiar. I'm pleased to meet you, Mr. Mallory. I'm Eve Travers."

For a moment, Logan thought she must be joking, but then he realized that she really didn't know who he was. That was refreshing in a humbling kind of way. He forced his ego to retreat, leaned forward, and offered her his hand. When she placed her small hand in his, Logan discovered that it felt fragile and warm, but her grip was strong. "The pleasure's all mine, Mrs. Travers."

"Miss Travers . . . Eve."

"I can't believe that no man's ever . . . What I mean is, that . . . you've never been married?" he finally asked, knowing she must think him a bumbling idiot. In fact, he was beginning to think that himself.

"I was married to my job, Mr. Mallory."

"Logan." He considered her answer. "I would have been better off if I'd been married to mine. Three ex-wives who are as greedy as a woman ever thought to be."

Eve chuckled and raised her eyebrows reprovingly. "Seems to me that you should have learned better. If not after the first, then certainly after the second."

Logan shrugged sheepishly. "I guess I'm just a fool where women are concerned."

Before Eve could reply, the young woman returned. "Miss Travers, Mr. Mallory? Mr. Carlisle will see you both now."

Eve jumped up, both magazines dropping to the floor at her feet. "Both? I have an appointment, Miss . . ."

Logan stood and glanced at the blanched expression on Eve's face. "I think there must be some mistake, ma'am. Miss Travers and I are not together. I'm with Jerry . . . Mr. Kent."

"He specifically asked to see you both at once. Come with me, please."

Eve fell in step behind the young woman and Logan followed after them. She didn't know what was going on, but she was beginning to become very suspicious. It was quite possible that this whole thing was an elaborate prank of some sort.

Grimacing inwardly, Eve realized that she'd fallen into a state of pessimism. She'd been turned down by every company that offered any sort of financial aid or charitable contribution, and that had taken its toll on her usually optimistic outlook on life.

But this was a new blow to her ego. She'd expected to see Mr. Carlisle alone. Last night she'd rehearsed a speech, one that she prayed would gain her the funds she needed. If not, she didn't know where she could turn. Tim Carlisle and Tennis Pro Athletic Equipment were her last hope.

Then she went through the door to Tim Carlisle's office. The two men were practically rolling on the floor with laughter. Color sprang into her cheeks.

Logan caught up with Eve and touched her shoulder. He looked as befuddled as she. "Miss Travers . . . Eve, I'm sure there's some perfectly logical explanation for—"

She turned and glared at him as if he were Satan himself. "I doubt that logic has anything to do with this situation, Mr. Mallory, but I'm sure as hell going to—"

"Ah, Miss Travers and Mr. Mallory. Welcome, welcome." Tim Carlisle stepped from behind his desk, apparently trying very hard to control his laughter, and caught Eve's hand and then Logan's. "I can't tell you how happy I am to meet you both."

"Mr. Carlisle, if this is some sort of joke, then I'm not amused," Eve stated flatly, wanting these men to know right away that she wasn't someone to be trifled with. If this was a joke, she wanted to know immediately so she could be on her way. She had a lot of letters to write to a lot of gifted students who were going to be disappointed.

Tim Carlisle's forehead wrinkled as if he didn't understand her attack. "I assure you, Miss Travers, that this is not a joke. Jerry and I were just laughing about . . . Never mind. Please, come in and sit down. You, too, Mr. Mallory."

Eve bit her bottom lip. She didn't want to look like a fool. Whatever she did was bound to be the wrong thing. All three men were looking at her, as if waiting for her to say or do something. She lifted her chin and settled into a chair at the corner of the desk. "Thank you, Mr. Carlisle."

Logan stared at Tim Carlisle and then at Jerry Kent before he took his seat. They were up to something. Knowing Jerry's warped sense of humor, it had to be no good. "I don't know what's going on here, guys, but whatever it is, I think has made Miss Travers feel uneasy. So, Tim, I'd suggest you get to the point of this little soiree."

Still chuckling, Tim returned to his chair and faced the people across the desk. "Well, I'd hoped for a friendly gathering. We tend to be a little . . . informal here, but I can see it's going to be all business."

Eve found her voice again. "Mr. Carlisle, I came here with the understanding that this meeting concerned my camp for gifted young people. I don't see the connection between . . . between . . ." Eve searched her mind for the headlines that were most frequently used to describe Logan Mallory. "Between my camp and this Casanova of the tennis courts."

"Bang, Logan, old boy." Jerry fell into another fit of laughter. "She just shot you down."

Logan spent a moment glaring at his manager and best friend before turning to Eve. "Casanova of the tennis courts?" She hadn't known who he was, but she certainly knew his reputation. Damn the newspapers for coining that nickname for him—even though it was deserved, or had been.

Tim cleared his throat. "Well, maybe we'd better stick to business after all."

"Fine," Eve said and placed her purse on her lap as she crossed her legs. "Thank you."

"I have an interesting proposition that involves Miss Travers and Mr. Mallory. May I call you Eve and Logan?" he asked, waiting for their nods. "Now, as you all know, most athletic footwear comes from overseas. We've succeeded in making a dent, albeit a small one, in the marketplace. We're ready to upgrade our dent into a chunk."

"But, Mr. Carlisle—"

"Tim. Call me Tim."

"But, Tim, what does that have to do with Camp Reach for the Stars . . . and how on earth could *that* have anything whatsoever to do with Mr. Mallory?"

"I'd like the answer to that question myself," Logan said, glancing from Eve to Tim. "I don't quite get the connection between . . . a Casanova of the tennis courts and a kid's summer camp."

"Ah, that's what's so interesting about this proposition." Tim rose and walked over to an easel. He showed them several graphs depicting the relationship between advertising and profit and between charitable contributions and profit over the past few years. "So, this is our grand scheme to combine the two. Actually it does something else. It combines the audiences. You see, Logan represents . . . the population as it grows older and the camp will attract a young audience. Voila'. Two birds with one stone when we introduce our new summer and fall lines of shoes. One line for adults and one for young people. There's a local angle as well. Logan lives in the area and the camp is nearby."

"Mr. Car . . . Tim, this is fascinating, but how does it relate to the camp?" Eve asked again, praying silently that the picture that was forming in her mind wasn't the one that had developed in Tim's.

"Don't you see?" Tim asked and sat back down. "This is the perfect way to do both. You, Eve, need money to operate your camp. You, Logan, need money, period. Tennis Pro Athletic Equipment needs a charity *and* advertising."

"All right, I'm beginning to get the picture." Logan rose and paced back and forth for a moment. "You want to hire me to promote Tennis Pro. You want to donate money to Eve's camp. But what has the one to do with the other?"

"Here's the picture." Tim glared at Jerry, who was chuckling again. "Eve's camp is a wonderful opportunity for us as well as for the kids who'll come there. She's drawn up a very detailed proposal concerning the activities. In addition to the outdoor events, which of course will include tennis, her kids will participate in the arts."

"Arts?" Logan asked, beginning to wish he'd never gotten up that morning. This wasn't working out at all as he'd thought it would.

"Yes, arts. The kids she proposes to bring to Camp Reach for the Stars are talented young people who are unable to pay their own fees, disadvantaged kids." Tim grinned at all of them. "You, Logan, are in your own little way, disadvantaged. You need big bucks. I'm willing to pay big bucks."

Eve gasped aloud. A smile refused to be quelled on her lips, but she managed to keep from dancing around the room.

"What's the catch?" Logan asked, returning to his chair.

"You teach Eve's kids to play tennis."

"What!" Logan shot out of his chair like a cannonball. "You want me to spend the summer with a bunch of geeky kids, teaching them tennis? Are you nuts?"

Jerry Kent finally broke his silence. He caught Logan's arm and jerked, showing much greater strength than Eve would have thought possible. "Sit down, Logan. Hear the man out. He said he was offering *big bucks*."

"There's not enough money in the world to make me spend the summer with a swarm of mosquitoes and a bunch of bratty kids." Logan started for the door.

"How does a three-million-dollar contract sound, Logan?" Tim shuffled through some files and held out a contract. "Have a look at this."

Logan stopped in his tracks. "How much?"

"Sit down and listen, Logan," Jerry urged.

Eve could only manage to stare in disbelief, frank disbelief. When Tim had mentioned that the advertising and the contribution could somehow be connected, she'd envisioned a commercial being shot at the camp, but nothing like he was proposing. She now suspected that her worst nightmare was about to come true. No, that wasn't exactly accurate. No matter how awful the nightmare, no matter what horrendous scenario, she never could have come up with anything even approaching this in terms of shock.

Spending the summer with Logan Mallory was the last thing in the world she wanted to do.

Two

Eve stared across the small lake on the camp property. She had only two more hours to make her decision regarding Tim Carlisle's proposal. Realistically, she knew that she had no choice; if her dream was to be realized, then she'd have to agree to his conditions. In fact, the decision was already made. She simply couldn't turn him down, no matter what conditions he attached to the funds.

The problem was that she wasn't sure about the stipulation concerning Logan Mallory. Even though Jerry Kent had assured her that Logan had changed, his behavior hadn't shown that to be true. Could she risk exposing a group of highly creative teenagers to his volatile temper? And what about his reputation for dating—and God only knew what else—young, very young women.

Some of the women his name had been

linked with were hardly of an age to vote. Some hadn't even graduated from high school when he'd started dating them. Well, maybe Eve was exaggerating a little, but there had been at least one or two who were reputed to be in high school and others in college. She couldn't watch him every single moment of the day.

"Maybe he'll refuse Tim's offer. After all, he said in no uncertain terms that he wouldn't work with kids." Even as she said the words aloud, she realized that Logan was nearly as desperate as she was—if the newspaper reports were to be believed. There was no possible hope that he would turn down all the money he'd be getting out of this deal.

She wondered what would happen if Logan refused. Her optimism surged forward, catching on to the slightest hope. Who then would Tim Carlisle choose to do the ads and teach the kids at the camp? Maybe he'd select an aging golfer. Those men were—reputedly—much more gentlemanly than Logan Mallory.

Eve tossed another stone into the lake and watched the ripples spread before her, almost like the rumors she imagined would result from Logan's association with the camp. Still, she had no other choice. She would either accept the terms of the Tennis Pro offer or cancel her plans to open the camp this summer.

Walking slowly up the path, she acknowledged that she'd made her decision; she wouldn't disappoint the kids who'd applied for the summer—even if she had to follow Logan Mallory around like his shadow. Eve reached her office and dialed Tim Carlisle's number. When his secretary answered, Eve spoke with a confidence she didn't really feel. "Please tell Mr. Carlisle that Camp Reach for the Stars will be delighted to accept his proposal. Tell him that—"

"Oh, Miss Travers, he wants to talk with you. Hold on, please."

Eve wasn't certain she was ready to discuss particulars with Tim yet. Even though she was accepting the offer, she still wanted some time to mull over how she would handle the situations that were sure to arise.

"Eve, I knew you'd come around." Tim Carlisle's voice was edged with happiness. "I've already talked to Logan. He's accepted as well."

"Wonderful," she said with much more enthusiasm than she felt.

"Well, I'm sending the contracts by courier. I suppose you'll want an attorney to examine them before you sign, but please don't wait too long."

"I'll try to get them back as soon as possible." Eve tried not to show how happy she was that he wasn't dragging his feet.

"Give me your bank account number and I'll wire you some money to keep things going until we can get the rest of the particulars ironed out," Tim said.

"That's very kind of you, but what happens if we can't come to terms on this—"

Tim chuckled. "Eve, a deal's a deal. You'll sign. There's no reason for you not to sign. I haven't put anything into that contract that we haven't already talked about."

When Eve hung up the phone, she sat at her desk for a long time, wondering if she'd done the right thing. Well, it was too late now. They had a verbal agreement, and she never went back on her word.

She looked at the desk pad and found the phone number of a handyman she'd interviewed. It was time she got some help to put this place in order. When the arrangements were made, Eve began a list of repairs her new employee could do, repairs that would relieve her of the heavier workload. She had a staff to hire.

Logan lay on his sofa, tossing a tennis ball in the air. It was too late to back out on the contract with Tennis Pro, even though he wanted to. "Why did I let you talk me into that deal, Jerry?" he asked, throwing the ball at his manager.

"Starvation, foreclosure . . . those kinds of things come to mind first." Jerry glanced around the neat apartment. "Having to do your own housecleaning."

Logan rose and began to pace. *"That* I'm doing intentionally." He picked up the tennis ball and started to toss it again. "You know, I never realized what a bunch of . . . airheads I've been dating, until just before Christmas."

"It's a genetic deficiency. Don't blame yourself."

"My mother isn't that bad," Logan said, grinning at Jerry. "Although she'll never make the ranks of Mensa."

"Your mother is a lovable nut."

"She's just eccentric. Artists are all that

way." Logan shook his head sadly. "That's the reason I avoid artistic types. I can't deal with their craziness."

"And athletes are saner, I suppose," Jerry chided with a grin. "Yes, sir, athletes are all pillars of society, all intelligent, articulate persons who are serious of purpose."

"All right, so we're not all consumed with a desire to solve the questions of deep space, but we're not nuts like artists are."

"Oh, sure, everybody knows that."

"Look, Einstein, have you ever known an athlete to stand for hours in one spot to paint feathers on a bird? Or have you ever known an athlete to huddle under a palm tree during a terrible storm, waiting for just the right wave to photograph so he can paint it later?" Logan noticed that Jerry got that pinched look around his eyes, like he was in deep thought. "Don't interrupt. I'm on a roll."

Jerry waved him on, as if he knew better than to try and stop Logan once he got wound up.

"And who, but a crazy artist, would paint a portrait of a woman with three boobs or with her nose on the side of her face?" Logan smiled with the obvious pleasure of someone who'd won a debate. "Athletes appreciate women—and their bodies, of course—more than that."

Eve hired several counselors who were talented in the arts. She found a man willing to teach photography for the summer. A woman who taught dance during the school year at her own studio contacted Eve and accepted the dance instructor's position. Even though Eve would be extremely busy, she decided to teach the painting classes herself. Now, she needed someone to teach sculpture, music, writing, and, of course, someone to coordinate the normal camp activities such as swimming, volleyball, softball, and other sports.

She loved this camp. Her father had founded it when she was a tiny girl, and she'd loved tagging after the older children. Those had been the happiest years of her life. She was thrilled to be bringing joy and laughter back to this campsite.

Camp Reach for the Stars was to be a creative camp, but the kids had to have some physical exercise, too. Eve decided to hire college students to handle most of the athletic activities.

And then there was Logan Mallory. He would coordinate the tennis program. She had Tennis Pro to thank for that.

Over the past few weeks, the entire property had been mowed, landscaped, bulldozed where appropriate for athletic fields, paved for the tennis courts, and imported sand, smoothing it out for the volleyball courts and the beach. All the cabins had been refurbished and outfitted with new lockers and beds. A large storeroom had been built and was brimming with all sorts of athletic equipment including new shoes and sportswear for the campers.

Her own quarters shone with new paint and furnishings, and Tim Carlisle had sent a beautiful desk with a matching credenza as a gift to her. With a part of her own savings, she'd bought material for curtains and sewn them herself. She also purchased new pots and pans, other cooking utensils, and a good quality of dinnerware for the dining room.

Eve sat at her desk, making careful notes to be transferred to the list of rules she was developing. She tried to remember the rules that had made her the angriest when she'd been a camper here. After a little thought, she discovered a way around some of them. But, there were some procedures that simply couldn't be changed, like the segregation of male and female campers, curfews, and that sort of thing.

Then she reviewed the applications for a camp nurse. The three most qualified candidates would come for interviews. Eve could hardly wait. Everything seemed to be coming together on schedule.

She heard a noise and looked up, expecting one of the construction workers to step through her door. Instead, she found herself looking up at Logan Mallory. "Mr. Mallory, I didn't expect you to be here for several days."

Logan grinned unexpectedly and settled into the chair across from her. "Neither did I. Is my cabin ready?"

"Yes, they just finished yesterday." Eve glanced at the work orders in the completed stack on her desk and then at Logan again. "It isn't much. I did manage to get you some pretty decent furniture, though. I can buy an air conditioner if you—"

"No, thanks. I love the heat." With a

grimace that expressed his true feelings, Logan averted his eyes. As much as he wanted to walk out the door and never see this place again, her sincerity touched him. "I appreciate your efforts, Eve. I'm sure it'll be fine."

"Would you like me to show you around?" She took a quick look at her watch. "I've got an appointment in about an hour, but we should be able to cover the camp in that time."

Logan wanted nothing less than to traipse all over a mosquito-infested kids' camp, but he'd promised Jerry that he'd behave. And here he was early, much earlier than he'd anticipated, but there didn't seem to be much else to do. And, to be truthful, he'd wanted a chance to settle in, get familiar with the place before the kids arrived. "I'd like that," he said finally.

"Well, shall we go?" Eve pushed her chair back from the desk and stood. "Thank goodness it's getting warm. I'd despaired of warm weather ever coming."

Logan followed her out the door, noticing her trim figure in the white shorts that just skimmed the tops of her thighs. Her cotton shirt was tucked in neatly, giving her a casual appearance without exposing too much skin. He recalled some of the women he'd dated. They'd shown more skin in their short skirts and spandex bandeau tops than this woman in her tidy shorts and shirt—and to his surprise, he found her very sexy indeed.

Much to his dismay, Logan found her figure intriguing. Her legs were long and lean, beautifully shaped, but what did that simple cotton shirt hide?

Worse, he discovered that he was getting out of shape. He hadn't had a real workout in more than three months and he was having trouble keeping up with Eve as she darted from her office over to the dining hall. He'd have to rectify that as soon as possible. Maybe he'd start jogging. He used to work out every day, but lately, he hadn't had the urge—now he had a real need.

"Meals are here. Breakfast from seven to eight," she said smiling.

Logan studied her. Her expression challenged him, as if she knew he hated to get up in the mornings. "I don't usually eat breakfast," he replied nonchalantly. "I suppose I can wander in and get coffee anytime."

"Pot's always on," she answered. "Lunch is from noon to one and dinner's at five-thirty. We're expecting about a hundred kids for each session of camp, so I'd get to meals early if I were you."

"Are you saying I have to stand in line to get my meals?" he asked incredulously.

"Yep. That's right." Eve leaned against one of the tables, crossing her legs at the ankles. She leaned forward slightly and grinned. "We all stand in line."

Logan was on the verge of telling her where she could stuff her meal plans when he noticed the generous contours of her bosom. At the vee of her shirt, he could just see her cleavage. Damn you for being a sucker for a great set of boobs. He rolled his eyes, stared at the ceiling for a moment, and then gazed at her. "Did Jerry put you up to this? I mean, are you joking or something."

She leaned forward and tapped a polished fingernail on his chest. "I never joke about food, Mr. Mallory." Eve stood, turned, and headed out the door, patting her behind a couple of times and laughing. "As you can well see."

He could see all right. Logan could see that this arrangement was going to try his patience. He'd sworn off the babes for a year in an attempt to pull his life back together. Now, here was one who was nearly as old as he, and he was panting after her like a puppy. Abstinence wasn't going to make his life easy this summer.

"Here are the tennis courts," Eve said with a proud smile. "We're waiting until just before the kids arrive before we install the nets."

Logan took a tennis ball out of his pocket. He was never without one, even though he hadn't played in awhile. He strode to the lines, eyed them critically. They looked as good as Wimbledon, except that those were grass courts and these were clay. He bounced the ball several times, first in one spot and then another. He looked at Eve and grinned. "Looks like they did a good job on the courts."

"They sure did." Eve waited as he paced around several more times and then rejoined her. "You like?"

"I like." Logan shoved the ball back into the pocket of his shorts. "I always preferred clay to grass."

"Well, I decided that grass would get too much wear and tear anyway." She surveyed the eight courts. "Besides, I knew which you preferred."

"Now, just how would you know that?" he asked, catching up with her as she left the court area.

She stopped beneath a huge oak tree and looked at him. "I do my homework, Mr. Mallory. I read everything I could find about you."

If Logan Mallory had ever blushed, he suspected he must be now. The skin of his face burned, but he fought the desire to touch it to see if it was really as hot as it felt. "I see."

"Come on, we've a lot of ground to cover yet." Eve hurried down the trail that led to the lake. This was one of her favorite parts of the camp. "Emerald Lake," she said, pointing to the small lake that stretched out before them. "It's a quarter of a mile across. We own the whole thing."

"We?" he asked, suddenly wondering why he'd never considered the possibility that she might have partners in this venture.

"We as in Camp Reach for the Stars," she explained and indicated that he should follow her.

They walked out onto the long dock.

To the right, several colorful canoes were tied to cleats, along with a few rowboats. To the left, a large square of water was marked with buoys to indicate a swimming area that went from the shallow edge of the shore to the deep water at the end of the dock.

As they stood there, Logan looked down into the cool depths of the water and saw something move. "What was that?" he asked, pointing down.

Eve glanced into the water and smiled. "A fish. Haven't you ever seen a fish before?"

"Only on my dinner plate." Logan smirked and turned to head back to the shore.

Eve chuckled, but by the time she'd reached him, she managed to stifle her outburst. "Then, I just might teach you to fish before the summer's out."

"Look, Eve, I'm here to teach tennis only because I have to be. I don't need to be entertained." Logan instantly regretted that he sounded so snobbish, so mean, but he was long past an age when sitting on the creek bank with a fishing pole appealed to him. "Besides I don't need a woman to teach me what's generally considered to be a man's hobby," he blundered on, wishing he'd discovered a way to control his mouth.

Eve blanched beneath his outburst. Far from being cowed by his display of temper, she smiled sweetly and nodded. "Well, if you need me, I'll be in my office." She lifted her chin defiantly and strode away.

She hurried up the path to her office, hardly noticing that the rhododendron was beginning to flower. Any other time, she'd have stopped to admire the beautiful blossoms, but now she strode past without hesitating.

Eve scurried along the rough pathway so quickly that she stumbled twice, once on an exposed root and once on a sharp rock. "Damn!" she exclaimed, hoping nobody was in hearing distance, but at the moment she didn't care.

When she reached her office, she sat down and glanced at the clock on the wall. She still had twenty minutes before the first nurse arrived for her interview. Forcing herself to concentrate, Eve went back to her forms. After a few minutes, she noticed the leather bags beside the door.

She hadn't shown Logan his cabin yet.

Sooner or later, he'd have to come back for the bags. For now, let him stew about his accommodations, she decided.

Mr. Logan Mallory was exactly like all the reporters said: arrogant and hot-tempered. He could damn well get over it. She wasn't going to put up with it from the kids and certainly not from him. He might get his way with the press, with tennis officials, and with the women who were always flocking around him, but Eve Travers wasn't one of his groupies—and she didn't intend to become one.

Wishing he hadn't been so smart-mouthed, Logan tossed a stone into the lake and watched the resulting ripples. He walked by the lake, staring down into the water for a short distance. The beach extended for a couple of hundred feet of freshly laid sand, compliments of this Tennis Pro contract, he surmised. The camp really did look nice.

Eve had done a great job. When he'd first heard Jerry and Tim talking about it, Logan had been afraid he'd have to live in the wilds with mountain lions and worse. In fact, the picture that had sprung to mind had been that of a small village in Borneo that he'd seen in *National Geographic* once when he was younger.

He sat down in the dry sand and stared across the lake. Three months of hell, that was what he had signed up for. There wasn't a decent-size town around here for miles. Camp Reach for the Stars, as Eve had so tritely named the place that was to become his prison, was about halfway between Charlotte, North Carolina, and Spartanburg, South Carolina.

Something moved close to him, and he sat stock-still, allowing only his eyes to scan the area around him. For a moment, he saw nothing. Then he noticed a scrawny cat, its fur gaped and torn as if it had been in a fight. "Get the hell out of here. Go home."

The cat simply sat down on its haunches and stared at him. Suddenly, Logan realized that he was very much like the cat. Though his skin didn't show the damage, as the cat's did, he was battered nonetheless. Even the years he'd spent on the tour hadn't been especially happy ones, though he'd won every tournament at one time or another. Now, here he was in another dead end—at least until the end of summer when he could collect his money from Tennis Pro.

He didn't even like kids. Every kid Logan had ever met had been spoiled rotten, totally ignorant, or just plain mean. Except for his son. No matter what happened, he couldn't get Brandon out of his mind.

Logan had been at his third Wimbledon, in the semifinal match when Brandon had become ill. Reina, his wife, had said that he should stay, she would take care of Brandon, but she couldn't. Nobody could. Brandon died halfway through the finals. Jerry hadn't told Logan until the match was over and he'd won. Logan's first Wimbledon title was tainted by his son's death—and the knowledge that he hadn't gone home when the boy needed him.

But even more painful was his wife's treatment of the situation. When Logan returned, he discovered that she'd lied to him about the child's condition. He'd had spinal meningitis. Reina had been at the opening of her exhibit at a gallery when he died. Brandon had died alone, with strangers. Logan could never forgive Reina—nor himself—for that.

Ever since then, he'd tried to maintain a

distance between himself and kids, especially boys. Logan couldn't stand the memories that always flooded in. And here he was, spending the summer with a bunch of them. How could he ever escape the devils that taunted him over his decision to remain in England when Brandon needed him?

Logan glanced at the cat again. Its scruffy black fur undulated gently as the animal rose and walked toward Logan, apparently undaunted by the admonition to go away.

Logan couldn't be mean to the animal. "Hell, you're in worse shape than I am. Come on. The least I can do is get you something to eat."

He reached toward the cat, halfheartedly hoping that the animal would shy and run. After a few seconds of hesitation, the cat rubbed against Logan's hand. He picked it up gently, not knowing how badly the cat was hurt. "You a fella or a gal?"

Petting the cat, Logan turned the cat over to check the sex. "Judging from the evidence, or lack of it, I'd say you're a lady." Logan rubbed the soft fur on the cat's stomach. "Why would you want to hang around the likes of me? I'm not much of a pet person."

Beneath his hand, he could feel something like a vibration. He heard a little sound and leaned closer. "What's wrong? Did I do something wrong? I never had a cat before, so I don't know what to do for you."

Logan continued to rub the cat, wondering what he should do. Maybe the cat was in pain. He stopping petting her. The noise stopped. "That's odd." When he began to rub her again, the sound resumed, along with the vibration. "Is that your motor?" He scowled at the cat and continued his ministrations. "I'll bet that's purring. Is that what you're doing? Jeez, I'm talking to a cat!"

Carrying the cat, who seemed perfectly content to allow him to do so, Logan headed back toward the office. He wanted to find out who owned the cat and why it was in such bad condition. There were several paths leading away from the beach, and Logan discovered he hadn't been paying attention when Eve had led him on the little tour. He was thoroughly lost.

* * *

Eve stood at the window of her office, watching the sunset. There was nothing quite like seeing a sunset from this vantage point in the mountains, but she couldn't concentrate. Logan's car was still in the parking area, and he was nowhere to be found. Visions of all the awful things that could happen nearly obliterated the beautiful palette of colors that grew more vivid as the sun sank.

She snatched a mesh shopping bag from its nail and shoved in a first-aid kit along with a thermos of hot coffee. On the way out, she grabbed her flashlight.

Eve decided to start at the beach. Maybe she could pick up his trail somehow. She jogged along the well-worn path to the beach, hoping to meet him along the way. When she reached the sand, she tried to force back her disappointment and offered a silent prayer for Logan's safety.

Scanning the beach with her flashlight, she soon discovered his footprints leading away from the beach. Instead of heading back toward the camp, he was following a path that led along the rim of the lake. For a few seconds, she was undecided about which way she should go. If she went the same direction as he, then she might miss him entirely. If she went the other way, she'd have to be careful about her tracking because he could cut away from the trail at anytime.

Eve chewed her bottom lip as she considered her options. This wasn't a time to make a snap decision and, therefore, a mistake. She decided to try to head him off.

The woods were growing darker. Her light produced a bright yellow beam as she threaded her way among the shrubs, vines, roots, and undergrowth that sought to obscure her way.

Her anger had long since dissipated, and she felt horrible about letting his remarks prompt such a response in her. She knew about his temper and should have expected him to make disparaging remarks. Eve was well aware that she wasn't the only person to have doubts about the feasibility of this venture; Logan didn't like it any more than she did.

The sun had set completely as she walked along the path and trained the beam of light before her. Maybe Logan would see the light and call to her—if he could. All around her, nocturnal animals awoke and began to hunt for their supper.

Owls hooted, frogs croaked, crickets chirruped, but there was no human sound other than her own cautious footsteps.

The lake lapped gently at the shore, and the mockingbird sang his diverse song as Eve continued her hunt. She was now getting truly worried. What if he'd left the path? What if he'd fallen in the lake? She didn't even know if he could swim or not.

Her anger returned. This was all Logan's fault. If he hadn't been so . . . so insensitive. No, that wasn't how it was. He'd been downright chauvinistic.

What would happen if Logan died? Would she still get the money for her camp? If his death had been at her hands, it would be different, she mused with a smile, remembering how angry she could get with him. As soon as the thought edged its way into her mind, she regretted it. That kind of thinking was how Logan thought. No matter what happened, she wasn't that self-centered. Logan's life mattered a great deal more than . . . well, it mattered a lot. She couldn't bear to think of how she would feel if he'd been hurt or killed because she'd reacted with anger to his needling.

It would truly be her own fault, too. She had nobody else to blame.

Logan had never in his life regretted having such a quick mouth. Why couldn't he learn to control his tongue? It had gotten him into trouble too many times. When . . . if . . . he got out of this alive—and he was beginning to wonder if he would—he was damned sure going to learn to control his mouth.

"Think before you speak, stupid," he scolded himself. Thorns scratched at his bare legs, leaving dark streaks along a path that would be obvious for a week.

The cat licked his hand as if to calm him down somewhat. "Yeah, I know. I'm an idiot."

The darkness was pervasive. He could hardly even see the light-colored fabric of his shirt and shorts, much less the dark blur that was the cat. "Maybe I made a mistake by leaving the path. How the hell do I know where the camp is? There aren't any lights."

Logan's arms were beginning to ache. The cat, though not heavy, was a burden because of the way he was trying to carry her. He considered putting her down, but wasn't sure she'd follow him. Holding her closer, he tried to convince himself that he was only carrying her to someone who could treat her wounds, that there was no connection between him and the cat.

Maybe if he couldn't find out who owned her, he'd keep the cat. The thought pleased him, though he didn't want to admit it. Owning a pet simply didn't fit in with the image he wanted to project, but then again, he was changing that image—or trying to.

"Damn briars!" came an epithet from her right.

It sounded like he wasn't too far away. Eve started to call out to him, but hesitated. How would she handle this? How would he like her to handle this? A man with as much ego as the magazines claimed he had just might not appreciate being made to look small. Being discovered lost and wandering around in the woods at night definitely qualified as making a man look small.

Then she smiled. She could handle this. Eve Travers could handle a man when she set her mind to it. "Logan? Is that you?" she called spinning around with the beam of her flashlight focused at eye level.

"Eve?" Logan answered, feeling more than a bit stupid.

"Over here." Eve hesitated, trying to train in on the direction from which his voice came. Then she saw him. Thank God he didn't appear to be injured. She waited until he got closer to her. "Gee, I didn't realize you enjoyed an evening walk in the woods. If I'd known, I would have suggested walking together."

Logan's forehead wrinkled for a moment and then he smiled. "Oh, yeah. Nothing like an evening stroll in the woods to get your appetite going."

Eve frowned. He was carrying something in his arms. "Is that a cat?"

"Cat?" he asked, looking down at the furry mass in his arms. "Oh, right. This is . . . uh . . . this is Muzzle."

"Muzzle?" Eve leaned a little closer. The cat was ugly, really ugly. Its coat was rough and uneven, maybe even torn. "That's an unusual name for a cat."

"Muzzle is an unusual cat." Logan hoped she'd invite him to walk along with her. Maybe she didn't know he was lost, though he considered that unlikely. If she did and was trying to avoid embarrassing him, he appreciated her effort. That was a likely scenario, considering her mesh bag containing what appeared to be a Thermos.

"Well, I'm ready to head back." Eve tried to smile reassuringly. "If you and Muzzle would like to join me, I'll fix something for dinner."

"Great. We were just getting ready to return as well." Logan fell into step beside her. "Muzzle isn't going to be a problem, is she? We're pretty much inseparable . . . these days."

"I suppose not, though I discourage our staff from bringing pets." Eve tried to recall if she'd ever seen anything written about Logan's pets, but couldn't. In fact, she recalled one article that quoted him as saying he didn't like animals. Well, journalists were known to be wrong occasionally. "You and Muzzle been together long?"

Logan gazed at her, the faint light from the flashlight's beam illuminating her face. He didn't want to lie to her, but he couldn't say that he'd just found the cat.

"Oh, longer than I ever thought possible," he said finally.

"Such devotion is an admirable quality." Eve reached over and scratched the cat behind the ears. "I hope she likes it here."

With a wicked little grin on his face, Logan nodded. "I think she'll like it here as much as I do."

Three

Logan awoke with cramping muscles and stinging scratches from his foray into the woods. He moved slightly, trying to get more comfortable on the narrow cot and wondered vaguely if Eve kept a first-aid kit on the premises. He could use some sort of antiseptic ointment and liniment.

Muzzle tiptoed up to his face and licked him several times before curling up on his crotch. He stared at the cat, wondering what he should do. "Do you want to go out? I guess I'll have to get you a cat-box or whatever they call those plastic things they put the sand in. If I'd known you were going to be this much trouble, I'd have left you out there in the woods."

Logan listened to the cat purr and was sorry he'd voiced his feelings aloud. "I apologize. But, you know, Muzzle, I get the feeling you're going to be as much trouble as a wife."

Muzzle purred again, rubbing her face against Logan's hand, as if to respond to his remarks. He lifted the cat and swung his legs over the edge of the cot. "Will you promise to stay close by if I let you out?"

Walking toward the door he shook his head in dismay. He was actually talking to this dumb animal. That made him as dumb as it was. He unlatched the door and set the cat down on the steps. "Don't wander away."

Logan sat down at the small desk and began to make notes of things he needed to buy to make his cabin more habitable. He'd sworn off liquor, but he intended to buy a small refrigerator for his mineral water and fresh fruit.

"God, who would have thought it?" he asked aloud, staring at the growing list.

"Thought what?"

Logan's head jerked up and he found himself staring through the screen at Eve. "Oh, I was just talking to myself."

"About what?" Eve asked, wondering if she detected a slight coloring in his cheeks. She decided it was her imagination.

"Come on in," he said and pointed at the door. "It's open. I just let Muzzle out."

"Thanks."

He waited until she was in the cabin. "Have a seat. I was just making a list of things I need to make this place seem like home."

Eve glanced around uncertainly. Home? What was home like for him? A well-stocked liquor cabinet, pornographic films, frozen dinners? "I don't understand," she finally said.

"Yeah, well, I'm going to buy one of those office refrigerators. You know, the half-size ones?" He pointed to the corner of his room. "For fruit and mineral water. That kind of stuff."

"I see." Eve really didn't see. She couldn't envision him sitting around at night, munching on an apple or peach and drinking Perrier. He didn't exactly seem like a beer and peanuts kind of man either, but she could easily envision him with a glass of Scotch in his hand.

"And I thought I'd get a new mattress, maybe even a new bed. No offense, but that one's not very hard." He studied her for a moment, trying to decide if she would take his purchase as a form of criticism. "I need a real hard mattress because of my back."

"I'm sorry. If I'd known earlier, I would have—"

"Well, we weren't exactly to the point in our relationship where we could discuss the pros and cons of mattresses." Logan grinned and added a few more things to his list. "Is there anything I can pick up for you while I'm gone?"

Eve considered him for a moment. "Where are you going?"

"Charlotte, I think. And I'll probably stop by my house in Tega Cay."

"Is that where you live?" Eve asked. Tega Cay was a small town, really a bedroom community about halfway between Charlotte and Rock Hill, reportedly very chic and expensive. "Do you live on the golf course?"

"No, I live on the lake. Tennis is my only vice." Logan glanced at Eve and grinned sheepishly. "Nowadays, anyway."

He and Jerry were both trying very hard to convince Eve that Logan had changed, but she found it hard to believe. A man who'd spent the better part of his life chasing women—sometimes girls—could hardly change overnight. Nor did she believe he'd stopped carousing around like a fraternity man.

"I hope so, Logan," she said and moved toward the door. "Are you planning to be gone long?"

"Not really, why?"

"I have a few things to do and I thought maybe we could go to Charlotte together."

"Great. Can you be ready in, say thirty minutes?" Logan didn't really know if he wanted her tagging along or not, but he couldn't very well refuse her.

She looked at him and smiled. "I can be ready in five minutes."

"Terrific. I can't stand a woman who keeps me waiting." Logan regretted the words as soon as they were out of his mouth. What had happened to his vow to think before he spoke?

"So I hear," she said and stepped outside. Muzzle came through the door and jumped up on the desk in front of Logan. "I'll be in the parking lot in thirty minutes."

Why had she said she would go with him? Eve glanced at herself in the mirror and made a face. "What a stupid thing to do. You could always change your mind."

But she did need to buy a few more things for the camp and having a man along to lug her heavier purchases was too tempting. After all, it had been her suggestion that she accompany him, so she could hardly back out.

Her main reason for going was the lawnmower. The old one her father had used was woefully inadequate, not to mention that poor Otis spent more time repairing it than he did mowing. Eve knew little about yard equipment. All the outside maintenance had been done by the apartment personnel back in Atlanta. Now, it was her responsibility.

She wondered what she should wear. After all, she'd said she would go with him without even knowing where they were going. Eve finally slipped into crisp white slacks and a red silk blouse, dressy enough, she concluded after a glance in the mirror, for nearly anyplace unless he decided to eat a meal at a really fancy restaurant.

Ten minutes ahead of schedule, she hurried out to find Otis Wallace, the handyman, to tell him of her plans. She spotted him, repairing one of the window hinges. "Otis," she called and waved to him.

He nodded and finished tightening the screw. "Checking the windows, Missy. Won't do for the shutters not to close if a rainstorm pops up. Don't want no rain-soaked young'un's, I reckon."

"Thank you, Otis. I appreciate your attention to detail." Eve watched him open and close the shutter several times. "I'll be away this morning, so if you need anything, I suppose you'll just have to wait."

"Don't worry 'bout a thing." Otis moved to the next window and checked the hinges. "I got plenty to do and I'll keep my eye on things 'round here."

"Thanks. Can you think of anything I should pick up while I'm in Charlotte?"

"Nope. Not a thing. 'Cepting the lawn-mower. It's gone again." Otis tried the next shutter, which seemed to be rusted in the open position. "Lacking that, I guess you'd better pick up some oil. Maybe some paint for the swings and jun-gle-gym in the playground."

"Guess what. I'm buying a lawnmower. And, I'll remember the oil, too." Eve hurried back to Logan's cabin in time to meet him as he walked out his door.

"I didn't expect you to be ready this soon." He walked toward her and stopped at his car. "I was going to pick you up at your place."

Eve smiled and walked to the passenger side of the car. She didn't want to remind Logan that she'd promised to be ready before he was.

Logan opened the door for her. The top was down on the Jaguar and Eve slid easily into the plush leather of the passenger seat. Somehow, she hadn't expected him to be such a gentleman. Of all the impressions she'd gotten from the newspaper and magazine articles she'd read, gentleman wasn't one of them.

The short ride to Charlotte passed quickly, with Eve chatting over the noise of the interstate highway and radio about her plans for the camp. Logan sometimes looked interested; other times he appeared bored. She couldn't understand exactly what the difference was, but soon found that as she discussed the sports portion of the camp program, he perked up. But when she spoke of her artistic projects, his expression changed subtly, as if he didn't want to think about such matters.

In Charlotte, they found a furniture store, with Logan trying mattress after mattress. He stretched out on one after the other, turning this way and that, curling up and straightening out. Finally, the clerk looked at Eve. "Wouldn't you like to try the mattress also, ma'am?"

Logan stifled a chuckle, but Eve simply smiled at the clerk. "No, sir. You see, this mattress is for one of my employees and I will never have occasion to sleep on it."

"Beg pardon, ma'am," the clerk said and glanced at Logan.

"Yes, well, we need something simple in a frame. Not a lot of money, but sturdy." Logan rose from the super firm mattress he had been lying on. "We'll take this one in a king."

Eve chewed her lower lip for a moment. "Logan, do you think there will be enough room if we put a king-size bed in that cabin?"

"All the room I'll need." Logan moved past her to look at the headboards. "I need to stretch out when I sleep."

Eve rolled her eyes. "I meant, will you

have a place to walk or work in the cabin if you put in such a large bed."

"Eve, I can't play tennis if I don't get a good night's sleep and I just can't sleep on a tiny bed." Logan felt like a fool discussing sleeping arrangements with a woman who might possibly—by stretching the terms of the contract a little—be considered his boss. He rankled at Eve mentioning it to the clerk, even though she didn't mention Logan by name. He'd managed to botch that up himself by insisting that *he* needed the large-size bed. Apparently the clerk didn't recognize him, and Logan was grateful for that small favor.

Still, it wasn't a comfortable situation. Logan regretted that she had made the trip with him. He could have come up with some excuse to prevent it, but hadn't considered the implications at the time.

Eve saw that he was embarrassed and assumed that it was because the clerk now knew, beyond doubt, that Logan worked for her, which wasn't precisely true. She'd tried to word her part of the conversation so that the clerk could infer nothing about her relationship with Logan, but he'd blurted out that business about needing the extra-large bed. Well, it served him right.

So far, neither she nor Logan had spelled out the terms of their relationship. She knew that he was more at ease with the knowledge left unsaid. The contract stated that any matters concerning Camp Reach for the Stars were her decisions, though she could consult him for his opinion.

Eve knew—or was pretty certain—that one clause had caused Logan the most grief. From everything she knew about him, he'd always been in charge. Even his manager couldn't exert much control over Logan where his temper or his social life were concerned. And that troubled Eve more than anything else about him: From everything she'd read, Logan Mallory seemed to have no control over his temper, nor over his libido.

"Will there be anything else?" the clerk asked.

What had gone on while she'd been off in her own little world of thought? Eve smiled, glanced at Logan, and removed her checkbook. "What's the total?"

"You don't have to do this, Eve," Logan protested. It was bad enough that he'd made such a fool of himself in front of the clerk, but now she was offering to pay for his bed. It was humiliating. Logan turned to the clerk and shrugged. "I nearly forgot. Do you have one of those office refrigerators? You know, the half-size ones? And a microwave."

"Certainly. Come this way."

Logan and Eve followed the man to the appliance section of the store and settled quickly on a small refrigerator and microwave. The refrigerator wasn't exactly the kind that Logan had in mind, but it was small and inexpensive. The small microwave was perfect.

When the clerk totaled the bill, Eve removed her checkbook again in spite of Logan's protest. "Nonsense. This is for the camp, so the cost will come out of camp funds." Eve wrote the check without waiting for Logan's answer.

In truth, Logan was glad she'd written the check. It saved him the potential embarrassment of using the last of his available credit. Most of Logan's credit cards were at the limit, some were even past due. He grinned lopsidedly at the clerk. "Never work for a woman."

While Logan made arrangements for

the items to be delivered, Eve stood silently, reluctant to do anything else that might embarrass him. He might well be the "Casanova of the tennis court" if the articles she'd read were correct, but something didn't really click. The Logan she knew, though he'd demonstrated his temperament a little, didn't really fit with the image the reporters had drawn.

Eve decided to try to put her research out of her mind. In fact, she was beginning to wish she'd never even looked up those articles. It would have been much better to meet him on even ground, with him knowing nothing of her and her knowing nothing of him. Except that they weren't meeting as man and woman; they were employee and employer—almost.

And, more than anything else, she wanted this arrangement to work. Logan would be a valuable drawing card for the publicity that the camp needed so desperately. Every tidbit of good publicity this summer would translate into donations— and dollars—next summer.

They arrived at the hardware store. Each time they stopped, Eve took a moment to finger-comb her short brown hair before getting out of the classic Jaguar convertible. "I didn't realize the wind would blow my hair so much," she explained as Logan waited at her door for her to get out. "I never rode in a convertible before."

"Yeah, well, I should have suggested a hat or something."

She glanced at his hair. Though hers was thoroughly windblown—as his must have been—his hair seemed to know its natural placement and return almost exactly, as if the wind had never affected it.

They walked into the store and Eve glanced around. She was lost here. Though she'd had to buy a few tools, hammers, screwdrivers, wrenches, and some hardware, she'd never even considered the merits or drawbacks of a lawnmower and she was a little apprehensive. "We need to look at lawnmowers."

"Lawnmowers?" Logan repeated and turned to stare at her.

"Yes. And some all-purpose oil." Eve spotted some signs suspended from the ceiling by chains. She looked down the rows as she walked along until she found the one marked "Lawn and Garden."

Logan followed along. This was one of the few times he'd ever been in a store that sold nothing but hardware. Many men counted their masculinity in terms of the number of saws and drills and other tools, but Logan perceived those items as drudgery and indicated a man with nothing interesting to do in life.

Eve stopped at a display of lawnmowers. There was a vast array, ranging from the simplest man-powered push mower, which the environmentalists favored because it emitted no fumes, to gasoline-operated mowers, to the self-propelled variety, and then to riding mowers. She walked along, glancing at the price tags dangling from handles or steering wheels.

Otis really needed one of the riding ones. There was so much to mow at the camp, particularly the soccer and softball fields, which had to be groomed frequently. But the price tag seemed so high. She looked to Logan. "What do you think?"

"Me?" he asked in surprise. "What do I think?"

"Yes. You've seen the camp." Eve glanced once again at the mowers and gestured expansively. "What do we need? No," she said, reconsidering her question. "What can we get by with?"

"You're asking me which lawnmower to buy?" Logan stared at first one of the machines and then the other. Green, red, green, and yellow. All were as alien to him as a man from Mars would be.

"Yes, I really want your advice." Eve walked by each one and read a little of the information attached to the handle of one mower. "I'm not sure. I don't know enough about lawnmowers to make an educated purchase."

Logan swallowed heavily and walked past her. He didn't know what to say, but he damned sure knew he was going to think before he spoke this time. "Well," he began, trying to buy a little time before he admitted his lack of knowledge. "Let's see. You've got a pretty big place. I think you need something sturdy."

"I know that." Eve grimaced. He was making her feel like a fool simply because she'd admitted that she didn't know anything about the subject. "Give me some concrete advice. Something I can base my decision on."

How did he get into this? he wondered. "Say, didn't you mention getting some oil for Otis?"

"Yes, but this is the most important item."

"Right. You run over and get the oil while I study the problem."

Eve chewed her bottom lip indecisively. "Men," she muttered and strode off toward the lubricants.

Logan watched her until she disappeared down the aisle. Then he hurried over to the counter and asked for help. He'd never cut grass in his life, not even as a kid. He'd been a tennis prodigy from the first time he picked up a racquet at age six. His mother had immediately employed a coach. Logan hadn't had the opportunity to grow up like other boys, learning the skills taught by fathers to sons.

But he'd learned one thing for sure: when in doubt, find an expert.

By the time Eve returned, he was squatting confidently beside a self-propelled mower with a wide cutting area. He fiddled with some sort of tube for a moment, unscrewed one of the caps—gasoline, he supposed—and then stood. "What about this one?"

"You've decided already?" she asked, gazing intently at him. His brown eyes were soft with humor, and she couldn't decide whether he was teasing her or not. She slid her hands along the shiny red handle. "This one's best for our needs?"

"I believe so."

"What is your decision based upon?" Eve asked, moving the mower back and forth for a moment as if that could help her make her decision.

"Eh, well, Otis has a great deal of grass to mow and this one is self-propelled. A little more expensive than the push-types, but a lot less expensive than the riding mowers. Sturdy, adequate, and affordable," Logan repeated the salesman's words exactly.

"I see." Eve glanced at the other mowers. There were several less expensive ones and she wondered longingly if one of them would be sufficient. No, you brought Logan along for his expertise. Accept his judgment. She knew that a man's judgment would be based in reality: this much yard, this much money, this much energy. "All right," she said, finally assenting to his will.

Logan smiled. "I'll just find a clerk to get one for us." He looked around. "I suppose we'll have to get one in a box instead of one already put together."

"Oh, I hadn't thought of that." Once again, Eve realized that a man's mind worked differently from a woman's. "Whatever you think is best."

Signaling to the clerk, Logan turned to Eve. "Find the right oil?"

"Right oil?" she asked and looked at the small can in her hand. She held it up. "This is . . . I think this is what Otis wanted."

Logan took the can from her hand and stared at the label. "Did he mention a brand name?"

"No, he just said an all-purpose oil."

With a shrug, he handed it back to her. "I guess this one will do then."

The clerk arrived and Logan listened while Eve told him which mower she wanted and then explained that they would like it in a box. He handed her a ticket and indicated that she should pay at the cash register and then pick the lawnmower up at the designated area.

Once again feeling that she was in control of the situation, Eve thanked him and then strode off to the cash register with Logan trailing behind.

He stopped here and there to examine some hand tools while Eve waited patiently. He looked at a power drill for a long time before putting it down with what he hoped was a wistful expression on his face. "I really need one of these, but I can see you're in a hurry."

Eve felt a little guilty. After all, they had come in his car. "No, please, take all the time you need."

Logan picked up another drill and then set it down. "No, they really don't have the model I'm looking for."

Glancing around for a clerk, Eve said, "I'm sure they can order it."

Damn you for showing off, Logan Mallory. He gazed at his watch, as if mentally calculating the amount of time such a venture would take. "I'll wait. I want to make sure I get precisely the right one."

"Whatever you think best," Eve said and waited for him to indicate that he was finished shopping.

They reached the checkout counter, and Eve handed the paper to the clerk, along with the oil. While she was writing the check, Logan went to get the car and the lawnmower. In a matter of minutes, they were speeding down Independence Boulevard.

After a few turns, he pulled into the restaurant he'd chosen for lunch. "This place is great."

Once again, Eve glanced in the mirror and finger-combed her hair. Her face seemed to be a bit pink, as if the strong sunlight had begun to make its mark.

"Sorry, I should have put the top up."

"No, I love riding with it down." Eve loved the feeling of the wind whistling past her, but even more than that, she was glad not to have to keep up a steady conversation. The noise of traffic and the radio had made hearing almost impossible. He pulled into the parking lot of a restaurant called the King's Court. Eve had heard of it, but she couldn't remember what had been said. It could have been good or bad.

When she got out, Logan closed the door and placed his hand on the small of her back as they walked into the restaurant. At first, Eve was a little unsure of what to do about the physical contact, but she took it as a gesture of a gentleman, rather than something personal. So far, Logan had shown no interest in her whatsoever, and she was happy with that arrangement. Emotional entanglements would cause nothing but trouble between them this summer, and Eve wasn't the kind of woman to settle for a one-night stand or an affair—not even with one of the handsomest men ever to play professional tennis.

Once inside the dimly lit restaurant, Eve realized that Logan must have come here for the comfort of a place he knew and where he felt at home. The owner or manager rushed up to them as soon as they walked inside.

"Logan!" the man called from halfway across the room. "How good to see you again."

"Nice to see you, Jack." Logan grinned and urged Eve forward. He was on his home turf here. In this sports-oriented restaurant, there were eight or ten television sets, all tuned to sports channels, which reminded him of another loss. He'd have to spend the summer without cable television, if he could get any channels at all on the top of the mountain. Forcing down a groan that threatened, Logan introduced Eve to his friend. "Got something good for lunch?"

"We got greasy and great or crunchy and healthy. Take your pick." Jack led them to a table and seated Eve. "Not exactly true," he said as an afterthought, as if Eve might object to the fare. "We have fine food, fine food. If it's not on the menu, we'll fix it. If we can't figure out how to fix it, you can come back in the kitchen and tell us how."

"I'm sure the menu items will be fine," Eve said, warming to the man's chatty style.

"Everything's great here." Logan slid into the chair beside hers and looked around to see if he knew anyone. He waved to one of the waiters, but saw nobody else even vaguely familiar. With a glance at his watch, he realized that they'd arrived before the regular lunch crowd. He smiled at Eve. "The Philly cheese sandwich is terrific. They tell me the salads are good, but until recently, I've been going for the greasy and great."

Eve gazed at him for a moment. "You know, I would have thought that a professional athlete would have to watch his diet. Why not you?"

"I do. Well, I did while I was on the pro circuit." Logan patted his flat stomach. "See what happens when you quit the rigid workouts and strict diet?"

"I see a very flat stomach. No beer gut, no paunch." Eve met his eyes again. "So what's the penalty for eating greasy and great and not working out?"

Logan looked down and shrugged. "I suppose you can't tell, but I've put on a few pounds lately. Eating my own cooking, I guess."

Eve recalled the day she'd met Logan for the first time. He'd asked to see a recipe in the magazine she'd been looking at. "You really do your own cooking?"

"Most of the time." Logan raked his fingers through dark hair shaded slightly at the temples with silver. "But I haven't been doing it for long. I have to admit I'm still learning."

"Burned beans and pot roast?" Eve asked with a tentative laugh.

"Well, I haven't gotten that far yet." Logan closed up his menu and took a sip of water. "More like grilled chicken and salad. I'm a whiz with a grill."

Jack returned with a waiter and Eve concentrated on the menu for a moment. The waiter spoke briefly with Logan before reciting a list of specials. She listened carefully and then ordered the fresh chicken salad plate.

Logan ordered the fettucine with a side salad. "Carbohydrates for energy," he explained.

"I see. But what about that rich sauce?"

"Jeez, do you have to point out my faults? So I love the Alfredo sauce." Logan leaned forward and whispered in a teasing voice. "I have it on good authority that if you eat a nice crunchy salad with it, the calories and fat in the sauce are dissolved."

"Oh, how exciting! I never knew that," Eve teased him right back. "Maybe we should write a cookbook that espouses that theory. Should sell millions."

Logan chuckled and shook his head. "Me? Write a cookbook? What a joke. My crazy mother never cooked. I never cooked. Who'd believe what I wrote?"

Eve laughed along with him for a few seconds and then studied him. "Maybe a lot of people, Logan. You know, books of any kind by athletes and stars sell very well. You could do something like . . . oh, I don't know. Healthy and filling recipes for unattached athletes."

Logan stopped laughing and stared at her. "You're serious, aren't you?"

"Sure I am." Eve saw the interest gleaming in his dark eyes. "Maybe I could illustrate it for you."

"What do you mean?"

"You know, take some pictures of the dishes or draw some athletic-type illustrations."

"You're an artist?" he asked, sagging back in his chair. "A real artist?"

"Real artist. Oil paints, pastels, watercolor, the works." Eve didn't understand the strange expression on his face. "Surely you knew that I was an artist? I mean, why would I want to start an arts camp if I weren't an artist?"

Logan stared blankly at her, barely seeing her face. "I never thought about it. I just . . . hell, I don't know what I thought."

Without knowing what had happened, Eve felt that she had somehow disappointed Logan. Many people had mixed reactions when they discovered that she was an artist, but disappointment wasn't one of them.

Maybe she was reading more into the situation. After all, she didn't know Logan very well and he might simply be disinterested. Not everyone cared for the arts, especially athletes.

Logan took a long drink of his mineral water as he collected himself. Why did she have to be an artist? What the hell did he care if she was an artist anyway? After the summer was over, he was back to living in style—alone. He was happy that he'd sworn off women. It happened to be a convenient excuse for not getting involved and, now, that was especially true.

There were too many problems with artists for him to allow himself to get close to her. He'd thought they might become friends, but now he doubted even that. After the childhood he'd had, the last thing he wanted was to get chummy with an artist.

Eve was thankful the waiter brought their meals. The silence was a bit strained. Not since that ridiculous mistake she'd made in Tim Carlson's office had she been so uncomfortable with Logan, not even when he'd gotten lost last night. True, she'd been angry with him for his rotten attitude, but not uncomfortable.

The best thing for her to do was to keep things on a strictly business basis with him. With his childish temper, there was no telling what he would do if she got close to him. None of the articles she'd read indicated that he was violent anywhere exccpt on the tennis court, but that didn't really mean anything.

All she knew about—or cared about at this point—was that she wanted her arts camp to be successful. And for now, that took getting along with Logan. She swallowed a lump of chicken salad that she would have otherwise savored and smiled at Logan. "So, Logan, do you have any good ideas about the tennis program and Camp Reach for the Stars?"

For a moment, he was taken aback. He could have sworn that she was about ready to vault over the table and attack him. "Ideas? You really care about my ideas?"

"Of course, I care about them." Eve nibbled on a cracker and studied him as he deliberately twirled a few strands of his fettucine.

Logan gazed at her for a minute and then glanced away. "Look, Eve, I'm there for the summer, nothing more. You tell me how you want the tennis program run, and I'll do it."

"Do you mean to tell me that you don't

even care enough to give me your ideas?" Eve asked, placing her fork neatly on the edge of her plate and trying to maintain her calm demeanor.

"I mean that I'm not getting involved. Not with you and not with a bunch of geeky kids." Logan gulped down the remainder of his water and then faced Eve again. He hated himself for acting like this, but he didn't want her to have any false illusions where he was concerned. "Let's just get this over with as quickly and as painlessly as possible for both of us."

Eve lifted her chin and let the words soak into her like vinegar. "Why did you accept this . . . challenge, Logan? I'm not stupid enough to believe you did it because of some . . . some sense of charity toward the kids who couldn't otherwise come. But if you have no feelings for this project other than—"

"Money, Eve. That's it, pure and simple." He put down his fork and wiped his mouth on the linen napkin. "Don't go attributing a bunch of motives to me that don't apply. I need the money."

"I see." Eve folded her napkin and placed it on her plate. "Well," she said, her voice a barely audible whisper. "It's good that we know where we stand."

She turned and signaled to the waiter. "Check, please," she said as he approached the table. When he handed her the bill, she removed her wallet and placed the proper amount on the table, along with a generous tip. She rose and stared down at Logan. "Let's go."

Logan scowled at her, but held his tongue for once. If that was the way she wanted to play, then he could give as good as he got. "Anything you say, Miss Travers."

Eve bit her tongue as she marched out of the restaurant. Jack, seemingly stunned by their behavior, trailed along after them into the parking lot.

"Hey, Logan, is something wrong?" Jack asked, trying to catch up to them.

"Nothing at all, Jack." Logan didn't want to discuss this in front of Jack. After all, in a few months, Logan would be a regular customer at King's Court again and he didn't want any gossip making the rounds to be whispered about when he returned from his prison sentence at the camp. He turned and waited for Jack to catch up, shook his hand, and shrugged.

"We're just in a hurry. That's all. See you again soon."

Eve said nothing, but strode to her side of the car and let herself in before Logan could help her—if he was going to. She settled in the seat and stared straight ahead. Logan started the car and they drove for three traffic lights before he said anything.

"Look, Eve, I'm sorry." Logan leaned back in the seat, his left hand draped over the steering wheel and his right poised on the floor shift. "I'm not the settling-down type, not even for a summer. Playing house isn't my idea of . . . I just don't want you thinking that—"

"Settling down? Playing house?" Eve erupted and turned to face him. "Why, you egotistical . . ." She bit back the epithets she wanted to fling at him, knowing that once the words were said they could never be taken back. "I don't know why you seem to think that I'm stumbling over my feet in an attempt to . . . to seduce you or whatever it is you think, but get over it."

"Whoa, hold on there—"

"No, you hold on. From the moment I met you, you've been a thorn in my side.

Drop this 'I'm God's gift to women' attitude with me because I'm not falling for it." Eve glared into his deep brown eyes, wondering how he was really taking her tirade. At the moment, she really didn't care, because she'd had more than enough of his childish behavior. "And, I'd better not hear of you trying anything with any of my campers or my counselors."

"What!" he exclaimed and shoved the gear shift into neutral. "I don't know what you're thinking, babe, but you got me all wrong. I'm not interested in you *or* any of the kids that will be here this summer. I'm just counting the days until I'm free again."

Four

Eve lay in her bed, thinking about her argument with Logan. She sensed that something was behind his words, something that was intended to warn her away, something that he might not even be conscious of. What had happened to him to make him isolate himself from people, from emotion?

She plumped up her pillows and rose to a sitting position, drawing her knees up and propping her chin on them. There were times when Logan was extremely likable, almost human. Then there were other times when he withdrew abruptly. Did it have something to do with living on the road for so many years?

With a weary sigh, Eve decided that she could spend the rest of her life speculating about Logan's psyche and never get any closer to the truth. Right now, that didn't concern her. What did interest her was how his condition—for lack of a better word—would affect his interaction with the kids who were due in about a week.

Thinking about the opening of camp excited her. She rose and began to pace back and forth in her room. There were so many questions that were unanswered and would remain unanswered until the end of summer. She knew how to handle kids, teaching school had taught her that, but a summer camp was entirely different.

When her father had opened this camp, he'd been a young man, in his twenties. As well as she could recall, the campers adored him. She adored him. He always had a cheery smile, could crack a joke with the best of them, and somehow knew when a kid needed to talk.

That was one thing that set him apart from the other adults. He listened. He was as energetic as any of the campers, and could participate in any of the sporting events and activities,

Could she be all those things? The campers who were coming were gifted in the arts, but they were all from financially disadvantaged homes.

In today's world, nearly every family was touched in some way by drugs or alcohol or violence. Was she up to handling the problems that might occur because of those familial complications?

She had let herself believe that Logan might be of help in that area, but now she knew she couldn't depend on him for support. He would teach the tennis classes, referee the matches, become dynamic and diligent and creative for the cameras when the advertising film crew arrived, but that was all.

For now, that would have to be enough.

Eve couldn't stand being inside any longer. She changed into a pair of shorts and went down the stairs. Outside, the air was cool and fragrant, resplendent with the sounds of insects and frogs and other night animals. Eve loved the nights at the camp. She loved the sounds and the energy that seemed to fill the air when the moon rose over the mountain.

She took her flashlight in hand and wandered away from her cabin. It didn't matter where she was headed; she just wanted to be a part of the night's vitality and fellowship—even if she was the only human.

A strong light came from the direction of the tennis courts. At first, she thought she'd go over and check to see if someone had left the lights on, but as she approached through the playground, she heard the unmistakable grunts and groans of a tennis player. When she got close enough, she saw Logan, banging a ball against the backboard with a vengeance.

She didn't know who or what he was angry with, but she was glad she wasn't a tennis ball. Changing her direction, she headed toward the lake. The moon would be beautiful this time of night, and she needed to be alone in her private world to think about all the things that were going on around her.

Tomorrow, Connie Edwards would arrive. Connie had been the nurse at her father's camp, and Eve had hired her the moment she walked into the office. Connie represented one of the happiest times of Eve's childhood and she was hopeful that those times would return.

Logan ran his hand along the top of the tennis net. The lights were hardly enough for an evening tournament, but he felt at home there between the white lines and the tall fence. This was where he belonged, where he excelled. This was his life.

When had he gotten so old? he wondered and bounced the tennis ball a few times. He moved back behind the line and tossed the ball high into the air. On its descent, he leaped into the air and pounded the furry ball across the net.

"Ace," he murmured and did it again. Over and over he served, each ball falling either on the line or just inside the service court.

He could still serve with the best of them, but he lacked endurance, especially when he knew he would have to play in tie-breakers that sometimes seemed to go on and on.

So, what was he going to do with his life? Become a commentator? He supposed he could do that, but he'd alienated one of the networks and the other two were reluctant to offer him a contract because of his disposition. He chuckled wryly and hit a few more balls. Didn't they realize that it had been his volatility that had kept him in tennis as long as he'd been able to play? Didn't people know that the passion that he called upon to beat his opponents was a direct result of his temperament?

"Logan, old boy, you could have exercised better judgment at times," he chided himself. How many times had his uncontrolled temper bought him time on the sports shows? Almost as often as his excellent play.

He was popular with the reporters, not because he was a helluva tennis player, but because of his outbursts. "Both," he answered himself to mollify his wounded ego. "No need to be *that* critical of yourself."

And what was he doing here? Couldn't he have found another company to represent? One that didn't demand he spend the summer in a godforsaken children's camp? The answer was no. There hadn't been any offers lately.

Word had gotten around that he was headstrong—hell, they already knew that—as well as being unreliable. But there was more. He hadn't even finished shooting his last commercial. After spending the night drinking, he'd shown up to shoot the spot and the director had refused to film. Logan's eyes were bloodshot and he reeked of alcohol.

That had been three years ago. Jerry had worked hard in a vain attempt to get another commercial for Logan, but had been unsuccessful until Tennis Pro made their offer. Hell, he'd jumped at the chance. Logan owed this to Jerry, if nothing else. For more than twenty years, Jerry had devoted himself to Logan's career. He had to succeed this time.

Somehow, he had to find a way, discover some common ground with Eve that would allow them to make this summer as pleasant as possible. He regretted the way he'd acted today, but it had been for her own good. Allowing her to get close to him would be a mistake.

He moved over to the bench at the side of the court and sat down to think. If he learned one thing this summer, Logan decided, it would be tact. He had to learn to communicate in a way that didn't offend people.

And, he needed to read people better. Had he mistaken her friendliness for a come-on? Or had he been right? Was that what set her off? Had he pegged her right and his correct assumption made her angry?

He forced himself to be honest. No, she hadn't been coming on to him.

The problem lay with him. Inside. And he didn't know what to do about it.

Eve and Connie Edwards completed their shopping and left the pharmacy. "Connie, do you think we have everything we need?"

"We've got plenty of everything." Connie smiled patiently at Eve and chuckled. "You're just like your daddy. That man was a worrier, if I ever saw one."

"Dad? A worrier?" Eve asked, unable to keep the surprise from her voice. "I never knew that. In what way?"

"He was just like you. Worried that some child would get hurt and he'd have to live with it the rest of his life."

"That is a valid concern, Connie," Eve reminded the nurse. She studied the older woman for a few minutes. "What made you decide to come out of retirement to take this job?"

"You," Connie replied simply. "I remember what a precocious child you were, always hanging around the older kids. You knew as much as they did. More."

"And you based your decision on that?"

"Well, I have to admit that if I didn't like the way you'd grown up, I'd still be sitting in the porch swing, crocheting baby booties to sell down at the store in King's Mountain."

"Are you saying that because of me, Cleveland County's babies will go barefoot this winter?" Eve joked. She turned her Bronco into the parking lot near the office.

Connie smiled, reached over and patted Eve's hand. "Pretty much. I suppose old Mrs. Cranshaw will have to take up the slack now."

Eve turned to face Connie and studied her deeply tanned face, a result of hours spent in the sun tending her vegetable garden and playing with the kids in her neighborhood. "All that sounds good, Connie, but it doesn't wash. Why did you want this job?"

"Well," Connie said, smoothing the hem of her freshly starched shirt. "I wouldn't want you to think it was for old times' sake or anything. Just say I didn't like retirement as much as I thought I would."

With a chuckle, Eve got out of the Bronco and walked to the back to start removing boxes of supplies. "I know exactly what you're talking about."

"You?" Connie asked, taking a box under each arm. "How on earth would you know?"

"I sort of got fed up with teaching, you know the paperwork and all that." Eve walked the short distance to the first-aid cabin and opened the door. "So, I quit. I'd saved my money, inherited a little from Dad. I was going to be a lady of leisure."

Connie placed her boxes on the counter and then turned to stare at Eve. "Sounds pretty good. You're young enough to enjoy yourself. You can still travel and all that."

"That's true enough, but I got in a rut." Eve dropped into the chair and crossed her legs, thinking about her retirement. "I started playing bridge every week, same day, same group. I joined an exercise class. I started teaching painting classes and workshops."

"Now, that's not much of a retirement."

"But, somehow, it wasn't enough. Something was missing." Eve fanned herself with a package of gauze, staring at her old friend for a long moment. "Then one day during a bridge game, my bridge partner mentioned taking a hiking tour of Mexico."

"Did you go?"

Eve laughed and shook her head. "No, and that's the problem. I just looked at her and told her I was too old for that sort of thing."

"Doesn't sound like it to me. You look like you're in pretty good shape for an 'old' woman." Connie leaned her rounded stomach on the counter and crossed her arms. "So what gives?"

"I heard myself calling myself old." Eve stood up, somehow energized by the recollection of what had spurred her into action. "I knew right then that I'd be in my grave before I was sixty if I continued to think that way."

"Good for you."

"So, I started to think of ways to stay young," Eve explained and peered out the window. Logan's sleek green Jaguar left a cloud of dust on the road and skidded to a stop in the parking lot beside the Bronco. "I decided that being around kids would keep me from thinking of myself as old."

Connie laughed so hard she nearly fell. When she righted herself, she sagged into

a chair. "At least you came to that conclusion before you got to be sixty years
old. I reckon I'm a slow learner."

Logan hesitated a short time before getting out of his car. He wasn't a man who
could apologize very easily, though he
knew Eve deserved to hear one from him.
He heard the sound of laughter coming
from a cabin near the parking lot and followed the musical tone, knowing it was
Eve's laugh. Who could she be talking to
that made her so happy? he wondered.

Well, that settled that. He was having a
hard enough time screwing up the courage to apologize as it was. There was no
way he could do so in front of a stranger.
He'd simply have to find a way to make
Eve know how he felt. Maybe she wasn't
a stickler for ceremony and would notice
his changed attitude. He'd worked out a
great deal of frustration last night on the
tennis court and had made his decision
this morning just before dawn. He would
become the model teacher at Camp Reach
for the Stars.

As he neared the cabin, he could make
out Eve's voice. She seemed so relaxed

and happy, chattering about nothing in particular. She and the other woman were obviously old friends, for they were bringing up names and asking what had happened to so and so.

Though he was reluctant to interrupt their joyful reunion, Logan felt that he needed to begin now to make Eve aware of his changed attitude. He knocked on the screen door. "Knock, knock."

Eve felt the color rise in her face. She had wanted her first meeting with Logan this morning to be alone. Not that she would demand an apology or anything like that, but she needed to understand where they stood. She turned to face him as he opened the door and came in without waiting to be asked.

"Hi," she said finally, glancing at Connie to gauge her reaction. "Sleep well?"

Logan shrugged. "I'll sleep better tonight. After they deliver my bed."

Eve introduced her tennis coach to the camp's new nurse. "Connie was the nurse here when my father ran this camp."

Shaking hands with the woman, Logan noticed that her eyes twinkled and her lips turned up in a ready smile. "Pleased to meet you, Mrs. Edwards."

"I'm thrilled to meet you." Connie glanced from Logan to Eve and back again. "Tennis hasn't been the same since you threw your last racquet at the judge."

"Now, Connie," he teased, catching the light intent of her jibe. "They never proved I threw it at him intentionally. It slipped out of my hand as I was going to put it away."

Connie narrowed her eyes at him and pointed her finger. "Tsk, tsk, Logan Mallory. Telling whackies will make your nose grow long and that would be a shame. Such a handsome face, don't you think, Eve?"

Eve could have joyfully strangled Connie for such a leading remark. "Certainly."

Logan threw his arms around Connie and laughed. "I think we're going to get along just fine, unless you stand at the side of the tennis court and criticize my technique."

"I'm sure I won't find a thing to criticize. Quite the contrary. I'm tickled pink." Connie disengaged herself from Logan's arms and backed away. "But, don't you go buttering me up. I know your kind."

"Me?" he asked in mock astonishment. "What kind is that?"

"You're just the sort," she said, removing four huge bags of lollipops from one of the boxes. "Just the sort who would fake an injury to get one of my lollipops."

Logan pretended that her accusation had wounded him. "How can you say such a thing? I'm perfectly innocent."

Connie opened one of the bags and dumped it into a large jar that sat beside containers of bandages and other medical supplies. "Innocent? Harrumph. You may be a lot of things, Logan Mallory, but innocent isn't one of them."

He sidled over beside her and peered at the jar. When she turned away, he poked his hand inside and swiped three purple ones.

Connie stood there, arms akimbo, staring at him in mock malice. "Innocent?"

"Well, I never could resist a grape lollipop." With a glance at Eve, Connie scolded him again. "I don't expect to come in here and discover that all my grape suckers are gone. You're not too old for a good old-fashioned whuppin'."

Logan tucked two of the suckers in the pocket of his golf shirt and opened the other. He raised his eyebrows suggestively.

"Sounds a little kinky to me. Wanna play doctor?"

Eve was about to stalk out of the cabin. What had happened to the Logan Mallory she'd spent the day with yesterday? Somehow, Connie's presence had transformed him into a lovable, laughter-filled man without the chip on his shoulder. Connie eyed him carefully and shook her head. "No siree, I don't fool around with the campers and I don't fool around with the counselors."

"Technically, I'm not a counselor," he countered, licking his lollipop playfully.

"Same thing." Connie studied Eve for a moment. She seemed to be angry about something. Could she be jealous? "Now, you two get out of here so I can get this mess straightened out. We have campers coming in a few days and I'm nowhere near ready."

As they walked away from the cabin, Logan glanced back. Connie was unpacking boxes and putting supplies away. "I don't know where you found her, but she's a treasure. The kids are bound to love her."

Eve swallowed her anger. He didn't seem to suffer from any residual bad temper from their disagreement yesterday, so she decided to pretend it never happened. "She is definitely a treasure."

Logan removed one of the suckers from his pocket. "Lollipop?"

Was that a peace offering? Eve wondered as she took it with a smile and removed the paper. After a few licks she looked at Logan. "I like grape, too, but I prefer Tootsie Pops."

"I'll make a note of that. Maybe on your birthday, I'll send you a truckload."

"Sounds expensive, but nice."

With a scowl on his face that said her assessment was true, Logan shrugged. "I hope your birthday comes after camp closes."

Eve shook her head. "Sorry, I don't tell my birthday to anyone."

"Well, that's a close-minded attitude to take, don't you think?" Logan wanted to tease her, as he had Connie, but somehow the banter didn't come quite as freely. And, with Connie, hugging had seemed natural. She was the kind of woman everybody hugged and you knew it immediately. But, with Eve, he wasn't certain.

"Close-minded or not, that's the way it is." Eve smiled and shook her head slightly.

"It's a policy I adopted when a friend of mine took me to dinner on my birthday and the entire staff came in banging pots and shrieking something about happy birthday. I was mortified."

"Banging pots, eh? Sounds like fun. Maybe we should do that here for the kids." Logan stopped and looked at her. "Do we have any way of knowing when their birthdays are?"

Eve stared at Logan. Coming from someone who'd declared himself to be completely uninvolved, this was a real surprise. "Yes, it's on the application."

"Great. Let's go and . . . what did you have to do this afternoon anyway?"

"I was going to finalize the schedules. There are lots of activities, and we need to shuffle these kids about in the most efficient fashion." Eve gazed at him pensively. Had she encountered a Jekyll and Hyde in this man?

"Scheduling, huh? I'm not the greatest in the world at mathematics and statistics, but I can try to help . . . if you need me." Logan studied her for a few seconds. Her eyes were an incredible color of blue, almost a cornflower blue or like the sky on a mid-August day. He'd always been a sucker for blue eyes. "I'm willing."

Eve smiled. He was trying to apologize without saying the words. Well, if he was willing to forget the past and start anew, then she was, too. She wasn't one to hold grudges for words spoken in haste. "I'd love the help."

For the remainder of the afternoon, Eve and Logan worked out schedules that balanced athletic activities with arts and leisure. She was adamant about working all three in daily. "I'm a firm believer that a well-rounded person is a happier person, so they all get arts and crafts and sports and fun and goofing-off time."

"I'm not sure about that, but it seems a sensible approach." Logan grinned at her and raised his eyebrows. "Well, what do you know? We almost agree on something."

Eve gazed at him, taking in the warm brown eyes and square cut of his jaw. He was a handsome man, especially when he was smiling. She passed the last list to him, and their fingers touched briefly and then their eyes met. She cleared her throat and smiled again. "We may even have an interesting conversation if we're not careful."

"Yeah, who would have thought it possible?"

Certainly not me, Eve thought, shuffling the papers before her. They'd sorted through all the applications for birth dates, put them on the calendar, established a policy for the birthday kids, and decided what to do about all the ones who were born during the other months of the year. Then they had pored over the activities until they'd developed a reasonable schedule for each day. It was almost as if she and Logan had been working together on projects for some time.

The phone rang. Eve answered it cheerfully and handed the receiver to Logan. "It's Jerry."

Logan took the phone. "Hi, Jer, what's going on in the real world?"

Jerry Kent laughed. "Everything's falling apart in the real world. What's it like in your 'summer-camp prison?' "

"Better than I thought."

Almost choking, Jerry hesitated until he could speak. "You mean you aren't ready to commit mayhem?"

"I have to admit that the idea crossed

my mind a couple of times, but things are really looking up." Logan didn't want to say too much in front of Eve. She didn't know how much he'd hated the idea of coming to the camp and it wouldn't do anybody any good for her to find out now. "You just call to shoot the breeze or is there something we need to discuss?"

"Just called to help ground you in reality. And to make sure you weren't in your bad-boy persona. You need the money too bad, old boy."

"I dropped him off at home this morning," Logan joked, recalling his quick trip to Tega Cay. He'd spent the morning trying to convince himself that this summer would be a learning experience for him as well as for the kids. It hadn't been an easy task.

"What were you doing at home?"

"I had a couple of things to pick up. Muzzle needed some food. So, since I was going out anyway—"

"Muzzle? Who the hell's Muzzle?"

"My cat." Logan glanced at Eve who had turned to watch him after he spoke the cat's name. "Surely you remember old Muzzle?"

"Logan, are you losing it? You don't have a damn cat."

"Oh, but I do." Logan knew Jerry was confused, but it didn't matter. Jerry could just wait for a real explanation or figure it out on his own. "Say, I gotta run. We're working on schedules and it's a bitch . . ." He glanced at Eve. "I mean, it's not an easy thing to do."

"We're?" Jerry asked, his voice incredulous. "You're actually helping Eve do something useful."

"Yep, I am."

"I don't believe it." Jerry chuckled and then continued, "Next thing you know, you'll be drinking chocolate milk and baking cookies

"That's right. I've got a great recipe for chocolate chip cookies." Logan winked at Eve. "I'll bake some when you come down to visit."

Eve stared at Logan in disbelief. She wasn't one to eavesdrop on personal conversations, but this one made no sense whatsoever to her. Even though she realized that reporters always chose the sensational to write about, she couldn't merge the public image to the Logan Mallory sitting across the desk from her.

Logan listened to Jerry's admonishment to behave himself like a gentleman for the remainder of the summer and then hung up the phone. He studied Eve a moment, wondering how much of the conversation she'd understood, but decided not to explain. He was resolved to do the best he could for this project, but he didn't necessarily have to become bosom buddies with the camp manager.

"How old are all these kids?" Logan asked, shuffling through some of the applications.

"Instead of ages, I restricted attendance to junior high and high school students. We'll have kids from about thirteen to eighteen years of age." Eve chewed her lower lip thoughtfully. That was a pretty vast difference in age. If she had thought about it at the time she would have divided the summer into two sessions: one for junior high and one for high school students.

As it stood now, she had one long session. From June 19 through August 13. At the time, she'd been of mixed emotions about the length of stay, but finally decided she couldn't help the whole world. This year, she'd start with a few students for the entire summer; next year, she might divide into two sessions, depending on how everything worked this summer.

There were several reasons for her decision. First of all, she remembered the homesickness that many of the campers experienced the first week of camp. They seemed unable to involve themselves in anything except moping around and wondering why they'd decided to come. The last week was generally devoted to gathering up their belongings and preparing to go home. If the campers had only one month of camp time, then their learning experience couldn't be much more than two weeks.

Of course, things could be different now. The kids might not be as susceptible to homesickness. In fact, some of her kids this year didn't even have permanent homes. One child in particular lived in a shelter for homeless families. But, for nearly two months, she would be on equal footing with the rest of the world—thanks to Tennis Pro and their generous donation of sports clothing and equipment.

That was the kind of child Eve was trying to reach. One with little hope, the child that sociologists predicted would drop out of school, turn criminal. A child born with artistic talent, but with little else to comfort him. Eve had corresponded with art teachers and principals in three states. They had identified most of the children whose applications were now resting on Logan's lap.

"Says here this child lives at Sister of Mercy Homeless Shelter," Logan said, his voice questioning. He stared at Eve a moment. "Is that true?"

"Yes. Heather Barton. Her father's dead and her mother has been ill." Eve rose and walked to the window. She didn't know if she had the stomach to take this girl for a couple of months, subject her to the comforts of being like everyone else, and then send her back. "Heather's case was the hardest decision for me."

"Why? I thought you were looking for artistic ability."

"That's true, but remember, all these kids are disadvantaged in some way." Eve leaned against the windowsill and breathed in the sweet fragrance that drifted on the breeze. She glanced over her shoulder at Logan and then turned back to the view out her window. She stared for a long time in the distance, through the trees to the sun glinting on the lake. "She's highly recommended as an artist by both her teacher and principal, but I just don't know if I've done the right thing."

Logan placed the stack of applications on the desk and leaned back in his chair to study Eve. Something about this child really bothered her. "Want to talk about it?"

"I don't know," Eve answered honestly.

"Well, I'm not a psychologist or sociologist, but I do know how to listen."

Eve chuckled and looked at him. "Hmm, that's not what the newspaper said about the last French Open. I seem to recall that—"

"Okay, okay, so I wasn't as good a listener on the tennis court as I should have been." Logan raised his hands in capitulation. "But I'm trying, Eve. Give me a chance."

Eve propped her elbows on the windowsill and leaned forward to rest her chin. "I'm not even sure how I feel. How can I explain it to you?"

"That's a good question." Logan considered her dilemma. "I know, why not start at the beginning and tell me everything? Chronologically."

With a barely audible sigh, Eve stood,

stared at him for a moment, and then walked over to the sofa to sit down. She tucked her left foot beneath her and wondered how to begin. "When I sent out my first inquiry, I received this note from Heather's teacher. She asked about financial arrangements for transportation."

"How's this kid getting here?"

"As I had no way of knowing that I could get such a good deal from Tennis Pro, I told her there were no provisions for transportation. I assumed that the child in question would have to find a way to get here if she really wanted to come." Eve looked at her fingernails. The nail on her index finger was chipped from typing and she began to pick at the remaining polish.

"And she couldn't?" Logan asked, wondering why he was even interested.

"No. She literally had no means whatsoever of getting here." Eve's lips tilted just a bit into a shadow of a smile. "I finally told the teacher that if she could bring the girl up or make sure she could get here, I'd find a way to get her home."

"So that's all arranged."

"Not exactly. I still don't know how I'm going to get her home." Eve continued to pick at her fingernail, the red polish chipping off in tiny flecks of color onto her white shorts. "I plan to take her myself. You see, she's only twelve." She gazed at Logan. "I can't risk putting her on a plane or bus back to Atlanta alone."

"Oh, I see. That is a problem." Logan considered the problem. "Well, it's only a four-hour trip each way. I'll take her back. I mean, how bad can a four-hour automobile trip be with a twelve-year-old kid?" He scowled, remembering some of the twelve-year-olds in his neighborhood. "Don't answer that."

"I wish that was all." Eve studied her index finger, now without polish. Still tinted a slightly orangish color from the constant use of nail polish, it looked alien among her other nails. She curled the finger into her fist, so Logan wouldn't see it.

Logan watched her make a fist and wondered what could make her so angry. She seemed to have such an even temper. "So? What is the real problem then?"

"The real problem is not the logistics of the how, but of the why. Here, she'll have a life like everybody else, then she'll have to go back. Is that going to make life easier for her or harder?" Eve leaned forward, her fingernail all but forgotten. She still wasn't comfortable with her decision. But even more of a problem was the environment from which the girl would come. "Why should a child have to live like that?"

Five

The next few days were a flurry of activity for Eve, as well as for the other staff members. Logan, Connie, Otis, Sharleen Jackson, the housekeeper, and Madora Singleton, the cook, who was also Eve's best friend, were each so involved in developing their own strategies for the summer that Eve hardly saw them.

For Eve, the level of excitement was almost unbelievable. She couldn't remember when anything had aroused her emotions to such a state that she was almost in a panic. Soft-spoken, cool headed Eve Travers, she mused, remembering the label given to her by her fellow teachers. Wouldn't they laugh now if they saw her with her hair uncombed, three chipped nails, and one nail broken at the quick.

No matter what had happened at school—or anywhere for that matter—Eve had always presented a manicured appearance from head to toe. Her hair was always exactly the right style and never out of place; her clothes were precisely the fashion required by the situation and fit perfectly; her manner was always impeccable; her nails were always manicured—fingers and toes. Eve often wondered why she went to such trouble to *appear* perfect. Maybe it was that she felt imperfect in so many other ways.

Well, she hadn't time to ponder about manicured nails and imperfections in personality; the camp was opening in two days. Madora's arrival had been a blessing. With her best friend around, Eve felt more normal. Madora's cheery disposition did a lot to calm Eve, as well as give her a positive outlook.

Madora and Connie hit it off well. It was easy to see that they'd become friends before the summer was over. But what had surprised Eve more than anything was the response Madora had to Otis. She actually flirted with him. There might even be a little lighthearted competition between Connie and Madora for Otis's attention.

Logan was more like a whirling dervish than she ever imagined he could be.

Every day he was at the courts, hitting balls, measuring the slack in the nets, testing the balls and racquets. Otis had helped Logan build a little addition to his cabin, and he'd moved in all the tennis equipment. He swam and jogged every day. It was almost as if he was preparing for a major tournament.

Eve, Connie, and Madora made numerous shopping trips to purchase food and all the other items that would be needed when the campers arrived.

Amy Owens, the nursing assistant, arrived along with the two head counselors, Kayla Hewitt and Bert Nelson. There were several college students from a variety of disciplines—sculpting, watercolor, oil and acrylics, drama, creative movement, and creative writing, who would get there the next day and serve as counselors.

The level of excitement was rising. Eve felt sure that Kayla and Bert were perfect head counselors. They had been well screened and seemed to be mature and energetic about the responsibility they would be facing.

They all met that evening for the first time in the dining hall. Madora had prepared a wonderful dinner for them and the camaraderie picked up quickly during the meal. Afterward, they split into small groups, talking among themselves.

Kayla was a slender blonde with vivid blue eyes that took in everything. She was an excellent artist, judging from the slides of her work Eve had seen prior to hiring her. She and Eve were instant friends, in spite of the age difference.

"I'm going to be an art teacher," Kayla confided to Eve. "Until I can really start selling my work, that is."

Eve nodded. She'd had the same dream when she started teaching school so many years ago. But there never seemed to be enough time to devote to her own work. That was when she'd made her decision four years ago to quit teaching and pursue her own art career. She'd scrimped and saved over the years until she had a nice little bank account, a few investments that were paying dividends, and enough jobs teaching art workshops to pay the bills. "I began the same way, Kayla. Work hard with your students, but don't neglect your own work. Keep your easel up and try to paint every day."

"I guess that's pretty good advice."

Kayla considered Eve's suggestions for a moment. "I suppose if you don't keep working, your creativity suffocates."

"Something like that." Eve looked proudly at her staff. She'd selected each of them with great care, not only for what jobs they were to do, but for what they could give to the students. She especially liked Kayla and her paintings.

Bert's work was incredible, too. He was a sculptor who worked in different mediums. Some of his slides had shown sculptures in bronze, some in clay, and some in an odd assortment of abandoned items. She liked the vitality of his work and found him to be just as exciting as his art.

With Amy, Eve was uncertain. She'd graduated from nursing school, but didn't have a job yet and was delighted at the prospect of spending a summer at camp. Eve had checked her references scrupulously and found nothing suspect, but something seemed a bit odd about the young woman. Connie, however, had no such reservations and the two nurses fell into an immediate discussion of medical protocol to be observed in the first-aid cabin.

Sharleen Jackson, the housekeeper,

joined in the conversation between Madora and Otis. After a few minutes, it seemed as if Sharleen had become a sort of referee when Connie realized that her newfound friend, the cook, was monopolizing the handyman's time. She and Amy insinuated themselves into the conversation.

Logan and Bert discovered a mutual love of a southern country band and launched into a lively debate about the effects of rock on country music. As their discussion progressed, Logan found that he liked the young man. "Do you play tennis?" he asked.

"I have to confess that I'm not much of a player. Not that I don't enjoy the game, but I'm more of a hack than a player, if you know what I mean." Bert seemed to be a little in awe of the famous tennis star. "Played a little in high school, but I haven't had much time since."

"Maybe we can get together for a game," Logan suggested, liking the young man more and more for his honest approach to everything. "I can give you a few pointers."

"Hey, I'd like that." Bert grinned and shook his head. "Boy, I can't wait to tell the guys back at school that I've spent the summer playing tennis with you."

"You think they'll even know who I am?" Logan asked, sincerely doubting that most college kids would recognize his name unless they were avid players.

"Oh, yeah. Most of the guys at school sort of admire your style."

Eve heard Bert's answer and turned to look at Logan. A frown creased his face, wrinkling his forehead and narrowing his eyes. She suppressed a smile; she didn't think Logan ever considered himself to be someone the kids would emulate.

"You're kidding!"

"No." Bert grinned sheepishly, chuckling a little to emphasize his answer. "They think it's real cool the way you handle yourself."

Logan stared at the young man. This sounded serious. "On or off the court."

"Both," came the reply.

"I see." Logan considered the answer for a few seconds. "Maybe I'd better get to work on this image business."

"Well, I think they admire a guy your age who still seems to be so active, too." Bert apparently sensed that Logan didn't exactly feel comfortable with what he was hearing.

"God," Logan said with a groan as he

leaned his head forward onto his hands. "A guy my age? What an insult."

"Hey, man, I didn't mean to insult you. It was a compliment." Bert scrambled to make amends. "Don't take it that way."

"Don't worry about it." Logan looked up at his new friend. "I won't throw a racquet at you when we play. A man my age?" he repeated incredulously.

Eve laughed. Obviously Logan's ego had been dealt a blow by the phrase. "Bert, maybe you should get Mr. Mallory a shawl for his shoulders . . . maybe a rocking chair."

"Thanks a lot, Eve," Logan said dryly. "Bert, I'm going to give you some advice. Never underestimate a woman."

Eve raised her eyebrows as if in surprise. "Why, Logan, how astute of you to have learned this first rule of getting along with a woman so early in life."

He grimaced and winked at Bert. "Right, after living nearly a half century, I seem to be figuring the creatures out."

"Wow, man, that's getting old," Bert said. "I hope I'm still as active as you are when I'm that old."

Eve stifled a chuckle behind her hand and said nothing. She could see by the color beginning to appear in blotches in Logan's neck that he was trying valiantly to control his temper. He, apparently, was sensitive about his age.

"Yeah, well, if you want to live to get this old," Logan finally said, "then be nice to us 'old' folks this summer."

This time, Eve couldn't help laughing. She'd seen the way Logan fought within himself before answering and concluded that Bert deserved the sarcasm he received for being disrespectful. When she finally suppressed her laughter, she looked at Bert for a moment. "Well, Bert, I guess you just found out how quick the 'old folks' wit can be."

"Yeah, who would have believed it?"

The kids would arrive tomorrow. Eve lay on her bed, tossing and turning. Finally, she got up. There was no sense in lying there when she couldn't sleep. Maybe a walk would relax her.

Eve changed into a pair of sweatpants and one of the short-sleeved T-shirts Tennis Pro had sent for the kids. The art department at Tennis Pro had worked out a neat logo for the camp, and Eve loved them so much, she'd been wearing her shirt one day and washing it the next.

Taking her flashlight, she walked down the path toward the beach. Not a sound could be heard; the world was asleep, except for the forest creatures. When she reached the lake, she sat down on the new beach and rested her chin on her knees.

The dream of her lifetime was about to happen, well one of them anyway. If she closed her eyes, she could hear the sounds of children splashing in the water, calling and shouting to one another. She could almost hear the snap of the sails as the wind caught and sent the cats gliding across the smooth surface.

As she considered her good fortune, she came to one conclusion. God had been kind to her. Not many people ever realized their dreams.

Logan stood at his cabin window and stared into the night. Why was he so nervous? With a smile and a scratch behind Muzzle's ears, Logan decided he couldn't sit or stand still any longer. He handed Muzzle a treat, slipped on a pair of shorts, and left his cabin. He needed to walk, to get some exercise, to clear his head.

Whatever happened had nothing to do with him. The success or failure of the camp really meant little to him. He got paid anyway at the end of the summer. The pittance he'd received as a signing bonus would hardly keep him in snacks for the next two months. That wasn't precisely true, but Tim Carlisle had been very niggardly with the signing bonus, citing Logan's penchant for spending money when he didn't have it as the reason.

But Logan knew the real reason: Tim didn't trust Logan.

That rankled more than anything. Logan tried to recall when his reputation had sunk to such a level as to be nearly nonexistent.

Before he knew where he was going, he reached the tennis court. He considered going back for his racquet, hitting some balls, but decided that wasn't what he needed and kept walking. He simply needed to think, really think for maybe the first time in his life.

Back in December, when he'd done all the soul-searching that had led him to make such stringent New Year's Resolutions, he'd looked at his life critically. What had he done? What would he do now? Did anyone care?

He discovered that *he* cared. For the first time in his life, he really cared about what happened to him, about the kind of image he presented to those tennis fans who might look up to him. Even though he was actually out of the mainstream of tennis now, he still had fans. He wouldn't let them down.

"You're a fool, Logan Mallory," he chided himself as he realized that the moon wasn't as bright as he'd first thought. From his cabin, it had looked light enough outside to see with ease. Now he lost the path and was stumbling along through the forest, unable to see hardly a yard ahead of himself.

He thought back to his childhood, or what little there was of it. He'd never had an opportunity to go to summer camp or even camping for a weekend, and as a result, Logan knew nothing about the woods. Feeling the sting of a briar, he wondered what in the world had possessed him to walk in the woods at night.

This summer would do two very important things for him: it would force him to think before he spoke and before he acted. If he got nothing else from the experience, he'd learn those two rules.

Logan saw the end of his stumbling. Just a short distance ahead, the woods gave way to beach and near daylight.

Eve heard someone—or something— tearing through the forest behind her like a wild boar. It probably wasn't anything as ferocious as a boar, but these woods weren't free of predators. For a short time, she listened to the crashing about, and then she heard a curse.

"Damn briars," Logan swore, pulling his shirt from the grasp of a blackberry bush. "How'd I get in this mess again?"

Suppressing a laugh, Eve turned around in time to see Logan literally fall from the clutches of one of the blackberry vines that grew wild throughout the area. "Hi," she called cheerily. "Having trouble?"

"You know, Eve," Logan said, sucking the back of his hand where yet another scratch started to bleed. "I just might buy a chain saw and go through the woods eliminating anything that resembles a briar or thorn."

"Commendable of you to be scouting the area for the kids." Eve smiled as he continued to examine his arms and hands for scratches. "Don't you think it would be safer to do so in the daytime, though?"

"What?" He practically barked the question.

"Well, if you're looking for anything that might be dangerous to the kids, wouldn't it be easier to do during the day?"

"Chuckle, chuckle, aren't you a barrel of laughs tonight?" he scolded her half-heartedly before sitting down on the sand beside her.

"Seriously, what in the world were you doing? I thought I was about to be attacked by a boar."

This time Logan laughed. "You were. I mean, you are. Being attacked by a boar, except that you spell it 'bore.' "

"I see." Eve chuckled along with him. "But I doubt very seriously if you would ever bore anyone."

"You'd be surprised," he admitted honestly. "I even bore myself sometimes."

"I don't get it. Every reporter in sports has called you the 'Casanova of the tennis

court.' So why do you think you're bor-
ing?"

"Still think I'm that person, do you?"
Logan leaned back on his elbows and
stared across the lake. "I haven't been in
a long time."

"Oh? How long?"

"Five months." He looked up at the
moon. "You know, it's really beautiful
here."

"Carolina Moon," she whispered almost
reverently. "I used to sneak out here when
I was a kid and stare at it for hours."

"Weren't you a little sleepy the next
day?" Logan asked, trying to coax her to
talk about herself.

"Always," she answered. "Somehow, I
could never get enough of watching the
moon. It's so majestic and at the same
time . . . soft. Do you know what I mean?"

"Let's see, majestic but soft." Logan
stared at the bright pathway riding gently
on the smooth lake. "Yeah, I kinda think
I do."

"I used to come out here and wish I
was a movie star or a great artist." Eve
sighed and smiled at him. "Most of the
time I was wishing to be a great artist."

"What made you want to be an artist?"

Logan sat up again and leaned on his knees. "I mean, movie stars make a lot of money and everybody loves them. Artists, well, they just spend their lives staring at a white canvas and splattering it with color."

"Is that what you think art is all about?" she asked, astonished by his definition.

"Not really, but to a nonparticipant in such ventures, that's pretty much the way it looks."

"Art isn't just paint and brushes and canvas. It's . . . it's a way of life." Eve knew she couldn't explain the way she truly felt. "Art consumes you. It filters into every part of your life."

"Now *that* I believe." Logan bit back the remainder of his bitter words. "The consume part anyway."

Eve turned slightly to stare at him. There was something he wasn't telling her, maybe something significant. "Why do you say it with that tone? Don't you think artists make a contribution to society and culture?"

"Sure. Sure they do."

"Why are you so bitter? You sound as though you'd been jilted by an artist."

"I guess I was, in a perverted sense of the word." Logan shoved the heel of his sneaker into the sand, pushing up a ridge ahead of his foot. He did that several times while he searched for a way to tell her why he felt the way he did. "Forget I said anything. Artists are great. They're the backbones of society."

"Logan, wait," Eve called, but he rose and darted off up the path. She sat there a moment, wondering about what had happened. Then she heard him cursing the briars and thorns again and smiled.

The summer wasn't over. Maybe he'd eventually confide in her and she could dispel whatever bad feelings he harbored about artists. For now, there seemed to be little she could do about his bitterness, except to continue to treat him as an equal, as someone she liked for who he was.

The strange thing was, she really did like him, in spite of her vow to remain aloof. For weeks, months, she'd been praying for a solution to her financial problems. Now, she'd received the answer to her prayers in Logan Mallory and Tennis Pro, but she wasn't sure whether it came from heaven or hell.

Eve liked Logan Mallory, really liked him, and it scared her to death.

Six

After Logan's abrupt departure, Eve sat for a long time assessing her feelings. Why, after all these years of enjoying being alone, did she feel so bereft when he left her?

Eve had never married. She was wedded to her work, thoroughly enjoying all the extra time she spent with her students. As a high school art teacher, she had duties other than her classroom time. She organized art shows, took her students on outings to the museum, all the things she could possibly devise to acquaint her microcosmic world with the one thing she loved better than any other: art.

She readily admitted that perhaps she'd been shortsighted in her view of life, that she might have been happier *now* if she'd rounded out her life with a husband and children. But would she have been?

Eve Travers had never been one to sit home on Saturday night, moping about life. She was energetic and enjoyed a full and happy schedule of activities, most of which were related to her school or church. Was that enough? She'd thought so at the time.

She looked at the lake, its tranquility spilling over into her thoughts. Had she married, would she have taken this daring step? Could she have left everything she knew behind to open this camp? If she'd had responsibilities, to a husband, to children in school, she couldn't have followed her dream.

Was it an equal trade-off?

There was no way she could find out. To do so, she would have had to travel both pathways. Eve, in her own philosophical way, knew that was impossible, that comparison of one lifestyle with another was futile. She'd trusted her instincts all these years; she'd continue to do so now.

Eve awoke to singing birds and knew immediately why she'd moved to King's Mountain. The sun was rising, the music of songbirds was filling the air, and the scent of sweet grasses and flowers and forest wafted on the whispering wind currents. She loved this place more than any other on earth.

She stretched luxuriously and stared at the exposed beams of her room, exposed because all the buildings were made as inexpensively as possible. The sturdy pine would hold up for years, had already in fact. Eve dressed quickly and hurried down the stairs. She still had a million things to do before the kids started arriving just after lunchtime.

For the thousandth time, Eve looked over her cabin assignments and schedules. Everything seemed to be in order. She rose from her desk and began to pace. What if the kids didn't get along? What if they didn't like the counselors or the food—or her?

"Hello!" Logan tapped on the screen door and went inside. Eve was obviously experiencing a case of opening-day jitters.

"Oh, hi. I was a million miles away." Eve smiled, noticing that Muzzle was artfully draped over Logan's shoulders. "Such a lovely fur collar you're wearing today."

"Oh, yeah. Muzzle is ready to meet her

new friends. She's well rested, which is more than I can say for you." Logan stroked the cat's forehead and grinned. "She's a bit nervous, though."

"Well, she's not the only one."

"Can Muzzle and I buy you a cup of coffee?"

Eve smiled. He could really be charming when he wanted to. "Thanks, but I need to stay right here. I'll just walk over to the dining hall and grab a cup."

"Where do you think I was talking about?" Logan grinned and raised his left eyebrow. "I can't afford anyplace else."

With a laugh, Eve walked over to Logan and scratched under Muzzle's chin. "How can I resist such a tempting offer?"

"What about me?"

Studying him for a moment, Eve smiled wickedly and scratched Logan under his chin. "Sorry. I should have . . . known you were like a cat."

"Oh? How's that?"

"You'd have to be to go bounding through the woods at night without a flashlight," she quipped and went out the door. When they reached the dining hall, she stopped and looked at the cat. "What shall we do with him?"

"Her. She's a her," Logan corrected and produced a leash.

"Cats won't stay on leashes."

"Muzzle will, won't you, my darling?" he cooed into her fur. Logan attached one end of the leash to her collar and then secured the other end to the garden hose. Muzzle began to roam around, the length of hose giving her plenty of prowling space.

"Now I've seen everything." Eve opened the door and went in. Once inside, she stopped and inhaled. "Hmm, smells like bacon, doesn't it?"

"That it is," Madora called from the kitchen door. "I saw you coming."

"Wonderful," Logan answered and hugged the cook. "If I promise to be a good boy, do I get eggs and toast, too?"

"Save your good boy routine for the younger ladies and sit down." Madora scuttled off to the kitchen, singing a pitifully off-key version of an Elvis Presley song.

Apparently the aroma of breakfast lured in everybody on the compound. Eve was delighted. Before she and Logan were served, Connie and Otis entered, followed shortly by Kayla, Bert, Sharleen, and Amy.

Once again, they enjoyed a light banter, teasing and taunting like old friends. Among her new friends, Eve felt warm all over, as if she truly belonged

After a while, the counselors wandered in, chattering like a gaggle of Canada geese at their wintering site. Eve liked all of them. They liked each other, too. She could see it in their eyes as they jostled and wisecracked while they waited for their food.

Suddenly, tears burned in her eyes. Sitting there, watching her dream take life, she succumbed to the emotion of the moment and a tear rolled down her cheek.

"Are you okay, Eve?" Logan asked, eyeing her suspiciously.

She took a few seconds to gather her thoughts. "Gracious, yes. I just burned my tongue on Madora's wonderful coffee. It's what I get for being such a pig and not waiting for it to cool."

Logan continued to study her for a minute and then shrugged. He didn't believe that for one second, but he was surprised by the emotions her tears revealed. She'd said this was her dream, but he never realized just how much this place meant to her. He resolved to be more helpful, if he could only figure out how.

The morning passed quickly, too quickly for Eve, and yet, not quickly enough. At times, the hands on the big clock over the sofa crept by as if they'd been drugged, while at others, they sped around the clown face. For a few moments, Eve stared at the clock and wished she'd never painted the clown. He seemed to be mocking her this morning, as if he were tormenting her with the frivolities of a clown's nature. She grimaced and re-read the directions to the counselors to make sure she hadn't left anything out.

Moments before the campers were scheduled to arrive, Eve's heart plummeted and played hide-and-seek with the butterflies in her stomach. How would she ever manage? What a fool she'd been to think she could pull this off alone.

"Hey, you're not alone, Eve," Logan called through the screen door.

"How did you know that was what I was thinking?" she asked, leaning forward to cup her face in her hands.

"Because you had that 'woe is me' kind of look that people get when they're launching a new enterprise." Logan let himself in, and Muzzle strolled into the room nonchalantly, as if she were there to inspect.

"Do I?" Eve rummaged through her drawer for a mirror and looked with dismay at her face. Even though she'd gotten a great tan, her face resembled parchment. "Oh, God, how will I ever get through this day?"

Logan dropped onto the sofa and slung his leg over the arm. "Oh, you'll manage."

"Thanks for the encouragement."

"Look, Eve, you've assembled a great team of people here." Logan patted the sofa and Muzzled joined him. "How can you lose?"

"All too easily, I'm afraid," she answered and then moved to sit on the sofa beside Muzzle. The cat crawled into her lap and lay down, as if she'd been waiting for Eve all along.

Logan watched with dismay and maybe a little jealousy. After all, he had rescued the cat, not Eve. "Traitor," he said with a scowl on his face. "Seriously, Eve, stop worrying. Torturing yourself won't help a bit."

"I know," Eve conceded, still stroking the cat. "But I can't help it. I was awake all night wondering what was going to happen."

"So? Maybe the rest of us were restless last night, too." Logan reached across the back of the sofa and patted her shoulder. "You're not alone here. You've got friends."

Hardly realizing what she was doing, Eve lifted her hand and rested it on his. "Thanks for the pep talk."

"Hey, it'll be great. You'll see."

The sounds of tires on gravel, of engines whining as the cars came up the last stretch of driveway, interrupted their talk. "Well, it sounds like the troops are beginning to arrive. Shall we?"

"Why not?" Logan lifted Muzzle and started out the door. "I think I'll drop her by my cabin."

They walked to his cabin and left the cat munching on some tidbits. Eve lifted her chin and strode across the parking lot to the van Otis had driven to pick up some of the kids at the bus depot. Behind him, several cars pulled up to logs that marked the parking lot and stopped.

Eve smiled and waved. Doors came

open and noisy kids burst forth like flowers blossoming on a spring day. Shouts and calls about luggage and who would beat whom rent the peace and quiet of King's Mountain as Eve and Logan stood watching.

Logan leaned down, his lips close to her ear. "Remember, you asked for this."

"I know," she whispered, recalling other summers when other groups of happy children had arrived. She could remember her father, standing in almost the same spot as she stood now, waving to the kids as they exploded out of cars, their energy somehow released the second the engines stopped.

Behind her came sounds of footsteps. She turned and saw her staff emerging into the parking lot. Kayla and Bert smiled at each other and began issuing orders. The other counselors helped the kids find their bags and then herded them into the dining hall, where room assignments would be issued.

"Looks like everything's working great." Logan paused to give directions to a woman who had a girl about thirteen years old in tow. "Shall we follow the throng? I have one stop to make, though."

They stopped at his cabin and retrieved the cat. "I hate to leave her locked up all day, but I'm not sure this place is safe for a cat."

"Safe for a kid, but not a cat?"

"Something like that." Logan didn't want to admit that he was really afraid the cat wouldn't come back if he let her go. When they reached the dining hall, he attached Muzzle to the garden hose again. "Shall we?"

"Why not?" When Eve entered the dining room, she smelled something wonderful. "What's that?"

Logan sniffed the air and grinned. "Smells like chocolate chip cookies."

Madora opened the kitchen door and brought in a tray of cookies. Otis was right behind her with several pitchers of milk. Madora placed her burden on a table and waved to the kids. "Come and get your snacks!"

"Looks like the food's going to be a great asset, if this is an indication." Logan gestured to the mob jostling to reach the cookies. When it looked as if they might get a little rowdy, he walked over and settled them down. "There's plenty for everyone." Then he glanced meaningfully at Madora "And there'd better be some for me."

She handed him a plate and two glasses of milk. "Like you said, 'plenty for everybody' and fresh, too."

Kids, parents, social workers, and staff stood around drinking milk and munching on Madora's wonderful cookies. Eve watched how smoothly the counselors circulated among the campers, introducing themselves and offering to help them in any way.

After draining her milk glass, Eve smiled at Logan. "Well, I guess it's time for me to get into action."

She walked over to one of the tables near where Madora had placed the cookies and climbed onto the bench. She greeted everyone and then introduced herself and her staff. "Those of you who brought campers may go with your child to his cabin. I know if I was a parent or, guardian, I'd want to know what kind of conditions I was leaving the child in. Then please meet back here at five for supper if you can stay. I know many of you drove long distances, so if you can't remain for supper, we understand. Remember, parents' day is only three weeks away and you're all invited back."

Eve watched as most of the kids and their parents left, picking up information sheets that were placed on a table beside the door. Counselors and staff followed along, answering questions and trying to be as helpful as possible without undermining the independence that was to be a part of the summer's program.

The sight suddenly energized her and she hopped down from her perch and walked over to Logan, who followed her out the door. "Well, what do you think? Will we have a campful of homesick kids tonight or not?"

Logan studied the question for a few seconds and shook his head. "You know, I don't think kids get homesick much anymore. Most of the parents aren't at home anyway. It's up to the kids to be at home wherever they go. What do you think?"

"I remember kids who cried every day for the first few days when my father ran this camp." She stopped walking and turned to face him. "I never could figure out why they would want to leave this place. To me, it had some sort of magical appeal."

"Now that's unusual. For a kid to think where she lives is magical." Logan looked around the verdant forest that surrounded the camp, encroaching on its boundaries in places. The wind rustled through the trees and sent dust devils dancing away from them as they stood there. "I think this is a magical place, too. I never imagined I'd get to like a place where the plumbing was . . . of the community sort."

"I know. I never minded when I was young, but it's a little different now." Eve looked ahead to her office. It centered the compound and was surrounded by the dining hall, first-aid office, camp store, supply hut, and maintenance shack. When she'd first come here as a child, there had been but one main building: the dining hall. "Lots of things have changed, but I think the magic is still here."

"Things change, whether we want them to or not." Logan glanced around. "Where's Muzzle?"

He walked back toward the dining hall, calling the cat by name. Eve followed and began to scan the terrain for the animal. "I don't think anything could have happened to him."

"Her," Logan corrected and smiled as

he found the water hose. "Where there's a water hose, surely there's a cat soon to follow."

Eve smiled and watched him as he traced the cat by way of the garden hose. There was a break in the underpinning of the dining hall and the hose led in there. "Is she in there?"

Logan got down on his hands and knees and peered into the hole. "Muzzle, are you in there?"

A tentative "meow" came first and then the cat peeped through the hole. Eve had to laugh. The cat, usually so fastidious, had dirt all over her face. "I think you'll have to give her a bath."

As Logan pulled her out, it was apparent that Eve had spoken the truth. The cat was covered in dirt, spiderwebs, and some sort of sticky substance.

After a moment of watching Logan cuddle the dirty animal, Eve said, "I suppose we should meet later for supper. It looks as if you have your afternoon's work cut out for you."

"Right." Logan released Muzzle's leash from the water hose and walked away, talking to the cat in hushed tones.

Eve chuckled as she walked into her office. Sometimes, life was simply too odd to predict. Who would have ever thought that Logan would become attached to a cat? He might think he'd convinced her that the cat belonged to him, but it didn't take a rocket scientist to see that it was Logan who belonged to the cat.

It was interesting to see this side of Logan.

This was what she'd come back for. Eve sat on one of the logs surrounding the campfire and stared at the happy, expectant faces of the children she was beginning to know. Of all, little Heather was the most haunting. As Eve had thought, the girl was a beautiful child, with huge blue eyes that seemed lifeless at times, especially when she withdrew.

When Eve had discussed the child with the social worker, something had emerged within, something that caught at her heart. No child should grow up not knowing where she lived. From one day to the next, little Heather and her mother never knew where home was going to be. In the past few weeks, home had been a shelter.

Before that, home had been cardboard boxes, bridges, and abandoned buildings.

Tears stung Eve's eyes. She realized that she couldn't cure the world's ills herself, but she damned well would make a start. Heather, whose bones were all too obvious through sallow skin, would be Eve's beginning place. This summer would be as a dream to the girl, painless and happy, perhaps for the first time in her life.

The counselors danced around the fire, invigorating the campers with song and jest. Heather peered through her great blue eyes in silence, occasionally brushing a wisp of blond hair away from her face. All the campers had put on their new tennis shoes, T-shirts, and shorts. Once again, Eve paused to thank God for Tennis Pro. Without their generous donation of money, clothing, and equipment, none of this would be possible.

Laughter bubbled forth, a sure sign that the kids were integrating well into the spirit of the campfire. As they sang and played games, Eve watched them. Tony Dean, a young black boy of about thirteen, and Dawn Anderson, a striking auburn-haired girl of fifteen, cavorted around the perimeter of the campfire in some elaborate scheme concocted by the counselors. When it was apparent that the joke was on them, they joined in the laughter and took their seats.

And then Kayla began telling a story—a ghost story. It was the story of a Revolutionary War soldier, a patriot, who'd fought in the Battle of King's Mountain. He was searching for his right arm, which had been amputated immediately after the battle. At first the kids laughed, but as Kayla began describing the man's plight in great detail, the laughter subsided into nervous smiles. As she proceeded, the smiles melted into wide-eyed fear.

At that moment, Bert burst into the circle, wearing a hook on his right arm. The silence exploded into shrieks and screams, followed by apprehensive laughter. Amidst the chattering of anxious kids, Kayla and Bert urged them to take their seats. They ended the first campfire with a song and a prayer.

The counselors led the way back to the cabins. For a long moment, Eve sat and stared at the dying flames. She volunteered to douse the fire after everyone was gone, but she hesitated, reluctant to leave the place of such joy.

"Staying all night?" Logan asked from across the fire.

"What?" Eve started, unaware that she still had company. "I thought you'd . . . that everyone had gone. I was just taking these quiet moments to think."

"Better take the quiet moments where you can find them, I suppose." Logan walked around the fire and sat down on the log beside Eve. "I haven't had a peaceful second since the kids arrived."

Eve laughed. "Nor have I. In a way, I'm glad. I love the energy that these kids create."

"They're energetic, all right." Logan tossed a stick into the fire, sending embers dancing into the sky until they winked out far overhead. "I know my tail's dragging."

"I must confess that mine is, too." Eve stared at the flames as they burned lower. Orange and blue ebbed and flowed within the fluid-looking flames, playing back and forth along the thick logs. "I used to say I was getting too old to do this or that." Eve hesitated a long moment. "That's why I decided to reopen the camp."

"Because you think you're getting old?" Logan leaned away and stared at her as if she had lost her mind. "Now, that makes no sense to me whatsoever."

"I guess not," Eve agreed. "But I kept hearing myself say I was getting older. Finally I decided that I *was*, not because of my age, but because I was talking myself into it."

"I would never have guessed it." Logan fidgeted to get more comfortable on the unforgiving log. His shoulder touched hers, but she didn't flinch. He glanced down at her. The firelight reflected on her face, giving it a warm and inviting look. Logan had to look away, or else risk breaking his New Year's Resolution. "It's a beautiful night for a bonfire."

"You're right," she said, her voice throaty. Eve gazed surreptitiously at him. His profile was clean, with good lines. No wonder women chased after him. Reporters had written that many times, the women were the aggressors instead of Logan. Her shoulder rested against his, but she couldn't seem to muster the strength to pull away. Somehow, it was comfortable, almost natural.

She was letting what she'd read about

him go to her head. Even if he were interested in her, which he definitely wasn't, he'd be gone after the summer ended, back to his rich lifestyle that included women who flocked after him. "I always found the sky lovelier here than anyplace in the world."

"Something about a Carolina moon as I recall," Logan teased. He discovered that for the first time in his life, a woman meant more to him than a convenience. Eve was different in many ways. Not that he hadn't thought of making love to her; she was a beautiful woman. What man wouldn't? But there was something else, an intensity that was indefinable.

"True. There's no moon any prettier." Eve watched the pregnant disc rise golden above the trees. Within a short time, the gold would change to silver, but for these few precious moments, the gold was hers to revel in.

A log shifted and sent sparks flying into the sky. The smell of wood burning permeated everything around her, its fragrance reminiscent of the happiest days of her life. And here she was again, reliving those memories and generating others.

That she was an adult now mattered little. Nobody ever grew up when it came to remembering, she decided. Childhood lasted a lifetime, if you were lucky.

"How long did you live here?" Logan asked quietly, almost reluctant to disturb the congenial silence.

"Too long and not long enough." Eve closed her eyes, remembering the pain associated with the camp. "My father refused to see that he couldn't make a living here. We weren't ever able to attract the wealthy kids; they went elsewhere. Gradually, our funds were depleted and the bank refused to lend him any more money."

"Sounds sad."

"Worse than that." Eve bit her lip, trying to maintain her poise. "My father . . . never could adjust to the outside world. I believe that the child in him refused to accept any real responsibility. He died in a car crash."

"Suicide?" Logan asked softly, regretting the word as soon as it was spoken.

"No, fortunately not that." Eve drew some comfort from knowing that, even though her father couldn't adjust to the outside world, he'd never given up. "He was struck by a drunk driver."

"Damn!" Logan swore.

"Thank goodness he never knew what hit him." Eve smiled wryly. "I lived with an aunt after that, but I never could get this place out of my blood. Fortunately, she knew how I felt about the camp and helped me to hold onto it."

"What about your mother?"

"She died not long after I was born. I never knew her very well."

"Sounds like a pretty traumatic childhood. I'm surprised you're still sane."

"Well, I'm not sure I'm sane, but you don't have to worry about me stealing into your room some night with a chain saw." Eve tried to lighten the tone of the conversation, referring to her most secret fear.

"Aha! You've thought about that, too."

"Who hasn't? It's pretty isolated here, but I think we're safe."

"How's that?"

"You have an attack cat and I have an alarm system." Eve fidgeted with the hem of her khaki shorts.

"Alarms?" Logan hadn't seen any evidence of any sort of alarm system. Usually, there were signs posted around a property that was protected by electronic alarms.

"Almost. The forest creatures tell me when someone is out and about." Eve laughed at her own morbidity. "And I leave a plate of Madora's cookies out with a bear trap."

"I'll keep that in mind if I get hungry during the night."

"Stay away from cookies if the platter is on a surface that looks suspicious." She glanced up at him, just in time for him to catch her, but she couldn't turn away.

"I will. Thanks for the warning." Logan gazed down at her and discovered that her face was turned up, her eyes glittering in the firelight. A more compelling picture he'd never seen. Her short, dark hair framed a heart-shaped face, lips slightly parted and eminently kissable.

Before he could stop himself, Logan leaned down, brushing her lips with a gentle kiss. Her fragrance surrounded him, blended with the aroma of smoke from the fire, tantalizing and taunting, coaxing him to deepen the kiss.

Eve didn't pull away, couldn't pull away. She remained there, luxuriating in the sense of emotion that hovered around them. His lips, contrary to what she'd imagined, were tender, not the least bit threatening.

Logan's arms stole around her, pulling her into the warmth of his embrace. Why? he asked himself, but the devil in him kept answering with a ready, "Why not?"

"Eve," he whispered against her hair, and then he kissed the lobe of her left ear.

Her heart pounding, she felt his answer as erratically. What was happening to her?

Logan kissed her again, this time more deeply, more urgently. He moaned when her arms slid around his neck and her fingers played in his hair.

A log shifted and thumped, jarring Eve's thoughts back to the present and she jerked. When she did, Logan tried to pull away, apparently without alarming her, but the commotion upset both of them and they fell backward onto the soft bed of pine needles behind the log.

Logan scrambled to get up and then pulled Eve back to a sitting position on the log. Picking pine needles out of her hair, he grinned lopsidedly, showing two dimples that she'd never noticed before.

Eve coudln't help smiling back. "I'm sorry. This is my fault—"

"Nonsense." Logan inhaled deeply to regain his senses. He should never have allowed this to happen. "I have to say one thing, though."

"What's that?" Eve asked, thankful for the ever-dimming light of the fire. She dusted herself off a little, feeling like the clumsiest of fools. This had to be the most embarrassing moment of her life. Not only had she let him kiss her, she'd encouraged him, and the result was humiliating. Imagine, Eve Mallory, kissing a man she'd sworn to avoid and then—as if that weren't bad enough—falling off a log like that.

He shrugged slightly and pulled her to her feet so they could walk back to their cabins. "When we're together, nothing is simple or ordinary."

Seven

Eve spent the night with little sleep. Not even the sweet songs of the frogs and crickets comforted her.

After she overcame her own embarrassment, Eve worried about how her indiscretion would affect the camp. Would Logan feel that he'd crossed some line of authority that would allow him to slack off or do less than his contract required? Would it change his attitude toward the kids? Eve felt that she'd been making headway with Logan, establishing a basis for breaking through the barriers he'd erected around himself, but now, she wasn't so sure.

And, how *could* she be sure? Of all the people she'd known in her life, Logan was the most enigmatic. On the one hand, she had read numerous articles written about him, and on the other hand, she had her own personal experience. Eve had been about to chuck the publicity and accept her own experience with him as real, but now she was confused all over again.

Eve got up and turned on her light. She had to stop thinking about Logan or she'd go crazy. There simply was nothing productive in rehashing the same incident over and over again in her mind. What would happen, would happen.

She paced back and forth, wondering what the coming days would bring at the camp. Everyone had seemed enthusiastic at the first campfire, but would that enthusiasm carry over through the weeks ahead?

Standing at the window, she peered out into the darkness. In a few hours, light would flood the campground, and children would pour over the entire area, running and laughing and playing. The thought brought a smile to her face, brought hope back into her heart. She sensed that all would be well.

Then she saw the beam of a flashlight bobbing up and down. It was coming toward her cabin. Eve pulled a robe over her gown and hurried down the stairs, envisioning disaster as she leapt down the bottom three steps and turned on the lights.

By the time she reached the door, there was a nervous tap. She swung the heavy door open and saw Heather Barton standing there with streaks of tears marring her face.

"Heather, darling, what is it? Come in." Eve stepped aside and the thin girl plodded slowly inside. "Here, sit on the sofa with me."

The young girl, dressed only in a nightshirt and Tennis Pro shoes, complied without a word. When she'd settled herself, she turned to look at Eve with huge blue eyes that sparkled with tears.

Eve put her arms around the girl. "Tell me what's wrong."

For a few moments, the girl said nothing. Her shoulders shook with great sobs as she began to cry in earnest. Eve let her have some time to compose herself. "Miss Travers, I want to go home."

Eve was shocked. The girl had no real home, unless you counted the shelter where she lived with her mother. "Why, Heather? Why would you want to leave Camp Reach for the Stars before your time is over?"

Heather swallowed another sob and stared at Eve. "Because my mom might need me."

Homesick, Eve thought. Homesick for a home that could be nothing more tangible than a couple of cots in a shelter for homeless women with children. "Heather, why would your mommy need you? Don't you think she wants you to have this opportunity?"

"Y-y-y-yes, but she needs me."

Eve simply didn't understand. "Darling, don't you think your mommy can use this time to . . . to . . . maybe to find a job?"

"Maybe. But she'll move."

"Won't that be wonderful? You can have a place of your own again."

"No. I mean she has to move now."

"Why?" Eve couldn't understand what Heather meant. "Are you afraid that she'll move and you won't be able to find her at the end of the summer?"

"No. I mean she has to move now."

"Why would she have to move now?"

"Because I'm not there." Heather sucked in air as if she'd been deprived of oxygen for hours. "She can't live there unless I'm there."

Rage flew all over Eve. What a horrible

burden to place upon a child. "You mean that she can't stay there even though you're coming back?"

"Only mothers and children," Heather explained wearily, leaning back against the corner of the sofa. "She has . . . had to leave today."

God, no wonder the child was so upset. This wasn't a simple case of homesickness, the child was concerned about her mother's welfare and had every right to be. The homeless shelter afforded a modicum of safety for Mrs. Barton, but the streets were vicious, if reports were to be believed.

Eve gazed at Heather, wondering what to say that would ease the girl's anxiety. "Heather, I'll call the social worker first thing in the morning and see what we can do. We'll make sure she's safe while you're gone."

"How will they find her?"

"They'll find her. I'll do everything in my power to make sure they do." Eve hugged the girl's frail body. One thing was sure: before Heather left camp this summer, she'd put on some weight. At least, the girl would have three balanced meals a day and would be safe. "Come on. I'll walk you back to your cabin."

Eve found her flashlight and looped it over her shoulder, letting Heather use hers to light their path. One thing her father had always told her was that camp should make children realize they can survive on their own if they have to. Eve wasn't sure that really applied these days, but in Heather's case, a dose of independence and survival skills would help.

They walked along the well-worn path and finally reached the cabin. "Thanks for talking to me, Mrs. Travers."

"You come and talk to me any time you feel like it." Eve hugged the girl again, letting her arms linger for a moment and hoping to make the child feel loved. "I'll call first thing. Now, you go in and get some sleep. Don't wake the other girls."

Eve waited while Heather tiptoed to her bed and pulled up her covers. Then Eve walked back to her own cabin, thinking about how terrible the horrors of being a child on the street must be. In a time when childhood brought enough problems, to have to face those problems without a supporting and loving family and a good place to live seemed an impossible task.

* * *

Logan rose early, before the sun appeared on the horizon. He walked down to the lake to watch the sunrise. While he was on the tennis circuit, he'd never done such a thing, but somehow, it seemed right that he should now, in this pastoral setting. This was the third time he'd sat on the lake and marveled at the colors in the sky. Only an artist could describe the picture that unveiled itself each morning over the mountains and lake.

Artist. Was his life to be plagued with artists forever? His mother had been an artist, the abstruse kind of person who'd had great difficulty communicating with her sons. He'd received little love, though he never doubted that his mother loved him. Somehow, she never had any time for him. She was always off at some art show or taking some class or teaching some class. Art was all important to her.

He'd vowed years ago to avoid artistic types. They were not for him. Give me the secretaries, the clerks, the . . . the anybody but an artist.

And last night he'd kissed an artist. He'd been drawn to her, inexplicably, ever since they'd met. She was pretty and she was intelligent. So what? He knew hundreds of women who were both—and more. But her attraction was unmistakable. He was like a bear searching for the honey pot and he'd run into the queen bee instead.

Logan knew he should avoid being alone with her. That was it. He'd just stay from her unless there were lots of people around. That should solve the problem.

Breakfast would be ready soon. Logan never realized how hungry he could get. It must be the mountain air. Even at the height of his career, he didn't eat as much—or as well—as he'd eaten since he came to camp. Madora was a fine cook. Maybe one of these days, Logan could hire her to cook for him full time, though he sort of enjoyed doing his own cooking now.

The breakfast bell rang out over the camp. Logan hurried toward the dining hall. Today, Madora was making pancakes.

As he neared the dining hall, he spotted Eve. "Hi," he called and waved to her. "Ready to start things up?"

"Yes and no," Eve answered honestly. She had hoped to avoid seeing him this morning, but apparently her wishes were being denied. "I've still got a million things to do. I thought that after the camp opened, my work would slow down."

"Yeah, well, it doesn't always work that way, does it?"

"I suppose not." Eve tried to smile, but she didn't feel very happy. Heather was still on her mind. "I've got a very important call to make about one of the campers, so I'm skipping breakfast."

"Skipping breakfast?" Logan shook his head. "No way. Make your call and then come to eat. You shouldn't skip the most important meal of the day."

"Mr. Nutrition speaks," Eve teased.

"Not exactly, but close." He glanced at his watch. "I'll wait for you."

"No need for that. I won't be long . . . I hope." Eve smiled as she returned to her office. She wanted the phone to ring at precisely the moment the social worker arrived at work.

She was in luck. At eight-thirty, she reached the Department of Family and Children Services in Atlanta. She told the receptionist why she was calling and was promptly put on hold. She waited and waited. As she was getting a little irritated about the long wait, the social worker picked up the phone. Eve explained the problem.

"Miss Travers, we understand your concern, but there's little we can do."

"But there must be something. Mrs. Barton's been put out on the street because Heather is no longer with her."

There was a sigh and Sara Thomas continued, "I realize that, but there's still nothing I can do. The rules of the center are their own. We can't control them."

"Is there any way we can find out where Mrs. Barton is staying?" Eve asked, finally realizing that her arguments to keep the shelter from throwing Heather's mother out were futile.

"She promised to stop by and see me every few days, for reports on Heather." Sara hesitated. "When she comes in, I'll call you. I'm really not supposed to do that, but I will."

"Great," Eve said, feeling a little bit of hope. "But I'm not in my office most of the day. How can we work this?"

Sara had no suggestions. In the end, Eve agreed to be at her desk each day at the same time. That way, Sara could reach her and they could discuss what to do if

Mrs. Barton came in. "Thanks for your help."

"I can't do much," Sara admitted sadly.

"Maybe we can work together to resolve this issue. I don't know what else to do, but Heather is so upset that I don't think she'll enjoy her time here if we don't get her mother settled."

Eve hung up the phone. She felt a little better, but not much. There always seemed to be so much red tape that the people somehow got lost in the shuffle.

"Knock, knock," Logan called from the open door.

"Come on in," Eve answered.

He wedged the tray he was carrying against the doorjamb and opened the screen. "Breakfast for madam."

Eve chuckled and gazed up at him. His eyes were a beautiful brown, surrounded by thick lashes. Laugh lines radiated from the corners of his eyes, as if he really enjoyed this moment. "I figured you'd get so involved you wouldn't eat."

"You're probably right." Eve removed the napkins tented over the food on the tray. "Breakfast for two, I see."

"Well, I'm just as hungry as you are."

Eve buttered her pancakes and poured

syrup over them. She took a sip of coffee. "That's got to be the best coffee in the state."

"I agree." Logan busied himself with his food for a few minutes. "So what was so important that it couldn't wait until after breakfast?"

Eve wondered how much he wanted to know. Was he merely curious or did he care? "Last night . . . this morning, really, Heather came to my cabin and was very upset."

"What's wrong with her?"

"She's the girl who lives in a homeless shelter in Atlanta."

"So? She's here with us, getting three meals a day and a bed of her own for a few weeks. What's to worry about?"

"Her mother." Eve ate a bite of the pancakes and was immediately glad Logan had brought them over. "Hmm. Thanks. Anyway, Mrs. Barton can't stay at the shelter unless she has a child. With Heather up here, she can't stay at the shelter."

"Wow. That's tough. Did you arrange for her to stay anyway?" Logan asked. He never considered that people could be so heartless. How could they throw the woman out of the shelter when her child would return in a few weeks?

"No. Sara Thomas, the social worker, says that the shelter has its own rules. Mrs. Barton was asked to leave as soon as Heather left."

"Damn. That's a bitch, isn't it?" Logan threw down his fork in disgust. "You do something to help a kid out and whammo, you tear her little mind apart because she has something like this to worry about."

"I know. It's breaking my heart." The wonderful pancakes suddenly tasted like mush. Eve got up and began to pace. "There's got to be something I can do."

"How is Heather going to find her mother when she goes back to Atlanta?"

"Oh, that's going to be easy enough. I hope." Eve peered out the window at the kids coming from breakfast. Classes would begin in a few minutes and she needed to be ready to teach hers. "Mrs. Barton is going to stop by the social worker's office every few days to find out how Heather is doing."

"So, you can get her a message then."

"Right. I wish there was something more I could do."

"Eve, you can't cure the world's ills. You

can only do so much, you know." Logan wanted to put his arms around her, to comfort her, but he wasn't sure how that would be received after last night.

"Doesn't this make you feel helpless?"

"Helpless, maybe, but not hopeless." Logan considered the problem. "Too bad you can't . . . Nah, that wouldn't work."

"What? I'm open to anything." Eve turned and placed her hands on Logan's shoulders, imploring him with her eyes to come up with a feasible solution to the problem. "What? Tell me."

"Why can't you get her up here. That would solve everything."

"Up here?" Eve walked around her desk and dropped into her chair. "Up here. Hmm. Maybe I could give her a job. Something that would . . . No, that won't work."

"Why not? Sounds like a great idea to me."

"Money, Logan. I don't have the money and I'm sure Mrs. Barton doesn't."

"Damn, that is a problem." He thought about the situation for a few seconds. "Won't the social services department give her the money?"

"I doubt it."

"What about you? I don't mean you

personally, but the camp. Can the camp afford to pay for a bus ticket or something?"

Eve closed her eyes and shook her head. "I've budgeted every single dime of the money Tim allocated."

"I guess we couldn't ask for a little more."

"No, I don't think so." Eve shrugged, feeling the weight of the world settle around her shoulders. "There must be a way."

"Call that social worker back and tell her to make sure Mrs. Barton doesn't leave." Logan jumped up. "You go ahead and tell her that Mrs. Barton is coming here. You'll send her the money to pay for the ticket."

"But where will I get the money? I'm being honest when I say every dime is budgeted." Eve couldn't help catching his enthusiasm, even though it seemed hopeless.

"I'll get it."

"Where?"

"I'll be right back. I need to go and make a phone call." Logan started toward the door.

"Wait," Eve exclaimed. "I've got a phone right here."

"Oh, I didn't think about that." Logan sat down and began to dial. "This is long distance. Pay you back at the end of the summer."

"Don't worry about it. If it gets Mrs. Barton up here, then I don't care about a long distance charge." Eve thought about that. "Unless you plan to call some foreign country and talk for an hour."

"No, I'm just—Jer? This is Logan." Logan winked at Eve. "Yeah, I just thought you might have forgotten. I need you to do me a favor." He looked at Eve and covered the phone. "How much money do you think we'll need?"

"I don't know. A hundred dollars, tops."

"Jer, can you get me a one-on-one with that tennis pro at the country club? Yeah, the guy who's always trying to get me into a game for money." Logan grinned and then held the phone out from his head. "Don't shout. I need the money for somebody else."

"Now, Logan, I don't think this is the way to—"

Logan held up his hand to stop her.

"Tell him I'll play him a match for two hundred bucks. Soon. This week."

When Logan hung up the phone, Eve couldn't speak for a moment. His proud grin told her that he was confident he'd hit upon the solution to the entire problem. When she found her voice again, Eve gazed at him for a second longer. "Logan, I can't let you do this."

"Do what?"

"Engage in a game of tennis for money." Eve wasn't a gambler and never had been, but this went beyond the scope of gambling. "It isn't right. Besides the right or wrong of it, where will you come up with the money if you lose?"

"Simple. I don't plan to lose." Logan flashed that smile again.

Eve felt her resolve begin to melt away, but this was something she considered serious. She'd heard about professional athletes who were ruined when the rumors of gambling got out. She couldn't let him spoil his career and reputation by such an act, even if it was in the best interest of one of her campers.

"Logan, aren't there sanctions against gambling? I mean for professional athletes."

"Let's just put it this way. It isn't looked upon with favor." Logan didn't understand her reticence. This was the only way he could see to buy a bus ticket for Heather Barton's mother. "It's *my* problem, Eve. Don't worry about it."

"But I do worry about things like this, Logan. What if Tim finds out? What if he decides that an athlete, even you, gives the wrong impression? I mean, if your reputation isn't the image that Tennis Pro wants for its spokesperson." Eve wanted to be sure that Logan didn't misunderstand her. "What will you do? I know you need this money as badly as I do."

"You've already got your money."

"I know. That's the point. You don't have yours yet." Eve racked her brain for the words to tell him what she truly meant. "I . . . I just don't want you to risk losing this contract because of something you're doing for us."

"A very nice sentiment," Logan said quietly. "But I understand the risks involved and I also understand a little girl's concerns about her mother's well-being. Can I turn my back on that?"

Coming from Logan Mallory, that was quite a profound statement. Not more than a week ago, he'd wanted nothing to do with the kids at the camp. What was it about this situation that was different? "No, Logan, you can't and I can't, but we need to think of a way that won't get you into trouble."

"Such as?"

"I don't know. Can we do some sort of benefit or something?"

He shrugged. "I suppose. But where will we hold this benefit and who will come?"

"We don't need many people." Eve considered the problem. "I guess we could hold it here."

"Maybe we could hold it at my tennis club. I'll call Jer and have him check on it." Logan picked up the phone and made the call. When he hung up the phone, he smiled as if he had solved the problems of the world. "I think Jer can talk them into it."

"Did I hear you mention another tennis star's name?" Eve asked hopefully. "Does that mean he might participate?"

"Yeah, well, he owes me a favor." Logan wondered why he hadn't thought of a benefit instead of a wager. Here was another clear example of speaking before thinking, and he'd sworn not to do that anymore.

Eve gazed at him with admiration. He was a man who saw a problem and set about taking care of it. No hassle, no waiting. "Thanks, Logan. That's more than I could have asked for."

"Don't get too hopeful. Jerry may not be able to pull this off."

Recalling the baby-faced manager who'd apparently masterminded this entire summer's project—bringing Logan together with Tennis Pro and then convincing him to work with Camp Reach for the Stars—Eve had no doubts. He could work miracles if he chose—and this might be such a miracle.

Eve called Sara Thomas and told her to find Heather's mother and then call back. Somehow, Eve would manage to have someone stationed at the telephone until that call came through.

Satisfied that she'd done all she could for the time being, Eve rose. "I suppose I'd better go to my class."

"Ah, and the tennis balls are waiting." Logan got up and headed to the door. He stopped and looked down at her. "You know, Eve, it's really nice to see an artist . . . I mean, someone who really cares about her fellow man enough to do all that you're doing."

With that, he bounded out the door like a teenager, leaving Eve to wonder about his meaning. Once again, he'd referred to artists as something less than human almost. Why did he feel that way?

She didn't have time to ponder about his comments. Heather was headed straight for the office. "Heather, I have some good news."

"What? Did you find my mom?" Heather asked, her slender face filled with hope.

"Not yet, sweetie." Eve straightened the barrette that held Heather's hair back off her face. "But we will. I talked to Mrs. Thomas, and she's going to find your mom and call back. When she does, I'm bringing her up here."

"Here?" Heather's face screwed into a grimace. "Does that mean . . ."

"That means that you'll stay in your cabin with your cabinmates. I'll find another place for her to stay." Eve hoped that her intuitive senses had picked up on the reason for Heather's scowl. "You'll still be just like everyone else."

"Cool," Heather said. "When will she be here?"

"That depends on a couple of things. Mr. Mallory is going to play a tennis game and the money from that game will buy your mom's ticket. As soon as we get enough money, she'll be on her way."

"Oh," Heather said, apparently trying to hide her disappointment. "I thought you meant she would be coming today."

Tears started to glisten in the girl's eyes, and Eve's heart went out to the child. "Listen, Heather, we're doing all we can as quickly as we can."

"I know. I'm sorry for being such a cry-baby, but I'm really worried about her." Heather hesitated for a long moment, chewing on her lower lip. "You don't know what it's like to sleep out there. Men . . ." Heather broke off in a rush of tears and buried her face in Eve's breast.

If ever Eve would have killed someone, she could have done so in that moment. Had the child been molested? Or forced to watch helplessly while her mother was raped? No child should have to live with that kind of threat. How many children were out there, facing those dangers every day? Eve simply couldn't think about it for very long. If she did, her heart would break.

To think that a beautiful child like Heather had been through the tortures she had at such an early age, Eve just couldn't believe it. But she'd seen the girl's face, heard the anguish in her voice. There could be no doubt about what had happened.

Eve knew that she couldn't stop the pain for every child, but, God willing, she could change Heather's life. For the moment, Eve didn't know how, but she would make this happen and soon.

"Heather, sweetheart, I don't know how I'm going to do it, but your mother will be here by the end of the week." Eve fought the tears that threatened to spill down her own cheeks. "I don't know . . . all the things that you do and for that, I'm truly sorry, but rest assured, as long as I can possibly do it, you and your mother will never have to go back to the shelter or to the streets again. I'll find a way."

Eight

For the first few minutes of her class, Eve ran through the basics of oil painting. She asked questions about primary colors, color complements, shading and tinting. When she was satisfied that everyone knew the rudiments of the art, she moved on to more complex concepts to assess their level of understanding and education.

She discovered that even though there was a diverse age group, all of them had apparently made art a priority and learned everything they could about the subject. She then talked briefly about other mediums, about selecting subjects, about balance, and composition. Some knew more than others, but the ones who were lagging behind when they walked into the room, quickly picked up the concepts.

"All right, I know you're eager to paint,

so we'll get started. I need someone who's willing to be my assistant for this week."

Heather's hand was first in the air. "I want to help."

"Heather it shall be." Though Eve hated the big name tags the kids wore, she found it much easier to keep up with names. "Heather will be my assistant this week. Next week . . ." Eve spotted a young black boy who was as eager as Heather. "Tony. Heather, write this down. The third week, Dawn. Rick will help the fourth week. When we get to week five, we'll decide what to do next."

Eve noted that Heather had copied the names down along with the scheduled week. "Here, Miss Travers."

Within minutes, the class was engaged in a spirited conversation about subject matter for their first painting. Eve listened to their suggestions, noting with interest how excited they all seemed to be. Finally she raised her hand for silence. "I suggest that we vote on the most popular components you've mentioned."

Eve listed the items on the chalkboard. "Cabin, stream, mountains, forest. We can do something quite lovely with those, I believe."

The students helped her to hand out the kits she'd so carefully put together over the last few weeks. Each child had a wooden box filled with paints and brushes. When everybody had opened their new kits, Eve began to call off the items that were supposed to be included. "Large tube of titanium white, cad yellow light, cad yellow medium, yellow ochre, cad red light, cad red medium, sap green, thalo green, thalo blue, cerulean blue, ultramarine blue, burnt umber, burnt sienna. You should also have a bottle of Lynne Pittard's Basik White and a color wheel."

Eve listed the brushes they should have and verified that everyone had all the paints and brushes they needed. "Now, we'll begin by passing out odorless mineral spirits."

When everyone was settled, Eve asked the students to sketch in the placement of the elements of their painting. When everyone was finished, she stopped at each easel and commented on the composition. She was very interested to see how much they knew. A lot could be determined by talking to a student, but the final analysis had to be in the execution, rather than the discussion.

Eve suggested that several students move this or that to avoid being in the exact center of the canvas; she told one young man to change the size of his cabin because it distorted the depth perception. Heather's sketch amazed Eve. Easily the youngest child in the class, Heather had drawn confidently, catching the line of the vanishing points without err.

Smiling with pride, for the child was every bit as good as her teacher had said, Eve moved to the window. She wanted to give every student a chance to pick his or her own palette of color before she talked about using complements, shading, and tinting in a little more detail.

The kids were busily at work, squeezing out little bits of paint, stopping occasionally to gaze at their sketches to see what might be needed. Eve inhaled deeply and was immediately immersed in her art world. The scent of paint, the texture of canvas, the feel of a brush in her hand transported her to a place where everything else was left behind, and she could see that many of her pupils felt the same way.

She wanted to give them a little more time to study the colors she'd given them.

Standing at the window, she answered a few scattered questions and then silence took over the room again.

Eve stared out the window. She couldn't see the tennis courts very well, but she could hear the laughter and occasional shrieks of dismay rising about the high fences. Apparently, Logan was better at teaching kids than he'd thought.

His face filled her mind. He was a handsome man, brown hair, brown eyes that glinted with humor, angular features that formed a strong face. She imagined him, leaping like a cat into the air as he served or streaking across the court like a gazelle to return a borderline hit. Though she'd thought he was out of shape when he arrived, Logan had gotten into shape quickly. His exercise regimen must be rigorous.

And then she thought of his kiss. Unexpected, but very satisfying. Well, until the end when they'd both toppled from the log. Eve smiled. Her smile widened as she remembered the embarrassing moment. At the time, she'd been humiliated by the awkwardness of not only the action, but the situation. She'd been nearly an hour picking pine straw and dead leaves out of her hair and clothes.

Eve began to laugh. What a sight they must have been, lying there in each other's arms, covered in leaves, shocked out of a first kiss. They were no better than pubescent kids, exploring the mysteries of the opposite sex for the first time. She wondered what the "Casanova of the tennis courts" must have thought of that event. What a laugh, though he probably wouldn't think so. Something like that could ruin his image.

By this time, her laughter was beginning to subside. Then she noticed the silence behind her. She turned to see every gaze in the room directed at her. "Finished?" she asked, quelling the laughter lest she have to explain.

"What was so funny, Miss Travers?" one of the kids asked, grinning along with her.

"Oh, I can't tell you."

A chorus of "why nots" and "please" rang from the students, but Eve knew she could never reveal that to anyone. Even though she thought it was funny, she wasn't prepared to be the butt of every joke for the remainder of the session. "Oh, maybe I'll tell you at the end of the season."

She strode back to the front of the class

and began to discuss color tints and shades before the kids could realize what she was doing. Eve adroitly diverted their attention from her to the work at hand. Thank goodness, the kids were so interested in their palettes that they forgot all about her laughter.

Logan reached for a return and hit it with his strong backhand. Some of the kids were pretty good, but most of them hadn't had much, if any, experience on the tennis court. He played a little with each student, giving tips on how to be more effective and, as he did so, he mentally arranged the kids into two groups. When he'd gone through with every student, he sat them down and talked to them about the basics of tennis.

A few of the kids didn't even know how to score a match. Within a few minutes, he'd divided them up, and they were playing their first sets of doubles. Logan sat down on the bench at the side of the court and watched. Even though they were beginners, for the most part, they were eager to learn and picked up on the points he'd made very quickly.

He studied them carefully, noting how gracefully or how awkwardly they moved. After a few minutes, he decided that he and Eve should rearrange the schedule a little if possible. There were a few pupils that he needed to work more closely with than the others. Those that had played before needed more of a challenge.

Wondering how that would work with her schedule, Logan began to make notes on his clipboard. He listed the students in groups according to ability. During the lunch hour, or perhaps this evening at dinner, he would discuss the feasibility of rescheduling.

As he watched the youngsters play, he smiled. They were enthusiastic, he had to give them that. Their laughter and squeals somehow lifted his spirits. In the beginning, he'd thought this was going to be as dull as teaching a bunch of spoiled brats, but he'd been wrong, oh so wrong.

The kids were on even footing here, all without great financial backgrounds, but each with a genuine desire to excel at tennis. He supposed that translated to the art studios, too.

Maybe this summer wouldn't be so bad after all. Logan had always wanted to go to camp, but his tennis had come first. School in the mornings, slavish hours on the tennis courts in the afternoon and evening, homework until the wee hours: all that had taken its toll on his free time. His summers were spent in three-a-day sessions on the court or watching films of great players.

Probably for the first time in his life, Logan realized that he'd been cheated of his childhood. He didn't necessarily regret it, because he loved tennis; it had been his life—a life he loved and wouldn't trade—for as long as he could remember. But, now, watching the joyful interplay among these kids who were probably happy-go-lucky for the first time in their lives, he felt a certain twinge of jealousy.

Well, he decided, if I missed my chances at summer camp because of tennis, it's right that tennis should offer me the opportunity to recapture those lost days of a regular kid's summer. That seemed fitting to him.

And, what of Eve? How did she fit into that kid's summer he was trying so desperately to recapture? Last night had been an interesting initiation into the romances that spring up at summer camp.

Logan knew that the youthful romances of camp weren't for him, nor for Eve; they were much too mature. But was she, as he was beginning to believe he might be, searching for the lost moments of childhood?

Could they find that innocent joy together, for just a few weeks? Logan rationalized that they couldn't. That sort of affair, if it could be termed that, was for teenagers. When adults ventured into romantic territory, the consequences were more often than not, lasting or painful—or both.

Eve showed the kids where to store their wet canvases and watched them put their supplies away before racing out the door. With a laugh at their exuberance, Eve followed them outside and ran into Logan who was trailing after his morning class.

"So, how did it go, Coach?" Eve asked, with a hint of humor in her voice. The morning had begun so well that she didn't want anything to interfere, but kids were always hungry.

Logan looked down at her and smiled. "Actually, it went very well."

Eve eyed him curiously. He sounded as if he really enjoyed the morning. "Am I to understand that your 'torture' isn't as bad as you first thought it might be?"

With a scowl on his face that was intended to show her she shouldn't recall those former unpleasant discussions, Logan grinned sheepishly. "I admit it. I'm having a pretty good time. I guess it's because of the kids. So far, they're great."

"Great? Great!" Eve chuckled. She knew it took courage to admit he was wrong. "I'm encouraged."

"Yeah, well, it's only the first day." Logan rested his arm on her shoulder as they got in the long line at the dining hall. "You know, tomorrow, I think I'll leave my class with five minutes of practice and sneak off to lunch early. I'm starved nearly to death."

"I know what you mean." Eve leaned over and looked down the length of the line. "We were so lost in our work that we forgot to take our snack break. I'll owe them an extra after today."

"Crap!" he exclaimed, shaking his head.

"I forgot, too. You'd think the kids would remind us."

"Apparently, we're going to have to get some timers so that we—"

"Eve," Kayla interrupted, striding toward them. "I'm so sorry."

"What happened, Kayla?" Eve asked, putting her comment about buying timers out of her mind.

"I didn't give my kids a break this morning." Kayla confessed as if she thought Eve would scold her.

Eve and Logan laughed, causing Kayla's forehead to wrinkle in puzzlement. "Kayla, my dear, both Logan and I forgot, too. I'll send someone in for alarm clocks or timers or something. Did Bert remember to give his kids a break?"

"I don't know. They're not even out of class yet."

Logan chuckled. "I think we need to install some sort of bell or electric system that rings in all the classrooms automatically. It seems that none of us are capable of keeping time."

Just then, another group of kids rushed into the dining hall, followed by Bert. His chagrined look told Eve that he'd forgotten, too. "I think I'll send someone out this very day. In the meantime, I need to go and ask Madora to increase the size of the portions or make sure to offer seconds. We don't want the kids to go hungry."

Eve left Logan standing with Kayla and elbowed her way into the front of the serving line where Madora was presiding over her servers. "Madora, it seems that we forgot to let the kids out for their snack this morning. Make sure they get plenty to eat and drink."

"You can rest assured that when Madora serves the meals, everybody gets plenty of everything." Madora watched the server place a dollop of mashed potatoes on a plate. "Put more than that. You heard Miss Travers. These kids are hungry."

Confident that Madora would take care of the matter, Eve returned to her place in line. "Gosh, I wish they'd hurry. I'm as hungry as they are."

Logan leaned down and whispered, "I'm even hungrier. I swear I could eat the north end of a southbound horse."

Eve stifled a giggle. "Well, I'm not quite that hungry, but close."

The line began to move, but not quickly enough to satisfy the hungry kids and staff. The dining hall was noisy with laughter and getting-to-know-you chatter, and Eve found the atmosphere energizing.

"Noisy bunch," Logan called above the din. "Enthusiastic, too."

Eve surveyed the kids surrounding her. "Seems as if they had a good time this morning."

"Me, too," Logan admitted with a grin. "Better than I thought I would, anyway."

"I know how you feel." Eve smiled at one of the students from her morning class. "It seems all that worry was for nothing."

"Yeah, well, with kids, you never know. Moods change quickly."

"And what makes you such an authority on kids, Mr. Mallory," Eve asked with a slightly sarcastic tone.

"I am one."

"I see." Eve had to laugh with him. Even though he'd been exasperating at first, Logan was coming around. He was almost human most of the time. "I'm not sure any of us ever grow up." She spotted Heather, standing quietly in line, biting her lower lip. "Then again, some of us grow up too soon."

Logan followed her gaze and saw Heather. She seemed to be such a sad child. He wanted to get her in his class and make her happy, even if it was only for the summer. "Yeah, I know what you mean."

Kayla said the blessing and the din of voices rose as the kids expressed their hunger. Lunch was a great affair. Madora and her crew had prepared boneless chicken breasts, mashed potatoes, fresh green beans, and a salad bar. On top of all that, there was fresh fruit for dessert.

"Something for everyone, it seems." Eve stared at the luscious array and tried to decide which fruit would be the best for her. "I'll take a peach to have later," she decided. "You should take one, too. They're from Sunny Slope Farms down in Gaffney. Nobody grows better peaches."

"If I've got your guarantee, then I'll have one for my afternoon snack instead of the corn chips I planned to have."

Eve and Logan reached for the salt at the same time. Feeling the color spring to her cheeks, Eve was amazed. It had been a long time since she'd blushed. The accidental touch immediately brought the kiss she'd shared with Logan to memory. Even though it had been brief, the feeling it caused sent a teasing shiver up her spine. And then there was the fall. Would she never get over the embarrassment of that clumsy effort? Maybe she should take that as a sign or omen to stay away from Logan. She averted her eyes, let him use the seasonings, and began to eat.

Lunch was tasty and filling. Eve watched Heather for a few minutes. She ate with vigor, as if she was afraid her next meal might never come. "It just breaks my heart to see these kids who are so obviously intelligent and talented, but have no financial resources to put a decent meal on the table, much less pay for college when the time comes."

"You know, Eve, since Tim is so interested in this camp, now that his money is invested, why not bring him down here to meet some of them?" Logan studied Heather for a moment. "Maybe he'd be willing to offer some sort of scholarship to the kids who're ready to go to college. It might not be much, but it's worth a try."

"You know, Logan, that's an idea." Eve felt suddenly lighthearted. "I could prepare a profile on each child. All these kids have good grades in school, too. Do you really think he might?"

"Who knows?" Logan answered honestly. "But let's work on it. We have a few days before we have to approach Tim. Why not get the kids to write something, too? I mean, after a couple of weeks, take a little time to let the kids express their feelings about what art means to them, about what coming to the camp means to them."

"That's a great idea." Eve considered it for a few seconds. "Maybe we should ask the kids to be thinking about it a few days in advance. That might help."

Just then one of the kids, a girl about sixteen, stood up on one of the tables and a hush fell over the room. "All right, gang, since nobody volunteered, I'll be the gossip reporter this summer." She looked around the room with a smile on her face. "*I* saw the movie about summer camp, so if you have a scoop, find me. My name is Julie."

A rousing cheer went up from the crowd. Apparently they liked the idea of a "gossip reporter" in their midst. Eve smiled. It might make mealtimes more interesting and would be a good way for her to know what was going on around her.

Bert made a few announcements and then the lunch crowd began to disperse. Eve had the afternoon free, so she went back to her office to look at the files. Logan's ideas were too good to pass up.

By the time she'd glanced at most of the files of the older kids, Eve had a good idea of what she needed to say when she talked to Tim. Maybe he would offer one or two scholarships a year. That would be really good publicity. Along with the scholarships, Tim could make some sort of commercial that featured Logan and the kids who were recipients of the scholarships, something about staying in school and trying to get grants and funding, almost a public service announcement.

The more she thought about it, the better she liked the idea. And the more she thought about Logan. the better she liked him. He was, she'd discovered, a very complex man. At the beginning, she never would have believed that he would come up with such a good idea, something completely devoted to helping the kids.

An unselfish act. Who was the true Logan Mallory? she wondered, biting into her peach. The slightly tart flavor filled her mouth. Eve loved the peaches from Sunny Slope. The ones that would ripen a little later would be even better, but for now, nothing could beat a peach for a snack.

She continued to make notes. There were several good candidates for scholarship. She couldn't tell them about it yet; there was no need to get their hopes up without reason. She decided to make time to talk with Logan again about the possibility of obtaining scholarships from Tennis Pro.

Supper came and went. Eve had a little time to gather her notes and put them in some semblance of order before the evening campfire, so she sat there studying what she'd written. She was amazed. What had begun as nothing more than a dream to give some underprivileged kids who were talented in the arts a summer of learning and fun, might transform into a way to help some of them on a more concrete level. She owed a great deal of thanks to Logan for his unexpected contribution.

She might have eventually thought of these ideas, but who could tell? It seemed so logical to her, but then again, Eve didn't consider herself a very logical person. She wondered what the difference was between them. He, in a way, was in an esoteric sort of career, not the usual assembly line kind of job, but he was more logical in thought. He seemed to look at a situation and grasp its possibilities without a great deal of hard thinking. It was almost instantaneous with Logan.

For now, Eve didn't care where the idea had come from. She was just glad it had come and that she might be able to implement it—if she was lucky and if Tim was amenable.

Eve loved the smell of the campfire. As she sat on her log watching the kids' antics, she couldn't help thinking of the last campfire when Logan had kissed her. Her gaze automatically sought him out. He was sitting with Bert and they were talking intently while Kayla and several kids put on a skit.

The breeze wafted the scent of burned wood all around her and she inhaled deeply. This was her dream; it was coming true for her. But its time was limited. What would she do at the end of the season? She'd given some thought to that, but not nearly enough.

Eve still maintained her apartment in Atlanta; her lease didn't expire until the first of October. She didn't want to go back there. Here was something else she'd have to consider as the weeks flew past. It wasn't a topic she really wanted to address, but was inevitable.

As the children were leaving, Eve strode over to Logan and asked if he might spend a little time discussing the suggestion he'd given her. He readily assented and they strolled through the woods to her office.

Logan glanced down at her as they walked into the office. There was an animation about her, something new. Even though she'd always been active, she was different tonight. He wondered what had happened to cause such a change.

Her blue eyes seemed bluer, if that was possible, and so expressive. Logan felt a tightening in his loin as he dropped onto the arm of the sofa. "So what's the problem?"

"Nothing, really," she admitted, wondering why she'd bothered him at all. He'd given her the idea, now she should simply take it and run. "I'm just trying to get this scholarship idea firmly implanted in my mind. When I call Tim, I don't want to make any mistakes. The kids' futures depend on me."

"Yeah, it is kind of a heavy burden, isn't it?"

She studied him for a moment. Was he feeling a responsibility for the campers? Some extra burden his contract didn't stipulate? "I don't mind the burden. It's just that . . . I feel so inadequate sometimes."

"It's hard to be confident all the time, Eve. Nobody's that sure of himself or herself."

"I know, Logan, but it's more than that." Eve considered the situation as she sat down on the sofa. He slipped off the arm of the sofa and came to rest beside her. "These kids deserve so much and I'm not really qualified to handle the financial questions that might come up."

"So? We'll get Jerry to handle the figures. He's a whiz at that."

"Do you think he would?" Eve felt a little better about the situation. "If I knew what to ask for, I mean, if I could have some specifics to give Tim, I'd be more confident. I know the need. I just don't know how much it will cost."

"I'll give Jer a call and ask him to check out the costs for some of the art schools. He'll do a real thorough job." Logan thought for a moment. "I'll ask him to come down and have a look at what we're doing here. After all, I'm proof positive that once you get someone involved, they become much more enthusiastic."

"I guess that's true."

"You know, Eve, I admire what you've done."

"I haven't done anything special. I saw a need for the kids and tried to fill it." Eve smiled a little shyly. "It happened to coincide with a dream of mine."

The phone rang. Eve reached over and picked up the receiver. "Hi, Eve, this is Jerry. Jerry Kent."

"Hello, Jerry. Nice to hear from you. Were you calling to talk to Logan?"

"Yes and no. I wanted to tell you that a film crew is going to be there tomorrow. They're going to be scoping out the place for the Tennis Pro spot."

"Tomorrow?" Eve echoed incredulously. "I . . . I figured they'd wait until we got things into full swing."

"I'm sure they aren't going to be filming tomorrow. Just setting up."

"Thanks for calling, Jerry." Eve handed the phone to Logan.

"Hello, you old cuss. What are you doing without me to browbeat this summer?"

"Logan, we've got some things working. I need to come down one day soon and talk to you."

"Sounds good. I've got a project for you, too. Why don't you come down tomorrow?" Logan glanced at Eve. She seemed distracted all of a sudden.

"I might do that."

Logan listened to Jerry's plans and then hung up the phone. "I guess we have a busy few days ahead of us."

"Logan, I don't know what to do. I don't know anything about film crews and . . . and commercials. What shall I do?" Eve asked, envisioning all her hard work going down the drain because of her lack of knowledge.

"Eve, it's a piece of cake. You don't have to be perfect." Logan gazed at the worried expression on her face. It was clear to him that she'd accepted this money and his presence at face value, but the film crew threw everything into chaos. "Look, just be yourself. They want to—"

"Myself? I'm an artist, not an actress." Eve rose and began to pace. "I expected to have some time to prepare for this. Why didn't they tell us earlier?"

"It's not the end of the world. They're just coming to look around. They'll see what equipment they need, set up the shots, and bingo, they'll be out of your hair for a few days."

Eve dropped back onto the sofa. "Do you really think so? I mean, you're used to cameras and that sort of thing. I'm a novice at this."

"Here's my advice. Ignore the cameras. You can't exactly ignore the director, but pretend the camera isn't there." Logan slid his arm around her and gave her an encouraging hug.

She looked up at him, thankful that she had someone who had some experience to guide her. She might be a fighter where her kids were concerned, but she was too inexperienced in dealing with media people for her own comfort. "Thanks, Logan. It's really nice that you're here."

Logan gazed down into her eyes and

smiled. "I'm glad to be here. Much more than I ever thought I would be."

Before he could stop himself, Logan kissed her. His arms were around her, his mouth pressed against her silken lips in a kiss that seemed more gentle, and yet more powerful, than anything he could remember.

Eve opened her mouth to him, allowing him to plunder gently into the recesses as she turned slightly to pull closer to him. Logan held her tightly, and Eve slipped her arms around his neck. For a few moments, she could hardly breathe.

Logan pulled away, still gazing into her eyes. "I shouldn't have done that," he said finally. "I'm sorry, Eve. It's just that . . . you're so different."

"Both of us should take control of this . . . this . . . whatever it is, before it becomes a habit." Eve breathed deeply, her blood tracing her veins with rippling sensations.

"Habit, hell. I enjoyed it. That's the problem." Logan rose and walked to the door. "When I sat in my house, alone, on New Year's Eve, I made several resolutions. The first was that I wouldn't get emotionally—or physically—involved for at least a year. It's hardly been six months."

Eve stood, as if that would give her some advantage. It would have, perhaps, had he not been at least four inches taller than she. "Then, let's forget it happened. I do want us to be friends, Logan. I think that anything else would ruin the possibility of a friendship."

"Yeah, you're right." Logan grinned and dimples appeared on his cheeks. "Friends. We can be great friends, Eve. No sex, no pressure. Just friends."

Nine

"Women," Logan thought as he tossed and turned in his bed. Why had he kissed her? She's extremely kissable, that's why, he told himself.

He punched his pillow and buried his head in it, trying to blot out the vision of her pretty face. "Damn it, I should never have made that resolution. That's the problem. I've been without a woman too long."

Muzzle yowled and then stretched, as if to warn him against waking her up again. She curled up against his stomach and settled down.

"Sorry, girl." Logan thought he was going nuts. First, he'd discovered the cat, made her his own, and now he was kissing the woman he'd thought he would hate. Hell, it would have been better if I hated her!

He never could hate Eve, Logan decided, turning over and disturbing Muzzle once again. She was much too kind. He tried to figure out what the difference was between her and the other artistic types he knew, particularly his mother. There was something that made Eve special. Maybe it was the way she tackled a problem. That had to be it. When she realized a problem existed, she jumped on it quickly, trying to find ways to resolve it.

Logan recognized that he was rationalizing. The fact simply was that he enjoyed Eve's company. But how could he reconcile that with the promise he'd made to himself to avoid entanglements with women for a year?

He sat up, threw the sheet back, and threaded his way between the big bed and the refrigerator. He pulled out a bottle of mineral water and sat back down on the bed, propping his pillows up behind him. Okay, Logan, old pal, so you like the dame . . . woman. Big deal.

He had to concentrate on friendship with Eve. That was the answer. They'd talked about being friends and he instinctively felt that was the best way to handle the situation. But could he remain that objective about her?

Logan had known a lot of women. None of them had ever affected him the way Eve Travers did. She wasn't the one-night stand kind of woman, not that he was looking for any kind of an arrangement. No, he'd decided that he wanted to stay free of entanglements for a year and then maybe . . . just maybe, look for someone who would mean more to him that anyone ever had. He considered Eve and knew she was this kind of woman. But he'd been wrong before.

He'd wait his year and that was final. Maybe then he'd start looking around. Not an active search, he reminded himself. He simply planned to be available if such a woman came his way.

Six months was a long time. He felt it sorely—especially after kissing Eve and holding her in his arms. It was going to be a long night.

What had she been thinking of? Eve paced back and forth around her narrow bed. "Careful or you'll wear a hole in the floor," she scolded herself, but she couldn't sit down, much less lie down.

Why had she let him kiss her again

when she'd sworn not to? Logan wasn't a settling down kind of man. At the end of the summer, he would jump into his Jag and drive out of her life forever. How could she be so foolish?

After she'd spent years developing a protective armor for her emotions, he'd managed to tear away a space big enough to play a tennis match in. But he was kind, he was thoughtful. Nothing like the stories she'd read about him. Who was right? Her instinctive feelings about him or the published reports.

There was too much at stake here for her to ruin it by becoming involved with a staff member. There, that distanced him a bit. He was a staff member, nothing more, nothing less. Somehow Eve had to think of him in those terms.

But his kisses burned in her mind, as did those beautiful whiskey-colored eyes, his enchanting dimples. He was far too handsome for her to fall for. He was trouble, pure and simple. Trouble. A troublesome staff member.

Eve awoke with a headache. She'd been awake until about four o'clock, unable to sleep because of Logan's kiss. It was as much her fault as his, she admitted. From now on, she wouldn't allow it to happen. If he sat on the sofa, she'd sit behind the desk. If he sat on a log, she'd prop herself against a tree. Getting close to him caused those problems and she could circumvent them by avoiding close contact.

She ran the tap a moment and filled a glass with water to take a couple of aspirin. Having a headache wouldn't help her when she had to face the film people this afternoon. And she had her morning class to contend with, too.

Eve slipped on a pair of shorts and a T-shirt and lay back down for the few minutes she needed for the aspirin to work. When she felt the easing of the muscles in her neck, she got up again and started moving around. By the time she headed for the dining hall, she'd almost forgotten she had a headache.

She was the first one to the dining hall and got her breakfast quickly. By the time the campers and staff started drifting in, she was finished. With a wave at everyone, she hustled out the door and back to her room.

Maybe what she needed was a swim. She

had about an hour before her class, so Eve changed into her swimsuit, snatched a towel out of her drawer, and headed to the lake. The beach was deserted.

She threw her towel down and waded out into the cool water. It took a moment for her to get used to it, but before long, she'd submerged herself and was swimming laps in the roped-off area.

As much as she would have liked it, Eve didn't go outside the marked area. She had plenty of time to make one lap across the lake and back, but since she was swimming alone, she didn't want to take any risks.

A splash interrupted her thoughts and she turned to see someone swimming beneath the surface of the water. Logan's head popped out of the water and he grinned at her. "Didn't you ever hear of buddy swimming? Never swim without your buddy?"

"Yes," she answered, feeling his penetrating gaze. "But I'm not going out far."

"Doesn't matter." Logan studied her a moment. "Looks like you're a pretty good swimmer. How about a race across the lake and back?"

Eve couldn't contain her happiness.

"That's just what I wanted to do, but I wouldn't swim that far alone."

"I'll give you a head start."

"Not at all necessary, sir," she said dryly and dog paddled to the rope. She swam underneath and floated with her feet touching the boundary of the swimming area. "Get out here. You and I both start with our feet touching the rope."

"Somebody got a gun?"

"Gun? You're going to shoot me if I win?"

"Yeah, right. I mean a starting gun, silly."

"We don't need one. We'll count to three and go." Eve treaded water while Logan swam to join her.

"One, two," they said in unison, but Logan reached over and caught her arm.

He scowled at her. "Is that one, two, three and go? Or is it one, two, and go on three?"

"Nitwit," she teased and pushed his head under water. "One, two, three."

It would have been better if they'd started by diving from the dock, Eve decided, but it was too late. Her quick count had caught Logan off guard. She glanced behind her, but he was holding his own.

"Not fair!" he called, swimming evenly. Eve was a good swimmer, probably better than he, but he wasn't about to give up. He'd fight to the finish.

The far shore was nearly a quarter of a mile. Eve had crossed the lake several times, but never in a race. Usually it took her about forty-five minutes to make the trip, but with Logan so close on her trail, she knew she could do it faster.

The shore approached. When Eve got to a point where she could stand up in the water, she turned around. Logan was right there. "Ready?" she asked, and dived beneath the surface. She swam under water for a few feet and then got back into her even stroke.

She wondered if he was holding back because she was a woman, but decided that he was such a competitor, there was little chance of that. Eve loved gliding through the water. It was like cool silk against her skin. She treasured each moment as the camp came more and more clearly into view.

Gasping for air, she walked to the beach and dropped onto her towel. She began to dry her hair and fluff it with her fingers. Logan trudged up the beach a few moments behind her. "Woman, you flat wore me out."

Eve watched as he fell onto his towel and lay there like he was dead. "Sorry." She breathed as evenly as she could, but her breaths still came in ragged gasps. "I was trying to make it easy on you."

He rolled over and glared at her. "Easy? Easy? You could have chased me down the mountain with your Bronco and it wouldn't have been any harder."

"Out of shape, are you?"

Logan pulled himself to a sitting position. "Yeah, a little, but I'm working it out."

"All those late nights and wild women, I suppose," she teased.

"Late nights, maybe. But the only woman causing me to lose sleep is you." Logan bit his tongue. How could he have said that? Once again, he'd spoke before he thought about it.

Eve pretended to be looking at something on the sand. She poked and prodded for a moment. "Why would you lose sleep over me?" She glanced up at him. There was no reason for him to have a sleepless night because of her. It must have something to do with the camp instead of her personally. "Are you that worried about my latest project?"

"Yeah, that's it." Logan was glad she'd thrown him an excuse. He wondered if she did it on purpose, but after studying her for a few seconds, he decided that she didn't realize how much she affected him. It was all innocence on her part.

Eve smiled sweetly, as if to say that she wasn't about to mention who'd won the race. She gazed at him a few seconds and then averted her eyes. He was too good-looking, his presence too powerful. If she didn't move quickly, she'd be in trouble. "This is wonderful, but I've got a class to teach."

"Me, too." Logan rose and extended his hand to her. "Same time tomorrow?"

"Right."

They hurried back to the compound, and Eve left him with a smile. When she reached her room, she pulled off her bathing suit and rinsed it, hanging it on the shower curtain rod. A glance at the clock told her she'd better hurry. She put on her clothes, dried her hair a little more, and gathered the items she needed for class.

* * *

Logan watched the kids serve. They'd improved even from the previous day. He sat there and thought about the morning. Why had he followed her?

That was easy to answer. The woman was gorgeous in a bathing suit . . . in anything. He'd followed her like a puppy follows a child with a cookie.

He almost wished she'd been a horsey-looking woman, one who was totally unappealing to him, bulging biceps, a slight mustache. That would have provided him with a form of protection that he instinctively felt he needed. Eve's attraction for him was too potent by far.

Logan grinned. She was one helluva swimmer, too. She'd beaten him fair and square, though he would have lied if she'd asked him. He vowed to practice. Before the summer was out, he'd beat her across the lake and back.

Maybe seniors tennis wouldn't be so bad. At least he'd have to keep in shape. Logan realized the need now. In the few short months he'd been "vegging out" at his house, he'd let his muscles go slack. Now that he really considered the situation, he understood why he'd done that. His pride had been wounded. Once the darling of the circuit, he was now a has-been.

No more. Logan rose, picked up his racquet, and told the kids to watch. For several minutes, he served, placing each service on the line or a couple of inches inside it. "Now, that's your most potent weapon. Long volleys tire you out. If you're going to play tennis, you should concentrate on learning to serve well."

The kids practiced their serves for the remainder of the time period. Logan had settled back on the bench to watch, but his thoughts continued to be of Eve. The summer was before them. If they didn't think of something to circumvent this attraction for each other, then . . . he'd be in big trouble.

Eve stared at her canvas. Behind her the kids were painting away, most of them far ahead of her. She was painting her camp, but nothing seemed to be working. There was nothing wrong with the painting, but she couldn't concentrate. Her thoughts kept drifting to Logan.

She asked one of the class members to hold up his painting. All the others critiqued it. In fact, it was an excellent work. Eve was proud of the boy. One by one, they discussed each other's work, including her own. When they were done, it was lunchtime.

They hurried out the door after putting away their supplies and canvases. Eve followed along as they headed for the dining hall. The kids were exuberant, flitting from one subject to another as they scrambled to be first in line.

Heather caught up with Eve. "Miss Travers, have you heard from my mom?"

"No, darling. I called Mrs. Thomas, and she promised to call back as soon as your mother came in."

"Do you . . ." Heather's voice dwindled into silence. "Do you think she's all right?"

"I'm sure she is, Heather." Eve stopped and put her hands on Heather's shoulders. "Look, sweetheart, I know your mother wants you to have a wonderful time. If you keep worrying about her, how can you have fun?"

"I can't help it, Miss Travers. She's never been by herself before." Tears were starting to form in Heather's eyes.

"Darling, you trust me, don't you?"

"Yes, ma'am."

"Well, I want you to promise me that you'll have fun. I want you to stop worrying about your mother." Eve hugged the child close. "Mrs. Thomas and I will take care of everything so you don't have to be concerned. You need to be concentrating on your art. You're very good, you know."

"Do you really think so?" Heather gazed up at Eve through a shimmering surface of tears.

"Yes, I do. I want you to work very hard. You have a great deal of potential as an artist." Eve caught Heather's hand and they walked on into the dining hall. "Why don't you eat with me, today?"

"May I?" Heather's eyes grew wide.

"Sure. Why not?" Eve looked at her class. They were clustered around her as they waited for Madora to open the line. "We can all eat together."

A chorus of happy voices surrounded her. Eve bowed her head as Kayla said the blessing and then they went through the line. "Looks good, doesn't it?"

"Country-style steak and rice?" A smile broke out on Heather's face. "My favorite."

"Mine, too." Eve helped herself to another peach and to a piece of chocolate pie piled high with meringue. "The pie, I mean."

Heather reached for a piece of chocolate pie, too. "I like chocolate a lot."

Lunch was fun with her kids, but Eve couldn't help worrying about the film crew. She didn't know exactly what time they would arrive, but she expected them momentarily. Logan was talking with Bert and a couple of boys from his morning class. As she gazed at him, she felt more confident. He'd told her not to worry, so she wouldn't.

Logan felt that someone was staring at him. He glanced up and found that it was Eve. She looked away almost immediately. How long had she been watching him? Did she want something in particular?

Eve felt silly, like a teenage girl who'd been caught staring at the cutest boy in class. Logan probably thought she was nuts. She vowed to avoid such conduct in the future—if possible.

Julie stood up and began to recite the gossip of the day. "And it looks like a relationship is on the horizon for two very cute head counselors. I don't want to mention any names, as there's nothing official yet, but their initials are Kayla and Bert."

Eve laughed along with the other kids, though she knew that Kayla and Bert probably wanted to huddle beneath the dining-room tables for the next hour. Maybe she should have put a stop to the gossip the first day, but everyone seemed to enjoy it so. As long as it remained harmless, Eve decided to let Julie continue.

Before lunch was over, the film crews truck crunched up the driveway. Eve heard the sound and turned immediately to see if Logan had heard. He smiled, rose, and said something to one of his group. Without taking his tray, he began to thread his way among the tables toward Eve.

Taking his cue, Eve turned to Tony. "Would you take my tray for me? I have an important meeting and I just heard the people arrive."

"Sure," the young black boy answered quickly.

"Thanks." Eve untangled herself from the bench and walked to meet Logan. She didn't want him to think she couldn't do this alone, so she said, "You don't have to interrupt your lunch, Logan. I can talk with them."

"I'm finished anyway." Logan placed his hand on the small of her back and they walked out of the dining hall.

By the time they reached the parking lot, several people had gotten out of the van. Eve hurried over to introduce herself, hoping she appeared more confident than she felt.

"And this is Logan Mallory," she concluded the introductions.

"Everybody knows who he is," Phil Underwood said, shaking Logan's hand. "Pleasure to meet you, Logan. This is my assistant, Dottie, Boogie the cameraman, and Lorna Peterson, producer."

"Well," Eve said, bringing the attention back to herself. "Would you like a walking tour of the camp first?"

"Sounds great," Lorna said, glancing around. "But first is there a place to get a bite to eat?"

"Is there!" Logan exclaimed. "Madora is the best cook in the South."

As they entered the dining hall, most of the kids were leaving. The campers glanced at the new adults, but streamed by them, laughing and talking about the afternoon's activities.

"Eve, I really love the idea of this camp." Lorna scanned the array of buildings. "My fondest memories of childhood are of summers at camp."

"Thanks, Lorna. I must say that things are working out much better than I ever expected." Eve glanced around. "Please sit down. I'll get someone to bring your—"

"Oh, no. No special treatment for us." Lorna spotted the sign that read "Entrance" and headed in that direction with her crew trailing after her. "You two sit down. We'll get acquainted with the facilities."

Eve dropped onto the bench. "Do you think we should serve them?"

"No. Let them go through the line like everyone else."

"I hope Madora has some steak left. Wasn't it good?"

"Terrific." Logan smiled at Eve. "I may invite her to live with me this winter. I could sure use some good food like that."

"I seem to recall that you were beginning a second career as a gourmet cook," Eve teased, a little anxiously.

"Oh, you mean the recipe I copied out

of the magazine on the day we met?"
Logan shrugged. "I tried it. Trust me, it
wasn't as good as it looked. But I've got
a great recipe for . . ."

"Logan Mallory collecting recipes?" Phil
Underwood asked, taking a seat beside
Logan. "I can't believe it."

Eve glanced at Logan instinctively. The
director's comments weren't meant to be
hurtful—at least, she didn't think they
were—but his tone had been a little deri-
sive. Before she could defend Logan, he
answered for himself.

"Well, Phil, we all gotta eat." Logan
leaned back and propped against the wall.
"I'm trying to uncomplicate my life, that's
all."

"Who would have guessed it?" Phil
asked.

"Guessed what?" Lorna sat down beside
Eve.

"That the great Logan Mallory has retired to the kitchen."

This time, Eve realized that Phil's intent
was definitely meant to be cutting. "Are
you married, Phil?"

"Who me?" Phil shifted a little under
Eve's scrutiny. "I got a wife and four
kids."

"Does your wife work?"

"With four kids? No way."

"Then you get three good meals a day when you're at home."

"Right."

Eve smiled. "I presume she gives you something other than peanut butter sandwiches or take-out Chinese."

"Sure she does. What's that got to do with Logan?"

"I think that he's doing the right thing. I mean, he's trying to eat a more healthy diet."

"Oh, I see," Phil said, looking from Eve to Logan. "This is a health kick, then."

"Exactly," Logan said, taking up where Eve left off. "If I'm going to get into shape for the seniors tournaments, I need to eat right."

"Oh, cut it out, Phil." Lorna reached across and smacked Phil's hand as she might a child's. "Stop baiting Logan." She turned to Logan with a big smile and raked her fingers through her long blond hair. "Don't pay any attention to him. He's just jealous."

Eve hurried to change the subject. "So, Lorna, do you have any specific plan?"

"Not really. I have a general—" She ate

a piece of steak and smiled. "Boy, I may never leave. This is great. Anyway, as I was saying, I have a general idea of what Tim's looking for, but until I see the layout, I'll have to wait."

Logan listened carefully. He wanted to help Eve as much as possible, but he hadn't expected her to have to come to his rescue. Obviously, Phil Underwood wasn't a fan of Logan's. "You'll love this place, Lorna. Eve's done a great job pulling this together."

"So, you're the moving force behind 'Camp Reach for the Stars,' eh?" Lorna asked, moaning with delight when she ate a bit of chocolate pie.

Eve couldn't help smiling at the woman's reaction to the food. "How long can you stay? We'll put you up in a cabin, or you can drive back out to the interstate and get rooms there."

"We've already got reservations at a hotel out there. I didn't realize you'd have room for us." Lorna scraped her plate with her fork and savored the last bite of pie.

"Whatever's best for you." Eve looked around the table. Everyone was finished, so she rose. "Well, now we'll go for that stroll around the premises."

As they walked, Eve explained her reasons for opening the camp, how she came up with the idea, and the difficulty she had with getting funding. "I was about to give up when Tim . . . Tennis Pro came through."

"So, Tim was the saving angel then?" Lorna asked, glancing back at her crew. "Keep up, guys. I want you all to get a good look around. We'll talk about specifics later."

"Tim has been very generous. Since all the kids are underprivileged, he's donated the T-shirts, shorts, socks, and shoes, along with miscellaneous other items."

"Bathing suits?" Lorna asked as they reached the beach.

"Yes. We have plenty." Eve glanced down at Lorna's figure. "We probably have one that would fit you, that is if you don't mind swimming in the lake."

"Sounds glorious."

Eve showed them everything she could think of. Logan had to break away after a short time because of his afternoon class, but Eve continued the tour. She introduced them to some of the kids, to the rest of the staff, and then took them back to the supply hut.

She scrambled around through one of the boxes and returned with a woman's swimsuit. "Do you think this will fit?"

Lorna glanced at the tag inside. "Perfect. When can we go?"

"Well, who's going? Do I need to get suits for everyone?"

Dottie bobbed her head. Phil grinned. "You don't think I'm going to miss this chance, do you?"

That left Boogie, who hadn't said much. "What about you?" Eve asked.

"I'm afraid I don't know how to swim."

"Afraid of the water, Boogie?" Phil asked, jabbing his elbow into Boogie's side.

"Just never learned," Boogie answered, returning the gesture.

Eve found swimsuits for all of them. "Boogie, you don't have to go in. Or maybe one of our counselors can help you learn. I promise it won't hurt and it doesn't take much time. You really should know how to swim."

He took the bathing suit. "I'll think about it."

The men and women separated. Eve took Lorna and Dottie to the office, where

they took turns changing in the bathroom.
Boogie and Phil changed in the boys' latrine.

When Eve emerged, Phil and Boogie
were heading toward the office in a hurry.
"What's the matter?" she asked, wondering what could have happened to make
them look that way.

"Lizard in the bathroom." Phil shivered
and grimaced.

Boogie grinned and raised an eyebrow.
"Afraid of a little lizard, Phil?"

"No, I'm not. I just don't like them."

Eve turned away so that Phil wouldn't
see her face. She was about to burst into
laughter. She gave everybody towels and
they walked the short distance to the lake.
After a refreshing swim, Lorna and Phil
got out of the water to sun themselves. Eve
approached Boogie, who'd come no closer
than the water's lapping edge. "Come with
me. I'll give you a quick lesson."

Boogie glanced at Phil. Eve saw that the
cameraman couldn't refuse without feeling inferior, so she said, "I used to be
afraid of water, too. When I lived here as
a child, some of the older kids would dunk
me."

Following along as she walked toward

the water, Boogie caught her hand. "You're not going to dunk me, are you?"

"No, of course not." Eve stopped at the water's edge and explained that fear was one thing that could cause a person to drown. "You know, Boogie, most people float naturally, whether they know it or not, so if you were accidentally thrown into the water, all you have to do is relax and let the water support you."

"Really?" He looked at her hopefully. "Don't go too far out."

Eve waded farther into the water. As she turned back to say something to Boogie, she noticed that Logan had arrived on the scene.

He glanced out at her and waved, said something to Lorna, and then ran into the water to catch up. "Going to swim the lake again?"

Boogie's eyes got really big. "No way, man."

Eve explained that Boogie had never learned to swim. Logan agreed to help her. Between the two of them, Boogie soon immersed his head in the water and came up grinning.

"Never thought I would do that willingly."

Before long, he was floating facedown. "Maybe if you get here early enough tomorrow, we can teach you to float on your back." Eve smiled at how quickly he'd caught on. She liked him a lot, much more than Phil, who seemed to want to antagonize everyone.

They joined the others on the beach. Lorna smiled approvingly at Boogie. "Looks like you're on your way."

"Looks that way," he answered with a glare for Phil.

They toweled off and went back to change clothes. Eve wondered if Phil was afraid to go back into the latrine, but said nothing. She couldn't wait to tell Logan about it later.

The rest of the afternoon they went from place to place, discussing the possibilities for camera shots. They wanted to shoot some stills, as well as a television commercial. Lorna listened and then mentioned the pros and cons of each location. She sat back and closed her eyes a minute.

Eve could see that the woman wasn't accustomed to so much physical activity. "Tired?" she asked quietly.

"Oh, yes. Wonderfully so."

"We're having fried chicken for supper. Interested?"

"Try and stop me." Lorna rose and wriggled her shoulders. "I'd swim the lake myself if I had to in order to eat in that great restaurant."

"Dining hall," Logan corrected with a grin. "I know exactly what you mean."

"Well, shall we go?" Lorna asked, smiling wearily at her crew. "This is a great place for the kids to go each summer, Eve," she said and put her arm around Eve's shoulders.

"You're right," Logan answered, looking down at Eve. "It is a great place."

Ten

The next few days were a buzz of activity for Eve. She worked long hours with the kids, giving tips to improve their painting skills, developing ways to increase their creativity.

One morning Eve tied blindfolds around all the kids' eyes and played classical music. While the music played, the students painted whatever came to mind. When the music was over, each child examined his canvas for interesting points. Then with a few strokes of additional paint, completed some portion of the painting.

Heather's work turned out to be a bowl of goldfish, while Tony's was a fireworks display. The enthusiasm the kids showed was contagious. Even Lorna and the film crew caught the fever. Dottie and Lorna begged for a repeat of the demonstration and took part themselves. All of this was taped for the television spots.

After lunch, Eve went with the crew to film the tennis portion of the commercial. As she watched the proceedings, Eve realized what a natural Logan was with kids. They clearly adored him.

"All right, gang," he said in his most commanding voice. "Now's your chance to get the coach. I serve, you volley."

He hit serve after serve past them, offering advice and encouraging words. Infrequently one of the kids would get his racquet on the ball, but none of them returned his serve. "Remember, your serve is the most important part of the game."

Logan continued to serve, each ball striking the court inside the lines by no more than an inch or two. Julie, the sixteen-year-old gossip columnist, whispered something to the kids around her.

When Logan realized they were plotting, he stopped and lectured them about paying attention. Each child smiled and apologized. With a somewhat smug look on his face, Logan continued to serve until all the kids dropped their racquets as one and leapt over the net to mob him. On his back on the court, Logan laughed and began to tickle whoever was closest, and the film rolled on.

When the hysterical tennis-neophytes calmed down, Logan started them in games against each other. He walked around, watching each child as he or she swung the racquet. Occasionally he would stop the action to correct some problem he saw in the backswing.

Eve watched as he prowled among his charges like a caged tiger, sleek and beautiful with a grace that belied his size. She could see that he practically itched to play, but he held back, still pointing out problems and helping them to improve their skills.

Hoping that the magic she saw transmitted itself to the film, she glanced at Lorna and Phil. Both of them were entranced. Boogie's face was buried in the camera as the film rolled, capturing each special moment. From what Eve could determine, the quality she noticed couldn't be rehearsed. She was witnessing an event that couldn't be repeated, no matter how hard they tried.

That night, Eve saw something else. Even Phil, the sarcastic director, began to feel the emotion the kids displayed at campfire. As the drama section presented yet another skit, Eve watched the expressions of their visitors. The skit was poignant and funny; the audience wept and then they laughed. And Boogie rolled film.

Eve and Logan watched the van disappear down the road back to the hotel where the crew was staying. For a long time, Eve couldn't speak. She was thrilled with the way the shooting had gone.

"Well, ma'am, what did you think of being a star?"

Studying his profile in the moonlight that filtered through the trees, Eve smiled. "I don't know about me being a star, but you certainly were."

"That was a dirty trick the kids played." Logan grimaced and slammed his fist into his hand. "Boy, will they pay tomorrow."

Eve turned and started to walk back toward her cabin, and Logan followed. "Yes, I can see that they're terrified of you. Where do you hide your bullwhip?"

"Spare the whip and spoil the brat, I always say." Logan chuckled and kicked at a stone. "They're okay, I suppose. Better than I thought they'd be."

"Right. Logan Mallory has a soft spot for kids. Who would have guessed?" Eve was teasing, but she caught the slight tensing of his jaw muscles as they walked into her office.

"A hazard of the job. Nothing more." Logan sat on the arm of the sofa and watched Eve for a moment. "Don't go giving me qualities that don't exist."

Eve studied him for a moment. She opened her little refrigerator and pulled out a bottle of champagne. When she handed him a stemmed plastic glass and filled it, she sighed. From all the things he'd said in the past, if she used his own words as accumulated evidence, she had to ask him a question. "Is there something you want to tell me about? Something about a relationship in the past with a child."

"No, Miss Inquisitive, there's nothing I want to tell you. Except that you're great on camera."

"And you're changing the subject." Eve started to sit on the sofa and then remembered her previous indiscretion. She walked to her desk and sat down, crosslegged on the corner. "You can talk to me, Logan. I don't kiss and tell."

Logan drained his champagne. "We've got a long summer ahead of us, Eve. I don't kiss and tell either."

With those words, Logan rose, kissed her forehead, put his glass down on the desk, and walked out. As he strode toward his cabin, he felt a moment of regret for not trusting her. Eve would understand his feelings about the kids.

She was right about one thing: Logan didn't want to get close to the kids, but he couldn't help himself. They were fun and bright and eager to learn. But the summer would end and he'd be gone, leaving nothing but memories for his scrapbook. Getting involved wasn't his style.

Long after Logan walked away, Eve stared at the door. She'd been so sure that he was ready to confide in her, but she'd been wrong. Maybe he never would. Maybe she was reading something into him that didn't exist, like he said, but she doubted it. There was a distance he tried to maintain between him and the kids, but today, it had been absent, and she was glad.

The picture the cameras caught was one of a loving arrangement: kids learning from someone they adored and that the feeling was mutual couldn't be disputed by anyone. Except Logan.

Before breakfast the next morning, Lorna came to Eve's office with a request. "Eve, what about letting the kids make a short film. It may work into nothing, but it could be an exciting event."

Eve considered the request. She sensed that there would be other uses for such a film and assented readily. "How long a film are we talking about?"

"Short. Probably fifteen to thirty minutes."

"Lorna, it sounds wonderful. How involved would the kids be in the project?"

"It can be their project entirely. We'll supply the expertise and the equipment. The kids can provide the creativity and everything else."

"I don't know what to say." Eve considered the multitude of possibilities. "Maybe we should announce it at breakfast." She rose and started toward Lorna, but stopped. "When would you want to do the actual filming?"

"Well, after this week we have a couple of commercials to do." Lorna removed her calendar from her purse and studied it for a moment. "How about in a couple of weeks?"

"Great. If we get the kids started now, developing the idea and that sort of thing, maybe we'd be ready in three weeks."

Lorna penciled in a few notes and nodded. "Deal."

Eve could hardly wait until all the kids and staff were gathered for breakfast. She stood on Julie's regular gossip table and made the announcement. The kids responded by jumping to their feet and shrieking with joy. "Now we've only got a couple of weeks to prepare, so be thinking about what you want. I'll try to arrange the schedule so that we have some time to work out an idea. The creative writing classes can work with the drama classes on production."

The kids tore out of the dining hall in a frenzy of conversation about what the film would be like, who would be in it, who would do the sets. Eve laughed as Logan helped her down from the perch where she'd delivered the good news.

"That sounds like a great idea, Eve." Logan hugged her briefly.

Eve could hardly catch her breath for a moment. "I can't take credit for it. Lorna came up with the idea last night and approached me about it this morning."

"Count me in. This could be a real breakthrough."

As Eve started to walk out of the dining hall, she noticed that Madora and Otis were involved in a very animated conversation. "I wonder what that's about?"

Logan glanced over his shoulder and shrugged. "How should I know? Maybe he doesn't like the way she makes biscuits."

Eve gave him a withering stare. "Did you eat her biscuits this morning?"

"Yes, I did. They were great."

"Then they must be talking about something else."

"You're right. They're talking about ways to stop the rain this afternoon."

Spinning to gaze at him, Eve felt her heart sink. "Rain? Do you think it's going to rain?"

Logan followed her out into the clearing that surrounded the dining hall. Overhead, clouds swirled in the wind that was rapidly picking up strength. "Maybe I was wrong."

"Wrong? It's clearly going to rain."

"Yeah, but I didn't think it would happen until this afternoon."

Eve considered the situation. "Okay, here's the plan. We'll get everyone back here to talk about the film. They can establish some committees and that sort of thing. Maybe by the time they get organized, the storm will have passed and we can get on with today's scheduled events." She looked up at the threatening sky. "The counselors should know to bring the campers here if it rains, but they're all new. Maybe—"

"I'll check on the kids from the tennis court and the soccer field. You go for the lake and the baseball diamond." Logan ruffled her hair as if she were a child and grinned. "I get to be lazy for a while."

"No, you don't. Run!"

Rain started to fall. Eve raced along the path to the baseball field and got everyone started back toward the dining hall. From there she ran through the woods to the lake. Nobody was in the water, thank goodness, for lightning started to crash and thunder shook the forest around her as she emerged onto the beach. "Back to the dining hall, everyone."

Logan gathered his crew and sent them back before heading for the soccer field. By the time he reached the field, he was drenched. "Dining hall," he shouted about the sound of the storm.

Kayla and Bert gathered the remainder of the campers and herded them into the dining hall. Eve spoke for a few minutes about the need to organize, since they had so little time. She set the creative writing class to work on a plot, while the drama department discussed open auditions, if necessary.

Lorna, Phil, and Dottie stood by as Boogie recorded the event on film. Eve stepped aside and let Kayla take over. The morning passed quickly, with shouts of ideas and suggestions for staging coming as fast as Julie could write.

Eve admired the way the kids approached the project. They were eager to do the film and wanted it to be perfect. Kayla asked if anyone had ever had any film experience. A couple of kids raised their hands. One had watched the filming of a movie, but the other had actually worked on a film.

Occasionally Lorna would offer a suggestion that would be met with a bevy of raised hands as kids took her idea and demonstrated their creativity. Eve realized that there were two processes in action here. The first was the development of a film. The second was a documentary of the first.

Lorna smiled at Eve and circled her finger and thumb in recognition of success. It was evident she liked the way the kids were working. Eve watched proudly as the campers displayed an amazing ability to adapt ideas and capture the spirit of the camp, which they'd decided was to be their story.

Eve leaned closer to Logan. "I need to call Tim. I want him to know what's going on here."

Logan nodded and they walked out of the dining hall. Standing under the porch roof for shelter, Logan looked down at her. "Are you sure you want to do this now?

Rain fell in sheets, but the thunder and lightning had lessened. Eve nodded. "Yes, I want to call him before it starts storming again."

Taking her hand, Logan ran across the compound with Eve until they reached her office. Once inside she threw him a towel and then took one for herself. "Wow, it's *really* raining out there."

"I'll say. I should have stayed in my room this morning."

"And miss all this fun?"

"You're right. There's nothing I like better than ruining a brand new pair of white shorts when the brand new red tennis shirt bleeds all over."

Eve glanced at her own shorts. The navy shirt she was wearing was bleeding, too. "Ugh! Well, what's done is done. We'll give them to the kids to tie-die or something."

"Yeah, picture me at Wimbledon in the finals wearing tie died tennis shorts." Logan sounded serious, but his grin was teasing. "Lucky for you these shorts came out of the supply shack."

"Well, mine didn't." Eve sat down on the towel and dialed the number for Tennis Pro.

"Eve? Is something wrong?" Tim asked before even saying hello.

"No, no, nothing's wrong." Eve briefly reassured him that everything was wonderful. "I have some news I thought you might be interested in."

"News? Like what?"

Eve explained about the commercial spot and the short film that was emerging as a result of Lorna's suggestion. She then mentioned that Lorna appeared to be making a documentary of the film process. "We're . . . I'm very excited about this. I thought you might want to know."

"I'm delighted to hear that everything is going so well."

"Tim, why don't you come down for a few days? I'd love to show you around." Eve hesitated a moment and then forged ahead. "I'm also interested in talking with you about the possibility of a scholarship of some sort."

"Scholarship?" Tim seemed to study the idea. "I like that. A scholarship to one of the campers, right?"

"Yes. I thought . . . Logan and I thought that you might want to consider running a public service spot about kids staying in school or something like that to coincide with the announcement of the scholarship."

"Eve, you're a genius. When are they filming this short movie?"

"In three weeks."

"You got a spare cabin?"

"I've always got a spare cabin for you, Tim. You just say the word."

"I'll be there on Sunday night before the filming starts."

Eve hung up the phone and stared at it for a long time. Everything seemed to simply fall into place. Nothing like this had ever happened in her life.

"Well?" Logan asked finally, when it appeared that she was not going to tell him what Tim said. "Are you catatonic?"

Looking up, Eve tried to smile, but tears were forming in her eyes. "Almost," she whispered.

"What gives? Is he coming?"

"Oh, yes. He'll be here on the Sunday before we start filming."

"Great!" Logan got up and began to pace. "Jer is already looking into the scholarship cost. He's checking with several art schools in the South. Or were you interested in other places, too?"

"No, the South has some fine art schools. Most of the colleges and universities have wonderful art programs. I know we'll find the right place."

"Who's going to choose the kid? I mean the recipient."

Eve stared at him for a few seconds. "I don't know. I hadn't thought that far in advance, but now I suppose I should. A panel would be best. A multidisciplinary panel."

The phone rang and Eve picked it up. "Hello?"

"Eve? This is Becky Gumm. Lynne wants to talk to you."

"Hi, Becky, put her on." Eve was surprised to hear Lynne's assistant. Eve hadn't talked to Becky or Lynne in a long time, almost a year.

After a few seconds, Lynne Pittard's voice came over the phone. "Eve, I just heard about your camp. I think it's great."

"Thanks, Lynne. We're having fun, learning a lot, and pushing your Basik White paint here."

"I appreciate that," Lynne said. "Say, you know I spend July and part of August in the mountains. Can I come over and do a workshop for your kids? I'll donate our time."

"Lynne, that's a wonderful suggestion. And very generous of you." Eve looked at Logan and smiled broadly. "You name the day."

When the date was set, Eve hung up the phone. "That was the most incredible thing. Lynne Pittard, are you familiar with her? She's an artist who has a television show."

Logan shook his head. "I don't exactly spend a lot of time watching art shows on television."

The phone rang again. Eve shrugged. "This phone hasn't rung the entire time I've had it, except for twice before today." She picked up the receiver. "Hello."

"Eve, this is Charlotte Adams."

"Hi, Charlotte, what's up in the big 'A' that I need to know about?"

"Nothing much. I'm calling about what's going on there."

"Did you talk to Lynne? She just called."

"Yes. I want to come up for a few days to help, too."

"Thanks, Charlotte. I really appreciate your offer. When can you come?"

"Anytime you need me."

Eve consulted her rapidly filling schedule book. "How about next week, say Wednesday?"

"I'll be there."

Eve put down the phone. "This is incredible. People from everywhere are offering to help. Somebody must be putting the word out about our camp."

"It's a good cause, Eve. No wonder people want to be a part of it."

Eve rose and walked to stare out at the rain. "I must say it's gratifying."

Logan watched her with a smile. She didn't know how magnetic a personality she had. "And it has a great deal to do with you."

"Me? What do you mean?" Eve spun to look at him. He was lounging on the sofa, relaxed and smiling.

"Well, damn it, Eve," he began, wondering how he'd gotten himself into this conversation. It had something to do with speaking without thinking again. "You're such a nice person that people just want to help."

"Oh, I don't think it's me at all. I'm sure they just want to be associated with such a worthwhile program." Eve turned back to the rain. "You know, these mountains are beautiful, even in the rain."

"I have to agree."

"There's a serenity here that pervades everything. And a creative energy that seems to flow out of the air and rocks and trees."

"Ah, Eve, you're beginning to wax poetic on me." Logan shifted slightly to a more comfortable position, which wasn't exactly easy in his tight, wet shorts. Watching her, he'd gotten aroused and he couldn't really understand why.

Eve wasn't really his type. She was the marrying kind, and he, of all people, wasn't. Maybe in the future, but not now. But she was so damned attractive, no more than attractive; she was beautiful.

She didn't seem to realize that her T-shirt was very revealing when wet, and he was glad she didn't. Eve was a lovely woman who clearly wasn't concerned with the artificial beauty so many women sought.

Her face, tanned with a kiss of sunlight, was devoid of makeup and as smooth as finest silk. Her hair was like a dark, fluffy cap barely touched with gray, crowning her with a radiance he would never have believed possible. Simply beautiful. Simple and honest and desirable. Her only concession to glamour was her fingernails, which were polished and neatly manicured, but instead of seeming at odds with the rest of her persona, they were an interesting quirk.

Rain pattered on the roof as Eve considered how fortunate she was to have such good friends. She was lucky to have Logan, too, though in the beginning, she'd been reluctant to accept him on her staff. Marveling at how kind fate had been to her and to her kids, she turned to Logan. "Thanks, Logan. You've been great. I don't know what I'd have done without you."

"You would have managed fine."

"Nonsense. You've given me a lot of good ideas, not to mention how well you're doing with the kids."

"Ah, well, the brats are okay."

"Why do you keep calling them brats?"

"All kids are brats until they get to be about thirty years old."

Eve laughed and recognized his nomenclature as another defensive mechanism. "Well, do you feel like braving the storm and running back across the compound to rejoin the brats as you call them?"

He raised up a little and peered out the window. "Not in this lifetime."

"What shall we do then?"

Logan watched Eve pace the floor. She obviously wanted to go back, but he knew she was as reluctant as he to go out into the torrential rain. He rose and walked to the window. Rain puddles he'd run through on the way over were now eligible to be called lakes or ponds. "I suggest that we sit down and relax while this storm passes."

"I suppose you're right. I could shuffle the schedule so that—"

"No, Eve," he interrupted and turned her around to face him. "You've worked too hard and without a break for weeks now. Why not just sit down and relax?"

Eve closed her eyes briefly. His hands still rested on her shoulders, comforting and warm against the cool, wet T-shirt.

When she looked up again, he was staring down at her, his eyes glinting in the firelight room. "I . . . I maybe we should—"

Logan fought with himself. He knew he should release her, back away, maybe even run to the dining hall and safety from his feelings, but he couldn't. Her eyes glinted of soft blue, fringed by dark lashes, and Logan couldn't even look away. His right hand slid up her shoulder and neck, coming to rest along her jaw and beneath her ear. Without stopping to consider the ramifications of his actions, Logan leaned down to kiss her.

When their lips met this time, Logan

moaned as he released the last of his barriers against Eve Travers. She smelled like soft flowers, gentle and enticing, and he wanted more from her than he'd ever anticipated. No matter what happened, he felt that he must trust his instincts, that he must allow her to become more than a friend. He deepened the kiss as her mouth opened to accept his probing tongue.

Logan rained kisses on her mouth, her cheeks, and her neck as he slid his hands down her back to pull her closer into his embrace. He wanted no distance between them, no clothing: nothing. Knowing that he couldn't take advantage of her, or of his own desire, Logan ended the kiss and backed away a little.

"Eve," he whispered, pulling her back into his arms. When he looked down at her again, he knew he needed to get away to sort out his feelings. "I'll be back."

With that, Logan strode past her and out the door. He ran across the compound, dodging the wide puddles when he could. Turning to take one last look at Eve, Logan twisted his ankle and fell headlong into a puddle. "Damn!"

Eve laughed. For some reason she felt free, maybe freer than she'd ever been in her life. She watched as Logan grinned rather abashedly and waved before continuing to his car. "Drive carefully," she called, but she wasn't sure he heard.

As Logan drove out of the parking lot, gravel flew up behind him and water splashed into the air. His clothes were drenched and he didn't care. All he knew was that he had to get away from Eve.

After a few minutes of waiting to see if he was coming back, Eve toweled her hair and then found her umbrella. There was no need to wait for Logan; whatever demons chased him had nearly caught him, she surmised, recalling the speed with which he'd left. He'd have to slay them alone, apparently.

Eve felt a great deal better as she walked around the puddles on her way back to the dining hall. The confrontation with Logan would have to take place later. She was suddenly very hungry, and Madora would be serving lunch soon. Happy sounds came from within, as if the kids were thoroughly enjoying whatever activity they were engaged in.

Hesitating a moment, Eve glanced back at the parking lot. Her feelings about Logan were mixed, were, in fact, a jumble of emotions battling inside, and she wasn't sure which was winning. But Eve knew that something had changed between her and Logan, some basic tenet that served to keep them apart had split asunder in the storm that brought such a fresh fragrance to the camp—and such a wonderful joy to her heart.

Eleven

"Women!" Logan skidded his car around a curve and decided he'd better slow down. Though the Jag hugged the road like a lover, the pavement was wet, and he didn't want to take unnecessary chances. "Oughta be kept barefoot and pregnant. That's what."

He slacked off on the accelerator. What was he thinking? That was the silliest thing he'd ever said, something a serious redneck might say. "Barefoot and pregnant?" Where had the thought originated?

Logan drove along more slowly now and reached a spot with a couple of picnic tables by the side of the road. He pulled onto the gravel parking lot, listening to the crunch of his tires as he skidded to a stop.

The radio was playing a love song, one with honeyed phrases declaring the undying love of one for the other. Logan reached out and snapped the radio off. He needed to think clearly.

He'd known Eve less than two months. Why did he feel this way when he was around her? In all his capering about with women when he was on the circuit, he'd never encountered a woman he simply couldn't be alone with in a room. Where was his composure? Where was his willpower? Where was his conscience?

Lightning flashed nearby, followed quickly by a resounding blast of thunder. Logan glanced out the window. The rain was driving down even harder than it had been when he and Eve had left the dining hall. The wind whipped the trees, tearing off leaves and small branches. For a while, it looked as if the storm would strengthen, but it gradually settled down into a comforting summer storm.

After watching the rain for a few minutes, he reclined the seat a little and lay back to think. Eve had bewitched him and he didn't know when or how it had occurred, but she'd managed.

What was different about her? he asked himself for the thousandth time.

* * *

Eve went through the line and got her food. As she gazed at the desserts, she simply couldn't make up her mind what she wanted. Nothing really appealed to her, even though there was peach cobbler—her favorite.

Outside, the wind howled and the rain beat against the side of the dining hall, but the building was sturdy and dry. The kids, at first concerned over the strength of the storm, had gradually gotten used to its blustering and had returned to their chatter. For Eve, it seemed to be fitting. With her emotions in such upheaval, the thunderstorm provided her with a new kind of energy to think about Logan. And that's all she'd done since he left.

This was the third time Logan had kissed her. But it was different. Before, the kisses had been spur of the moment, almost as if they'd just happened of their own accord. Eve knew that wasn't possible, that it was her imagination.

As she recalled the latest incident, as she termed it, she remembered those long agonizing moments when his lips hovered above hers. She'd been so sure she didn't want him to kiss her, but equally positive that she'd die if he didn't.

Her arms still tingled where he'd held her, almost as if the contact had singed her skin.

"Miss Travers?" Heather repeated, staring up at her and tugging on her shorts.

"What? Oh, Heather, am I holding you up?" Eve hardly glanced at the table of desserts as she finally decided on a small bowl of peach cobbler. "Sorry. Too many decisions, I suppose."

Heather stood silently, staring at the array of desserts for a second. "Did my mother call this morning?"

"No, darling, she didn't." Eve looked down at Heather's concerned face. Somehow she had to divert the child's attention. "But some other people did, and I'm thrilled about it. You will be, too, when you meet them."

Eve wasn't ready to tell anyone about the phone calls yet, but she couldn't help smiling. She considered the offers from Lynne and Charlotte to be a coup of sorts. They were both women who cared about the human condition, and their offers of help proved it. But Eve knew it went beyond simply caring: they both loved people.

"Is that what you were thinking about?"

"What? I don't understand what you mean?" Eve glanced back at Heather. Apparently she'd drifted off into her own world again and forgotten the girl.

"You were just standing there like you were daydreaming or something."

Eve quelled her embarrassment and smiled down at the young girl. "Daydreaming? Of course not. I was . . . thinking of a way to fit some guest instructors into our schedule."

"Oh."

As Eve walked to the table, Heather followed. Lorna soon arrived with her lunch and placed her tray on the table. "I must say that I'll miss this place when we're gone."

"I'm glad. I wanted it to be a happy place."

"It is. And the food is marvelous." Lorna sat down and took a bite of yeast roll, closing her eyes as if she relished the wonderful taste more than anything else. "I'll probably gain ten pounds this week."

"I doubt it," Eve said, noting the woman's slender figure. "Even if you do, you can use it. But I think you stay busy enough to burn the extra calories. At least you do while you're here. You're the busiest person I ever met."

"Where's Logan?" Lorna looked around the dining room and then stared at Eve with a questioning gaze. "I haven't seen him since the two of you left this morning."

"We had to speak with Tim Carlisle. After that, he left to run a few errands." Eve hoped she wasn't blushing. Could the woman see how uncomfortable Eve was with the topic of conversation? She hoped not. Until she could sort out her own feelings—and determine what Logan's were—she didn't want to talk with anyone about her relationship, or lack thereof, with him.

"I must say I'm amazed to see how well he fits in here." Lorna neatly ate a couple of rows of corn on the cob and then placed it back on her plate. "I mean, with all the stuff that's printed about him, I hardly pictured him with a bunch of kids piling on top of him on the tennis court. You know what I mean? He just seemed so . . . untouchable where kids were concerned."

"I must confess that I was surprised, too."

"He's lots of fun," Heather said and looked at Eve. "I think he likes you a lot."

"Heather!" Eve didn't know exactly how to handle the girl's candidness, but she didn't want the child saying anything to the other kids. It wouldn't do for rumors to get started and hit Logan in the face when he returned. He wouldn't like that at all. "Logan likes all of us."

Heather shook her head stubbornly. "Not like he likes you. He looks at you different."

"The girl's got a point, Eve," Lorna said with a canny smile. "I've noticed it, too."

"Both of you are imagining things."

"I'd think about it, if I were you." Lorna studied Eve for a few seconds and then smiled. "You know, Eve, he may really be changing."

"That may well be, but I doubt seriously if I have anything to do with it."

"You're wrong. The more I think about it, the more I realize that he likes you an awful lot. Maybe more than he knows." Lorna pushed away her plate and patted her flat stomach. "God, I'm stuffed. What's for dessert?"

"Lorna, that's preposterous. We . . . we

hardly know each other," Eve blustered, knowing how limp her argument sounded. Time wasn't really an element that determined how one person felt about another. She'd known for . . . how long? Several days? Several hours? Several minutes? that she liked Logan more than she was comfortable with. No matter what happened, he'd still drive out of her life when the kids left at the end of the season. She had to change the subject. "How'd the movie session go this morning?"

With a knowing grin, Lorna said, "Changing the subject, eh? Well, it went great. We've got a plot that seems to be viable. The kids are enthusiastic. And Boogie got some great footage."

"Fantastic. I talked to Tim and he's as eager as the kids are. He's coming down the week we do the actual filming." Eve was silent for a minute. "You know, Lorna, I have to thank you. This project may be the one that pulls this summer together for us."

"Now you're the one that's being preposterous," Lorna countered. "I came in here to a well-run, well-planned camp. The kids were happy, they're talented, they're bright. What more could you ask for?"

Eve glanced at Heather who was happily eating her second bowl of peach cobbler. "Oh, there are lots of things that I could ask for. But will I get them? Who knows?"

"Before I leave here, I'd like to have a nice long chat with you." Lorna rose and picked up her tray. "I like you, Eve Travers. Well, gotta run. Staff meeting with Phil, Boogie, and Dottie. The wicked never rest."

Watching her go, Eve leaned forward and rested her chin on her hands. How fortunate she was to have encountered such wonderful people along the way to the success of her dream. Maybe the old adage was right. What did it say? Something about, when the need arises. . . .

By the time of the evening campfire, Eve was beginning to get nervous. Logan hadn't returned, nor had he called. She'd expected him to be back by suppertime, for sure. He loved Madora's cooking too much to miss more than one meal unless he couldn't help it.

Eve considered calling Jerry to see if he'd heard from Logan, but decided to wait until later. After all, she had no chains on Logan. If he wanted to take off for the afternoon and evening, he had that right. Besides, she didn't want to worry Jerry unnecessarily.

This would be the first campfire Logan missed. She sat down on the plastic-covered log and searched the area for him. It wasn't the same without him. Though they didn't always sit together, she had but to glance around the circle and catch his eye. That was a comforting luxury, she decided, one that she missed more than she wanted to admit.

The fire wasn't very big because of the heavy downpour during the morning. The counselors had gotten firewood from deep in the stack, hoping to get the driest wood possible, but had met with little success. The damp firewood didn't burn nearly as well as dry logs. Eve made a mental note to cover some of the logs to prevent them from getting saturated every time it rained. The kids' spirits seemed to be down tonight, too, maybe an aftereffect of the morning's energy-sapping creative session or the daylong storms, but maybe it was because Logan wasn't there. Had he insinuated himself into their lives, too?

She made her way back to her cabin, walking out of her way to go past the parking lot. Logan's Jaguar wasn't there. Eve tried hard not to be disappointed, but she was. She went on to her room. At first she thought she'd stop downstairs in her office to work a while, but her heart wasn't in it.

Her heart wasn't in it. Why that expression? Why would that cliché be the one that came to mind? Was she getting more involved with Logan than she'd thought at first? Was Lorna right about his feelings?

Eve changed into a short gown and sat down to think. It had been ages since she'd stopped to consider her love life—or her lack of one. When had she lost interest? And why?

Devotion to one's job was certainly a commendable attitude, but Eve wasn't sure that was all that had kept her from falling in love. She'd been busy, of course, but it was something more. It was almost as if she'd been waiting for someone, that special someone who'd charge in and make her life complete. That thought astonished her. If that was the case, she'd never realized she was waiting.

Madly dashing about the school, involved in this activity and that, had given her purpose in life. Her schedule had been filled with school events that she adored sponsoring, but her own life had been sacrificed to permit that indulgence. She supposed that some people simply weren't equipped to handle both a career and a relationship. And she was one of them.

Then she heard the sound of a car on the gravel parking lot. Lights flashed through her windows, making interesting patterns on the wall as the car turned into a parking space and stopped. Was it Logan?

She fought the urge to run out and tell him all about her thoughts, about her confusion, but she knew he had enough to clutter his own mind without adding her problems. Or was that what had kept him away? She had no way of knowing. He may have left to get out of the claustrophobic isolation of her office. Or he may have remembered some errand. Or he may have simply wanted to get away from her.

Eve rose and peered out the window. It was Logan.

Dropping onto the sofa so he wouldn't see her, Eve felt like a child caught hiding beneath the Christmas tree, waiting for Santa Claus to appear. She ordered her pitter-pattering heart to be still. So he was back. Big deal, she told herself, but she was glad, maybe more than she should be.

The idea that she was making more of this than the situation warranted had crossed her mind several times. The isolation of the campsite, her starting over might have a great deal to do with her feelings about Logan. Or maybe she was simply infatuated, like a tennis groupie or teenager. God, but I wish I knew.

She rose and peeked out the window again, but he was nowhere to be seen. It was hard to contain her disappointment. Had she really expected him to come racing across the compound to her cabin?

Waiting for his light to come on, she wondered if he'd had any luck resolving the questions that plagued him. She certainly hadn't. In fact, she was no closer than she'd been when he left. There was one certainty, however: Eve was very fond of Logan. That was all she was willing to admit at this time, even to herself . . . especially to herself.

Something bounced off the screen. "Eve!" came a furtive whisper. "Open up."

Eve looked down. Logan was standing just below her window, tossing pebbles at the screen. "Just a minute."

She snatched her bathrobe from behind the bathroom door and hurried down the stairs, wishing she'd bought a longer robe for the summer. This one exposed nearly as much of her body as the short gown did. She flipped on the light switch and opened the door. "What is it? Is something wrong?"

"Wrong? Yes, there's something wrong." Logan stepped through the door and put his arms around her. He held her for a long moment, not knowing what to say to her. Hell, he'd been out for hours, driving and then parking in strange places, and he still hadn't figured out how he felt.

"What? What happened? Where did you go?" Eve bit her lip. She had no right to ask those questions, none at all. "I'm sorry. I don't mean to pry, but I was worried about you. Come in. I'll fix us some coffee."

Eve plugged in her coffee pot and turned to face him. His white shorts had been changed, so maybe he'd gone home. Tega Cay wasn't too far from King's Mountain for him to go to change clothes. "I see you changed clothes."

Logan looked down and then chuckled. "Yeah, well, I did stop at home and shower." He leaned closer, close enough to catch the clean scent of her perfume. "You know, those puddles out there really are dirty," he said innocently.

"Didn't your mother ever tell you not to walk in mud puddles?"

His expression changed immediately; it became hardened and inscrutable to her. What had she said that caught him off guard? Or had it made him angry? Could it possibly be the reference to his mother? "I'm sorry. Did I say something wrong?"

"Wrong? No, I guess not."

Eve knew she had. Whatever she'd said, he acted as if it had almost physically cut into him. It had to be the comment about his mother. Was there something wrong there? Was that why he was so reluctant to get close to the kids? It very well could be, but she sensed something else. Eve's intuition told her that he was a very complex man, a man with many more problems than the press had ever discovered or reported.

The silence was uncomfortable, but the coffeepot began to perk and soon the scent of fresh coffee filled the cabin. "It'll be ready soon," she said to break through the painful silence.

"Good. I need something warm."

"The rain cooled everything off, didn't it?"

"Sure did. It was a nice storm, though." Logan watched her pour the coffee. Her robe barely skimmed the tops of her thighs, and he was having a lot of trouble concentrating on his reason for coming there so late.

"Look, Eve," he began as he took the cup from her. Their fingers touched momentarily and he almost dropped the cup. "Sorry."

Eve poured her own coffee with shaking hands. She knew Logan wanted to talk to her as badly as she wanted to talk to him, but for now, neither of them really knew if they could trust the other. They were, she supposed, at that critical point in the beginning of the relationship when trust was still an unknown quantity.

"Logan, talk to me. I need to talk to you.
There are things that I feel . . . I mean,
that I think I feel . . ."

She couldn't say the words either. The
problem was that one of them would have
to take the chance and neither of them
was willing to take that step just yet, at
least she wasn't.

Logan put down his cup. He walked over
to Eve, took her cup out of her hands, and
pulled her close. "Eve, I spent the day . . .
well, what I mean to say is, I think that . . .
I never really felt . . . Oh, hell!"

Kissing her soundly, Logan then lifted
her into his arms and carried her up the
stairs. "You asked me earlier what was
wrong? I can't get you out of my mind.
That's what's wrong."

Eve glanced behind her. The bed was
a single bed and hardly big enough for
the two of them. *My God! I'm seriously
thinking of making love with Logan Mallory.*

"Damn but that's a little bed." Logan
laid her down and then settled beside her.
"I don't know if what I'm doing is right
or wrong or indifferent, but I have to do
it."

With that, Logan kissed her again. And again. And again.

All notion of resisting fled in the span of a breath, and Eve thereafter invited his kisses, returning them as passionately as they were given. Not a novice by any means, Eve recognized that there was a difference in this moment, a difference from any other intimacy she'd ever experienced.

Logan was amazed. He'd expected her to knee him in the groin and then whack him over the head with a hammer, but she was responding as if she desired him as much as he wanted her. He'd spent the better part of the day telling himself how much he *didn't* need to get involved with her, reminding himself of his New Year's resolutions. "Damn the New Year's resolutions!" he whispered.

Eve's eyes fluttered open in question, but they soon closed again. Logan's epithet didn't diminish her passion one whit. Before long, she was helping him undress, much to her own astonishment.

And then they were blessedly naked together, and Eve reveled in the touch of his hands on her skin. The music of the night creatures serenaded them as Eve and Logan explored each other's bodies for the first time. Her breath caught in her throat when his hand slid across her breast, cupping it momentarily and then moving ever so gently down her stomach.

Logan mentally cursed the darkness. He wanted to watch her face, gauge her reactions when they made love.

His body joined hers. Their union sent shivers down Logan's spine. Was it the waiting, the anticipation that made it all the sweeter?

Eve felt like a feather caught upon a wind drift. Higher and higher she floated on the music offered by the night creatures, now a chorus that sang in unison with her and Logan as they made love. Never had she experienced such a phenomenon. She sensed a change in their rhythm, a subtle prelude to the crescendo that would mark the end of a wonderful, incredible experience.

Logan waited until he knew that Eve was fulfilled, perceiving the pulsating of her body as she cradled him inside. A few seconds longer and his own gratification seized him with a powerful grasp that shook his entire being.

A soft aura of diffused light from the

outside lamp surrounded them on the tiny bed. That, along with Logan's fluttering kisses, brought Eve down slowly from the cloud where she'd found herself but moments before. Still shuddering from the profound experience, Eve opened her eyes slightly, reluctant to obliterate the security of their lovemaking and its aftermath.

Logan was staring down at her, unwilling to move lest he spoil the glory that shone in her face—and his as well. For a flitting second, he wondered why he'd taken so long to make the decision to do this. But, he realized, Eve had a voice in the process as well. Never again would making love be his judgment alone.

When he lay beside her at last, still smothering her with fervent kisses, she smiled. Never before had she known such fulfillment. She might never again, but she had these moments to treasure for a lifetime. Eve turned slightly in his arms, kissing him full on the lips and lingering there as long as he allowed her.

He rose and pulled on his clothes. "I don't want anyone to catch me leaving."

"I suppose that's best," she murmured sleepily.

"Well, Eve," he leaned down and whispered against her mouth, gently pulling at her lips. "This is certainly going to be the most interesting summer I've ever spent."

Twelve

Eve rolled over again and punched Logan's cold pillow. While he'd been there, it had been warm. It still smelled of his cologne.

She couldn't believe what Logan had said as he left. An interesting summer? Was that all making love to her meant? A fling?

How could she have ever thought that he might be interested in her? Didn't she know about his numerous affairs? Hadn't she read numerous articles that mentioned his flagrant dalliances with too many women to count?

Now her problem was how to act toward Logan. Should she pretend that their precious moments together meant nothing more to her than a casual fling? Until he made some declaration to the contrary, Eve would be forced to treat him as if nothing special had happened. She had no choice if she was going to protect her fragile ego.

It was nearly time for breakfast, and Eve was dressed—had been in fact since about five o'clock—but she couldn't make herself go out the door. Logan would be there, she was sure. He never missed Madora's biscuits.

Eve had contemplated skipping breakfast, but realized that she needed to be there for other reasons. Pacing back and forth, she wondered if she could sneak in at the last moment, see the staff and get them started—all without seeing Logan? How silly, she decided and, lifting her chin proudly, started toward her door.

The phone rang. Thankful for the momentary reprieve, Eve picked up the receiver and, to her relief, found that Sara Thomas was on the other end. "Gracious, I'm glad to hear from you. Heather's been very concerned."

"Sorry to take so long, but when you don't have an address on a person, they can sometimes be hard to track down."

"Did you find her?" Eve asked, crossing her fingers with hope.

"I've got a lead on Mrs. Barton. I found out that she's been showing up at one of the shelters to eat dinner some nights."

"That's wonderful." Eve closed her eyes and said a brief prayer of thanks. "So what's our next move?"

"I've asked the shelter manager to have her contact me as soon as possible." Sara sighed and continued, "But, Eve, these people are so damned independent. I just don't know when she'll call or come in."

"Do whatever you can. Heather is worried to death about her mom." Eve remembered all too well the tears glistening in the child's eyes. "I've promised to do something quickly."

"You mentioned having her come up there. What about the expenses?"

"Don't worry about them. I'll send you a check today. When you find her, put her on a bus and let me know when to pick her up." Eve took out her personal checkbook. She didn't know for sure whether they could raise the money or not, but this problem had to be solved and she was determined to do it.

Eve jotted down the address on an envelope and stuffed the check inside. She put it in the letter box outside her office. Sometime later in the day, Otis would take all the letters from the kids to their parents and whatever other mail was there to the post office in town.

She needed to see Otis right away about making a cottage ready for Mrs. Barton. Eve didn't know what the woman was trained to do, if anything, but she'd find a job for her at the camp and pay her a modest salary, which should help the Bartons get back on their feet. For two months, Gayle Barton would have an income and almost no expenses. That should give her a big boost toward independence.

Eve hurried over to the dining hall. Otis was sitting with Logan and Connie, lingering over coffee. Ordering herself to remain calm, Eve went through the kitchen line and got her breakfast before joining the group at Logan's table. The conversation was light and she listened for a few minutes while she ate.

She could hardly keep her eyes off Logan and he seemed to be watching her as well. To her dismay, nothing in his demeanor gave her a clue as to how he felt about their intimacy but, to be perfectly fair to him, she guarded against giving any clues, too.

After a few minutes, Madora came and

sat down by Otis. He grinned at her and handed her the cream. "I know what you want."

Madora smiled her sweetest smile. Eve couldn't believe it. For all the years they'd been friends, Eve never saw the usually pragmatic Madora flirt so openly with any man.

Eve realized that she'd been so preoccupied with the opening of the camp and getting everyone started off right, that she'd overlooked the relationship that was blossoming before her eyes. Now that she considered it, she could recall several times when they'd bristled at each other, as if each was measuring the other. They'd obviously gotten past that stage and had progressed to the sweet maturing of like into love.

When she turned to look at everyone else to see if they'd noticed, she caught Logan staring at her speculatively. She smiled and shrugged as if she was conveying an "I just didn't know about this" remark without speaking.

Logan watched Eve. He wondered why she acted so cool toward him. They'd spent most of the night together, involved in the most passionate moments of lovemaking, the most tender, the most . . . well, the most. Was she pretending that it hadn't happened? It seemed that way to him.

When he'd left her last night, she'd been a little distant, but he felt sure that was because she was falling asleep. Now, he didn't know. He was sure that she'd had experiences before and he was equally sure that nothing had been as mutually satisfying for either of them. So why the charade?

He decided to venture into conversation, to see if he could pick up some clues from her words. "You're running a little late this morning. Rough night?"

Eve nearly swallowed her tongue. "Rough night? Not really. It began well, but deteriorated somewhat as the evening progressed."

What could she possibly mean? Logan was definitely confused now. He was almost afraid to ask her questions, for fear she might reveal something he didn't want to hear. But he was sure she'd enjoyed their lovemaking. What could have happened to change her feelings? "Something you want to discuss?"

"Not right now." Eve sipped her coffee,

demanding that her fingers not shake. She couldn't afford to give away her insecurity in front of all these people. "Oh, you mentioned that I was late. I had a good reason."

Logan grinned. Now she sounded more like herself, more assured and confident. "What good reason?"

"I talked to Sara Thomas, the social worker who's helping me to find Gayle Barton, Heather's mother."

"Oh, I see." Logan didn't see. She was purposely changing the subject. Of course, she might not want to talk about their evening together in front of all the other people, but they were involved in their own conversations. "So what's the scoop?"

"I'm putting a check in the mail this morning to pay for Gayle's bus fare." Eve smiled with confidence. Everything seemed to be moving in the right direction, everything that is, except for her personal life, which had taken a very wrong turn last night. "Sara's found the shelter where Gayle eats her dinner. We should hear from her soon."

"Sounds great," Logan said without much conviction in his voice. He wanted to talk about last night, make plans for tonight, but she obviously had other ideas. Maybe she needed a little time to think about it.

Logan watched her a moment. He hadn't used a condom. In recent years, he'd done so out of protection. AIDS was too big a threat to fool around with. But he didn't even have one now. Eve wasn't a woman who made love promiscuously, so he felt he didn't have to worry there.

Was Eve protected? How old did a woman have to be to stop having children? He studied her, catching her bright smile and then responding as if nothing other than breakfast was on his mind. Eve was an intelligent woman. If she wasn't protected she'd have told him, wouldn't she? Sure she would.

Eve turned to Otis. She waited until there was a lull in his conversation with Madora. "Otis, I need you to do something for me and it should be done fairly quickly."

"What's that, Eve?" he asked, seemingly reluctant to take his attention away from Madora.

"I need cabin fifteen fixed up. I know it's going to be a chore, but it can't be helped."

"You got more kids coming in?"

"No. Heather Barton's mother is coming soon from Atlanta and I want to give her a place to live." Eve glanced at the expectant faces around the table. "We'll have to find something for her to do, something productive. I want to give her a small salary, so she'll feel like she's a part of our team. Any suggestions?"

"What's she trained to do?" Connie asked, tenting her fingers in front of her.

"That's the problem. I won't really know until she arrives and I have a chance to talk with her." Eve glanced at her staff, her friends. "Another thing. I don't want to tell Heather until Gayle arrives. Something could happen at the last minute and I don't want to get her hopes up for nothing. Agreed?"

Everyone murmured their assent and Eve turned to Connie. "I doubt seriously if she's got any nursing skills. If she did, I'm sure she'd have a job in Atlanta. They're practically begging for nurses there."

Logan shrugged. "Well, I guess I'm out of the loop on this one, too. I wouldn't expect her to be a tennis player either."

"You're right, I'm sure," Eve replied,

trying very hard not to notice the new definition in his muscles. In the few weeks he'd been at the campsite, he'd been working out, running, lifting weights, swimming, and it appeared to be paying off. It would be interesting to know why he'd let himself get so out of shape. "The only real choices that are left are kitchen help and housekeeping. I can't imagine that she'd have any art skills that we could use, though Heather is certainly talented."

"She's always got a place with me," Madora volunteered.

"Thanks, Madora. I appreciate that. We may work some sort of split schedule for her. Maybe she can help Sharleen with the housekeeping in the mornings and you in the afternoons."

"Whatever you think best." Madora rose and winked at Otis.

"Well, I've got things in the kitchen that need my attention."

Eve could hardly believe she actually saw that. She couldn't wait to get Madora alone to ask about her relationship with the handyman. Apparently Connie had given way to the two lovers because she smiled approvingly as Madora walked away.

Class time passed slowly that morning for Eve. She wanted an opportunity to talk to Logan alone before classes, but the chance never came to pass. She had to be content to wait until they had a break at the same time.

Heather gazed at Eve with a question in her bright blue eyes. As she studied Heather's painting, Eve noticed a trend of soft subtleties in color. The girl had a gentle touch, one that spoke of wistfulness or dreams or tenderness. While she was there, she hugged the child. "I talked to Mrs. Thomas this morning. She tells me they found a place where your mother is eating dinner nearly every night. We should hear something soon."

Even though she had decreed that nobody should tell Heather of the new information about her mother, Eve couldn't withhold anything that would bring a smile to the child's face. Though she didn't repeat her vow to Heather that the chances were good that her mother would arrive this week, she did try to reassure the girl. When Heather left the classroom, her spirits were visibly improved.

Eve ate lunch with some of her students. Across the room, Logan ate with his. On several occasions, she caught his eye and he smiled at her. She couldn't seem to help herself. Her gaze was drawn there, across that cheerful group of chattering kids, to Logan's face. She memorized every line, every plane, every nuance of expression before she finally forced herself to concentrate on her lunch.

Eve realized that their worlds were too far apart to ever come this close again. For this summer, for the sake of about one hundred children, Eve Travers and Logan Mallory had come together to make magic. For an evening, that magic had extended into her cabin, into her narrow bed.

Should she allow that to happen again? And, if she did, at what cost to her?

Lorna stopped by to show Eve some of the footage the crew had captured for the commercial. The only place that could be made dark enough to view the film was the dining hall. Eve walked across the yard with Lorna into the hall.

After telling Madora what was going on, Eve and Lorna sat down to look at the footage. Eve was entranced. Lorna, her editors, Phil, Boogie, everyone had done a splendid job of capturing the spirit of the camp. A pastiche of images flashed across the small screen, colorful and stylistic. It was a collage of events that began with sunrise and ended with an evening campfire: all in one minute.

To Eve's surprise, there were several such clips. "How did you do this in so short a period of time?"

"Tim's in a hurry, but we did it." Lorna grinned and sat down. "Eve, we're all infected. We all want to be a part of the success of this camp."

"You don't know how delighted I am to hear that."

"It's wonderful. We've gotten to know some of the kids and they're incredibly creative. What a wealth of talent lies in those hands and brains!" Lorna shook her head slightly. "I have to confess that this wasn't a plum of an assignment as far as I was concerned, but my opinion has changed one hundred percent."

"That's good to know." Eve patted Lorna's hand. "I don't think you realize what this has done for the kids. They're working away on their plans for the short film. By the time you come back to tape it, they'll be ready."

"I want to ask a favor." Lorna shifted in her chair slightly and leaned forward to prop her elbows on the table.

"Ask away. How can I refuse?"

"Easily enough, I'm afraid."

"Ask anyway."

"Here goes." Lorna breathed deeply for a moment and then closed her eyes briefly. "I want to be a bigger part of this program next summer."

"You mean . . . like teaching a class in film?" Eve slid forward on her chair, feeling the excitement rise in her like a thousand butterflies taking flight at once.

"Yes. I think I can get funding for some equipment, maybe a sponsor who'd donate enough money to pay a crew to help the kids."

"Lorna, that sounds wonderful. I'm deeply moved by your offer."

"I'll donate my time if you'll give me a cabin and meals."

Eve laughed and hugged her new friend. "Say, is this just a way to assure that you get to eat Madora's cooking for the whole summer?"

"I confess. I've been found out." Lorna

laughed, her voice a sweet girlish trilling. "That's what I consider the icing on the cake. I'm crazy about the idea of this camp, about your philosophy. And, I do like the kids, too."

"In that case, I accept." Once again, Eve knew that fate had dealt her a winning hand when Lorna had first stepped onto the premises. "We'll be delighted to have you aboard."

"I've got to head back to Charlotte." Lorna rose and began to pick up the materials she'd brought in. "We're going to duplicate these tapes and then dub in sound and graphics. After all, Tim isn't paying for a commercial that doesn't have one word about Tennis Pro."

"I saw it written on the T-shirts and tennis shoes the kids were wearing," Eve protested good-naturedly.

"Actually, Eve, you've probably got a point. I think he really wants to showcase the camp, so there will be a minimum of voice-overs."

Eve got up and followed Lorna out to the van. "I can't thank you enough. I believe that your work will be more beneficial to us than just about anything I could have done."

"I'll get you some footage to use in your grant applications and funding requests. Something really neat and flashy, so that the stodgy folks who make those decisions will see what a worthwhile and necessary project this is."

"We appreciate anything you can do."

When Eve returned to her office, she was humming a jaunty tune. Connie hurried past without speaking and Eve called to her. "Say, what's the hurry?"

"Got a patient."

"Serious?"

"Bee sting. Not bad." Connie grinned and raised her eyebrows. "Unless you're the one who got stung and you're a kid."

"Go to work then. You've had it too easy this summer." Eve couldn't sit behind her desk any longer. She had to move about.

Without paying much attention to where she was going, she walked down to the lake and watched the kids splash and play for a few minutes. The counselors were teaching some of the kids to swim, while others were diving and swimming on their own. Eve noted that the lifeguard sat vigilant at his post, and for that she was grateful.

After a few minutes, she walked up the

hill and stood outside the sculpture class. Bert was working with the kids to make busts of someone they admired. She smiled at some of the likenesses of Logan, one of Madora. One of them might be of Eve herself.

Without disturbing the class, she continued to the athletic fields. The softball game was well underway. She stayed a few minutes to cheer both sides before going over to the tennis courts. As she approached, she could hear Logan talking to the kids.

"You've got to practice if you're going to be any good." He looked at the kids in the semicircle in front of him. "How many of you picked up a paintbrush and were . . . Picasso on the first day?"

Laughter erupted from the kids. Logan held up his hands as if to fend off their verbal attack. "All right, all right. Maybe . . . Chagall."

Heather tugged on Logan's shirt. "Logan, Chagall paints weird things. I mean, he has people floating in the air and stuff like that. He had an uncle that he loved who played the fiddle. He painted 'Old Uncle' as he called him in several paintings. Sometimes up in the corner or just anyplace he could tuck him in."

Logan gazed at Heather very seriously. "You've got a good point, Heather. Marc Chagall painted weird things. Isn't that what creativity is all about?"

"Yes, I guess so."

"Right. Do you think the first time Chagall, or any of the painters we study today, was born knowing how to paint masterpieces? Or were great writers born knowing how to write the wonderful books we love so much?"

The kids looked at one another. Eve surmised that they were a little surprised that their tennis coach had taken such a philosophical bent to his instruction. They hadn't seen her yet, so she continued to listen.

"No, they have to learn."

"That's partly true. Whether you're born with it or whether you learn it, you've got to practice. Without practice, nothing is worth the effort."

"How did you get so good at tennis, Logan?" Rick Carter, a lanky boy of about seventeen, asked.

"I practiced. My mother saw that I had some talent for hitting the ball, so she signed me up for a private coach near where we lived. I had to practice hard every day." Logan stood up and began to juggle three tennis balls. "The more you practice a sport or art, the better you get."

"How much did you practice, Logan?" another child asked.

"I started out practicing fifteen hours a week when I was six. That was in addition to school and homework and everything else."

Eve could see that the little group huddled around Logan were calculating the time. Heather frowned and gazed at him with her mouth open for a minute. "When did you play?"

"I didn't. The older I got, the more I practiced. By the time I was fifteen years old, I was on the court about thirty to thirty-five hours a week."

Eve gasped and everyone turned to look at her. Thinking as quickly as she could, she reached down and swatted her thigh. "Ugh! Mosquitoes."

Trying hard to appear as if she'd walked up the path at that very moment, she strode to the fence behind Logan. "What are you **guys talking** about?"

Heather smiled. "We were talking about how Marc Chagall had to practice his tennis thirty hours a week so he could paint his 'Old Uncle' well."

Everybody laughed, even Heather, who'd apparently been poking fun at all the serious talk. She continued, "So, I figure when I can paint and shade that ball well enough for it to look like a round ball instead of a flat surface, I'll be able to play professional tennis."

"That makes a certain amount of sense to me, Heather," Logan said and reached down to tousle her hair. "Okay, gang, get to it. You'll never improve your serve by sitting on the asphalt."

Leaning back against the chain-link fence, Logan watched the kids for a few minutes, but he was very aware of Eve's presence. Finally, he turned slightly so he could see her. "You know, that's a bright kid."

"Heather?" Eve watched the child serve. Though she wasn't the best on the court, she was as good as most and better than some—and she was the youngest. "I've noticed. She's . . . she seems old for her age, like she never had a childhood."

"I suppose that living on the streets

does a lot to help you grow up. How long has she been homeless?"

"I don't know, but from the way she talks, she and her mother have been on the streets for a while." Eve watched the kids serve to one another. Even she could see that they were improving. "I think you're doing a splendid job."

"Thanks."

"What was all that jabber about Marc Chagall and painting tennis balls?" Eve really wanted to ask other, more personal questions, but realized they'd have to come later when she and Logan could be alone. She wasn't sure she could ask the questions that were in her heart even then.

"I was talking to them about practice. We got off on the arts. You know, if you want to be an artist, you practice making noses or trees. If you want to be a musician, you play scales, arpeggios, and practice fingering." Logan turned to face her through the fence. "If you want to be good at other things, you practice those things, too."

Eve met his gaze and her smile faltered. She knew what he meant. His suggestive remark directly addressed the question that had dogged her all day: should she or should she not make love with him again? "Well, maybe if you have some spare time, I'll meet you on the court and you can give me a few pointers."

"We'll talk about it later." Logan grinned at her, raising his eyebrows as if to tease her. "Later."

Eve lingered long enough to make sure the kids knew she was interested in their progress, but the entire time she was standing there, she felt Logan's gaze on her as if he were gauging her response to his remarks. With a smile and a wave, she strolled away as if she hadn't a worry in the world.

Several days passed. Eve's routine was firmly established now. She rose, showered and dressed, ate breakfast, and then taught her class. After lunch, she tried to look in on all the classes or athletic activities. Sometimes she had shopping to do or errands to run.

The hours had run to days and she hadn't had a chance to talk seriously with Logan. Every time they had a moment, someone would interrupt with a problem.

She decided that fate had decreed that she and Logan would have no private time together at all. For the moment, that was all right with Eve. She still had a great deal of soul-searching to do.

There was still no word from Sara Thomas about Heather's mother. Then the call came.

"I've found her, Eve," Sara said, a proud note in her voice. "She's here right now. I'll let you tell her what you have in mind."

"Hello?"

"Mrs. Barton? This is Eve Travers from Reach for the Stars Creative Camp."

"Heather's all right isn't she? I mean, she hasn't been hurt or anything?"

"No, she's fine. But actually she's the reason I asked Sara to track you down." Eve didn't think Gayle Barton would accept charity, so she wanted to broach the subject carefully. Actually, Eve was glad that Sara hadn't said anything. That made it easier for Eve.

"If she's fine, then why did you need to talk to me?"

"Heather came to me the other night and was a little upset."

"Upset? Did someone do something to her? She's very sensitive about—"

"No, she was worried about you."

"Me? Why was she worried about me?"

Eve hesitated. How much could she say without getting Heather in trouble? "I think that she was concerned because you weren't going to be staying at the sh . . . place you'd been staying. I told her I would see if I could . . ." Eve paused, trying to find the best way to phrase what she had to say. "Well, we need some help here and I asked Heather if she thought you'd like to come for the summer and give us a hand? We'll pay your traveling expenses, of course, and a salary when you go to work."

"A handout?"

"No, Gayle, not a handout. A hand up." Eve kept her voice calm and tried to sound convincing. "That's what we're giving all these kids. A hand up. And I'm extending that hand to you. You'll have your own cabin, meals, and a salary." She waited a moment for that to sink in and counted to five. "Will you come to King's Mountain?"

"What about at the end of the summer?"

"You're free to do whatever you choose. If you want to return to Atlanta, I'll pay your expenses." Eve's mind was racing. "If you'd like to stay in this area, I'll make sure you get situated and have a fresh start."

"Thank you for the offer, Mrs. Travers."

"Eve," she said, her heart spinning like a ferris wheel. The woman actually sounded like she was going to turn Eve down. "Please come, Gayle."

"All right, Eve. I'll come. But if it doesn't work out, you've got to send me back to Atlanta immediately."

"Gayle, you've got a deal. When can you be here?"

"I'll leave on the next bus."

Eve could have done cartwheels around her office, out the door, and all the way down to the lake. She felt as if a weight had been lifted off her whole body. She arranged to pick Gayle up at the bus station in Spartanburg and hung up the phone.

She searched the compound for Sharleen and finally found her in the washroom. "Hi, Sharleen, how's it going."

"I never saw such a bunch of messy kids

in my life. I found a chocolate bar stuck to a pillow this morning, a frog squashed between a sheet and a mattress, and three jars of dead lightning bugs." Sharleen transferred the last of the clothes from the washer to the dryer. "And I love every last one of those rotten little scoundrels that cause me to have to work so hard."

Eve smiled appreciatively. "I know what you mean. I caught one of the kids with a garter snake in his pocket during art class."

They talked about the kids for a few minutes and then Eve got to the point. "Gayle Barton is arriving tonight. I'd like to have some sheets for her bed. Oh, and some towels, too. Whatever you think she'll need."

"I'll take care of it." Sharleen turned to Eve and studied her a moment. "You're doing a good thing, Eve. That child is worried to death about her mother."

"Please don't tell her. Something could still go wrong."

"I won't speak a word. When's she getting here?"

"About midnight."

Eve wasn't fit for anything the rest of the day. She flitted from place to place as if she didn't know what she was supposed to do.

Logan had been searching for Eve all afternoon. He finally tracked her down in her office, though he'd been there three times already.

"Can I see you a minute, Boss?"

"Boss? Where did that come from? You know that's not true and if you—"

Logan chuckled, interrupting her flow of words. "Whoa, woman, don't get so riled up. I was joking."

"Oh, I see." Eve felt a little foolish. She was on edge, probably because she didn't know whether Gayle would want to stay once she saw the small cabin that was to be her home for the rest of the summer. Nor did she know how Heather would react to having her mother so close by. "Sorry, I'm on edge, I guess."

"What's the problem?" Logan lounged across the arm of the sofa like he always did. "Maybe I can help."

"I don't know." She gazed at him for a few seconds. Why did he have to look damnably handsome? Deeply tanned, lean and muscular, he could easily steal a girl's heart. "I guess I'm upset because I'm go-

ing to pick up Heather's mother this evening."

"So? What's the big deal?"

"The big deal is, I don't know how
she'll like her cabin. don't know if she
wants to be around this sort of camp,
with all the kids and the arts and . . . I
suppose I'm nervous for Heather's sake."

"I see. Well, I can't do much to help
with your nerves, except maybe go and
pick her up for you."

"That's a nice offer, but I wanted to
spend some time talking to her on the
way back. You know, sort of get a sense
of what she can do. That kind of thing."
Eve leaned back in her chair and stared
ahead at nothing. Her thoughts were too
scattered for her to think sensibly.

"Okay, so I'll drive, you talk."

"You don't have to bother. I'm going
to Spartanburg to pick her up and her
bus doesn't arrive until midnight."

"That settles it. Unless you really don't
want me to go, I'm going. We can go in
your Bronco, since the Jag's a little small
for the three of us."

"Thanks, Logan." Eve studied him a
moment and smiled broadly. "You're a

nice guy in spite of what the press says about you."

"How right you are, woman. And I'm working on the press. You just wait, the bad boy of tennis will soon be . . . guess what?"

"What?" Eve couldn't help laughing at his antics.

"A little drum roll, please." He patted his hands on the sofa as if it were a drum. "The bad boy of tennis is about to change into the bad boy of seniors tennis."

"No change from the bad boy, eh? Just the age group."

"Well, actually, the bad boy is changing, too. I just like the idea of being called a bad boy."

"You know, I don't think you're a bad boy. I think the press just labeled you that way." Eve rose and went to sit on the edge of her desk, right in front of him.

"Hey, you're right. I never threw a racquet at a judge. I never cursed a spectator for throwing a cup of ice on the court. I never—"

"Hold on," she said, interrupting the regurgitation of his more infamous exploits as a tennis player. "I believe you."

"It's a good thing, too. I was running

out of bad stuff to say about myself." Logan stood up and placed his arms around her. It felt good to have her in his arms again. "I've missed you the past few days, Eve."

"I haven't been anywhere but around here." Eve could hardly catch her breath. The scent of spices filled the air around him. The touch of his embrace sent shivers skittering down her spine like baby squirrels after a pecan.

"True, but you haven't been here, either," he said quietly, wondering how she'd take his gentle chiding.

"That doesn't make much sense." Eve knew very well what he was talking about. They hadn't been alone in several days, not for any length of time.

He leaned down, lifted her chin with his fingertips, and kissed her. "Now, that makes sense."

Thirteen

Eve held her breath. Logan's kiss melted her resolve to avoid being alone with him. But in this she really didn't have much of a choice. She didn't want to go alone, and he was the logical person to make the trip with her since he didn't have any responsibilities in the evening.

Eve considered a timetable. The trip to Spartanburg would take about forty-five minutes, so they needed to leave about eleven o'clock.

"Let's leave earlier. We'll have dinner at a restaurant I like." Logan liked the idea of being alone with her for several hours.

"You'd actually miss Madora's cooking to eat in a restaurant?" Eve wasn't sure she believed him. He'd made a point of being in the dining hall for nearly all his meals. "I understand she's having coconut cream pie tonight."

"She'll save a piece for me." Logan leaned down and rested his cheek against her hair. She smelled so clean and incredibly sexy. "Indulge me on this. You won't regret it."

"All right. We'll go early." Eve tilted her head to one side and looked up at him. "Did you have something in mind in the meantime?"

"Boy, do I?" Logan grinned devilishly. "Well, I guess not that. Sure as I throw you over my shoulder, some urchin will come wandering in and ask a silly question."

"In that case, let's leave a little earlier." Eve reached back and snatched her purse. "I need to do some shopping."

"Me, too."

Eve arranged for Connie to be in charge. Kayla and Bert were competent and usually needed no special direction, but Eve didn't want to leave without designating someone who had the final say in case of emergency. Connie was the best candidate for the job. She'd worked in camps for years and, of course, was a registered nurse.

When Eve met Logan at the Bronco, he had a big smile on his face. "What's so amusing?" Eve asked as she turned on the ignition.

"Nothing really. That Madora is a real card, you know that?"

"What does that mean?" Eve backed out of her parking space and shifted the vehicle into drive.

"She said she'd save us a piece of pie for a price."

Eve glanced at Logan briefly. "Did she name the price?"

"Nope."

"You didn't agree, did you?"

"Sure I did. You don't think I'm going to miss a piece of her coconut pie, do you?" Logan reclined slightly in the seat and propped his knees against the dashboard.

"That woman's crafty. You can't give her free rein on anything."

"What do you mean?"

"I mean, she'll devise something awful for us to do."

"Like what?"

"Oh, I don't know. But it'll be awful." Eve thought back to her childhood fondly. "Once she made me clean all the garbage cans."

"Yuck! That sounds awful for a kid."

Logan remembered the mess in his refrigerator and wondered if Eve had been as creative at finding a solution to her problem as he had been at solving his.

"It was at first. The smell was horrible." Eve chuckled. "But I ended up having a ball."

"Now, this story I have to hear."

"She'd given me a rag and a bucket of soapy water. I just couldn't put my hands in those trash cans, even with gloves."

"So, what did you do?"

Eve drove past the entrance to the King's Mountain National Park. "We need to bring the kids down here one day. We'll get Madora to pack a picnic for them."

"Great, so what's the story on the trash cans?"

With a wide smile, Eve continued, "So I put my devious little brain to work. I sneaked into the kitchen and took the broom and a bottle of dishwashing soap. I dragged the hose around to the back of the dining hall and scrubbed those cans out with the broom."

Logan laughed. He hadn't thought of using the broom when he'd recently faced a similar problem. "I admire your creativity. So you've known Madora a long time then."

"Yes, she came here just before my father closed the camp. When we left, she became our houseckeeper and cook." Eve's mind flooded with a hundred memories of Madora all at once. "She's been my best friend for more years than I can remember."

"I thought I'd stop at a toy store on the way. When the kids don't have anything to do, maybe they'd like to play games or work puzzles. We can set up a puzzle table and a game table in the dining room. Anybody who has some spare time can come in and have fun."

"That's a great idea." Logan had his own agenda this night. He'd bribed Madora into telling him when Eve's birthday was and he planned to make good use of that information.

When they had arrived at the toy store at Westgate Mall, Eve was surprised that Logan took off on his own, but didn't question him.

Eve stopped at the puzzles. There were thousands of them. She selected several and put them in her shopping cart. Some were photographs of landscapes, buildings, flowers. Others were the more difficult puzzles like baskets of cherries or were double-sided or were so nearly the same colors and patterns that it would take the kids a long time to work them. Some of them could be instructional, she decided, looking at the balance and composition in the landscapes and postcard pictures of cities.

She realized she needed to stop at a bookstore as well. When she reached the checkout counter, Logan was waiting. "I want to get some art books."

"How about a couple on tennis techniques." Logan watched her as she tried to unload the cart from behind. He placed his package on the counter and took over. "It's easier from this side of the cart."

Eve drove to the bookstore and they found several books in each category. "These are expensive, but I think it will be worth it. Maybe we can let the kids check them out."

"Why don't you start a library? I mean, just for the kids. I guess you couldn't really buy a lot of books at first, but maybe you can add to the collection each year." Logan placed their purchases behind his seat and got in. "Where to now? I think we've got about two hours before we have to pick up Mrs. Barton."

"I really need to step into Belk's. There are a few things I'm running out of." Eve studied Logan. He didn't appear to be upset at the idea of going into a department store.

"Great. I'll tag along."

Eve meandered through the clothing department. She found several dresses she'd love to have, but her budget crunch prevented her from buying them. There was one silk dress, a deep berry color, and she had a hard time passing it by. She went back to it several times, but knew that the price was too high. Besides, where would she wear such a dress? To campfire one night?

Logan saw Eve's eyes when she spotted that purple-looking dress. It was pretty, he had to admit, and he thought it would look great on her. Maybe that was the answer to his question about what to get for her birthday. But what size? Eve herself had stated that she had to try something on before she could buy it. That, too, was a dead end.

From there they went to the jewelry

counter. Logan noticed the items she seemed to linger over. She spotted a gold charm that she wanted. It was an artist's palette. She looked at it longingly, but moved on to the perfume counter. Telling Eve that he was going to the men's department, he waited until she was out of sight and bought the charm and a bracelet on which to hang it.

He took the small box to gift wrap. By the time he got to the men's department, he knew Eve would be looking for him. He quickly picked out a few pairs of shorts and swim trunks that were on sale, a jogging suit, and some shirts to match the shorts.

Thank God Jerry came through with some cash, he thought as he returned to the cosmetics counter where Eve was making a purchase. Logan spotted his favorite cologne and bought a bottle while he waited for her.

"Ready?" she asked as she walked over to him. She'd had to pick up a bottle of her favorite perfume. She wanted to smell nice for Logan.

Logan took his change and turned to Eve. "Ready and willing."

He took her arm and they walked out

of the store. Glancing down at her, he saw that she had several bags and selfishly hoped that she'd bought some of the wonderful perfume she'd been wearing ever since he met her. The scent never failed to entice him.

"Looks like you found something you needed." Eve pointed to his bags.

"Yeah, well, they had swimsuits and shorts on sale. I guess they're getting ready to put out winter stuff." Logan held her packages while she opened the car door. "We're off to the Beacon, I guess."

"What's that?" Eve asked, pulling on her seat belt. She started the engine and then hesitated. "Which way do we go?"

"It's a great restaurant. Go out of the shopping center at the light. I'll point the way."

Eve did as he directed and they were finally driving down a divided highway toward the city of Spartanburg. Noting that they were on Highway 29, which turned into West Main Street, Eve spotted several businesses that she'd like to visit on her next trip. At Reidville Road, Logan told her to turn right. Within a couple of blocks, Eve saw a sign like a lighthouse: the Beacon Drive-In.

"Park on the upper side of the lot," Logan told her. He waited for her to pull into a parking space and then said, "I need to warn you about this place."

"Warn me? Isn't the food good?"

"It's the greatest, but this is a different sort of place." Logan got out of the Bronco and walked to her side to let her out. "You give your order at one end of the line, pick it up in the middle, and pay for it at the end."

"I see." Eve didn't, but she thought she could muddle through.

Once inside she could see that the place was filled with frantic activity. Over the hum of the crowd, she could hear a loud voice, in a singsong sort of litany. "Talk to me. Talk to me." The voice came from a black man who was taking orders.

Logan handed her a menu. "That's J.C. He's legally blind, and he's been here for longer than I can remember."

"How long is that?"

"More than twenty years."

Eve was fascinated. The man seemed to have no disability at all. He took orders, rushed back and forth between work stations, and then was back for more orders. "What do you recommend?"

"I always get a hash-aplenty, heavy on the red."

"I'll take one, too, whatever that is."

When they reached the spot where J.C. was taking orders, Logan spoke a moment with the man before he repeated the order in his singsong way and went off to get things started.

Eve shook her head in disbelief. "I'm amazed."

"You should be."

Above her head were signs of all descriptions, including one that said it was fine to pass in line. She figured out pretty quickly what that meant. Logan handed her a tray and they passed several people and went to stand at a second spot.

"Hey, Willie," Logan called and shook hands with the black man who turned and grinned. "How's it going, man?"

"Hot. It's hot, but my Braves are winning, so I can't complain."

"Willie's a big Atlanta Braves fan. Eve, this is my friend Willie. And back there piling up the onion rings is another buddy of mine, A.J."

When Willie placed the paper plate on

Eve's tray, all she could do was stare. She'd never seen so much food on one plate in her life. The sandwich was hidden beneath a pile of onion rings and French fries. Logan said goodbye to his friends and they walked farther down.

"Tea?"

"Fine," Eve answered, still wondering how in the world she would eat all that food.

Logan snared two styrofoam cups of tea and placed them on his tray. "Keep moving."

They finally reached the cash register. Eve could see a slender white man practically dancing as he rung up the price of the meals. He, too, was a friend of Logan's.

"Hi, John, looks like business is good. Oh, John White, this is Eve Travers. She's running a camp for underprivileged kids."

"Pleased to meet you, Eve. Where's your camp?"

"King's Mountain. It's the Reach for the Stars Creative Camp."

"Sounds like a worthy cause to me."

"It is. We've got a wonderful group of kids this summer."

"Yeah, I'm the most wonderful," Logan said, snatching an onion ring and popping it into his mouth.

"What do you have to do with it?" John White looked at Logan in surprise.

"I'm coaching tennis."

"I never figured you'd do something like that."

"He's great at it, even though he probably won't admit it."

"Oh, he'll admit it," John said with a laugh. "His ego won't let him be bashful about taking credit for something, right, Logan?" He looked at Eve. "Nice to meet you. Hope you'll stop in often."

Eve and Logan went into one of the dining rooms and sat down. High on one wall was a television set showing a baseball game. Eve bit into an onion ring. "Oh, this *is* good."

"Everything here is good."

"You know, for someone who's supposed to be such a bad boy or spoiled brat kind of man, you seem to have lots of friends."

Logan shrugged and dug out his sandwich. "Hash, heavy on the red. Mmm, good."

Eve did the same and found that he was

right. The sandwich was delicious and the meal had been inexpensive. "Logan, tell me about yourself. All I know is what I read about you before you arrived at camp."

He wiped his mouth. "What's to tell? I played professional tennis and now I don't anymore."

Knowing that she was going to have to confess to overhearing a part of his conversation with the kids, Eve hesitated. She *did* want to know more about Logan. But he always seemed to cut off every overture. "I heard a part of the conversation you and the kids were having. About practice. How do you know so much about art?"

"What's to know? Picasso obviously knew nothing of anatomy, but his paintings sell for millions. Everybody knows that."

"I understand that part, but you were talking about Marc Chagall. And before that, you were discussing things that are common knowledge in music circles or art circles, but not in normal life."

"There's your clue, Eve. People in the art circles and music circles aren't normal. There's something wrong with them." He stared at her for a long moment. "That's why I have such a hard time figuring you out."

"In what way?" This was news to Eve. She'd never considered herself hard to understand.

"You're an artist and you still make sense. Most of the time, that is."

"Thanks for the vote of confidence." Eve considered his remark. She sensed that she was closing in on something important. "What makes you think that all artists and musicians are so strange? I think that Kayla and Bert and I disprove your theory."

"Okay, so a few of you are all right, but the majority of you are just about too weird to live in a civilized nation." Logan didn't like the direction the conversation was taking. He liked Eve an awful lot, more than he wanted to in fact. But he kept being reminded that she was an artist and that was one taboo he'd observed religiously for ten years until he'd made love to her the other night. "So how's your dinner?"

Eve picked at her onion rings, wondering how to convince him that he could confide in her. She saw the shadow of something in his eyes, a vulnerability that was obviously associated with artists. "It's fine, Logan," she said softly, still thinking about his dislike for her craft. "But why are you shutting me out? We were . . . we were about to cross a bridge and suddenly you put up a toll booth and I can't figure out what the toll is. I'm a friend and good listener, Logan."

"See? You're talking about something . . ." Logan let his angry words drift away into silence. He wasn't really angry with Eve, but with the situation that generated the conversation. Why did the first woman who really interested him in years have to be an artist? But the better question, he chided himself, was why did he have to continue feeling this way about artists? "Look, Eve, I'm sorry if I snapped at you, but . . . that's the way I feel and I can't really change it."

Eve began to understand. Some woman, an artist, had jilted him. No, she thought, looking at the lines etched in his face, it had to be worse than that. An artist had done something so horrible that he couldn't even talk about it with a friend. "Logan, for the moment, let's put aside careers and just be good friends. Remember? We talked about it before? Nothing permanent, nothing that entangles one with the other for an extended period of time, and . . . no promises of forever."

"No woman is willing to settle for that kind of relationship, Eve. I know women too well." Logan admired her for making the offer and respected her even more than he had before.

Eve wanted to reach across the table and shake him. "Logan, I'm not like other women. Don't judge me by someone you . . . met before." She glanced at her watch. "I think it's almost time to go."

They cleaned off their table and left. During the short drive across town, Eve tried to think of something to say that would convince Logan she could be trusted with his innermost fears, but was unsuccessful. Everybody has secrets, vulnerabilities, she thought. Would she be willing, at this point in their relationship, to confide in Logan?

That was a question Eve couldn't answer, particularly since she didn't know what dreadful secret he held within his heart. Trying very hard to understand, she glanced over at him, his strong profile visible in the glow of a street light they were passing. "Logan, I'm here. Just re-member that."

"Thanks, Eve. I appreciate your offer; it's just that this is something that . . . well, I can't talk about it."

Eve heard the pain seep through his words like poison. Whoever had hurt him, had done a great deal of damage, and she felt that pain in her own heart for him. The utter helplessness of the situ-ation angered her, but she couldn't force him to confide in her, even though she was certain that talking about it would help.

To Logan's dismay, they arrived at the bus depot much too early. Sitting in the dark Bronco without speaking really both-ered him. He felt that he should find some way to make it up to Eve for his outburst and for his distrust, though that wasn't really true. He trusted her, more than he'd trusted a woman in many years, maybe ever, but he couldn't extricate the awful emotions that were held in check in his heart.

He couldn't trust himself. That was the bottom line.

After a moment, Eve turned on the ra-dio and found a station that played country music. The pressure of the silence was like an anvil on her heart; she could hardly stand it any longer.

The music didn't really help. Eve found the songs were targeted to point out the chasm that seemed to be widening between her and Logan. She played with the dials and found a classical station with soft music that was even worse than the country songs; the classical music made her want to put her arms around Logan and kiss away his pain—and hers.

"Look, Eve, I'm really sorry. I came along to keep you company and now, I'm being a pain in the ass."

"No, you're not. Forget it. We'll talk about something else." Eve scoured her brain for another subject. She glanced at his profile, barely visible now in the neon sign outside the bus station. Without saying another word, she leaned across, placed her hand on his cheek, and kissed him. "Blame it on the music," she whispered, her lips still pressed against his.

Fourteen

Logan thought that Eve's sultry voice would melt a tennis court. Her voice—along with a liberal supply of her kisses—had brought about a painful situation he could hardly correct in the parking lot of the bus depot.

"Eve," he said tenderly, stroking her hair and neck. "I think we need to . . . think of something else to do."

Sitting up abruptly, Eve gazed at him, the hurt apparent in her eyes. "I . . . I'm sorry."

"No, don't take it the wrong way." Logan pulled her back into his arms and kissed her forehead. "I have a problem that is a direct result of our making up or making out, whichever the case may be."

"Oh, I see. Well, no, I don't really see, but I'll take your word for it for now." Eve giggled like a schoolgirl and sat up straight. "Maybe we'd better behave before we get caught."

"Spoken like a true high school girl. Tease me, put me in agony, and then giggle and say 'no, thank you.' " Logan grabbed her and kissed her soundly. "You're getting away with this for now, but I make no promises for later."

"Then I'd better behave for sure." Eve heard the sound of a diesel engine and kissed Logan quickly. "Sounds like our prayers are answered. A chaperon."

Logan groaned. *"Your* prayers, maybe."

Eve started to get out. "Hmm, you might want to stay in the car and do something about that problem we were talking about. I'll find Gayle."

Before Logan could protest, Eve was gone. He did have a problem, worse than she could ever imagine.

She was the problem!

Eve scanned the faces of people getting off the bus. She didn't know why she hadn't thought to bring a sign. Unless Gayle resembled Heather, Eve didn't have the first clue about determining which woman was Gayle Barton.

"Are you Miss Travers? Eve?" one of the women asked, her voice timid and so low that Eve could hardly hear her.

"Gayle? Yes, I'm Eve." The woman favored Heather a little, almost enough for Eve to recognize. "Welcome. We'll get your luggage and—"

Gayle smiled weakly. "I don't have anything but this."

Eve glanced at the plastic bag and her heart almost burst into fragments. To be reduced to carrying all your worldly possessions in a plastic trash bag seemed to be the final insult among a throng of them. "Good," Eve said finally. "I like a woman who travels light."

Gayle glanced around. "You didn't bring Heather?"

At once Eve knew she should have. "No, I didn't and I'm truly sorry. But, Gayle," she began, wondering how she put this as gently as possible. "I didn't know what might happen. Anything could have prevented you from getting on the bus, and I was afraid Heather would be distraught."

"You did the right thing." Gayle slung her bag over her shoulder and followed Eve. "I almost didn't get on the bus."

Eve stopped and turned around. "Why not? What could possibly—"

"Pride." Gayle smiled more openly now and patted Eve's arm. "Don't worry. I'll pull my weight."

Holding her tongue, Eve decided that it would be better if she waited to complete this discussion later—when Gayle was at the camp. "That was never an issue."

She introduced Logan and Gayle before starting the Bronco. "We're only about an hour from home."

"That's good. I'm pretty tired after that bus ride."

Logan had gotten into the back seat. He was glad to see that Gayle wasn't grungy looking. Apparently she wasn't like some of the street people he'd seen. "Heather will be ecstatic when she sees you."

"I hope so. I missed her so much."

"Gayle, we need to figure out a way to make Heather realize that she's still at camp even though you're on the premises. What I'm trying to say, and doing a lousy job of it, is that I really want Heather to establish her own set of friends based on equality." Eve knew she wasn't making good sense, but she'd been trying to figure this issue out for days with no success.

"You mean, you don't want her to visit me or anything?" Gayle sounded heartbroken.

"No, no, of course not." Eve racked her brain for a way to explain her feelings. "Look, here's the scenario. All these children come from poor homes. All year they have to fight for their own identity, mainly because, whether we like it or not, class lines are still evident in our society. I want them to be on equal footing at camp."

"I see. For once in their lives, these kids are the cream instead of the clabber."

"Precisely. Here, we have no class lines. All the kids dress alike, live in like cabins, eat the same food, share the same facilities." Eve stopped at a traffic light and turned to look at Gayle. "Nobody's special here, and yet, everybody is. Does that make sense?"

"It does and I'm thrilled for Heather." Gayle peered out the window for a moment. "So where do I fit in?"

"I'm going to level with you, Gayle, because I think you're an intelligent woman who deserves honesty." Eve took a deep breath, praying that she wasn't making a mistake. "On the first night of camp, Heather came to me in the middle of the night. She was crying."

"I knew she would," Gayle said softly.

"She was worried about you, about where you would live." Eve bit her lip to keep from crying herself as she recalled that awful night. "She knew that you'd have to leave the shelter because she wasn't with you."

"That's true, but she didn't need to worry. I can take care of myself."

"Damnit, you shouldn't have to!" Logan could no longer contain his anger. This situation had gotten under his skin and he hated the whole stinking mess. "Your lives should be stable. Heather should have a safe place to call home."

"There's very little safety on the streets, Mr. Mallory."

"That's the problem, Gayle," Eve said, catching Logan's anger herself. "I can't do anything about the multitudes, but I could do something for Heather. That's why you're here. Because of Heather. I knew that she'd be so worried about you that she couldn't take advantage of our program."

"You're a kind woman, Eve," Gayle said quietly. "And you're very kind, too, Mr. Mallory."

"Logan. Heather's a great kid." Logan sat back and relaxed a little. "Helluva tennis player for a little sprite like she is."

"Heather excels at everything she tries. I just wish I could offer her the advantages that other kids her age have. Unfortunately, I can't."

Eve listened to the words and to the emotion that carried the words. "Gayle, why are you on the streets?"

"My . . . my husband lost his job. It wasn't so bad at first. He was able to keep his insurance up for a while. He looked for a job, but couldn't seem to find anything. He got discouraged and then depressed. And then I got injured." Gayle caught a tear with her fist and bit her lip. "He killed himself."

"Oh, God, you poor dear. And Heather," Eve reached over and gripped Gayle's aim for a moment. "You don't have to talk about this if you don't want to."

"I think it will help. Getting things out in the open frequently makes them less painful."

Eve glanced at Logan in the rearview

mirror. "That's exactly the way I feel. Go on when you can."

Logan caught Eve's gaze. He knew exactly what she was thinking, but it didn't apply to him. She didn't know how awful the truth could be.

"When I got out of the hospital, we had no money and I couldn't work. Our mortgage company foreclosed. I tried to get disability, but couldn't." Gayle hesitated for a long moment. "This has been worse on Heather than on me. I can take care of myself, but that haunting look in her eyes just kills me."

"It couldn't be helped," Logan said, trying to assuage her guilt.

"I couldn't apply for welfare. I tried, honestly I did." Gayly buried her face in her hands. "Those questions and those awful social workers. I couldn't go through with it. I just couldn't. And, now, look what I've done to my daughter. My pride. My foolish pride put us on the street," she said, sobbing.

"Gayle, you've got a place for the summer. I can pay you a small salary. We'll find a way to get you and Heather back on your feet." Eve turned off of Interstate

85 and headed through the black night toward King's Mountain. "I promise."

By the time they pulled into the parking lot at camp Gayle had fallen asleep. Apparently she felt safe for the first time in a long while. Eve was happy about that.

Logan got out and gathered up their purchases. They could sort them out in the morning, except for the one special box he kept with him. "I'll see you ladies to your cabins."

Gayle looked around sleepily. "Can I see Heather before you take me to my cabin? I won't wake her, I promise."

"Of course." Eve grabbed her flashlight and led the way through the woods. "Keep up, Logan," she teased.

"Gayle, you don't know what a vicious woman Eve Travers can be. Watch out for the brambles and briars."

They reached the cabin and Eve shined the flashlight through the screen. Heather lay sound asleep, her face angelic in slumber. When Gayle touched Eve's arm, they walked back the way they'd come.

"Thank you. She looks wonderful. I think she's put on weight."

"Madora's cooking will do that for you, too." Eve patted her own stomach. "I fight it every day, but I never miss a meal."

"Eve, before we take Gayle to her cabin, let's go into your office."

"Whatever for?"

"Surprise." Logan loved springing surprises on people.

Eve opened the door to the office and switched on the light. A whole coconut pie sat on the desk and beside it were three plates and forks, and a thermos of coffee. "Bless your heart, Logan. And Madora's, too."

They all sat down and Eve sliced pie for each of them while Gayle poured the coffee. After the first bite, Eve moaned with joy. "Nothing like Madora's cooking."

"Hmm, this is wonderful," Gayle said and continued to eat.

"You girls owe me for this. I'll probably be cleaning garbage cans for three weeks because I asked her to do this."

"Oh, this is the secret, eh? I can imagine she'll have some particularly *delicious* torture for you, Logan."

"This Madora sounds like an interesting person," Gayle said, looking from Eve to Logan.

"She's wonderful. You'll love her like we all do." Logan scraped his plate clean and finished his coffee. "When you ladies are ready, I'll escort Gayle to her cabin."

"I'll come along to make sure everything's all right." Eve finished her pie and sighed. "Oh, I don't think I'll ever be hungry again."

"I can't wait for breakfast!" Gayle exclaimed. "If all her food is this good."

"We have well-balanced meals here. Lots of vegetables and fruits."

"And pies and cakes," Logan added with a grin. "Especially the pies and cakes."

They were soon at Gayle's cabin. When she went inside her face lit up and her smile made her beautiful. Eve gave Gayle a quick hug. "Welcome to the Camp Reach for the Stars family."

"I don't know what to say. This is wonderful. And it's mine?"

"For the rest of the summer. The camp closes on August nineteenth, but I'll be here probably through September. You and Heather are welcome to stay and help me close down for the winter." Eve considered Gayle's tired face. "Gayle, why not stay here in this area? I'm sure we can find you a job."

"You're a real friend, Eve. You're a woman people can count on. I'm privileged to know you." Gayle's wan smile lasted but a moment. "I couldn't get a job in Atlanta because I couldn't leave Heather alone. When I could get away to apply, nobody would hire me because I didn't have a permanent address and phone number. Thanks for everything, Eve."

"Don't get so excited. You haven't started to work yet."

"Well, if Madora puts Logan on garbage can cleaning detail, I'll happily do it for him."

"That reminds me. What do you want to do, Gayle?" Eve asked, wondering if she should have waited until morning. "You think about it and let me know tomorrow. That's a better idea. After you've seen how we run things, you'll be able to make that decision."

"Whatever it is, Eve, it's better than living on the streets and never knowing if your only child is going to be safe."

Logan felt as though a knife twisted in his heart. He could certainly understand that feeling. He'd thought Brandon was safe at home with his mommy, but Logan had been wrong and was still paying for that mistake. He knew how Gayle felt.

Eve could hardly wait to get to breakfast. She hurried down to Gayle's cabin and knocked gently. If she was still asleep, Eve planned to let her be. God knows when a woman could rest on the streets.

She found Gayle dressed in a pair of shorts and a T-shirt exactly like the campers wore. Apparently Sharleen had left some clothes for the newest staff member, just in case.

"How do I look?" Gayle asked, twirling around. "Do I look like I fit in?"

"You look great." Eve smiled and hugged Gayle. "Don't you love the logo? Tennis Pro, that's the company that's sponsoring the camp this summer, had their art department work it up combining their logo and ours."

Gayle looked down at her white legs. "It's been a long time since I wore shorts."

"Are you ready to meet the rest of the crew and the kids?"

Gayle gulped and nodded. "Have you told Heather that I was here?"

"No, I thought I'd let you do that yourself." Eve linked arms with Gayle and they headed to the dining hall. "After breakfast, I'll take you on a little tour. We'll have about an hour before my first class starts."

"I'm really interested in seeing what Heather is doing. She has a fixation on Marc Chagall."

"Believe it or not, I just found out about that yesterday. Logan was talking to the kids on the tennis court about practice. He mentioned a couple of masters and Heather brought up Chagall." Eve shook her head and waved to Connie who was coming out of the first-aid station. "Here's Connie Edwards."

After the introductions, Eve could see that Gayle would fit in. Before they reached the dining hall, Eve stopped and turned to Gayle. "You said last night that you'd been sick and couldn't work. I'm concerned about putting you to work here."

"Don't worry. I broke my back when a scaffolding fell. My company had no workers' comp." Gayle reached around and rubbed her lower back almost involuntarily. "It still bothers me some, but I'm much better. That is, unless you want me to lift something really heavy."

"Not here. Otis usually manages that."

Eve opened the door to the dining hall. Most of the kids hadn't arrived. They went through the line and settled on a table where they could spot Heather as she came through the door. Several other staff members came in and sat with them.

Then Heather came in leading a few of her fellow campers. She was telling them about Chagall's paintings. She spotted Gayle and broke into a run. "Mom!"

Gayle hugged Heather close to her and held her for a long moment before pushing her back so she could see her face better. Both of them had tears in their eyes. "My, but you've grown and it's hardly been a week."

Heather wiped her eyes and glanced at her mother's attire. "You're dressed like me. I mean, like all of us. Do you have on the shoes? Tennis Pro makes great shoes. I love mine. When did you get here? Isn't it great?"

"Whoa, Heather, one question at a

time." Gayle hugged her daughter again. "I arrived last night."

Gayle made a concerted effort to answer the jumble of questions that Heather asked, but finally laughed and hugged the child again. "Go and eat your breakfast. I'll see you at lunchtime."

Heather stared at her mother for a moment. "You don't want me to eat with you?"

"No, you can eat with your friends and I'll eat with mine." Gayle bit her lip. She did want Heather to sit down, never to leave her side again, but her daughter needed to maintain her independence. "I'll see you later."

As she started to walk away, Heather hesitated and then returned. She looked at Eve with a big smile. "Thanks for bringing my mom here."

"My pleasure, sweetheart. Now, get going. The line's getting longer all the time."

"She looks great, Eve," Gayle said as she watched Heather romp across the room and get back in line with her friends. "She looks like she adjusted well, too."

"She's been fine, Gayle." Eve pointed

to Gayle's plate. "Now, eat your breakfast. We've got lots to do."

Logan came in shortly. He looked as if he hadn't had any sleep. Eve waved at him and motioned for him to join them.

He grabbed a cup of coffee and sat down. "I'm hungry, but I'm not waiting in that line. I'll eat when the monsters leave the dining room."

"You're welcome to do that. Gayle and I were getting ready to tour the grounds. Would you like to bring your coffee and walk with us?"

"Are you kidding? I'm not even awake yet." Logan leaned forward on his elbows. "Wake me up when classes start."

Eve got up and took her tray. As she walked by Logan, she whispered, "Shouldn't stay out all night."

He reached out and caught her hand, pulling her back toward him. With a malicious grin, he murmured, "We'll see about that tonight, won't we?"

Their tour ended, Eve took Gayle to class until something else could be worked out. They were sketching with charcoal that day and Eve handed Gayle some supplies and

told her to have fun. Eve had set up a still
life, with a milk pitcher, bowl of fruit, and
a small bouquet of wildflowers.

She sat there, sketching and thinking of
Logan. His face filled her mind and his
pain filled her thoughts, but her hands
were busy sketching.

They'd both been too tired, and maybe
a little too keyed up, last night to talk.
She'd lain awake, considering some of the
things he said and trying to relate them
to what she'd read in the articles.

The only thing of consequence that she
could connect was that his son had died
at a very young age with spinal meningitis. Could that be the reason he shied
away from most of the kids? He was doing better about talking with them, but
she still sensed that he held himself away,
as if shielding himself from an emotional
attachment. With the older kids, those
seventeen or eighteen, he seemed more at
ease.

And then there was the chasm that had
opened between her and Logan. At times,
he acted as if he liked her a lot, but at
others, he drew away with the same sort
of shielding that she noticed in him with
the kids. His pain must have been a ter-

rible one if it still affected him so devastatingly. No wonder his relationships never worked out.

When she glanced critically at her work, Eve was astonished. Her first few strokes had been intended to form the pitcher, but Logan's face had been the result. She hadn't been paying too much attention to her sketching, but she'd always been able to think about one thing and draw another.

The sketch was a good likeness. He seemed to be in a somber mood, but that took nothing away from his appeal. She'd captured the bad boy of tennis as well as if she'd been drawing from a live model.

Eve turned the page quickly. It wouldn't do for the kids to catch her sketching Logan. They might read more into the accidental drawing than it really meant.

She couldn't concentrate on apples and peaches and flowers. Her mind remained on Logan, and her fingers followed her thoughts. This time, however, he seemed more at ease, happier. Was that wishful thinking on her part? She'd seen little of that part of him over the past few weeks.

"Miss Travers, why are you drawing Logan?" Heather asked, her face screwed into a questioning gaze.

Eve had to think fast. "I was . . . making sure my portrait skills were good enough to teach. Would you kids like to do a charcoal portrait?"

A resounding chorus of "Yes" made her smile.

"Well, then who should we use as a model?"

They discussed that for a moment and finally decided on Kayla. "I'll ask her if she's willing," Eve said and closed her sketchbook. She walked from one to the other of the students and noted their progress. "You've done well today."

As she collected their drawings, to be sprayed for protection, she caught a glimpse of Gayle's sketch. It was rich with detail and extremely well done. "Gayle, why didn't you tell me you were an artist? That's wonderful."

"I'm not, really." Gayle beamed at Eve's praise. "I studied art in school, but artists can't make much of a living, so I got a real job."

"As far as I'm concerned, you just got your *first* real job. I want you to teach one of our classes." Eve sat down beside Gayle and studied the drawing. "This is just great. Will you teach?"

Gayle smiled, her lower lip trembling slightly. "I'd love to."

"Terrific. That will give all of us a break. We were scheduled pretty thin." Eve waited until everyone's work had been checked, but hers and Gayle's. "Okay, guys, time for lunch. Put up your supplies."

They walked over to the dining hall together. Madora outdid herself for lunch. Eve shook her head and grinned. "Great job, Madora."

"Eve, is Gayle going to be helping me?"

"Oh, no, I forgot." Eve went back to speak more quietly with Madora. "She's going to be teaching art. She's wonderful." Eve leaned a little closer to make sure that nobody heard except Madora. "Don't think I haven't noticed this little . . . shall we say, affair that's going on between you and Otis."

Madora blushed and growled something about Eve's imagination, but Eve knew she was right. She walked to the table and sat with Logan, Gayle, Sharleen, and Connie. Their conversation was light and fun, but there was a certain tension between Eve and Logan. She knew that it had to come out sooner or later. She decided she could wait.

Lunchtime was gossip time. As Eve ate her lunch, Julie yelled out today's version. For her efforts, she got cheers and boos, with a few catcalls between. The kids seemed to look forward to lunchtime for that reason.

Eve had plenty to do. Charlotte Adams was arriving that afternoon. She and Sharleen went out to the guest cabin and straightened everything up, made the beds, put towels and washcloths in the bathroom, and a fresh arrangement of flowers from Eve's scraggly flower bed.

When she heard the crunch of tires on gravel, Eve knew her friend had arrived. She met Charlotte at the parking lot and they hugged for a long moment. "Glad you could come, Charlotte. You'll love it here."

"I'm so excited about this," Charlotte said, unloading her trunk. "What do I need out of here?"

"Just your clothes. We've got everything else, unless you have some special paint you want to use." Eve hugged Charlotte again. "What are you going to paint?"

"We're going to do a collage with things we find on the campsite." Charlotte gave her a beautiful smile. "You know how I love that sort of thing."

"They'll love it." Eve took Charlotte's bag. "I'll show you to the palace. That's what I call the guest cabin."

"As long as it's got an indoor toilet and a bed, I'll be happy."

"You're in luck." They chatted amiably as they walked the short distance to the guest cabin. "Charlotte, do you want to lie down for a while?"

"No, I'm ready to go. Sitting in that car has me all cramped up." She shrugged her shoulders, rolling her head to one side and then the other. "I need to stretch."

"Then we'll go and you can meet everyone."

Charlotte's classes were wonderful. The kids responded well to the gathering of unusual items to be used in the collage. For dirt, some of the kids used sand or brown dirt gathered from the beach, but others used coffee grounds. Some of them used leaves, pine cones, bark, and dried grasses, but others found newspaper and made papier-mâché.

Eve took the time to write some letters,

to return phone calls, and to rest. She was exhausted. It wasn't necessarily the physical effort of running the camp, but more a combination of that and the tension that still hung between her and Logan.

The campfire that evening was delightful as usual. The moon was full, hanging like a silvery medallion over the camp. When she thought about it, the full moon signified that Logan had been at camp for a month, though the kids hadn't been there that long. Eve could hardly believe that much time had passed.

Her birthday was coming up very soon and she was in a pensive mood. Watching the kids' antics around the campfire that night did little to take her mind off her situation with Logan. She kept wondering why he wouldn't talk to her. Eve finally decided her conjecturing was useless and tried to concentrate on the kids. They were having a ball.

Studying Eve, Logan sat across the campfire. She seemed to be deep in thought, apparently focusing on something that displeased her. He instinctively felt that he was the cause of her consternation.

Logan wished he could do something

to relieve her concerns, but he simply couldn't talk about some things. Brandon's death. Nor could he talk about why he disliked artists so much. It was still too painful—and futile. Artists were all people with their heads in the clouds; nobody could talk sense to them. Maybe one day, but not now.

Eve had said she would accept whatever occurred between them, without asking for any promise of the future. Like the fanciful name of the camp, Reach for the Stars, she just didn't know what she was saying.

Reach for the stars, he thought. What does that entail? Wishful thinking. And, Logan, of all people, knew wishing wouldn't make it so, no matter how hard you wanted something.

As she walked away from the campfire, Eve sensed that Logan was waiting for her. He'd been with some of his favorite kids, but had dropped back to join her.

"Mind if I tag along?" he asked, looking down at her.

"No, I'd like the company." Eve controlled the shiver that started to tease her. "How are the tennis classes going? I haven't had a chance to stop by in a couple of days."

"Good. No, great." Logan touched Eve's arm and stopped. "I need to talk to you about something important."

"Go ahead."

"Not here. I don't want this to get around." Logan waited until all the kids had gone past them. "Can we have a cup of coffee in your office?"

"Sure, why not?"

For the remainder of the stroll back to her office, first one thought and then another flitted through her mind. What could be so wrong that he didn't want the kids to hear him? Was there some problem with one of them, something so awful that it required secrecy to be discussed?

Eve tried to think of something that was that bad, but couldn't. The kids were too nice to cause trouble, so it had to be something else. Maybe it was personal. Maybe he needed to leave for a few days or borrow some money or . . . it could be a million things. Eve was wasting her mental ability by wondering. She would find out in a couple of minutes.

When they reached her office, she put on the coffeepot. Seconds later, it was perking merrily, as if there were no problems in the world, much less one of such magnitude that it required secrecy. While it perked, they talked about things in general. Eve thought she would scream.

Finally she poured two cups of the steaming brew and sat down on the opposite end of the sofa. "Okay, Logan, what gives? You're making me crazy, wondering about whatever has happened."

Logan took a sip of coffee and set the mug down. "Tony tells me that his father won't come up for parents' day."

Relief that nothing catastrophic had happened made Eve relax a little. "Is that all?"

"All? It's important to him." Logan got up and began to pace. "He was counting on his dad coming. Now, there's some hassle about it."

"It's definite? Mr. Dean isn't coming?"

"Nope. I even talked to him on the phone myself."

That information surprised Eve. "You did? When?"

"This afternoon while you were out doing whatever it is you do."

"And Tony isn't taking it well?"

"He says he's going to hitchhike home."

Eve leapt to her feet. "Logan! We can't let him do that. Go get him."

"Easy, easy, he's not going now." Logan settled Eve down and then flopped down beside her. "We need to find someone to stand in."

Eve considered the problem. She could understand how the boy felt. After all, there were lots of events scheduled that required two people: an adult and a child. Tony would be excluded from all of them. "Logan, you'll just have to be the stand-in. You can be Tony's dad for a day."

If she could have taken back the words, she would have. Logan looked as if she'd asked him to lay down his life for the boy; maybe that would have been a better suggestion from his expression.

"I can't, Eve," he said, his voice barely a croak.

"But, Logan," she insisted. "It's just for a day. What can that hurt?"

"Don't ask me to do this, Eve. I can't."
Logan felt a tear slide down his cheek. "I
can't," he whispered.

Fifteen

Eve felt tears form in the corners of her eyes and then slide over her eyelids. How much pain could one man stand without sharing it?

From the set of his jaw, Eve could tell that Logan still wasn't ready to talk about this problem, so she slipped her arms around him and held him tightly, as if she were comforting an injured child. Mentally cursing whoever had caused this condition, she drew his head down on her shoulder and said, "You don't ever have to do anything you don't want to do, Logan. You're safe here from whatever devils haunt you in the outside world."

Logan gazed at her. He hadn't meant to be so foolish. He prayed she hadn't seen that damned tear, but considering her reaction, he suspected she had. "Thanks, Eve. You're the greatest."

For a long time, he sat there wrapped

in her arms. She was right about one thing: he felt better around her, even if she was an artist. Leaning against her made something else obvious. Even though he was agonizing over Tony's dilemma, Logan's body was responding to Eve.

What did that say about him? he wondered. Was he truly the lecher . . . well, maybe not lecher, but "Casanova of the tennis courts" that the media made him out to be? As the thought crossed his mind, Logan knew it wasn't so, at least not where Eve was concerned.

There was no doubt that he wanted her physically, but it was the emotional craving for her that didn't go with the Logan he knew so well. "Eve," he said quietly, noticing that anyone who happened to walk by could see them. "Maybe we'd better turn out the lights or continue this discussion upstairs."

That seemed like an odd request, but when she followed his gaze, she understood. "Good idea."

She extricated herself from him and rose. Which should she do? If she only turned out the lights, would he believe she thought less of him for his vulnerability? Or, if she took him to her bed-room, would he think she was doing it out of pity? Her instincts told her to for-get both concerns and take him upstairs to bed. Was that her libido talking or her mind?

Eve turned out the light. "Logan, I think . . . hell, I don't know what I think. Let's go upstairs and try to sort this out."

She heard him rise from the sofa. Within seconds, his arm was around her and they were walking up the narrow stairs. Smiling to herself, she leaned closer to him. "I'm glad we think alike, on this matter anyway."

Eve realized that Logan needed comfort. He wanted to be pampered in a way that could only happen between a man and a woman. It wouldn't occur to him that by satiating his physical needs, she was feed-ing his spirit, but Eve knew. There was a connection between them, much deeper than the lust that she was about to quench—for both of them.

When they reached her room, she shed her clothes without fuss and began to re-move his. As if his energy had been sapped, Logan withstood her ministra-tions until she reached the waistband of his pants.

"I'll be glad to assist," he murmured, dropping his pants around his ankles to the floor.

Taking her face in his hands, Logan kissed her. It was his way of saying "thank you" for something he didn't really understand. She had, in the lapse of a few minutes, softened the pain that he'd dug from deep inside himself.

It was her unquestioning understanding. That was it. That was what he liked most about her.

Logan lifted her and lowered her on the bed, joining her immediately. Their bodies melted together, each seeking comfort in the other. With a groan of surrender, Logan allowed her to turn him on his back and cover his face with kisses. She played her fingers across his chest, toying with the light thatch of hair.

Eve smiled at his sighs, knowing that with each caress, she relieved some of the tension that bunched up his muscles and held him so taut. She traced down the muscles of his chest, his stomach, and teased into the patch of hair at his groin. Then she realized something else. As the nervous tension drained out of him, it was replaced by another kind: sexual tension. She smiled, knowing she had some slight power over him.

"Eve, you don't—"

"Shh!" she warned, and kept up her ministrations.

Logan felt his body lighten, almost as if a weight had been lifted from him as he lay there and relaxed while her fingers danced across his skin. He wanted to throw her on her back and make love to her for hours, but he held back, letting her enjoy the moments of pleasure she was giving him.

Knowing his great need, Eve pushed all thoughts aside and slid over him, allowing him to fill her. She gasped in surprise as she leaned back and moved her hips gently back and forth. Logan's moans turned to groans of ecstasy beneath her. And her movements quickened.

Logan could stand no more. He turned her on her back and smothered her with kisses for a long moment. She returned his caresses in full, massaging his back with her fingers before tracing a trail around to the front and to his nipples.

Speeding his pace, Logan felt the surge that carried him over the threshold and transported Eve along with him. Their bodies met, and he felt the sweet slide down from the lofty heaven of his gratification. That Eve had experienced the same spectacular moments pleased and excited him.

For a long time they lay there, not speaking. Her fingers occasionally caught his nipple and teased it, but for an extended interval they simply lay there and touched.

Eve had set out to relieve some of Logan's pain, and had won her own release in the bargain. Floating softly in the afterglow of fulfillment, she hoped he wouldn't leave her to go back to his cabin. She wanted to fall asleep in his arms and to wake up to find him still there in her tiny bed.

In time, she slept, peacefully for the first night in awhile.

Logan tried to rise before the sun came up, but Eve pulled him back down for a repeat performance. After they'd come down from their lovemaking, he kissed her gently. "Good morning, love," he whispered. "If I don't leave now, our secret will be out."

"I hope not," she said with a nervous laugh. "I'd hate to hear about us on the noon gossip report."

"Then I shall clothe my satiated body and flee in darkness," he teased, kissing her longingly one last time. "Until later."

When he was gone, Eve hugged herself. The night had been wonderful. She could only think of superlatives when she recalled, with a wicked blush, how she'd made love to Logan Mallory not once, but twice during the night.

Eve dragged herself out of bed and peered at herself in the mirror. Instead of the sexually satisfied woman she expected to see, a woman with sleepy eyes and bedraggled hair glared back. "Well, so much for the lovely afterglow," she said to the person in the mirror. "A shower and you'll look presentable—maybe."

Eve appeared at breakfast, dressed in crisp black shorts and a red top. Her class was being conducted by Gayle this morning, so she had a little time to linger over her coffee. That was when she got the biggest surprise of her life.

She walked into Madora's office, expecting to have a nice chat with her friend, but she found Madora and Otis in an embrace. "Oh! Sorry," she stammered and backed out.

So much for work this morning. She took her sketch pad and walked down to the lake. Sitting on the edge of the beach, propped against a tree, she began to draw. The first picture was of the lake, still and beautiful in the morning sun. The second was of a playful Logan, who appeared to be ready to take on the world.

She liked that expression. It was very similar to the one he'd had when he dressed that morning. Eve knew that she'd been responsible for putting that smile on his face and felt like she was in flight. She couldn't recall when she'd been so happy about anything.

Recalling her idea about Logan's cookbook, she began to sketch him in action. Instead of the serious drawings she'd done earlier, these were more like caricatures. Most were of him at the tennis court, reaching to serve or running full tilt to backhand a ball. Some were of Logan in the kitchen. One showed him with a befuddled look as he gazed at a huge turkey on a table with only one place setting. Others illustrated him tossing a salad.

Maybe she'd collect a bunch of these and let him look at them. The idea appealed to her. After all, the summer was drawing to a close.

Charlotte had come and gone. She'd been a public school teacher, too. That was where Eve met her. Now she taught art full time. The kids loved her.

Soon, Tim would be there to talk about the scholarship program. Jerry had gotten the estimated cost from several schools, but there didn't seem to be anything cheap. Eve would have to do a real job of selling this idea.

She put down her sketch pad. The summer was turning out to be more incredible than she ever thought possible. The only problem was tomorrow: parents' day.

Logan still refused to act as Tony's surrogate father for the day. Even though Eve felt that she was leaching away some of Logan's pain, there was enough residual there to last a hundred people a lifetime.

It would be up to her to stand in for Tony's parents. She didn't know how the boy would respond, but she intended to make it work, no matter what it took out of her. He was a talented boy, only thirteen, and this summer had been wonderful for him. Like Heather, he needed the chance to be equal to everyone around him.

Eve gathered up her sketch pad and charcoal. Her growling stomach told her it was lunchtime. And she didn't want to miss that.

Of everything she'd been so worried about, her birthday had to be shoved aside. Sunday, she'd be forty-six. She still didn't know how she felt about that. How old was old? When did you get there?

Logan spotted Eve in her usual seat in the dining hall. He hurried through the line and took the seat beside her. "I'd kiss you, but I think a hundred dirty-minded kids would put their little imaginations to work and think bad thoughts."

"I'd be willing to bet that the kids aren't the only dirty-minded people in this room." She smiled knowingly at him. "Eat your lunch, Romeo."

"Ah, Juliet, I'd abandon food for the

remainder of my days for thee," he quipped and raised his eyebrows.

"Yes, Romeo, I can see how thou wouldst, except for the coconut pie, which resideth on thy tray." Eve laughed and snatched his slice of pie. "Now, how willing art thou to make that statement."

"I confess, dear lady, I lied to gain your favor." Logan wrested the pie from her hands. "Never touch Romeo's coconut pie, woman."

"Ah, how fickle is man. He declares his undying love in one breath and takes it back in the next." Connie dropped into the chair beside Logan. "I heard all that claptrap. Eve, don't you believe a word of it. If he told you he'd give up spinach, maybe you could trust him, but I know how much that man loves Madora's coconut pie."

"Sorry, pal, you heard my adviser. You're history."

"Alas, poor Yorick, betrayed by a slice of coconut pie." Logan burst into laughter and hugged both women. "I never realized I'd have this much fun up here. I may volunteer to come back next year."

Eve gazed at him in astonishment. For him to have changed his opinion that much in a few weeks was startling indeed.

They were joined by several other staff members and settled down to eat.

Pretty soon the kids were pounding on the tables for gossip. Julie climbed to her perch on the first table and held up her hands for silence. "I've got a real scoop for you guys today. What handsome tennis instructor was seen sneaking out of which camp director's cabin before dawn this morning? I promised I wouldn't tell, but here's a hint: her name's Eve and his name is Logan."

Color sprang to Eve's face. How had Julie found out? Eve felt humiliated, but Logan smiled and nodded, as if he were caught and knew it.

To her surprise, the kids began to cheer. It appeared they liked the idea of Logan and Eve being a couple.

Still, it didn't ease her embarrassment. How could she ever teach her class again?

Logan swallowed his chuckle. Of all people, he was accustomed to gossip, but he could see that Eve was chagrined by the "local gossip reporter" who had somehow discovered their secret. As he watched her he realized what a deeply private person she was. This very public airing of something so intensely personal might be the one incident that could terminate their relationship without further discussion, no matter how he—or she, in fact—felt about it.

What could he do? His denial of an obvious truth would do nothing but billow this gathering thundercloud all the more quickly. Yet, from the blanched expression on Eve's face, he realized he had to do something fast. He rose and held up his hands for quiet. "Now, all this is real cute, but I think we need to examine the facts here."

The lunchtime crowd gradually quieted. "Anybody who might have seen me sneaking around Miss Travers's cabin would also have seen a leash in my hand. My poor Muzzle got out last night and I went looking for her. Miss Travers very kindly consented to help me look." He glanced down to see what effect his words were having on Eve. From what he could tell, the kids were caught somewhere between wanting to believe the gossip and knowing they should believe him. "Unfortunately, we didn't find her."

Julie stared at Logan in disbelief. "But

I saw her this morning sitting in your window."

"Yes, the little prowler had returned by the time I got back to my cabin. She's probably going to sleep the day away." Logan started to sit down and then was struck by a flash of brilliance. "I'll probably be coming to look for some of you guys in about two months to offer you the result of this night."

Heather looked at Logan, her mouth pursed as if she didn't understand. "What result?"

Logan smiled. "I imagine that Muzzle will become a mommy in about sixty days."

As he sat down to a discordant shout of congratulations, he glanced at Eve. Her color had come back. The tentative smile she gave him told Logan that she appreciated his valiant effort, whether it worked or not.

Eve had listened to Logan's fanciful tale with a grateful heart. It wasn't that she didn't want anyone to know she was . . . what were she and Logan doing? Dating? Seeing each other? Having an affair. She knew their times together couldn't technically be called dates, but as far as she was concerned, they were as close as they could be.

His story reminded her of something she hadn't considered. What if she got pregnant? Forty-five, well, almost forty-six wasn't too old physically for such a thing to happen. The news media frequently aired reports about women in their forties getting pregnant.

Eve tried to remain calm about the subject. It wouldn't do for her to jump up and run out immediately after Logan's explanation. She smiled at several of the kids and shook her head as if to chide them for their belief in gossip, but she wanted to run. She wanted to find someone who could give her information—right now.

Chatting amiably with several campers and then the staff, Eve felt that she could never get away quick enough. Then she thought of Connie. She could trust Connie.

Excusing herself with a lie about having to discuss a child's problem with Connie, Eve hurried away. Where was Connie anyway? She hadn't been at lunch.

It seemed that everything and everyone got in her way as she crossed the compound to the first-aid cabin. When she finally reached the place, Connie wasn't there. Amy, Connie's assistant, said that Connie had gone to buy some additional antiseptic spray or something equally inane, Eve thought. She jotted a note for the nurse and returned to her office to wait.

She had bills to pay and that should take her mind off her problems, but it didn't. As Eve began to write checks, she realized that her time would be better served if she waited until she was in a better frame of mind. After putting the electric company check in the envelope with her Bronco payment, she set aside the checkbook and stared at her desk.

Idle hands are the devil's workshop, came a familiar phrase her father had repeated time and time again. Eve wasn't the kind of person who could sit around doing nothing. After pacing for about a hundred laps back and forth across her office, she dropped into her chair again. She was being foolish and she knew it.

With a sigh of resignation, she decided to work on her budget for next year. Her results were no better than with the checkbook. In disgust Eve put all her paper-work away. She took out a bottle of polish remover and stripped off her nail polish. Pushing back her cuticles and filing her nails came next, and with those tasks came a sense of calm, temporarily at least.

Next she put on a base coat, thinking all the while about the possibility of pregnancy. What would she do? Could she manage a child? She'd discovered this summer that she had a great deal of patience, but babies were different from teenagers. She scrunched up her nose at the idea of changing a dirty diaper.

By the time she got to the first color coat of nail polish, she'd calmed down considerably and was able to think rationally. Statistics very plainly showed that women over thirty who had never given birth usually didn't conceive as readily as those twenty-nine and under. That much was in her favor.

But as she glanced at her calendar, she saw that her cycle was favorable for her to get pregnant. Eve erupted from her chair and began to pace again. Swishing her hands about in the air to dry the first two coats of polish, she strode from the door to the sofa and back again.

Maybe she didn't have to worry. Logan could have had a vasectomy. "God knows, he's had enough affairs to need one," she said and swatted at a fly.

"What in the hell are you doing?" Logan asked, peering through the screen. "Is that some kind of native fertility dance or something?"

Stunned, Eve spun around to see his cheerful smile. She could very easily have choked him at that moment, but thought better of it. If she tried something like that, she'd obviously mess up her nail polish. She attempted a smile. "Come in. I'm drying my nail polish."

"Oh," Logan said and opened the door.

He came in as if nothing was wrong, but he couldn't know the turmoil Eve was in. He probably thought she took birth control pills or something, if he worried at all. Eve decided that, for the moment at least, she wanted something solid between them, so she walked around her desk and sat down.

Logan watched her silently for a few seconds. "Something wrong?"

"No, why do you ask?"

"You're as fidgety as a dog in a porcupine den."

Eve had to smile. He still thought that she was worried over the gossip at lunch.

Little did he know that the problem had long since been shouldered to one side by reality. "Thanks, Logan. You saved me a great deal of embarrassment." She hesitated a moment and glanced at her fingernails. In spite of her efforts, one of them had a scratch in the polish. "I'm a pretty private person."

"Yeah, well, don't worry about it." He grinned and shrugged. "What I told them was plausible enough to cause some doubt. There is no way they can prove I wasn't telling the truth."

"Thanks anyway." Eve studied him for a minute. "It proves one thing, though."

"What's that?"

"That you're a lot more creative than you ever thought."

"Yeah, I guess I am." Logan crossed his legs. "I think we need to get away."

"Logan! How can you say such a thing? That would only fuel the gossip fires. That's the last thing I need."

"Aw, Eve, don't worry. Even if the kids find out, it wouldn't be the end of the world."

Eve was responsible for the camp and could think of lots of problems such knowledge could make. She doubted seriously if

Tim Carlisle would like hearing that she and Logan were sleeping together, to say nothing of the parents. "Logan, how do you think the parents or Tim would feel if they knew that two of the instructors were having an affair practically within view of the kids?"

"I guess you're right about that." Logan rose and looked outside. "Maybe I'd better go. Besides, I've got a class."

"I suppose so." Eve didn't want him to go, but she couldn't think of a way to stop him. "Have fun!" she called as the door slammed shut behind him.

"You should have asked him, silly," she chided herself. In that moment, Eve realized she wasn't a nineties woman, whatever that was. She couldn't just come right out and ask him if he'd had a vasectomy. No, Eve wasn't that kind of woman.

Having the kids openly speculating about the possibility of an affair between her and Logan was embarrassing. A modern woman probably would have laughed it off and gone on with her lunch.

Eve settled back in her chair and began to think about all this again. She was in a dither over nothing. The sooner she forgot all this pregnancy stuff, the better off she'd be. But, in case she needed them, Eve decided to find a drugstore and purchase some protection—if she could manage to do so without humiliating herself too much.

Connie came merrily in, as if she hadn't a care in the world. "What's up, Evie?"

Eve smiled at the use of her childhood nickname. Nobody had called her that in a long time. "Nothing." Eve chickened out when it came down to telling Connie about her worries.

"Really? Amy said you seemed upset when you stopped by a while ago." Connie eyed Eve speculatively. "Does this have anything to do with a certain tennis pro that we all know and love?"

"Don't be silly." Eve rose and started to pace. There was no need in telling anyone since the problem had sort of resolved itself, in Eve's mind anyway. She could get condoms and one of those home pregnancy tests. "I just stopped by."

Connie took a piece of paper out of her pocket, unfolded it with a determination that made Eve regret writing the note. "It says here, that—"

"I know what the note says, Connie. I

wrote it, for goodness sake." Eve watched her lifelong friend sit down as if she didn't intend to move until she had a satisfactory explanation. "All right, all right. You're worse than a mother hen."

"Yes, I am. And right now, one of my chicks is in trouble." Connie patted the sofa. "Sit over here. I think we can talk better if that damned desk isn't between us."

Eve complied, curling her left foot beneath her as she sat down. "I . . . gee, I don't think I ever had this much trouble talking to anyone about a problem before."

"Eve, tell me about Logan. I know a part of the 'problem' as you call it, but I can't for the life of me figure out why it's bothering you."

"Connie, I don't . . . well, you see I haven't been . . ." Eve stammered, trying to broach the subject without embarrassing herself further.

"You don't take birth control pills, do you?" Connie said, finishing Eve's sentence for her.

"No. I don't. In recent years, I simply haven't needed to take them." Eve picked at the scratch on her nail polish. A flake of color chipped off and fell on her white shorts. "Now I'm worried."

"When's your period due?"

"I know the facts of life, Connie. I'm not trying to figure out if it's possible. I *know* it is. My problem is, well that really is the problem. I'm at my peak time for conceiving."

"Evie, you're in your midforties. Women your age, especially women who've never had a child, have a great deal of difficulty conceiving." Connie smiled reassuringly and tucked the paper back into her pocket. "I think you shouldn't worry about this unless you skip your period. Or if you're really worried, get a pregnancy test."

"Great, you sound like a high school guidance counselor." Eve rose and began to pace again. "That's only part of the problem, a major part, but still only a part. The other thing is, I need to get some protection now."

Connie chuckled and watched Eve pace for a few seconds. "I never thought I'd see the day that you were this upset over a possibility."

"To my way of thinking, it's a probability until it's proven to be untrue."

"I suppose you'd see it that way." Connie

stood up and hugged Eve. "Look, Eve, we'll cross that first bridge when we come to it. In the meantime, I'll make you an appointment with a doctor for birth control pills if that's what you want."

"I need something, that's for sure." Eve closed her eyes for a moment, picturing herself making love to Logan. "I don't see any change in my behavior patterns in the near future. Until the end of the summer, anyway."

"If you're not planning to continue this relationship after the end of the season, why not use condoms?"

"I could, I suppose. In fact, that's exactly what I was thinking, but . . ."

"But, what?"

"How do you think Logan will feel about that?"

"I think he should have thought of it himself. He's an adult. It's his responsibility as much as yours. More." Connie started for the door. "Maybe I should have a talk with him."

"Connie! Don't you dare!" Eve rushed over and caught Connie by the arm. "I'd be humiliated beyond anything I can imagine."

"Then you do it, Eve. You're an adult,

too. Both of you need to think of the consequences of your actions. And soon."

Eve watched Connie walk away. The
nurse was absolutely right. Eve, as well as
Logan, had acted irresponsibly. But if
their actions resulted in a pregnancy, Eve
would be the one who would have to deal
with the situation.

As she sat back down on the sofa, she
decided that she might like having a baby
after all.

Sixteen

Eve didn't have a great deal of time to think about babies during the afternoon. Lynne Pittard arrived in her white Riviera and navy blue top. At the sight of the car, Eve's mood improved considerably. Lynne was a very special lady.

Becky Gumm, Lynne's assistant, climbed out of the car first, her purse and a mystery novel tucked under her arm. Then Lynne popped out, a happy smile on her face. "Hi, Eve. Great to be here."

Eve chatted with them for a few minutes and then took them on the grand tour. "I've walked this way so often, I sometimes fail to notice how beautiful it is. Then I stop, look around me, and marvel at the beauty of nature. This," Eve said, gesturing widely, "is why I love this camp."

Lynne looked at the wildflowers dotting

the edge of the path that led to the lake. "I can see why. This is a gorgeous view."

Eve took them to the guest house and got them settled in. "I've saved the best for last."

"What's that?" Becky asked, looking around the neat room.

"The art gallery." Eve smiled with pride and led them down to the dining hall. "We were working so hard and producing so many beautiful things that I didn't know what to do with them. Here's the result."

"Wow! I'm impressed. How old did you say these kids are?" Lynne asked, walking past the pictures and stopping occasionally to look more closely at one here and there.

"Teenagers. Junior high and high school." Eve was proud of her students' accomplishments. "They're very creative."

"No animals, I see," Lynne noted with a smile.

"Not yet. We were planning to paint some, but we haven't gotten around to it yet."

"You'll love what we're doing." Lynne removed a photo book from her purse. "Look here."

Eve opened the little book and found several pictures of Lynne's daughters in wedding dresses. "Still paying for the weddings?"

"You know it. The pictures I want you to see are farther on."

Finding the ones Lynne was talking about, Eve broke into a grin. "These are great. The kids will love them. Which ones are you going to do?"

"I'm going to let them decide. I've got everything we need."

Becky turned from the picture she was looking at. "What's that smell?"

"Dinner," Eve said and hugged Becky. "You'll love it. Fresh cooked vegetables and baked chicken."

Logan walked in and threaded his way over to the ladies. "Hello! You must be Lynne."

Eve smiled. "I've been talking about you nonstop." She remembered the past few hours of tension. "Well, almost nonstop. This is Logan Mallory, resident tennis pro. Lynne Pittard and Rebecca Gumm."

"I've heard a lot about you, Logan."

"All untrue. Just ask Eve. She'll tell you the truth."

With a sly smile, Eve decided to get

back at Logan for all the little barbs he threw. "He's exactly what the newspapers say, Lynne. A rogue. Watch out for him."

After supper, they set up for Lynne's workshops. Becky bustled about as usual, issuing orders that Eve dared not disobey. Logan even offered to help.

Becky handed him a roll of paper towels and a pair of scissors. "Cut these into fourths."

Logan sat down, took a paper towel and cut it into four pieces. Becky watched for a moment, her hands on her hips while Lynne and Eve stood back to view the scolding. "Are you nuts? That'll take all night." Becky tore off about ten or fifteen sheets and cut them all at once. "Men just don't know how to do anything right," she muttered.

Logan grabbed her and gave her a big hug. "There are some things that we excel in, Becky."

"See! I told you he was a rogue. Watch out for him, Becky." Eve turned her back on Logan's withering glare.

"You just wait, Eve," he teased, throwing an empty paper towel tube at her. "I'll get even."

When the room was set up, Eve took

them to the campfire. Logan sat beside
her and she felt a little shy, like a schoolgirl on her first date. Since the pro-
nouncement at lunchtime that Logan and
Eve were an item, the kids seemed to accept it without question. Eve still had a
problem with a relationship that was being played out in front of everyone.

As they walked back to the cabins, Eve
and Logan said good night to Lynne and
Becky before continuing on. When they
reached Eve's cabin, Logan whispered. "I
won't come in tonight. Too many eyes, if
you know what I mean. Good night,
love."

Eve didn't know whether to laugh or
cry. Waking up wrapped in Logan's arms
was something she had looked forward to
all day, even if they had to be sneaky
about it. After her initial shock, Eve had
calmed down considerably, and thought
she could accept a more open arrangement—if nobody started to poke fun at
her.

People did fall in love, didn't they? It
was a natural thing to do. *Fall in love?*
Where did that come from? Eve stood in
her doorway, watching Logan walk toward
his own cabin. Could she really be falling

in love with him? That this might not be infatuation or lust, but true love—if such a thing even existed—stopped her cold.

Eve awoke early. Her body clock told her she hadn't slept more than two hours, but she couldn't lie in bed any longer. She rose, pulled on her warm-ups, and then left her cabin.

She aimed her flashlight on the trail that led to the beach. After a moment of standing there, she found a beach towel that had been left and sat down. Watching the moonlight ride the gently undulating surface of the lake, Eve thought about Logan. She'd really thought of little else for the past few days.

Ever since he'd come into her life, everything had changed. Was it for the better or for the worse? No matter how she felt personally, he'd had an impact on her life that was more unsettling than anything that had ever happened to her.

Hearing a noise behind her, Eve turned around to stare at the path. She could hear Logan cursing as he stumbled through the brambles. Stifling a laugh, she found her flashlight and turned it on.

"Here I am, Logan," she called softly and rose to shine the flashlight at him.

"Didn't it ever occur to you that a flash-light would come in handy when one walks through the woods at night?"

"I'm roughing it. No artificial light."

Eve giggled as he yelped again. "I'm sorry, but this is too funny."

"Yeah? You wouldn't think so if you walked in my briar- and bramble-scarred legs." Logan disengaged himself from the prickly shrubs and walked, as decorously as possible, to where Eve stood with the flashlight.

"Logan, why in the world don't you keep to the path?" Eve picked a few thorns out of his legs and then looked up at him. "Trust me, it's much better than trying to forge new ways through the woods."

He took her arm and walked her back to the beach towel where they sat down. "Eve, I'm going to be perfectly honest with you. I *do* start out on the path, but I lose it somewhere between here and my cabin. It's . . . I don't know. It's like every time I think I've got the direction figured out, somebody changes it on me."

"First thing tomorrow, I'm getting you a flashlight." Eve took the corner of the towel and dabbed at a spot of blood from one of the scratches. "Use it next time."

Logan leaned down and kissed her. When he drew away again, he breathed deeply. "Now why would I want to do that?"

"To keep from bleeding to death comes to mind almost immediately." She could hardly speak above a whisper. Her body was responding to Logan's presence, and she wanted nothing more than to lie in his arms.

"What? When I get to play doctor with you afterwards?" He kissed her again. "That's worth any amount of scratches."

"How about we make a deal?"

"I'm game . . . well, maybe I should listen to it first."

"From now on, you take better care of those manly legs by bringing a flashlight when you insist on strolling through the briar patch. Or better yet, use the light to help you keep to the path."

"I like the sound of that so far," he conceded, wrapping his arms around her and lying back to look at the moon.

"And," she whispered suggestively, turning in his arms to bring their bodies closer together, "I'll continue to play doctor anyway."

"You got a deal, doll." Logan kissed her again several times, each one more wonderful than the last. "We've got to stop meeting like this."

"What do you suggest?"

"I suggest we go out to dinner on Saturday night and then stop by my house at Tega Cay for the rest of the weekend."

"Logan, I can't be away from the camp that long."

"Yes, you can. You've got a staff that's great." Logan shifted so that he could prop on his elbow and look down into her eyes. In the moonlight, he could barely see them, but the twinkle of warm light was still there. "We could spend Sunday working on administrative stuff. You know Tim's arriving next week."

"That's right. Lorna and her crew will be back, too." Eve could feel herself giving in. Saturday was parents' day. Maybe she could work some sort of deal with Logan about Tony. "All right, Logan. I'll do it on one condition."

"Anything you say, love." Logan kissed her forehead. He could hardly keep from running up and down the beach. The

idea of a weekend all alone with Eve at
his apartment sent his pulse racing. He'd
make it perfect for her. After all, it was
her birthday, and Logan had already
made certain arrangements to make it the
best party she'd ever had.

"I want you to stand in for Tony's father."

Logan disentangled himself from Eve
and sat up. He drew his knees up to his
chin and propped his elbows on them. "I
can't do that, Eve."

Eve sat up. She knew that he was in
pain about something, but she felt that
she had to make him see how different
this was from anything that had ever happened to him. "Logan, whatever happened in the past has nothing to do with
this one day of . . . befriending a kid
who really needs you. You can't let him
down. He's counting on you."

"Yeah, but that's the reason I can't do
it." Logan stared across the lake. Somewhere in the distance, he heard a dog
howl, and the plaintive sound seemed to
fit his mood.

"Logan, I don't know what happened
to you. I can't pretend to know what has
made you this miserable, but nothing,

nothing is so bad that you can't talk about it with me." Eve put her arms around him and rested her head on his shoulder. "I care about you a lot, Logan. Trust me, please."

"Eve, you're one of the kindest, most caring people I ever met, but I can't talk about this. Not to you and not to anybody."

The pain in his voice brought tears to her eyes. What could have happened that was so horrible that he couldn't speak of it to anyone? "Logan, I want to . . . be more than friends with you. We're compatible in so many ways, but if you won't trust me, how can I fulfill my end of the bargain?"

Logan turned slightly so that he could see her. He wanted to tell her; he really did, but to give voice to the nightmare that had haunted him for twenty years would bring it back fresh in his mind again. There was no way he could withstand that agony a second time. He instinctively knew it would be the arbiter of his sanity—and he would lose.

Lynne's classes were delightful. The kids learned some new techniques and ended up with great paintings. In the two days she was there, they managed three paintings: a beautiful horse with a flowing mane, two bunnies huddled together in the snow, and a fawn.

As Lynne and Becky drove away, Lynne shouted, "We'll be back next year."

Eve walked back to the office. Tomorrow was parents' day, and Logan still hadn't agreed to serve as Tony's surrogate father. There was always a possibility that other parents might not come, but with the excited chatter among the kids about their parents, Eve saw her concerns grow.

She would wait until the very last moment. If Logan still refused, she would stand in herself. That, she felt, would be cheating Tony, but there was no help for it. Whatever plagued Logan refused to loosen its grasp for a half second.

After campfire that night, Eve was in a melancholy mood. She'd tried to bargain with Logan over a weekend together and felt horrible for it, especially since he was in such pain over the entire episode.

When she felt sure the kids were sleeping, Eve stole out of her cabin and crossed the compound in the shadows. As she passed Madora's cabin, she heard a rash of giggling.

"Otis, you behave!" came Madora's girlish voice.

Eve smiled. Some people, it seemed, were able to put aside their problems and fall in love.

When she reached Logan's cabin, the lights were out. As she raised her hand to knock on the door, she hesitated. What if he was asleep? No this is too important. I've got to tell him *now.*

Eve inhaled deeply and tapped on the door. "Logan?"

"Come on in. It's open." Logan scrambled from the bed and began to search for the light switch.

"Don't turn on the light," she whispered. Tilting her chin upward, Eve opened the door and walked in. "I don't want the 'gossip princess' to find out I'm here."

For a few seconds, Eve stood still while her eyes adjusted and then she walked over to the shadow that had to be Logan. "I need to talk."

"About what?" Logan led her the few steps to the bed and pulled her down beside him. He didn't want her stumbling over the cat-box or something.

"About . . . what we were talking about on the beach last night."

"Forget it, Eve, I'm not—"

"No, no, that's not it. I did something . . . I mean, I said something I shouldn't have and I'm sorry. I've come to apologize."

"About what?" he repeated, this time truly confused. "What do you have to apologize for?"

"For trying to bargain with you." Eve reached out and put her arms around him. "Logan, I never should have done that. I would love to go away for the weekend with you. No strings attached."

"Why the change of heart?" Logan asked, feeling suddenly better about the whole incident.

"Because, Logan, I was demanding that you trust me and I've never done anything to earn that trust." Eve looked at him in the darkness. She could see little of him, except where the outside light filtered in. From what she could tell, he was puzzled. "Trust has to be earned. I want you to trust me and if I barter with you over this, my actions send the exact opposite signal from the truth."

"That's a brain-full for openers." Logan slid his arms around her. "Eve, I really do trust you, but I'm protecting you. You don't want to know this. You really don't."

"Logan, if you told me you killed a man, I'd have to trust that you did it for an honorable reason. What could possibly be worse than that?"

"Not much, but don't ask. This is worse." Logan stood up. He began to pace in front of her. The space was narrow, too narrow. He stumbled over her feet and fell half-in and half-out of the bed. "Damn!"

"Logan! Are you hurt?"

"Only my pride, Eve. Only my pride." Logan righted himself and sat down again. "Look, let's agree that we can't talk about this yet. All right?" Logan rubbed his shin. "Damn, but that hurts. If we don't get this relationship started on an even keel, I'm going to be a good candidate for the hospital."

"Relationship? I thought you had sworn off relationships for one year."

"I swore off women completely for one

year, but somehow that doesn't seem to apply to you."

"Logan," she whispered, praying that she was interpreting him correctly. "I want to spend this weekend with you. Please accept my apology for trying to bargain with—"

"Hush, Eve," he said and kissed her soundly, drawing her down on the bed at the same time. "You talk too much."

Eve left after making love with Logan. This day was too important to start off by being discovered skulking outside his cabin. The campers were early risers and would surely see.

Her only consolation for leaving his bed and the pleasure he brought her with his body was that they would be together again that very night. After the parents left in the afternoon, she and Logan would leave as well.

She considered telling him that today was her birthday, but decided that if they were going to dinner, he might feel compelled to alert the restaurant manager and she would have to suffer the consequences. I'll tell him *tomorrow,* she de-

cided, when the deed is done and I can't
be embarrassed.

When breakfast was over, the kids were
restless. There were no classes today, but
the camp was festooned for a great festi-
val. There were to be games and sporting
events, an open house, lots of food and
fun for the parents and for the kids. Even
the counselors were excited.

Eve dressed carefully. She wanted to appear to be the perfect camp director,
though she could only judge by her own
father who's attire had been haphazard at
best. She checked with Madora about the
lunch menu and heartily approved. Today's selections were some of Eve's favor-
ites.

She stopped on her way across the compound. Why was Madora serving Eve's favorite foods? Did she remember that
today was Eve's birthday? It was possible.
Madora and Eve had been friends for
many years, though she seldom made a
big deal over her birthday.

And where was Logan? He hadn't been
at breakfast this morning. She'd even gone
to the parking lot, but his car was there.

Otis had gone to town in the Bronco. Maybe Logan had tagged along, but that didn't make much sense.

Nothing today made much sense, come to think of it.

Eve crossed to the first-aid cabin. Connie was ready for almost any eventuality. Amy was bustling about on some errand for Connie.

"I had to get her out of my hair," Connie explained. "She's a treasure, but she'll worry you to death when she's nervous."

"I'll see you soon," Eve said and backed out of the cabin. There was no need to worry about Connie's preparations; she could handle almost anything.

The cabins were decked out with welcome signs that gave the name of all the campers who resided there. As she passed by, she could see that the cabins were spotless. Kayla and Bert had done a good job in making sure that preparations were ready.

Eve went from there to the beach, where a swimming competition would take place. The whole area was decorated with brightly colored umbrellas, hand-painted paper by the art classes. At the end of the summer, each child would have his or her own umbrella to take home. She could never remember the beach looking this pretty.

Her next stop was the parking lot. People would begin arriving anytime now. For the rest of the morning, the kids would show their parents around the camp. Eve was proud that the camp looked so cheery. The campers were obviously as eager as she to show off their summer home to its best advantage.

Cars began to arrive. Eve stood at the edge of the parking lot with her campers. She didn't see Tony anywhere, nor did she expect to. She'd have to go looking for him if they were to enter the afternoon's events.

Eve looked everywhere. Worry for the child shoved aside her own desire to preside over the day's activities. She'd searched his cabin, snared another boy to check the latrines, been in and out of every building on the premises, and still hadn't turned him up.

A glance at her watch warned her that it was near lunchtime and she would be expected to make some sort of welcoming speech. If he wasn't in the dining hall, she planned to go looking for him. He might have really left as he'd said he would.

Despairing of finding him on the campsite, she went into the dining hall, trying desperately to hide her apprehension. When she stepped inside the door, a rousing cheer went up from all the kids and parents alike. Eve was stunned. Why were they cheering her?

And then she saw it. There was a banner that had to be five feet long and two feet wide that said HAPPY BIRTHDAY, EVE.

Heather and Gayle rushed over to guide her to a spot of honor. Eve stumbled along dumbly, barely able to understand what was going on. How had they discovered that today was her birthday?

Then she saw Connie, Madora, and Logan standing behind a huge birthday cake. Eve started to turn and run, but Gayle's grip was firm.

"Not a chance, Eve," Gayle whispered and started dragging her toward the cake.

Logan saw that Eve was about to bolt and hurried over to help Gayle, who still hadn't gained enough weight to withstand Eve's tugging. "No way, Eve," he said. "Come on and take your medicine."

"Medicine?" Eve murmured with a glare at her dearest friends. "More like poison."

"Yeah, right. I know you're not ashamed of your age, so just march right in there like a good girl and take all the honors due you on this day." Logan leaned down and blew in her ear. "The kids have been about to bust. I was afraid they couldn't keep the secret."

Eve stood facing the mob of people who'd gathered to wish her well and she couldn't help smiling. With a wave intended to tell them that she wasn't angry, she turned to Connie and Madora. "I'll deal with you traitors later."

To Eve's very great surprise, a group of about ten kids marched out of the kitchen wearing pots on their heads and banging pans with huge spoons. When they spotted her, they launched into an off-key version of "Happy Birthday," which the entire crowd helped them to finish.

Smiling sarcastically at Logan, Eve stepped soundly on his toes. "I seem to recall telling you something about how humiliating all this is."

"I suppose it's the price you pay for being loved."

Being loved. The words echoed in Eve's

mind. Nothing could have improved her spirits as much as that did, except if he'd said that *he* loved her.

Too late, Eve noticed that Lorna and her crew were filming the entire embarrassing event. But even more surprising than all this, she saw that Tony was tracking every step of Logan's. She glanced at Logan questioningly. He simply shrugged and smiled.

As if all the hoopla wasn't enough, Eve couldn't stop the tears from flowing as Tony struggled forward with a huge box. With a round of encouraging applause, Eve blew out all forty-six of her candles and grinned foolishly as the cameras rolled and still cameras flashed.

The box was taller than she. Eve couldn't imagine what could be packed in a box that was the size of a refrigerator, but was light enough for Tony to carry. When she opened it, she began to cry in earnest. It was a brand-new easel, an expensive one.

Then she noticed that Tim was there, and Jerry Kent. They were laughing and applauding, too. Logan guided her to a table laden with small presents. Each one contained a new tube of paint or a brush or something she could use in her art.

The last present was long and narrow. She opened it and found a gold palette knife from Logan.

Wondering what she'd done to deserve such a wonderful surprise, she slumped down into her seat and buried her head in her hands. How in the world could she get through the remainder of the day? She was spending tonight with Logan at his house.

And she felt like a virgin bride.

Seventeen

Logan and Tony won some of the events, but lost more than they won. The decision for Logan hadn't been easy, but he couldn't stand to see the kid so devastated that he was willing to leave camp.

Eve's words had helped, too. Though she hadn't said so, he realized he was selfishly letting his own personal tragedy come between the possibility of a happy memory for Tony and a new sorrow for a child who'd already seen too many.

By the time the parents began to leave, Logan was tired and dirty, but it had been a very satisfying day for him, as well as for the boy. Tony was a competitor. Logan had seen that from the beginning. He had a great deal of talent as an artist, but he showed a stunning prowess on the tennis court.

Logan showered and changed into a suit for the first time in nearly two months. He and Eve were going to dinner at the nicest restaurant in Charlotte.

He hadn't stopped to wonder what she would wear. It didn't matter to him. She was beautiful in everything she wore—or didn't wear. Logan assumed she had a dress or something a little fancier than shorts and a T-shirt. Beyond that, he was as eager as a teenager on his first date. He wanted to get started.

Carrying the corsage Otis had picked up this morning on the mail run, Logan knocked at her door.

Eve heard the knock and was panic stricken for a moment. What should she do? "Come in," she called finally. "I'll be down in a moment."

Tucking clean clothes and toiletries into a small tapestry bag, Eve glanced at her room. Was she leaving anything?

Unable to think of any vital item that she might be leaving behind, she walked down the stairs. Logan looked resplendent in his black suit. Eve studied him as she approached. He seemed so different, dressed like this.

"I'm ready," she said, her voice barely above a whisper.

"You're beautiful," he answered, his

voice breaking with anxiety. He laughed lightly, a little embarrassed by his own demonstration of emotion. "I sound like an adolescent."

She moved closer and touched his face gently, pulling him toward her. After kissing him with the lightest of touches, she smiled. "You look wonderful to me, no matter how old or young you are."

Logan watched her move as gracefully as a dancer, turning out the lights in the office. "That's a beautiful dress. It looks great on you. Oh, before you turn the lights out, let me pin this on you."

Happy that she'd selected the black silk dress, Eve looked down at the orchid; it would show wonderfully against the dark background. "Oh, Logan, this is lovely."

"Not as lovely as you." He pinned the corsage on her dress and then kissed her soundly. "If we don't get out of here now, we never will."

With a happy smile, Eve nodded. They slipped away in silence. Thanks to Logan, Connie and Madora had corraled the kids in the dining hall, making Eve and Logan's escape much easier. The drive into Charlotte was a quiet one, too quiet for Eve. She leaned over on Logan's shoulder and fell peacefully asleep.

Logan felt as if he held a treasure in his arms. The trust that meant so much to Eve was so evident in her face, an angelic picture in the lights of the oncoming traffic. What had he done to earn that trust? His mind echoed Eve's criticism of herself.

What did trust mean between two people in love? *In love?* Logan nearly slammed on the brakes. He glanced again at the woman lying tranquilly against his shoulder. Did he love Eve Travers?

That was a startling thought. Logan hadn't loved anyone in a very long time. There was no doubt that he felt protective of Eve, that he craved her body close to his own all the time, making his tennis lessons a painful separation from her instead of the joy he'd experienced at the beginning of the season.

He eased the Jag into the parking lot of the restaurant and slipped it between two cars. He hated to move, for fear of waking her. Maybe he should have taken her directly to his house instead of the restaurant. But that wasn't fair to her. She deserved to be treated with kindness, respect, and love on this day of all days.

He moved Eve a little and then slid the gear shift into neutral. Turning the ignition off, he glanced over at Eve. She was waking from her slumber. "Eve, darling, we're here."

"Where?"

"At the restaurant." Logan pulled her into his arms and held her for a moment. She was wearing lipstick, and he didn't want to embarrass her by smearing it with a kiss, so he brushed his lips against her forehead. "Sit where you are."

He got out and went around to her side of the car to open her door. When she was in his arms, he held her for a long moment. "We'd better go in. We don't want to miss our reservations."

She took his arm obligingly and then stopped. "You didn't tell them it was my birthday, did you?"

"No. I swear, Eve." Logan put his arm around her and urged her forward. "After what we did today at the camp, I wouldn't dare."

Eve glanced up at him wryly, her eyebrows knitted together. "Well, I suppose I'll have to trust you or starve to death."

"We can always go to a drive-thru some-where."

"Not on your life." Eve stopped again. "Logan, this is a rather delicate question, but—" She was embarrassed and didn't know exactly what to say to him. "Logan, do you . . . I mean, can you afford this restaurant?"

Logan laughed. "I guess I deserve that. Yeah, I can. Jerry gave me an advance on my Tennis Pro money."

"Bless his heart. I always knew he was a good man."

"He gave me something else, too."

"What?"

"A check to cover all Gayle's expenses and even a little extra."

"But why?" Eve asked, halting once again.

"Look, Eve, if we don't take more than two steps at a time, the restaurant will be closed before we ever get inside," Logan teased and gazed down into her beautiful eyes. "We can talk later."

When they stepped inside the restau-rant, Logan waved to several people. Eve felt a little odd; she wasn't used to being seen in public in the company of a celeb-rity. The maître d' seated them at a nice secluded table and immediately brought a bottle of champagne along with the menu.

Eve sipped her champagne as she studied the menu. Finally she closed it and looked across the table at Logan. "I presume you've eaten here before. You choose."

"I have and I will." Logan closed his menu and when the waiter arrived, he ordered a shellfish pastry for an appetizer, followed by a house salad with the Parmesan dressing, and lobster tails for the main course.

"My, that sounds like a lot of food."

"It is, but it's all great."

"Thanks, Logan," Eve said in a low voice.

"For what?" he asked, sliding around the semicircular booth to sit closer to her.

"For doing what you did today."

"The party?"

"No, well, yes. Thanks for the party." Eve touched his hand and smiled up into his face. "But, I mean, thanks for being Tony's friend today."

"Don't mention it."

"But I need to talk about it." Eve didn't want to cast a pall over their dinner, but she felt as if she had to express her feel ings on the subject. "I know what that must have cost you emotionally. Thank you."

Logan shrugged and fingered his silverware. "Just say that I'm working toward earning your trust."

"But you already have it," she protested.

"I realize that, Eve." Logan slid his arm around her. Her lovely scent filled his nostrils and he wanted to take her away where they could be alone. "But I haven't earned your trust yet. You told me in the wee hours of the night, that trust had to be earned."

"I was speaking of me. I feel that I need to earn your trust."

"You've done everything in the world already. You don't owe me anything." Logan leaned forward to kiss her, but the waiter approached with their appetizers. Frustrated by the necessity of eating, Logan concentrated on his food—and on banishing the potentially embarrassing evidence of his desire for Eve.

Eve couldn't remember eating a meal as delicious in a long time, except of course at the camp, but Madora's cooking was different. It was good, hot, nutritious, and filling. This meal was one to savor, to linger over. A dribble of butter caught on her lip and she licked it off with relish. This night would become one of her fondest memories, of that she was certain.

Logan watched Eve eat. When she licked the glistening butter off her lip, his problem renewed itself in full force. With each sip of wine, he knew he was getting more deeply into trouble. If something didn't happen soon, he'd find himself unable to leave the restaurant.

Eve leaned back against the plush leather of the booth. "I don't know when I've enjoyed a meal more."

Logan shifted in his seat to adjust his discomfort. He'd given up on banishing it and had decided to try to manage it instead. "Neither do I."

The ever-alert waiter came and took their plates. "Coffee with dessert?"

Logan glanced at Eve and then nodded. "Yes, bring us each a serving of the raspberry mousse."

"Oh, Logan, I don't think I can eat another bite," Eve protested, though she thought the idea of the mousse sounded wonderful.

"Then bring us one serving and two spoons."

Eve smiled. "Maybe I can handle that."

The waiter reappeared quickly with their coffee, and Logan winked at Eve. "This place is great, isn't it?"

"I love it. I think it will become one of my favorite places."

Logan reached into his pocket and pulled out the small package he'd been carrying all evening. The little bow and flower were a little flattened, but it was still pretty. "This is for you."

Eve stared at the gift in astonishment. "But, Logan, I already got a present from you. Back at the camp."

"That was nothing. This is special, from me to you."

Eve's fingers trembled as she tried to remove the wrapping paper without tearing it. When she realized her efforts were futile, she ripped through the pale lavender paper and pulled out the small box. "This is too much," she murmured as she removed the lid. When she looked inside the box, she saw a gold charm in the shape of an artist's palette. It was attached to a fine gold bracelet. "Oh, Logan, this *is* too much."

"It's perfect. A perfect gift for a perfect lady." Logan smiled happily as she continued to stare at the charm. "Let me help you put it on." He lifted the bracelet from the box and fidgeted with the clasp.

"Here, let me." Though her fingers still quivered, she managed to open the clasp.

Logan took the bracelet, enjoying for a moment the fluid weight in his hand, and then latched it around her slender wrist. "There. Perfect. Just like I said before."

Eve looked up at him and then closed her eyes briefly. "I don't know what to say. It's the loveliest gift I've ever received. Thank you."

She inclined her head toward him and met his kiss. Eve would have lingered there, but she sensed a presence and drew away. When she turned around, there was a woman standing there staring at them.

"Excuse me, but Logan, I'd like to introduce myself. My name is Cora Whitfield." The pretty woman giggled and held out her hand. With hardly a glance at Eve, she simpered, "My grandson needs a tennis coach so badly. We're members of the Country Club of—"

"Mrs. Whitfield," Logan interrupted,

"It's lovely to meet you, but I'm not a tennis coach." He caught Eve's hand in his and squeezed it gently. "And, as you can readily see, my friend and I were enjoying a quiet dinner to celebrate a very special occasion. So, if you don't mind—"

"Oh, really? What's the occasion?" She took a moment to assess Eve and apparently decided that she was insignificant. With her Marilyn Monroe looks, she leaned forward, showing a great deal of cleavage. "I'll bet I can . . . talk you into coaching my grandson. You know, make you a deal you can't refuse." She pouted suggestively. "He's a prodigy if I ever saw one."

"Pardon me, madam," the waiter said, edging between the woman and the table. "I apologize for the delay in bringing your dessert. Please enjoy it."

Logan glanced meaningfully at the waiter who nodded almost imperceptibly. The woman chatted on, as if she and Logan were the best of friends.

Eve wondered how Logan ever managed to go anyplace without being recognized and then mobbed. Maybe that was one of the reasons he'd gotten the reputation of being a bad boy. People usually didn't want anyone with so foul a temper around them.

The maître d' came over to the table. "Madam, would you please come with me?"

"Why? Why should I want to go with you? Can't you see that Logan and I are having a conversation?" The woman's voice rose to a threatening level.

"Mrs. Whitfield," Logan said quietly. "I do apologize for cutting our conversation short, but my friend and I are in somewhat of a hurry. We'd like to finish our meal and leave. If you want something from me, contact my manager, Jerry Kent."

"Oh, I understand," the woman said, glaring at Eve. "I'll be in touch."

Eve watched the woman stalk away. "I never imagined you'd have such a problem just eating a meal in a restaurant. Does that happen often?"

"Often enough. Not usually here, though. People usually realize that such behavior is inappropriate." Logan glanced around the room and saw that the other patrons were staring at Mrs. Whitfield in open distaste. Several nodded, as if to say that they believed Logan handled himself well in an awkward situation.

"Well, we won't let her spoil our meal." Eve picked up her spoon and smiled at Logan. "Race you to the middle."

Eve could hardly believe the dessert was so delicious—or that she still had room for it. "I'm stuffed."

"Hardly," Logan said derisively and signaled the waiter. "Let's get out of here before someone else decides I'm open game."

He paid the bill and rose to help Eve from her seat. Without glancing the way of Cora Whitfield, he picked up the box and handed it to Eve. "Do you want the box?"

"I'd better put it in my purse." Eve didn't want to show how foolishly sentimental she was. She'd already decided to fill the box with sand, rewrap it, and use it as a paper weight on her desk back at the camp.

Logan placed his hand on the small of her back and they walked out of the restaurant. Furious over the encounter, Logan forced a smile. "Would you like the top down?"

"Oh, yes. Please."

He helped her into the car and then got in on the driver side. "Anything you want, birthday girl."

In moments, the top was down and Eve looked up at the sky. "It's a beautiful night for a ride with the top down, isn't it?"

Logan's anger was gradually dissipating. "It's a beautiful night, period." He threaded his way among the cars that jammed the Billy Graham Freeway and then turned onto Interstate 77 heading south.

"How long does it take to get to your house?" Eve asked, beginning to get the flutters in her stomach again. Sleeping with him at the camp had been one thing, but this seemed like such a big step. It was almost as serious as being taken home to meet his family.

"Not long. It's about a fifteen-minute drive."

"That doesn't seem like very long. I mean, Tega Cay is in South Carolina and Charlotte is in North Carolina."

"Yeah, but they're both hugging the state line."

Eve watched the miles roll by quickly as the car sped down the highway. Soon they crossed the state line and were back in South Carolina. As they headed away from Charlotte, the ambient light interfered with her stargazing less and less. "Oh, Logan, what a magnificent sky."

The moon had risen and was like a large opal against an ebony sky scattered with diamonds. The wind whistled by them as they sliced through the night, all alone for stretches on the freeway.

He exited at Gold Mine Road and turned right. "It's not far at all now."

Eve leaned back and relaxed. There was nothing she could do for now except enjoy the ride and the view.

After they passed a shopping center at an intersection with a traffic light, Logan stopped. "Better go back and pick up a few things. I'm afraid the cupboards are bare."

"Fine," she said, in a dreamy mood.

They went into the grocery store and picked a cart. Hurrying down the aisles, Logan selected an array of fresh vegetables and fruits. "Don't want to eat junk food, do we?"

"Anything is fine with me."

Logan looked at the meats, picked up a couple of steaks, some fresh shrimp and scallops, bacon and eggs. They stopped at the dairy counter and took milk and cheese. "I think we need a bottle of wine and we're set."

After paying the cashier, Logan loaded the groceries into the car and they sped off. He glanced at Eve. She seemed a little preoccupied, and he didn't understand why. "Did that woman bother you, Eve?"

"I don't know, Logan. A part of me was jealous, I think." That was a revelation to Eve. She never thought she'd be jealous of anyone. "Did it bother you?"

Logan slowed down as they entered what looked to be a housing development. "This is Tega Cay," he said, not sure yet how to answer her question. "A bedroom community."

Eve glanced out the window. They were passing a neat little police station. The divider in the road was well manicured and dotted with young trees. Every now and then they passed the entrance to a subdivision. "So it's just a village made up of several subdivisions?"

"That's about it. We have a mayor, city government, and a police force. I'll take you down to the *city* sometime if you'd like." He turned left and drove by the clubhouse and through a part of the golf course.

"This is a beautiful community."

Logan nodded. "It's quiet. There's only one way in and one way out. Kind of makes you feel safe."

She noticed the pretty houses, clustered among huge trees. Soon they went down a road that led to the lake. Compared to the little lake at the camp, Lake Wylie looked huge.

Logan turned into a parking space. "We're home."

Eve glanced at him. *We're home*. That had a nice ring to it. "I'm happy to hear that."

They each took grocery bags and Logan unlocked the door. He flipped on the light switch. "Make yourself at home."

She followed him into the spacious kitchen. Eve could tell in an instant that he was at home in the room. Apparently he hadn't been just flirting when he'd asked for that recipe on the day they met. "Nice kitchen."

Logan smiled. "One of my favorite rooms." He put the groceries away and then turned to her. "Ready for the grand tour?"

"By all means." Eve took his hand and they walked from the kitchen into the dining room. They went through a pair of sliding glass doors opened onto a deck that ran the length of the house. "This is really nice."

"Another one of my favorite places." Logan led her back into the dining room and then into the living room.

Eve glanced around. There was a fireplace in one corner of the large room. It's vaulted ceiling had skylights and exposed beams and sliding glass doors onto the deck. She liked the warm decor. Logan was smiling proudly. "Another one of your favorite rooms?"

"Yes, how did you guess?"

"Because you were grinning so foolishly."

"Foolishly, eh? I'll have to remember that." He took her hand and they walked across the plush carpet into the bedroom. Looking down at her, he started to speak again. "Another—"

"One of your favorite rooms," she said in unison with him. "I think you just love this house."

"Actually, I do." Logan pointed at the sliding glass doors. "I like my view of the lake."

From there they went downstairs. He showed her the great room that divided two bedrooms and an office. There were sliding doors off each of the bedrooms and the great room. "This porch is screened to keep the bugs away."

"Logan, your home is beautiful. I love it," Eve said honestly. Each room had huge closets and there were closets lining the wall between the staircase and the office. "Plenty of storage space."

"I like it because it's so spacious." Logan led her back upstairs. "I'll go get your bag out of the car."

While he was gone, Eve did her best to still the butterflies fluttering in her stomach. She loved this house. She loved Logan. Dared she believe that they could ever live there together?

She glanced around. The place was spotless. Even the inside of his refrigerator had been so clean a surgeon could have operated in there. He must have a maid, she decided. But then she realized that the place was very much like him: immaculate in every way. Maybe he did his own housekeeping. After all, he was a bachelor. How much cleaning could he need to do?

Eve gazed at her new bracelet. Logan had seen her look at it when they'd gone shopping. He was very kind to buy it, but even more than that, to wait until he saw something she liked and to select that item. Not many men took that much time to decide on a gift for a woman.

Logan returned. Eve was standing in the middle of the room, looking all around. He couldn't figure out exactly what she was looking at, but she seemed to be examining each component of the room in detail.

"Eve, where should I put your bag?" he asked, hoping she'd say to put them in his bedroom.

She hesitated a moment and then turned around to face him. "Put them wherever you think . . . best."

"I'll just put them in my room, then," he said and took the small piece of luggage to the master bedroom. When he returned to the living room, he put some CDs on the stereo. "Have a seat. I'll pour us a glass of wine."

Eve sat down on the sofa and listened

to the first strains of *Rhapsody in Blue* by Gershwin. She laid her head back and closed her eyes. When she felt that Logan had returned, she opened them again and turned to glance toward the door to the kitchen. "I like your taste in music."

"Great. I love good music, too." Logan walked over, handed her a tulip stem glass of wine, and sat down beside her. "When I came back into the room, I thought you might be asleep. You were so still."

Eve sipped her wine and smiled. "I'm not that far gone . . . yet."

"Pretty rough day, eh?"

"The day was bad enough, but last night was worse."

"Last night?" Logan asked, recalling their wonderful lovemaking. "What was so wrong with last night?"

"I didn't get any sleep, silly." Eve laughed. "Do I detect an ego that might have been injured?"

"No might about it." Logan kissed her on the tip of her nose. "My memory of the event was something akin to spectacular. I hope yours was, too."

"Hmm," she said and cut her eyes at him. She was seeing something she'd never seen before with Logan. Uncertainty. It was nice to know that she didn't suffer that malady alone. "My memory makes me want to . . . curl up in bed and think about it."

"If you're sleepy, you can take a nap."

"Nap?" she asked, her eyebrows rising in astonishment.

"Only a short one." Logan stood, offered his hand to her, and pulled her up. "Otherwise, why don't we go and relax in the hot tub?"

"That sounds wonderful." Eve waited while he went and grabbed the bottle of wine.

He led her through the bedroom into the huge bathroom. The water in the hot tub was swirling around. "I turned the Jacuzzi on while I was in here a while ago."

"Aha! You planned this, did you?"

"You bet your life, I did." Logan took her glass of wine and placed it on the edge of the tub. "I have something I need to check on. Why don't you go ahead and hop in?"

Eve watched him walk out of the room. She knew he was trying to put her at ease by allowing her to undress alone. "Logan," she called after him. "You don't have to leave."

He turned and hesitated. "I thought you might feel more comfortable having a few minutes alone."

She walked to the edge of the bedroom and took his hand. "I may need help with this dress."

"I'd be happy to oblige." Logan slid his arm around her and they went back into the bathroom.

He unzipped the dress for her and watched it slide to her feet. She was wearing a pair of matching black lacy panties, a dainty garterbelt, and a filmy bra. "I can see how you might need help."

Eve smiled. She'd bought the sexy garments, thinking that she might need them one day, at Belk's when she and Logan picked up Gayle Barton. Maybe she was looking forward to this night.

Logan pulled her into his arms. "I see that you're wearing your conservative 'black' tonight."

"You would have preferred pristine white?" she teased and kissed his chin. "Or, perhaps, very serviceable cotton undergarments."

"Not in a million years." Logan held

her back and gazed at her. "I've seen women dressed in less, but nobody has ever done to me what you do."

"Should I take that as a compliment or be angry about your other lady friends?" Eve teased, with a pouty look on her face. His expression was worth more compliments than she'd ever received in her life.

"Eve, you have to believe me when I tell you I haven't been with another woman since before New Year's Eve." Logan noticed the smile teasing the corners of her mouth. "You'd better watch that saucy attitude, woman. I'd hate to have to bring you down a notch or two."

"And how might you do that?"

"I might just beat you the next time we race across the lake." Logan pulled her roughly to him. "You're not dealing with a wimp anymore."

"I don't think I ever was, Logan," she whispered, willing him to kiss her. "I know I never was."

Logan kissed her long and hard, his mouth covering hers hungrily. Plundering her sweet mouth, he stripped off the remainder of her clothes. He could hardly wait to remove his own.

"Here, let me help you," she said her

lips still pressed against his. Eve unbuttoned his shirt and then slid it down his arms. "Don't keep a lady waiting."

Needing no persuasion, Logan quickly took off his clothes and led her to the hot tub. "Easy, don't slip."

He helped her into the tub before following her. Once inside the whirling water, he pulled her into his arms again. The water swirled about them, foaming and bubbling as he kissed her again and again.

For once in his life, he didn't want to rush the moment when they'd come together. Anticipation, with Eve in his arms, was nearly as wonderful as making love.

Her response surprised him. She'd always been a willing lover, but something had changed and he didn't know what it was, nor did he want to stop and ask about it. All he knew and cared about was that she was his, at least for now.

Eighteen

Eve slid easily into Logan's lap. She was as hungry for him to make love to her as he was for her. She vaguely wondered why they even bothered to go out to dinner, but the thought vanished quickly when he kissed her breasts, one and then the other.

That she could no longer think rationally didn't bother Eve; she simply wanted to feel instead of think. She wanted to be cherished, if not for a lifetime, then for a short while and she wanted Logan to be the man who did so.

His fingers worked magic on her body and she soon found herself filled with him, taking her breath away. They moved together in a rhythm enhanced by the frothy water caressing them and by the beautiful strains of Gershwin, as well as by their own ministrations. Eve could hardly remain in his grasp. The water added a fluidity to his touch, a silken grasp that sought every nerve ending at once and set it to singing within her.

In a frenzy now, Eve wriggled in his arms, longing, begging for the release she knew he withheld from her. "Now, Logan," she whispered, writhing in his embrace.

Eve matched his increased motion. Thrusting herself headlong into the merging of their bodies, she felt the coming tide of satisfaction welling within her. When it reached its crest, she cried out with relish as she felt him spill his seed within her.

Something was wrong, but she couldn't think clearly. She was supposed to have done something.

In the euphoria of the afterglow of lovemaking, Eve tried to think rationally, but all thought abandoned her to her senses. She could feel Logan still within her. She could smell his spicy cologne. She heard the sweet sound of his voice as he whispered loving words in her ear. She still tasted his kisses.

But she couldn't think.

They got out of the water and Eve stood there dreamily while Logan toweled her dry. Their lovemaking still held her in its sweet cocoon of rapture, and she was unwilling to break free.

Logan carried Eve to his bed. As she lay there with her eyes closed, he admitted to himself that he loved her. No, his feelings were much deeper than love; Logan Mallory adored her.

When he was dry, he climbed in beside her on the big king-size bed and wrapped his arms around her. "Are you awake, my love?"

"Sort of," she replied dreamily.

"I adore you," he whispered, kissing her earlobe and then the hollow of her neck.

Eve heard the words in her silken cocoon and opened her eyes. Had she heard him correctly? "What did you say?"

"I said that I adore you, you beautiful, bewitching woman." Logan held her close, inhaling the fragrance that clung to her hair.

"And, I you, Logan Mallory," she answered in a soft voice. "I adore you."

Eve awoke to Logan's kisses. She cuddled against him, their arms entwined, her legs laying across his. "Morning."

"Do you expect breakfast in bed?"

"Hmm," she said, opening her eyes but a sliver.

When she came fully awake, she smelled bacon and coffee. Eve propped herself up on her elbow and glanced around. She was alone in Logan's big bed, though his scent clung to the sheets and pillows around her. "Logan?"

He walked into the room carrying a tray. "I bear nourishment for the sleeping beauty."

"Smells divine." Eve pulled herself into a sitting position. "I can come to the table."

"Not on your life." He placed the tray on her lap and climbed in beside her. "You asked for breakfast in bed and that is exactly what you get."

"You are a gentleman and a scholar," she said, taking a piece of buttered toast and slathering it with strawberry preserves.

She ate with relish. "You're a good cook."

"Do I detect a note of surprise?"

"Yes, I confess I didn't really believe you did a lot of cooking." Eve remembered the day at Tennis Pro when they'd first met. "I thought when you asked for the magazine you were poking fun at me."

"I wondered why you got so steamed." Logan leaned over and kissed her lingeringly. "Usually it takes people a lot longer to get that angry with me."

"It was partly because I was carrying a lot of emotional baggage that day." Eve finished her breakfast and then looked at Logan. "I'd been turned down by every company that I could find that had ever given a grant or donation to charity."

"Yeah, well, we all have our baggage to carry, don't we?" Logan moved the tray and slid into bed beside her. "Do you want to talk or make love?"

"What do you think?" Eve kissed him, for the first time teasing him with her tongue as he had done so often with her.

"I say, forget everything else but you."

To Eve's surprise, their lovemaking was every bit as passionate as the night before. They luxuriated in each other's bodies, Eve taking her turn at tempting and teasing Logan as she improved her prowess in bed.

When Logan finally roused her from the bed, they showered together. Dressed in shorts and a fresh shirt, Logan wrapped his arms around Eve from behind as they looked out over the deck railing to the lake. "Want to take a civilized walk?"

She looked up at him, over her shoulder. "What's that supposed to mean?"

"It means, my dear nature lady, that I don't intend to take you into a bramble patch."

"I never did that to you."

"Oh, yes, but you did," Logan protested, tightening his grip. "Many times."

"And just how did you arrive at that erroneous conclusion?" Eve wriggled until she could turn in his arms and look him squarely in the face.

"By going to that damned beach so much."

"What does that have to do with you?"

"I had to try to follow you," he said, kissing her forehead and then her nose and then her lips. "I couldn't resist."

Eve and Logan walked for miles it seemed to her. The terrain and streets around his house were steep and hilly. "You should get a good workout here."

"Yeah, I should, but I never have done much walking here."

"Why not?"

"Well, I haven't lived here for very long." Logan stopped at the top of the hill and peered out across the lake. "I moved here after Wimbledon last summer."

Eve recalled the articles that told of Logan's ignominious defeat at the racquet of an unseeded player. "What made you choose this place?"

"I've always lived in or around Charlotte, but I liked the isolation here."

"But there are houses all around you."

"True, but I don't know anybody and they don't know me." Logan shrugged his shoulders and caught her hand. As they started walking down the hill, he remembered the horrible events that had precipitated his move. "I swore never to play tennis again."

"Logan!" she exclaimed, stopping and gazing into his brown eyes. "That's absurd."

Even now, the memories were painful. "No, it isn't Eve. I was the toast of tennis at one time. Reporters were referring to me as the grand old master of tennis, not the young hotshot that I once was. I admit that I was astonished to discover just how right they were."

"So you came here."

"I ran. I came here, hid out." Logan walked with her down into his yard and then into the house. "I sat here for months, eating and drinking and doing nothing but feeling sorry for myself and letting my well-toned muscles turn to jelly."

"You have nothing to be sorry for. You were a wonderful player. You still have a lot to offer the world." Eve tried to recall the articles. "What's wrong with the Seniors Tennis Circuit?"

"I was too proud to admit that I belonged there."

"And now?"

He looked down at her and grinned foolishly. "I'm learning that I'm not as proud as I thought I was. I'm looking forward to playing next year."

"I'm glad to hear that." Eve was happy for him, but that made her wonder about her own life. Where did she fit into his scheme of things?

When they were inside, Logan told her to make herself at home while he prepared dinner. He scrambled around in the kitchen for a moment and then went back to the living room. "Do you need anything?"

"No, but I thought we were going to throw a couple of steaks on the grill."

"Even that takes preparation." Logan blew her a kiss and returned to the kitchen.

Eve sat down on the sofa. There was a huge scrapbook on the coffee table. She picked it up and began to look through it. He'd included many of the articles she'd read when confronted with the fact that he was coming to Camp Reach for the Stars. There were others she hadn't seen, some a great deal more complimentary than the negative press she'd found.

She was fascinated by the pictures of Logan as a young man, some from the time when he was just a boy. He'd won plenty of championships in his junior high school days before he'd turned pro.

In all the material, she found there was little or no mention of his private life. That one article she'd discovered that revealed that his son had died was conspicuously absent from this album.

Eve sat back and thought about that omission. Why would he purposely eliminate the one group of articles that referred to his son's death? Was it because he simply couldn't bear to be reminded of his son? There had to be a connection between that tragic event and the way he felt about the campers he was forced to deal with this summer.

More than anything she could think of, Eve wanted to understand his feelings, to comprehend the reasons he shied away from contact with children. Was it that he couldn't face the memories that the children brought?

Why? Why couldn't Eve figure this out?

Logan put the steaks on the grill where the potatoes had been cooking for some time. He went back into the kitchen and poured the heavy cream into the pan, blending it with his whisk until he dumped in the noodles.

He poured the seafood fettucine into a bowl and placed it on the table outside. His salad was ready to be tossed and the dressing added. "Eve, go and wash up for dinner," he called.

Eve washed her hands and went into the kitchen. "Smells heavenly."

"Take the salad bowl and go out on the deck. We're eating there."

Logan grabbed the steamed broccoli, a bottle of wine, and two glasses, and followed her outside. "Sit anywhere you like."

Glancing at the table, Eve was pleasantly surprised. There were two candles, ready to be lit. The table was set with a pretty geometric pattern and the silverware was lovely. "How beautiful."

"Only for you. Otherwise, I eat on paper plates."

"Somehow, I doubt that." Eve sat down and allowed him to serve her. "Logan, this is wonderful."

"Don't say that until you taste it." Logan placed a filet mignon on her plate, followed by a baked potato. "The seafood fettucine is sort of an appetizer."

"I'm glad we took that long walk or I'd never be able to eat all this."

"You keep telling me stuff like that. I've seen you eat at the camp and you never put on an ounce." Logan tasted the fettucine. "Here, let me grind some fresh Parmesan cheese for you."

Eve ate until she thought she would explode. "Now I need to go jogging or I'll be miserable for the rest of the night."

"Bring your plates. You can help clear the table."

"I'll do the dishes."

Logan swung around and glared at her. "No woman does the dishes in my house."

"I didn't mean anything by it. I was just offering to help." Eve couldn't believe he'd gotten so upset by her proposal to do the dishes. Every man she knew anything at all about would have jumped at the chance to have his date—or whatever she was—clean up the kitchen.

"I'm sorry. It's just that I'm a little touchy about that." Logan followed her into the kitchen. "Eve, I'm going to level with you."

"I would appreciate that." She put her stack of dishes on the counter and turned to face him.

"I'm, well, I *was* a true bachelor. When the house got messed up, I'd bring some chick home for the weekend. Usually she would clean up my messes." Logan rinsed the dishes and put them in the dishwasher. "When I made my vow to stay away from women for at least a year, getting someone in for the weekend was my greatest temptation. I had to learn to clean up the place myself. I don't want to fall back into my old ways."

Eve studied him for a minute. "Then I'll just go in the living room and put on some music."

As she walked from the room, Eve felt a little funny. Logan was like no man she'd ever met. That he was tortured by his son's death was an understatement, but she could see that he was trying to work through whatever devils plagued him about that. And then there was the scene she'd just witnessed. How many men, no matter how many resolutions they'd made, would refuse to accept a woman's help in the kitchen?

How could Eve help him? She'd never had any psychology courses other than those required for classroom teaching on the high school level, and that gave her very little basis for knowing which way to go, what questions to ask. Maybe if she didn't press him about it, he'd feel more at ease to talk to her.

Damn, but she felt so helpless.

Logan walked into the living room. Eve was standing with her back to him, facing a cold fireplace. He felt terrible about snapping at her like he had, but it had come from deep down within him, another result of speaking without thinking.

"Eve," he said finally, knowing that she must be furious with him. "I'm sorry. I'm truly sorry, but I am like I am."

She turned slowly and looked at him, measuring the depth of emotion cradled in his words and etched in his face. "Logan, I'm going to say this one time. And, when I do, you can throw me out or take me to your heart, but I must say and do what I think is best for us . . . for me."

Logan said nothing. For once his quick tongue abandoned him.

"I love you, Logan, but for our relationship to have any meaning whatsoever, you have to be honest with me." Eve saw the lines deepen around his eyes and mouth and forehead. Fearing that he would throw her out before she finished, she still knew that she had to tell him what was in her heart. "You've got to trust me. And you don't."

"Eve," he began, but stopped. How could he answer that? Did he trust her? Of course he did, but was it the kind of trust that she was talking about?

"Take me back to camp, Logan."

* * *

Logan sat in his cabin and stared at a bug marching across the wooden floor. The bug seemed to know where he was going. Did Logan? He made vows he didn't keep. He made promises he forgot. He accepted responsibilities that he couldn't handle.

No wonder Eve was so angry with him. He thought back to the reasons he was the way he was. It began when he started playing tennis. A power-hungry mother threw him into lessons at the cost of everything else in his life. But Logan could forgive that. She saw a talent and wanted him to make the most of it.

His childhood had been nonexistent practically. After more than two hours of contemplation, he realized that he didn't care about that, nor did Eve. What he had become, as a result of his instant adulthood, was a problem.

Perhaps his other troubles stemmed from that time in his life. If that was true, then his lack of ability to trust might also come from that. Simplistic, he decided. Maybe even wishful thinking.

And what about little Brandon? Pain

tore through Logan as he remembered the towheaded child with huge brown eyes, so loving, so dependent. Logan had let him down. More than once.

Tears formed in Logan's eyes as he remembered the innocent hugs and kisses that could hold the world at bay, that made a Wimbledon loss seem like a sand castle caught in the tide, like nothing. And the trust. Brandon had trusted Logan.

Could he recapture his own childhood? Logan stared out his window at the trees swaying in the cool summer night air. Where did one begin to go back and find his lost youth?

He gave Muzzle a couple of treats, feeling that her scorn was lessening enough for her to take his handout. She purred and licked his fingers. The cat trusted him. Eve trusted him. Did that make him trustworthy? No, not by a long shot. What, if anything, did?

Logan stroked the cat for a few more minutes before she jumped out of his lap and curled up on his pillow. His thoughts were scattered, but they all led back to the same thing: his childhood.

So, he'd had a rotten childhood. Lots of kids had it even worse than he could imagine. Heather and Tony were good examples. But what could he do now that he was nearing fifty?

He leapt to his feet. Be a child. That was what he could do. Logan Mallory, the middle-aged tennis professional, was going to learn to be a child.

Where could he start? He'd already proven, beyond doubt, that he had no business rambling around in the woods. He was too old to become a boy scout. What was left?

Logan didn't know, but he couldn't stay cooped up in his cabin any longer. "Sweet dreams, Muzzle," he said as he fled out the door in pursuit of his childhood.

Eve heard a noise outside her window. She'd tossed and turned from the moment she lay down, unable to put Logan out of her mind. She listened quietly and heard what sounded like a moan or groan, and it came from nearby.

Without turning on her light, Eve got out of bed, slipped on shorts and a T-shirt, and stole down the stairs. At the front door, she hesitated, her ear cocked to pick up the slightest sound. Then something fell outside her door, a twig or branch from the large oak that shaded the office and her room.

It must be an animal in the tree, she thought and started to return to bed. But what if it was Muzzle?

Eve found her flashlight and hurried into the yard. She aimed her flashlight into the tree, expecting to see the big yellow cat perched on a high limb.

"Oh, my God!" she exclaimed when she spotted the "animal" in the tree. "Logan Mallory, what in the world are you doing in that tree in the middle of the night?"

"Hi, Eve," Logan said, feeling even more foolish than he must look. "I seem to have a slight problem."

"What would that be? That you're a Peeping Tom and someone called the police?" Eve asked, trying to keep the humor of the situation from showing in her voice.

"No, that's not it at all." Logan heard the mirth in her voice and it grated on him. "Keep your voice down. Do you want to wake the entire camp?"

"Depends on what you're doing there," she retorted, peering into the branches. "What are you doing there, Logan?"

Logan didn't want to admit that he had done something completely ridiculous. Any idiot would have waited until daylight to do such a stupid thing—if ever. "The problem is not what I'm doing here, but how I can get down."

"You're stuck?"

"No, I like sleeping in trees." His voice was heavy with sarcasm. "Of course I'm stuck."

Eve bit her lip. He was in trouble, and she was about to burst into laughter. Even though he'd used extremely poor judgment, he didn't deserve to be ridiculed. "Hold on, I'll get a ladder."

She hurried out to the supply shed and dragged out an extension ladder. It was bulky, awkward, and heavy.

The noise was bound to wake someone, so she needed to hurry. What could she say if someone did spot her and Logan? Eve didn't have time to stop and plan a logical excuse. There were none that she could think of. She continued to drag the ladder, mentally cursing the person who'd selected the distant site for the supply shed.

Eve finally managed to get the ladder back to her cabin. With great difficulty, she propped the ladder against the tree trunk. She wondered whether Logan would attempt to climb down alone or if she'd need to call the fire department. At least the power company lights offered some illumination for Logan to see.

Instead of waiting for him, Eve began to climb the ladder. Without *asking* if he had the courage to climb down, she joined him on a huge limb that overlooked the compound. She slipped her hand in his and fluttered her eyelashes. "This is really a neat place. You come here often?"

Logan chuckled. Somehow her presence made him feel a little better. Damn it, Logan, you're too much to be believed. You've gotten yourself up here and can't get down. What a knucklehead. "Not often enough, if you frequent the place."

"I didn't realize I had friends in such high places," she quipped and began to laugh.

"You're the queen of comedy tonight, Eve, you know that?" Then Logan began to laugh, too. "I look like some kind of prize fool, don't I?"

"I've seen you look better, I believe." A noise alerted Eve. She listened carefully and then whispered, "Shh! Somebody's coming."

Logan rolled his eyes. This was all he needed to make his humiliation complete. "No wonder kids think their childhoods are awful?"

"What?" she asked in a low voice.

"Nothing. I'll tell you later." Logan shifted slightly, gripping the tree limb as tightly as he could. "Maybe we'd better climb down."

"I'll go first," Eve offered and scooted back toward the trunk. She clung to the limb and swung her legs over, hoping Logan could see how she was managing. She'd hate to have to tell him in front of whoever was approaching.

It was too late. Sounds of people were coming from two directions.

"Stop where you are," came Otis's gruffest voice. "I've got a shotgun."

"Me, too!" Madora shouted from the door of the dining hall.

Astonished, Eve peered around the tree trunk. A gun? Two guns? To her knowledge there were no guns of any sort on the premises. She looked more closely at where Otis was standing. In the illumination provided by the outside lights, she could see that he was carrying some sort of wooden gardening tool. The glint of stainless steel was on whatever Madora had in her hand, probably a kitchen utensil. "Otis, Madora, for goodness sake, it's me."

"Miss Eve? That you?" Otis asked suspiciously.

Madora stepped out of the dining hall. "Eve Travers, what on God's green earth are you doing in a tree at one in the morning?"

Eve glanced up at Logan. "Follow me," she whispered.

Logan kept his gaze riveted on her. She seemed so lithe, moving so gracefully over the limb and then starting down the ladder as if it was something she'd done all her life. But she had done this all her life. She grew up here, playing in the woods. Logan decided that she was part monkey as she deftly made her way down.

"I'm coming," he called softly, praying that if he fell he'd survive.

Eve jumped the last couple of rungs and landed on the ground. "What am I doing? What are you two doing?"

Otis glanced at Madora and nodded.

"We're protecting you. You still haven't told us what you were doing up a tree."

By this time, people were coming from everywhere. The commotion was like the concentric circles in a lake after she'd thrown a stone. The main staff had heard her and Logan; the first circle of campers were awakened by the staff; the other campers were disturbed by the noise in the other cabins. Pretty soon, everybody was standing in the compound. Everybody except Logan, who was still in the tree.

No matter what she said, nobody would believe her. It was just too unbelievable, even for her. Well, that's understandable. You haven't heard Logan's excuse yet, she rationalized.

Logan scooted back toward the trunk as Eve had done. This was going to be humiliating. He considered staying where he was. As of now, nobody had spotted him. That was a chicken-hearted thing to do, though, and Logan refused to take the coward's way out.

Hugging the trunk, he put one foot on the next limb down and then stood there. As he began his descent without mishap, he became a little more confident. Finally, he was on the ladder, well on his way down, and felt almost safe. Almost.

Eve glanced up at him with a reassuring look and then turned to the gathering crowd. She smiled her most cheerful smile, hoping that she could at least stop the questions before they started. The only way to do that would be to say something so preposterous that nobody could think of a reply.

"Logan and I were looking for tree sprites. Good night, everyone."

Nineteen

Eve walked slowly into her cabin and up the steps without turning on the lights. When she reached her room, she fell onto the bed and buried her face in a pillow to muffle her laughter.

As she laughed she heard the questions start. Poor Logan. She'd left him to explain what she meant by that ridiculous remark. Well, it served him right for climbing a tree in the middle of the night. That was one explanation she could hardly wait to hear.

Logan's deep, masculine voice cut through the yammering of the sleepy crowd. "I want everybody in bed in two minutes." He glanced at his watch. "Starting now!"

Eve stifled her laughter to see if his ploy was working. The level of mumbling seemed to be growing lower and lower. Good one, Logan, she thought and flopped over on her back. What on earth could he have been doing in the tree?

She almost expected him to come storming up the stairs to demand an explanation of her actions. Eve supposed she deserved a rebuke for pulling such a stunt. Still, this night would become a legend, exaggerated and retold by the campfires of years to come, if the camp were to continue in operation long enough—and she discovered that she liked the idea immensely.

Logan probably wouldn't, especially if someone discovered the reason for his being in the tree. The embarrassment would probably get the better of him, she thought.

Had he gone back to his room? She wanted to go and comfort him, but after the scene at his house, she couldn't until he came to her of his own accord. Was that what he'd been doing?

Logan sat in his cabin for a long time. He'd never been so humiliated in his entire life. Tree sprites, she'd said, and then left him to explain. What in the hell were tree sprites anyway? Still, she'd gotten him out of the tree without asking questions that would have made him feel silly.

He glanced at his watch. An hour had passed since she'd left him standing there in that curious crowd. Dared he go back to her cabin now? Feeling a little mischievous, he left his cabin and ran from one shadow to another until he reached her door. What fun! he decided with a grin. He should have done something like this years ago.

Eve heard a noise again. What in the world was Logan up to now?

She sneaked down the stairs and swung the door open as quietly as she could. "Logan," she called softly, hoping that if he was nearby he'd answer.

"Here I am." He came around the corner, grabbed her, lifted her in the air, and spun around. "Can you come out and play?"

Eve knew he'd sworn off hard liquor for at least a year, but he had to be drunk. "Logan, are you drunk?"

"Just having a good time with my best girl." Logan put her down, grabbed her hand, and began to run. "Come on. Let's go. We don't have all night."

Happy that she'd left her sneakers on, Eve hurried along after him. She didn't know what he was up to, but he seemed to be happy about it. He was headed through the woods toward the tennis court.

Thankful that she knew the trails as well as the fingernails on her hands, Eve suddenly stopped. "No way, Logan. You're not pulling me out into the brambles with you. Go right on and enjoy yourself. I'll meet you at the tennis court."

"Brambles?" He glanced around in the darkness and then turned back to Eve. "Am I headed off the path again?"

"You are."

"You lead then. I'll follow." Logan moved aside to allow her to pass. As he backed up slightly, he got his pants caught on a thorn. "Damn! Will I never be rid of those things?"

"Hush. Do you want to wake everyone up again?"

"Not on your life. Get moving, little girl."

"Little girl?" she asked, standing stock-still. "I'm not budging until you tell me what this is all about."

Logan leaned closer. "I'll tell you when we get to the playground."

Eve had little choice but to lead him down the path he found so elusive. They'd gone but a few steps when Logan stopped her.

He pulled her into his arms and looked down at her in the darkness. "Isn't this fun? Can you come out and play every night?"

Eve laughed. Whatever prank he was up to might be childish, but could be fun. She decided to play along. "Only if you don't be mean, little boy."

From there, they fairly raced to the playground. When they arrived, Logan turned on the light so they could see and then surveyed the area. "I'm glad there's a light here. I'd hate to break a leg playing on these things."

"Me, too." Eve studied Logan. He seemed more animated than she'd ever seen him, but she couldn't decide what had changed. "Well, what do you want to do?"

"Let's play on the slide."

Eve ran to the slide, but Logan beat her. She followed him up the steps, waiting while he positioned himself and then slid.

"Whee!" he shouted, just like a child.

Shaking her head slightly, Eve followed. Before long, they were on the whirligig. They both ran round and round, jumping on and coasting until it almost stopped. Eve was almost drunk when they staggered off and tried to walk to the seesaw.

Always a gentleman, Logan allowed Eve to sit down on the seesaw first. When he took his place, his end fell to the ground and hers flew straight up, nearly sending her headlong into the air. "This won't work."

Logan tried to figure out a way that they could work the seesaw. Eve was much lighter than he, so he looked around for a large rock to add weight to her end. "Sorry, Eve, I think we have to forgo the seesaw for tonight."

Eve ran from there to the swings and sat down. Logan pushed her, and she went higher and higher. "I'm flying, Logan."

They changed and Eve pushed Logan for a while. She felt almost like a child again as she played on the playground she'd loved when her father ran the camp.

For an hour, the two of them danced

and played from one place to another, hanging from the jungle gym, flying on the swings, racing down the slide, and spinning on the whirligig.

Madora and Otis watched from the path. She thought that both Eve and Logan had taken leave of their senses, but they seemed to be having fun. Pretty soon, Madora and Otis joined Logan and Eve.

"Hey," Logan shouted, jerking Eve's short hair. "I think we can work the see-saw now."

Logan and Eve got on one end while Madora and Otis got on the other. It worked. They played for a long time, laughing and having great fun.

And then Eve noticed others. Counselors at first, but they were soon followed by campers, first one or two and then more and more as the level of noise rose. Almost all of them were in their pajamas. The playground was full of people of all ages and it was nearly four o'clock in the morning.

Eve stood with Logan at the edge of the playground and watched in wonder. "Where did they all come from?"

He shrugged his shoulders and put his

arm around her. "Just out to have fun like us, I suppose."

"What do you think we should do now?" Eve asked, watching Madora moving down the slide.

"How about if we go to the dining hall and start some hot chocolate. It's a little chilly out here." Logan hugged her close and kissed her on top of her head. "Who started all this anyway?"

"I'll tell Madora," Eve said and slipped away. She walked through the throng of playing teenagers and found Madora about to slide again. "Logan and I are going to start some hot chocolate. Give us a few minutes and then bring the kids to the dining hall."

Eve and Logan strolled back to the dining hall. As she walked along, Eve felt invigorated by all the physical activity. It had been a long time since she'd played with that much energy. "Did you have fun?"

"Sure, did you?" Logan asked, taking her hand. "Don't forget, I'm still foundering in the woods in the dark."

"Why did we do that, Logan?"

"I'll tell you about it later maybe."

"What's wrong with right now? We're

moseying through the woods, without a care in the world. Now's the time to talk about stuff like that." Eve led him around the turn where he'd gotten off the trail on the way to the playground. "Come to think of it. Now would be a good time for you to tell me why we had to climb that tree."

"Would you believe I suddenly felt the urge to climb a tree?"

"Don't think so." They reached the edge of the compound that separated the dining hall from her office and the supply hut.

Logan stopped and pulled her into his embrace. "Would you believe I was trying to sneak a peak into your bedroom?"

"Don't think so. My light was out, remember?"

"Oh, yeah." Logan thought for a few seconds. "Would you believe I was trying to recapture my childhood?"

Eve tried to see his eyes. In the dim light, she could hardly see his face, much less his eyes. Of the things he'd said, that made the most sense to her. "I think I believe that." She could hardly keep from dancing around the compound. But she didn't want to scare him away from her confidence when he appeared to be nearing a breakthrough. "Can you talk about it?"

"I suppose." Logan released her and began to walk toward the dining hall. "After I brought you home tonight, I couldn't get some of the things you'd said out of my mind. I began to think back to the beginning, to figure out where things started to go wrong."

"And you settled on your childhood as being the culprit. An unhappy childhood?"

"No, that's not it. I was pretty happy, I guess. I loved tennis and school." He stopped and stared down at her. Even in the dim light he could see the concern on her face and in her eyes. "I just never had a childhood."

"So that's why were playing children's games. Climbing a tree and romping in the playground." Eve smiled up at him, hoping that her face showed her love and understanding. "Anytime you feel the need to climb my tree, come ahead."

"That's another thing." Logan could hardly breathe. Eve's soft floral scent was driving him wild. He wanted to forget the hot chocolate and take her up to her

room and make love until the sun rose.
"Thanks for getting me out of the tree.
I guess little boys have their first experience climbing trees when they're six or
so. We didn't have any trees to climb."

"I think it's very touching that you
picked my tree to climb."

Logan chuckled and shook his head.
"Don't be too flattered. I picked that tree
because it had a bench beneath it that allowed me to reach the lowest limb."

"Well, you were looking around for the
tree near my cabin, so I choose to think
it had something to do with me."

"Maybe. I refuse to say on the grounds
that you might call me a Peeping Tom
again."

"Logan, I had a good time, really I
did." Eve wanted to reassure him, but she
didn't know exactly how. Had the evening's fun cured the need to recapture
his childhood? "Would you like to take a
short trip tomorrow?"

"Where?"

"It's a secret."

Logan had to accept that, for Eve would
say no more on the matter. Sooner than
he had expected, the campers and staff
came in from the playground, almost

dragging themselves in sleepy languor. The hot chocolate would help them to fall asleep much more quickly, he thought.

Later, as Logan settled into his bed, he recalled the riotous adventure he and Eve had shared. When nodding off to sleep, he remembered that he hadn't asked her what a tree sprite was.

Eve made arrangements for morning classes to be skipped. She set up an abbreviated afternoon schedule that allowed the campers to have as easy a time of it as possible. After all, almost none of them had slept the previous night.

"Connie, I may not be back tonight. Logan and I will be away for the afternoon and evening. If our business isn't concluded, then don't expect us back until morning."

With that, Eve hurried out to her Bronco where Logan awaited her. She intended to drive. Before they reached the interstate highway, Eve stopped at a drugstore and bought several packets of condoms. Just in case, she told herself.

Logan looked at her with a question in his umber eyes, but didn't voice it. The short ride to Carowinds Amusement Park didn't take too long. The expression on Logan's face when she pulled through the gate was one she'd never forget.

"Haven't you ever been here?"

"No," he answered peering ahead. "I just never thought about stopping."

"This place is ten minutes from your house and you never came here?" she asked in disbelief. When she'd decided this would be a good trip for Logan to release the child in him, she had no idea it would truly be for the first time.

She parked the Bronco and got out. "Let's go."

Once inside the amusement park, Logan's eyes were childlike. He seemed to be interested in everything.

"Eve, this place is great." They walked hand in hand, stopping for an ice cream. As they sat on a bench, Logan turned to look at her with new admiration. "What made you think of coming here?"

"Our wonderful evening at the playground. If that was fun, this is bound to be even better." Eve surveyed the throng of people. "I just didn't anticipate this many people. I suppose I forgot what summers were like at an amusement park."

"Would you consider leaving?"

"Leaving? We just arrived." Eve turned to look at him. "Why would we want to leave."

That was a good question. He didn't even know himself. All he could answer was, "I feel the need to talk, rather than play today."

Eve would have raced him to the Bronco if she'd thought it feasible. "Great. Me, too."

They bought a couple of souvenirs on the way out, but Eve was almost impatient. She could feel Logan's need to talk, almost as if it were a physical presence. What had happened? Had a single night of play changed him that radically?

He seemed to be in a pensive mood as they rode the short distance to his house. When they arrived, Logan offered to grill some hamburgers for lunch. Eve happily heated chili in the microwave and peeled an onion. "Chili-burgers!" she announced when she placed the bowl of chili and plate of onion on the table.

"You got that out of my freezer?"

"I sure did. Thawed it in the microwave."

Logan grinned at her. "That took guts after the last time you were here. I apologize for being such a bear."

"I'm fond of wildlife," she said raising her eyebrows suggestively.

"And I'm beginning to wonder about you."

Logan put the burgers together and she spooned on the chili. For a few moments, they ate in silence.

"Logan, you said you wanted to talk."

"Not while I'm eating this chili-burger." Logan held it up. "It's almost gone."

When they'd finished their meal, Eve cleared the plates from the table and took them into the kitchen. "You need some help?"

"Help? I cooked. You wash the dishes." Logan stared at her for a few seconds. "You can put them in the dishwasher if you like."

"Boy, things have changed around here," Eve complained good-naturedly. She flashed him a smile. "For the better."

When the dishes were all tucked away in the dishwasher, Eve went into the living room where he was selecting music. She pointed to the Gershwin. "I like that. To be honest, I like most music."

"We'll stick to classics. That way, you won't be singing along while we're trying to have a serious conversation." Logan put the CDs on the player and went to pour some wine. When he returned, she was sitting on the floor in front of the sofa. "Something against the sofa?"

"More homey on the floor," she answered and pulled a pillow off the couch. "Here. Sit with me."

He put their glasses of wine on the coffee table and sat beside her. "I think it's a little warm for a fire, but it seems like we should have one."

"Oh, this is going to be one of those kinds of talks."

"What kind?"

"A fireside chat."

"Make that a cold fireplace chat and we're in business." Logan slipped his arm around her and she leaned back against him. "I hope you have a good imagination, Eve."

"I do. Trust me on this."

Logan closed his eyes, trying to bring all the things he wanted to tell her about into his mind. There seemed to be so much, but they had all afternoon. "I did a lot of soul-searching last night and this morning, Eve."

"That's a good sign." She was almost afraid to answer, for fear that her words would put him off or make him regret his decision to talk to her.

"Well, it's about time. I've been an abject asshole for going on two months now. Longer than that actually, but this conversation is directly related to you, so all that other time doesn't count."

"Logan, don't think you have to sugar-coat this conversation. I . . . I love you. Nothing you can say will change that."

Logan gazed into her beautiful dark blue eyes and relished the truth he saw there. "And, I love you, Eve, but love isn't enough sometimes." He saw that she was about to interrupt and kissed her into silence. "Don't stop me when I'm on a roll."

For a moment he considered where he wanted to begin. "As I told you, my childhood was sadly lacking in, well, childhood. When I started taking tennis, I became an instant adult. But I wasn't ready for that. The 'bad boy' image comes as a result of the lack of learning to deal with anger as a child. I know this now."

"Maybe it's a good thing. I'm glad for you." Eve saw the pain as he began thinking of what to say next.

"I made some bad choices." He turned aside for a moment and swallowed hard. "I married a woman, an artist. For a while, I thought it was wonderful, but I gradually saw that she didn't consider our marriage anything but another show piece."

"Logan, you don't have to tell me this now."

"Yes, I do. I've got to trust you. I've got to say this to someone and you're the only person I can trust."

"That's not true, Logan. You can trust Jerry, too. In fact, there are lots of people who love you."

"Yes and that's because of you." He smiled down at her. "You've changed me, Eve."

"No, you've changed yourself. You started last winter, remember?"

"Yeah, but I wasn't doing too well until I met you." Logan kissed her lightly. If he didn't get on with this conversation, he'd forget that he intended to talk first and make love second. "Reina and I had a baby, Brandon. God, I loved that kid. He looked just like me."

Logan took his arm from around her and leaned forward, propping his elbows on his knees. He could see Brandon as easily as if he were still standing there. "I took him with me as much as I could, but that wasn't always possible. Reina had her career, too. Then there was that cursed Wimbledon, when I won my first title."

"Logan, I know this is hard, but I want you to know that I know about Brandon's death." Eve was trying to think of any way possible to make this easier. Giving him the information she already had should ease the burden of saying the words.

"That's not all." Logan turned to look at her, taking comfort from the tear that slid down her face. "I was at Wimbledon. He . . . he got sick. Reina told me it was nothing. She stayed with him at the hospital, but she had a gallery opening that weekend and left."

Eve closed her eyes to blot out the image of the child alone in the hospital, cringing in fear of the unknown and with nobody to comfort and console him. "There was nothing you could do. You didn't know—"

"I shouldn't have stayed, Eve. When I found out he was sick, I should have taken the first plane back to Charlotte."

"No, Logan, you were doing your job. She told you he was all right."

"He died while I was finishing the final set. While I was being cheered by the crowd, my baby was lying dead without a single person who cared about him there to ease him into death."

Eve's heart was breaking with the weight of Logan's agony. How could he have endured this all these years alone? "Logan, this is tragic, but not your fault."

"What would you have done?"

"Had I been his mother, I would have sent you off on your tournament just like Reina did."

"And then?"

"I would have spent every moment with him at the hospital. When his condition worsened, I would have called you home."

"Right. That's what *you* would have done." Logan leapt to his feet and crossed to the opposite wall. He leaned his head against it, his body trembling. "That's what most parents would have done." He turned to gaze at Eve. "I wanted to kill her, Eve. I still do. That's how bad I hate her. She killed my baby.''

"No, Logan. She used poor judgment, but she didn't kill him. The disease did."

''I said I wanted to kill her.'' He laughed derisively. "She did it herself, depriving me of even that measure of revenge.''

"Revenge digs two graves, Logan. You've got to let go of this hate." Eve rose and went over to him, pulling his head down on her shoulder. "It's not your fault," she repeated over and over until she felt him begin to relax. "Logan, you've got to believe me. It's not your fault. Even if you'd been here, you couldn't have changed what happened.''

"Yes, I could, Eve. I would have been there to hold him during his last minutes. I would have been the father I should be.''

Eve closed her eyes briefly. How could a man endure such agony and still lead a productive life? She hurt for him, but there wasn't any way she could really ease that pain. He had to deal with it himself, deal with it rather than suppress it.

Eve said nothing, but led him to the bedroom, undressed him, and put him in the bed. She stripped quickly and joined him. Once there, she cradled his head on her shoulder and they cried together. For a long, long time, they lay there, tears mingling, until she felt him begin to breathe easier, his anguish subsiding a little with each tear.

When he finally slept, she thought over what he'd said. If Eve had the capacity to hate, Reina would be the person she hated. She'd put her career ahead of her son's health and her husband's mental health. Not only had the woman deprived Logan of the right to be at his son's bedside when he died, but she'd caused him to mistrust and hate artists.

No wonder Logan had been so sarcastic about the camp. Eve considered the summer program and Logan's part in it. He'd shown great courage by doing whatever she asked. Even the effort he put forth to be Tony's surrogate father must have reopened all Logan's wounds, if they'd ever healed.

Now, maybe they would. Eve felt helpless to advise him. She could only love him, but would that be enough?

* * *

When Logan awoke, he was surprised to find Eve sleeping with her arms around him. For a moment, he was a little disoriented. Then he remembered their talk. He'd told her his worst, that he wanted to kill his wife and would have, had she not taken the privilege away from him.

Now, as Logan slid out of her embrace and walked to the sliding doors, he wondered if he really could have killed Reina. For years he'd promised himself that if she'd given him the chance, he would have. But after talking about it, after voicing his intentions to do that very thing, he realized something: he couldn't do it.

He looked back at Eve, lying like the sweet nymph she was on the pillows with her hands at odd angles where he'd left them. She'd listened to him. She'd heard every hateful word and had cried with him, shared his anguish.

That gnawing ache inside him was lessening. He could feel it even as he stood there. What had Gayle said to Eve? Something about sharing pain lessens it. Eve had looked meaningfully at him in the rearview mirror as they'd been driving down the highway. She knew it, too.

All summer long, she'd tried to tell him

that nothing was too bad to share, and that the sharing made it bearable. Logan considered himself lucky. She loved him. Thank God, she'd stuck with him long enough to make him realize that there might be something left inside of himself that was worth loving.

Her perseverance had taught him something else, too. He'd learned that he still wanted to play tennis, even though he'd vowed never to do so again. He'd learned that he wanted to teach his skills to someone else, maybe even Tony. The boy was a natural—and he'd had plenty of chances to learn to climb trees.

Eve had given him a great gift. He'd never be able to repay her for that.

Logan tiptoed out of the room, picking up his shorts along the way. In the living-room, he went to the telephone and called the camp. Filled with a renewed confidence, he felt the need to conspire with Madora again.

When he hung up the phone, he spotted the little bag Eve had brought out of the pharmacy. Even though he experienced a little guilt, he looked inside. Condoms.

Logan dropped into a chair. She didn't

take birth control pills. They'd made love
several times, and she hadn't been protected. God, what a fool he'd been. He'd
spent his entire adult sex-life making sure
that no accidents happened, and she'd
made him forget to even ask about protection.

He counted the condoms and smiled
broadly. There were a dozen of them.
Lusty wench, he thought.

Taking the bag into the kitchen, he
looked into the refrigerator and found
what he was looking for: Eve's birthday
corsage. He removed the long pin from
the orchid. Then, very deliberately, he
stuck the corsage pin into each Mylar
packet and grinned.

Conspiring against Eve might just become his favorite pastime.

Twenty

Eve awoke, her eyelids still heavy from sound sleep. The sun had long since begun to set and she stretched luxuriously. And sat up abruptly.

Where was she? Then it came back to her. She was in Logan's big bed, the one at his house. But where was he?

She rose, pulled on one of his long-sleeved oxford cloth shirts and started to look around. As she walked from room to room, she rolled up the sleeves that hung almost to her knees. She searched the upper level and then the lower, but Logan was nowhere to be seen.

Eve went to the window and glanced out. Her Bronco was gone.

Where could he be? She curled up on the sofa and pulled a pillow into her lap to prop her elbows on. Their conversation had been a breakthrough, something she'd been trying to generate for several days.

Had he been so upset that he'd left in anger or depression?

She considered every ramification of the possibilities. Eve didn't think Logan was suicidal. She was grateful for that. When he'd fallen asleep, she'd thought that he had at last accepted that he wasn't responsible for his sons death. Many scenarios passed through her mind, some to be discarded as quickly as they came.

Almost an hour passed without his return. Eve called the camp, just to make sure he hadn't called or been there.

"Connie, have you spoke to Logan this afternoon?"

"No, Eve, I haven't. Maybe he just went to pick up some groceries or something. Or to rent a movie."

They talked a few minutes more and then Eve hung up. She went into the kitchen to look in the refrigerator. Taking a bottle of mineral water, she noted how clean everything was, almost perfect. As she returned to the living room, Logan crept through the front door.

She met him at the passageway between the kitchen and livingroom. "Oh, Logan, you're safe."

Logan stared at her a moment and then

put down the groceries he was carrying. "Yeah, but I tell you, I never thought I'd get out of the meat market alive."

Eve laughed with him and collapsed into his arms. "I was worried about you."

"Didn't you read my note?"

"I didn't see a note."

He took her by the hand and led her to the bedroom. There, pinned on his pillow was a folded piece of paper. He slipped the note off of the corsage pin and handed the hastily scratched memo to her. "See? I was a good boy."

Eve read the note: *Dearest, gone hunting for food. I promise to climb no trees while I'm gone. Make yourself at home. Love, Logan.*

"I suppose I was worried all this time for no reason."

"That's what you get for jumping straight out of bed. You should linger there for a while." Logan eyed her shrewdly. "Isn't that my shirt?"

"I think it is. I found it in your closet."

"Damn thing never looked that good on me." Logan pulled her into his arms. "Thanks, Eve. I know that I haven't been the most pleasant person who could have taught tennis this summer, but I promise

to do better if you'll let me teach next
summer."

"Next summer," she repeated, feeling
the words surge through her. She gazed
into his loving eyes. "I never let myself
think past this year, Logan. I couldn't.
Somehow, I had to get through this year
and then maybe think about next year."

"I've been talking to Jerry about that
benefit tennis match." Logan turned Eve
around and they walked to the sofa and
sat down. "We can do a lot of things, Eve.
I have some ideas and the benefit will
give us enough money to implement some
of them."

"Like what?"

"Like maybe having a shorter arts session and making time for an athletic session."

"Athletic?"

"Yeah, basketball, baseball, tennis, golf,
swimming, all those kinds of things."

"I wouldn't know how to—"

"But I do." Logan hugged her. "There
are so many things I want to do, Eve."

"I see." Eve smiled up at him. "And
when did you do all this profound thinking?"

"Mostly this afternoon while you slept.

But I've done some serious thinking over the past few days. I like the kids. I like being around them." Logan lay down on the sofa and pulled her with him. "I don't want to be a loner the rest of my life, Eve. You've shown me that I need people. I need you."

"I never could have pulled this off alone, Logan. I realized that now." She looked at him with renewed confidence. "When I found out that you were to be my tennis coach, I thought I could have done better with a trained 'possum."

"You may be right."

"Silly. The problem was, I believed all the awful things I read about you."

"Those things were true, Eve. *Were* true."

"No they weren't, Logan. On the surface, maybe, but the Logan Mallory I love has always been there, skulking behind the 'bad boy' who was so flashy."

"You're quite the philosopher, aren't you?"

"I am, when the occasion demands it."

"Well, I can't lounge around here all evening. Somebody in this place has got to fix dinner. Can you make the salad?"

Eve smiled with pride. He was changing. "I'm a whiz with lettuce."

They worked together in the kitchen, occasionally bumping into each other. The companionable silences made Eve happy. When she was near enough to Logan, she stood on tiptoes and kissed him. "The 'bad boy' is changing."

"I'm happy to hear that."

"Well, I fell in love with the 'bad boy,' so I hope he doesn't disappear completely."

"Whenever you feel the need to experience life with the 'bad boy,' I'll be delighted to throw a tennis racquet for you."

"As long as it's not at me."

Logan studied her for a moment. "Is madam dressing for dinner?"

"I don't think so."

"In that case, we'll eat on the living-room floor."

Logan went into the living room and started a fire. He stopped by the thermostat and turned the air conditioner as cold as he could get it.

Eve watched with interest. "Isn't that a little—"

"Romantic," he said, completing her sentence.

"That wasn't what I was going to say, but it works for me."

She spread a linen tablecloth on the floor in front of the fire and set out plates, silverware, and glasses. She found napkins and tucked them through napkin rings. "An elaborate picnic, if I ever saw one."

Dinner was a triumph for Logan. His new recipe for pasta primavera made Eve rave. "Well, it's the combination of food and company."

When they were sipping wine over the cheesecake he'd bought at the deli, Logan watched her. Every movement was so dainty, so feminine. The shirt she wore—over nothing but her pride—set his libido to working overtime.

When they were finished, he poured her a glass of champagne. While she was staring into the fire, he brought the champagne over, dropped in a few fresh raspberries and a heart-shaped diamond ring.

"Oh, how lovely," Eve said, gazing at the champagne with the raspberries. "Such a nice touch. I've often wondered why" —Eve stared at the glass. Something in the bottom glittered. A ring! "Logan! A ring!"

He knelt down beside her and took her hand. Clasping it to his heart, he stared into the depths of sapphire eyes he'd come to love. "Eve, I love you. I swore I'd never marry again, but you've bewitched me. You are the kindest, most generous, most caring person I ever met. Please, say you'll marry me. Share the rest of your life with me."

Eve could hardly breathe. His words were meant from the heart, that she couldn't not doubt. "Logan, this is . . . I love you, too. I've loved you ever since that day you asked for that silly recipe."

"I'll make it for your wedding dinner."

"Yes, I'd love to share the rest of my life with you."

He rose, reached down and picked her up, and walked toward the bedroom. "You won't regret it. I'll make you the happiest woman on earth."

"I already am, Logan." Eve laid her head on his shoulder and as she did, she spotted the picnic spread before the fire. She smiled, raising her eyebrows suggestively. "Don't you want to clear away the dishes first?"

"Damn the dishes," he replied and lowered her on the bed. He lit several candles, removed his clothes, and lay down beside her. He pulled her toward him and bunched up his pillow. "Damn!" he exclaimed, jerking his hand back and sucking his thumb.

Eve suppressed a giggle. "The 'bad boy' returns?"

He chuckled with her. "Very funny. I lie here bleeding to death from that damned corsage pin, and you're making jokes."

"Sorry. I'll try to be more serious." She looked at the lavender head of the pin sticking out of the pillow. "I may regret ever keeping the corsage."

Logan eyed her for a moment and then disposed of the corsage pin. He recalled his next to last use for the pin. "Yes, you may, my darling. Yes, you may."

Eve came alert. The bag! She started to rise. "Logan, I know we've never talked about this and it may already be too late but—"

"I found them. I confess to snooping." Logan held her down and reached over past her to the floor. He produced a little basket decorated with flowers. Inside the basket were the condoms she'd bought. "Looking for these?"

"We haven't talked about—"

"There's not much need to talk about that."

"Then you don't object to—"

"Object? Me? No." Logan watched as the color in her face changed to a bright red. "I'd like to warn you about them, though."

"What about them? Aren't they . . . I asked the pharmacist and he said—"

"I know for a particular fact that those condoms aren't safe."

"How can they not be?" she asked, wondering what she could do now.

"It might have something to do with the way I used the corsage pin earlier."

"What?" Eve stared at him, trying to understand what he was telling her. "Corsage pin? You mean, you—"

"I did."

"But, Logan, what if—"

"I'll be the happiest man alive if you get pregnant." Logan propped himself on one elbow and kissed her. "Eve, I've always protected myself when I was involved with other women. This isn't exactly the time I would have chosen to talk about it, but we do need to talk. I *never,* not in the last twelve years, had unprotected sex. I didn't trust the women, even though most said they used some form of birth control."

"Very sensible." Eve smiled. This meant

he trusted her. She could have sung an aria—if she could have carried a tune.

"Not sensible, but sure." Logan kissed the tip of her nose. "I don't want that with you. I trust you. That's hard for me to admit, but I do."

"Logan, I don't take birth control pills."

"I know." He kissed her soundly, crushing her to him and relishing the lingering taste of champagne on her lips. "And I'm glad."

Eve had too much to think about. Tonight was the last campfire of the summer. She was of mixed emotions about it. The campers were ready to go home, but she knew they'd all want to come back. Almost as much as she wanted them to return.

This summer had changed her life. It had changed a lot of lives. Heather and Gayle Barton were staying in King's Mountain where Gayle would be teaching art at the local high school. Eve was especially proud of that accomplishment. Gayle still needed to get her teaching license for North Carolina, but it was almost assured. She needed to take several courses at a nearby college to get the credits she needed, but she would work in the meantime under a special arrangement.

Madora and Otis were getting married soon and would move into the caretaker's cottage. Eve was delighted about that. She never knew two more deserving people—and she was happy that the camp would be taken care of during the winter.

The kids had completed their film. Lorna had shown it tonight at dinner. What a triumph. She'd previewed it for a producer of a pay cable channel, and they were going to show it in the spring. The money would help to build some additional buildings for the camp—like a film lab and a place to teach movie making.

Tim Carlisle and Tennis Pro were elated over the results of this year's venture. The first commercials were airing this fall. He'd already offered new contracts to Eve and Logan for next summer.

Eve and Logan were going to be married at final campfire. Eve would move into Logan's house with the understanding that housework was a shared responsibility. She was proud of that, though she knew she'd come to a point where she would wish that he hadn't been so *kind* in dividing up the duties.

"All's well that ends well." Eve remembered the famous quotation and smiled happily. Her life was just entering a new phase and she looked forward to it with confidence.

She pulled on a pair of white stockings and attached them to the lacy white garter. Over that, she put a pair of white silk walking shorts that just touched her knees. The campers had attached lace and seed pearls to the shorts. Her T-shirt was elaborately decorated with pearls, lace, and sequins. Gayle had designed Eve's veil and arranged the flowers in the bouquet.

Madora poked her head in. "Ready?"

Eve grinned and nodded. "I'm not sure. I think I'm getting too old for all this."

"You're just getting cold feet."

Eve glanced down at the sequined tennis shoes Tim had provided. "In these?"

"I'll tell you one thing, Eve Travers." Madora folded her arms across her chest. "When Otis and I get married, it's going to be at the judge's office. I don't intend for you to put me in something like that getup."

"It's the spirit that counts, Madora."

"It looks great on you. I never thought tennis clothes would look that good."

"Well, they've been altered considerably." Eve looked down at the cleavage that was exposed by the princess neckline the kids had cut from the T-shirt. "Let's go."

When Eve arrived at the campfire, she almost laughed. Logan's attire was similar to hers, except that his was black. He wore a top hat, just to lend a formal air to the occasion.

Jerry Kent was Logan's best man. Eve never thought Jerry had looked so happy. He winked at her when she took Logan's arm.

Madora served as Eve's matron of honor. The kids were all decked out in "formal" sports clothes. It was a sight to behold.

Lorna Peterson and her crew were filming. Eve glanced up at Logan and smiled. This night, too, would become a camp legend, and Eve was thrilled.

Logan looked down at Eve. He'd never seen her so beautiful. The firelight glinted and glimmered in the sequins of her wedding . . . shorts and shirt, and he loved it. Nothing could have been more perfect. Their rather unusual attire was a combination, a compromise between art and sport.

What could have symbolized their love any better?

He recited his vows in his mind, praying that he wouldn't bungle them and embarrass her. When they'd decided to write their own vows, he hadn't considered having to remember all of them. Now, he not only had to remember them, he had to recite them aloud on the most unsettling night of his life. He almost wished they'd decided to stick with the "I will and I do" ceremony.

But when he looked at Eve again, he knew better. Their vows were special to their situation, a situation that included not only the two of them, but slightly more than a hundred others. Nothing else would be appropriate.

The minister, from a local church, glanced at Logan with humor in his eyes. Logan had told the man that the ceremony would be a little unusual. The minister's expression told Logan that it was even more unusual than first thought.

Their vows, maybe a little corny to some, spoke their true feelings. Their love and humor would be evident in the words they spoke, words that would echo for the rest of his life in his mind and Eve's.

The minister began, "This is an occasion of joy. Two people from worlds apart have discovered that love bridges differences far better than anything else. The love they bring to this union will abide with them forever, unmarred by hardship, or sickness, for better or worse and will grow with each day and the challenges it brings.

"Eve and Logan have chosen you to share in the expression of their joy. Join with me and partake of their love as they give voice to their feelings."

Logan gazed down at Eve. Her happiness gave him courage. "On this the most important day of my life, Eve, I give to you whatever is mine. We shall walk together down life's trail, accepting and sharing with love whatever boon or bramble fate places in our path."

Eve's smile deepened at his reference to brambles. "And as we walk this path, we shall always take time to stop and drink in the beauty that surrounds us. We shall endeavor to breathe in that beauty, to make it a part of our lives, for without beauty, life is colorless. The painting of our lives together begins tonight, though the preparation of our palette and canvas began when we met. Our experiences together will guide the brush that records our joy together."

"Love knows no boundaries," Logan said, taking up where her lines finished. Squeezing her hand, he paused a moment to gather his thoughts. Love for her surged forth as she watched him with glistening eyes. "Our love began as a tight bud, a promise of a more beautiful life to come. With the joining of our hands and lives, comes the joining of racquet and brush. For me, that is a sign of trust and of an enduring kind of love that Eve inspires in me.

"We look to our future, a future that will bring us back to this spot to renew our vows and our love each year. With the promise of that renewal comes the anticipation of including friends like all of you in our circle. We pray that this circle grows each year, but that those of you already joined with us will always remain good friends."

Logan looked out at the kids, at the people who, along with Eve, had started the transformation of his life. "This moment, though the most precious of my life, would be lessened without each of you and the influence you've had. With my vows to Eve, to the heart of my life, I include one other. I will endeavor for years to come, to carry on the work of her vision and I will do it with the joy you've given me . . . us this summer."

"I join in that vow." Eve felt a tear slide down her cheek. "And to you, Logan, who has made my life complete in a way I never knew love could, I vow to support all your choices, to bring a cheerful heart to the decisions you make about your career, for I know that tennis is a part of the fiber of your being, as art is a part of mine."

"I love you, Eve. I declare it before these witnesses. I will cherish you with every part of me. I honor your right to be the woman you are."

"I love you, Logan. I declare it before these witnesses. I will cherish you with every part of me. I honor your right to be the man you are."

"Our two lives are now joined. The rings we wear bear witness to the love in our hearts." Logan slid Eve's ring on her finger and waited while she put on his. He continued, "As long as birds sing and beauty abounds."

With a smile, Eve took up where he left off, "As long as tennis balls bounce."

"As long as art endures."

"As long as we have trees to climb."

"I will love you always, from the depths of my soul and the heart of my heart."

"And, I will love you always, from the depths of my soul and the heart of my heart."

As she gazed up at Logan, he grinned down at her, his dimples showing for the first time during the ceremony. She nodded almost imperceptibly.

Logan kissed her, long and hard, cherishing his first kiss with the woman he loved more than life itself. When he drew away, she smiled with love and mischief in her eyes. They stepped a short distance out of the clearing, leaving everyone staring at them.

Eve looked back at the kids, at Lorna and her film crew, at Jerry and Tim, and Madora and the rest of the staff. "We love you all and welcome you to our family."

Logan kissed the top of her head. "We hope that we will one day have a child of our own, but for now, you all belong to us."

He reached up and caught the rope ladder that hung from the limb above.

Had it not been for Eve's idea, they would have had to do this without help. He gave a mighty jerk and helped her into the tree with him. They stood on the thick bottom limb of a huge tree.

They began to shake the limbs above and the one they were standing on. Confetti, candy, miscellaneous school supplies and art supplies, tennis balls, and a variety of tiny gifts fell from the nets Logan and Eve had strung in the trees that morning. The campers scrambled to pick up their bounty, and Eve took Logan's hand. While everyone was busy, they climbed down again.

"So much for throwing rice," she whispered and ran with him up the path. "You're leading?"

"You bet. This may be the first and last time in my life that I get to lead through the forest, but I'm doing it and that's that."

"Yes, sir," she said and saluted. She stifled a giggle when he took a wrong turn, and she kept her mouth shut. They might make a lot of wrong turns in the future, but at least they'd be together.

"Damn!" he shouted and stopped abruptly, picking brambles out of his scratched legs. "Why didn't you tell me we'd gotten off the path?"